THE
GRAVE
DIGGERS
UNION

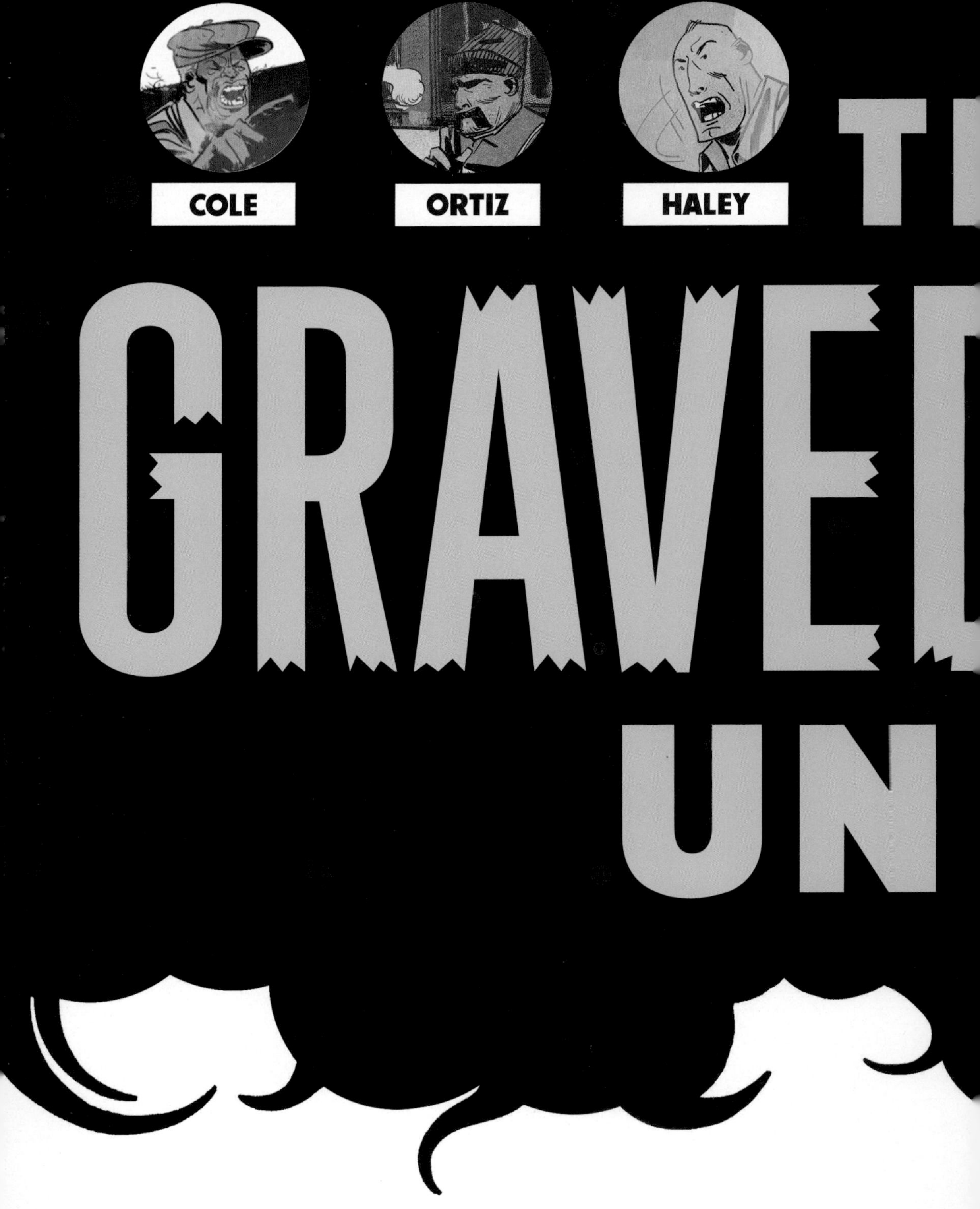

COLE **ORTIZ** **HALEY**

GRAVED
UN

IMAGE COMICS, INC. • Robert Kirkman: Chief Operating Officer • Erik Larsen: Chief Financial Officer • Todd McFarlane: President • Marc Silvestri: Chief Executive Officer • Jim Valentino: Vice President • Eric Stephenson: Publisher / Chief Creative Officer • Corey Hart: Director of Sales • Jeff Boison: Director of Publishing Planning & Book Trade Sales • Chris Ross: Director of Digital Sales • Jeff Stang: Director of Specialty Sales • Kat Salazar: Director of PR & Marketing • Drew Gill: Art Director • Heather Doornink: Production Director • Nicole Lapalme: Controller • IMAGECOMICS.COM

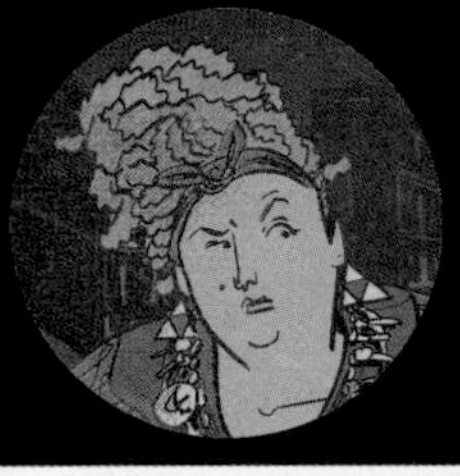

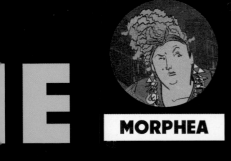

MORPHEA

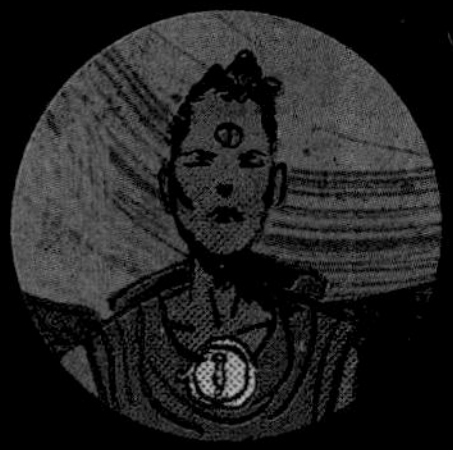

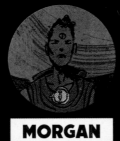

MORGAN

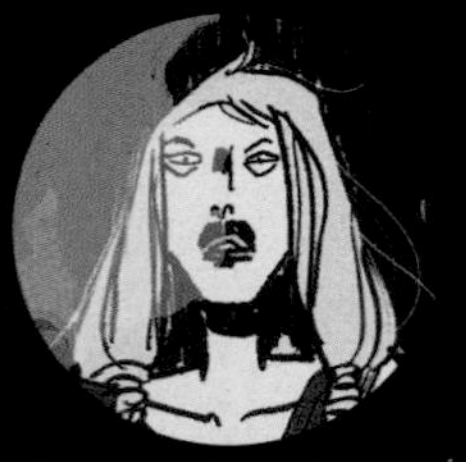

ZEPHON

IE IGGERS ON

WRITER + FLASHBACK ARTIST
WES CRAIG

ARTIST
TOBY CYPRESS

COLORIST **NIKO GUARDIA**

LETTERS **JARED K. FLETCHER**

CHAPTER

BURIED DEEP

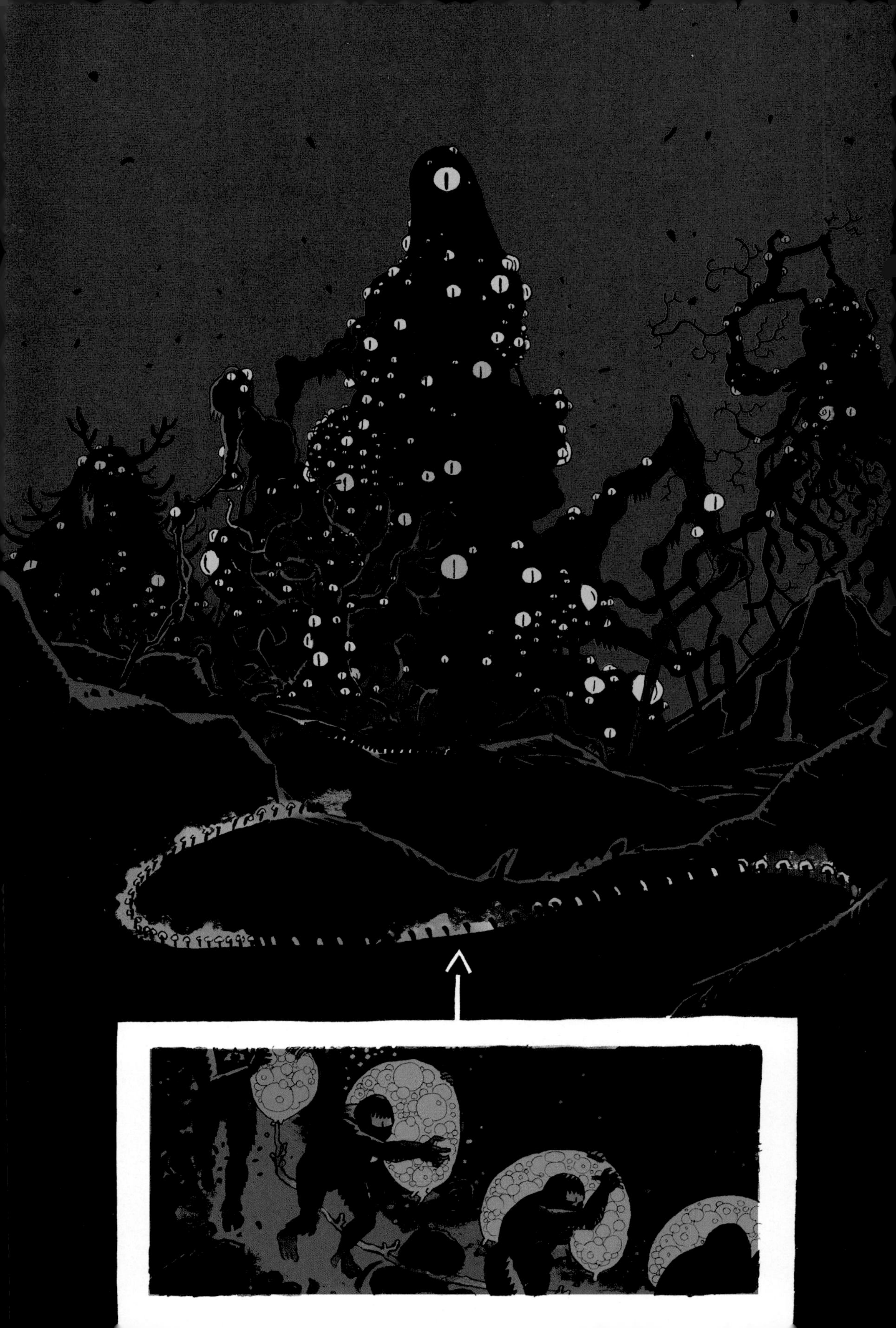

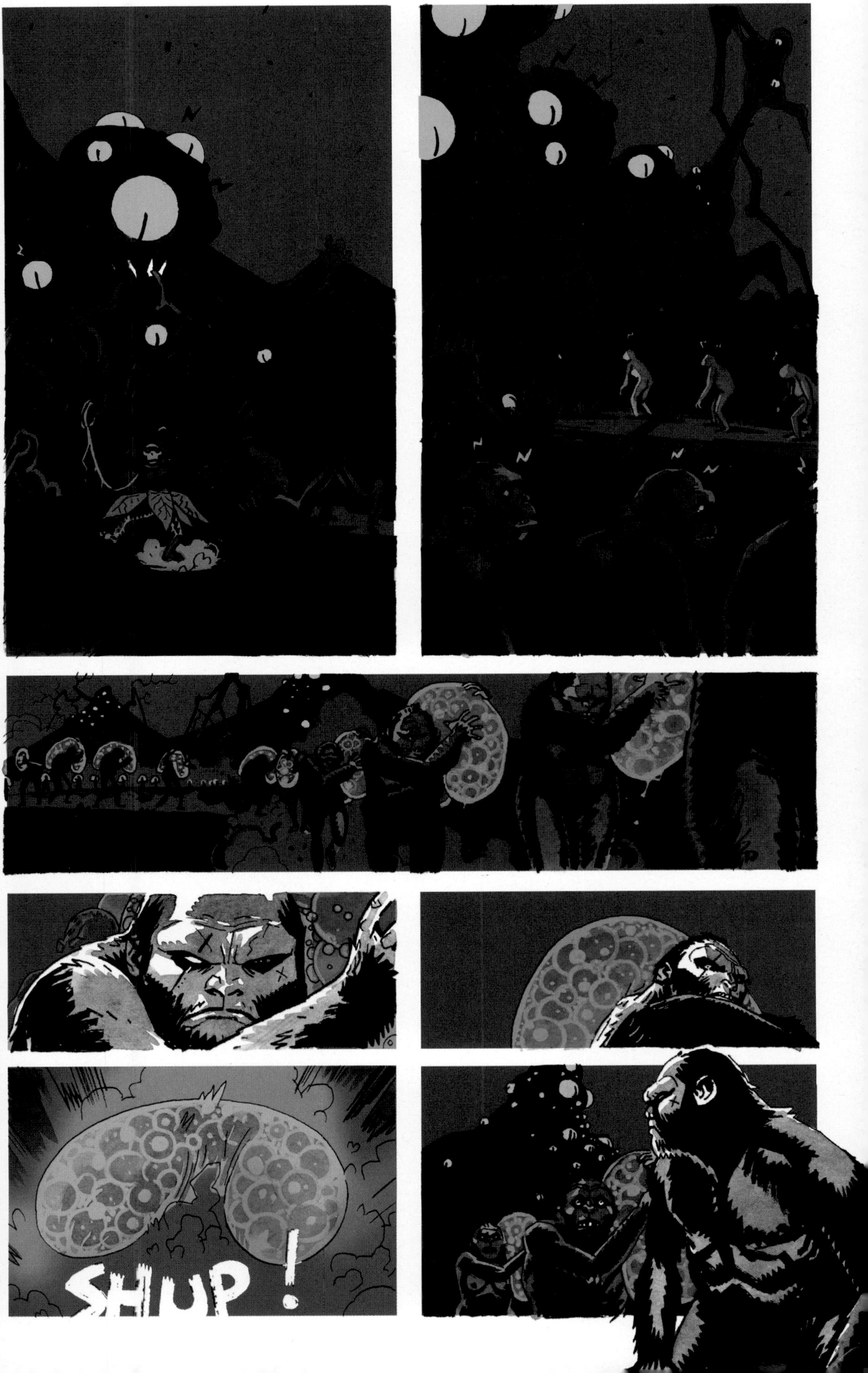
SHUP!

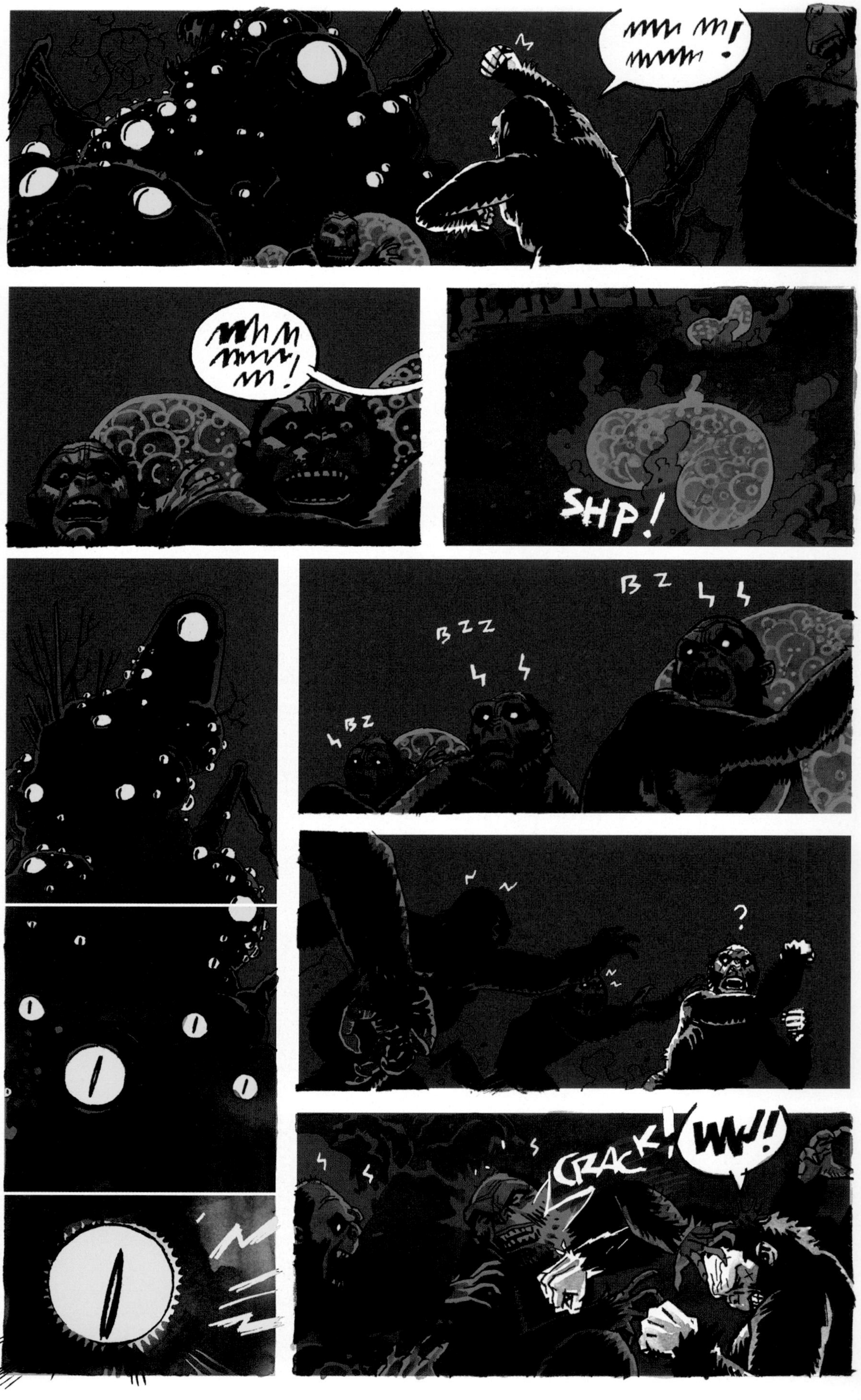
SHP!
BZZ
CRACK!

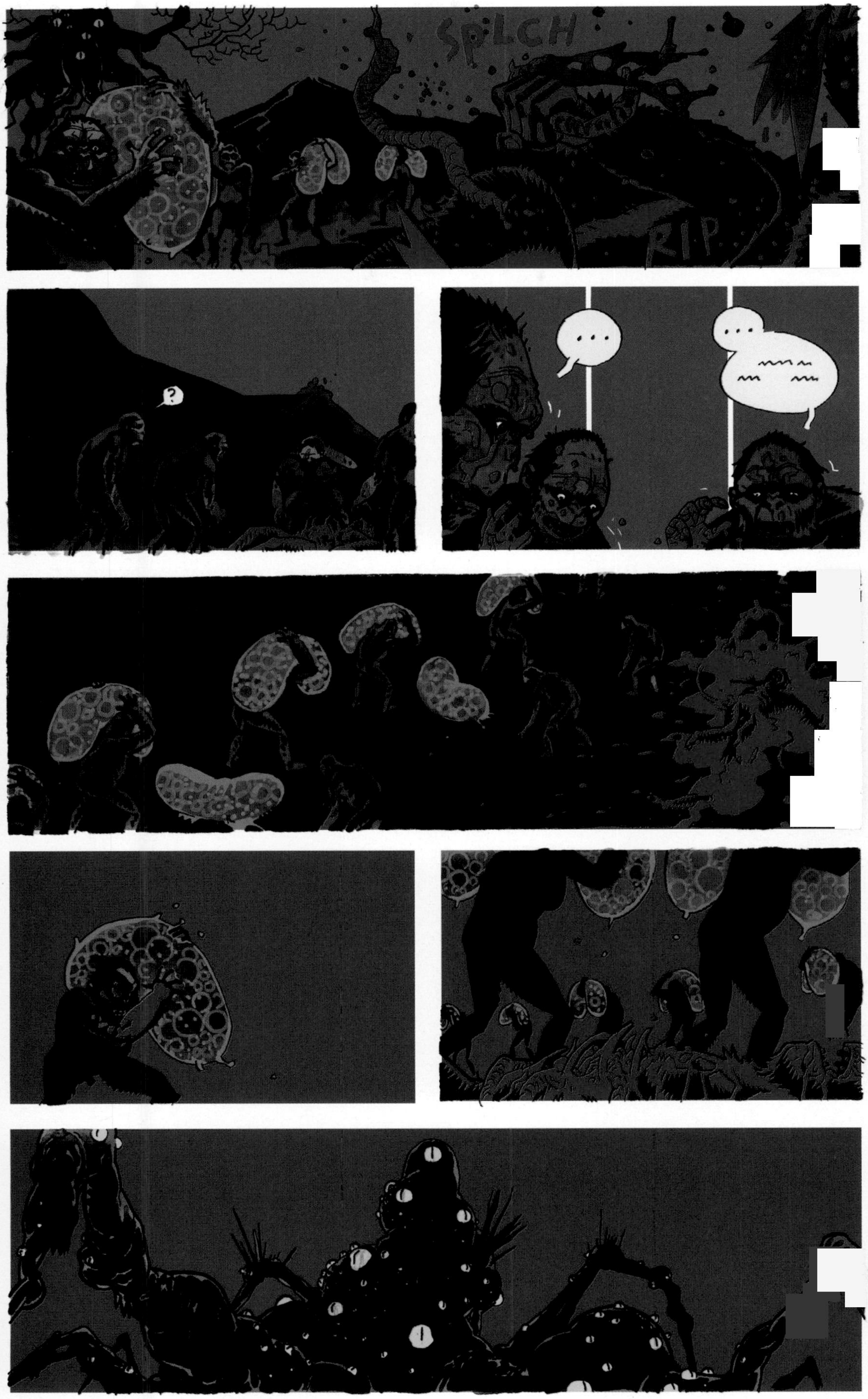
SPLCH
RIP
?
...
...

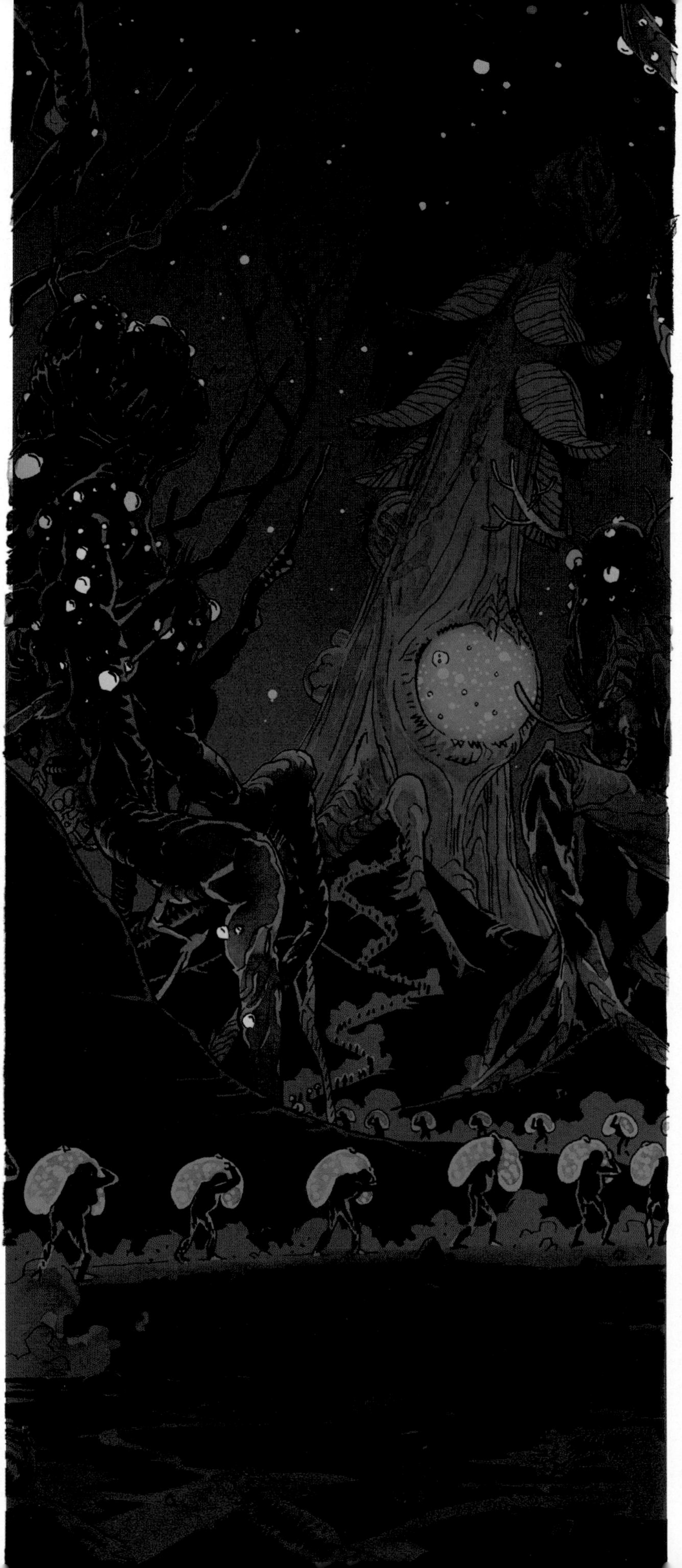

IT'S THE END
OF THE WORLD...
BUT WHAT ELSE IS
NEW, AM I RIGHT?

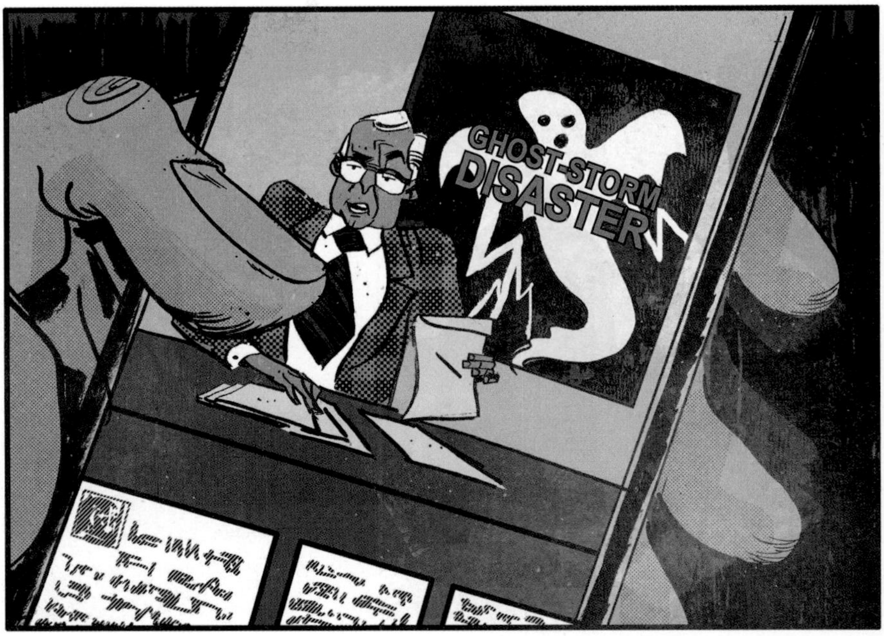
GHOST-STORM
DISASTER

STILL...
GHOST-STORMS
EVERY OTHER WEEK?

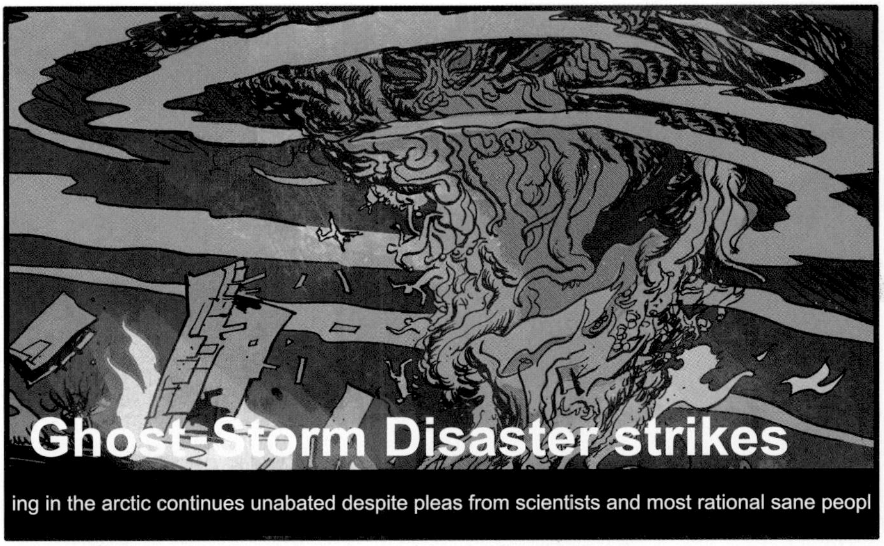
Ghost-Storm Disaster strikes
ing in the arctic continues unabated despite pleas from scientists and most rational sane peopl

ZOMBIES SHAMBLING
ACROSS AMERICA?

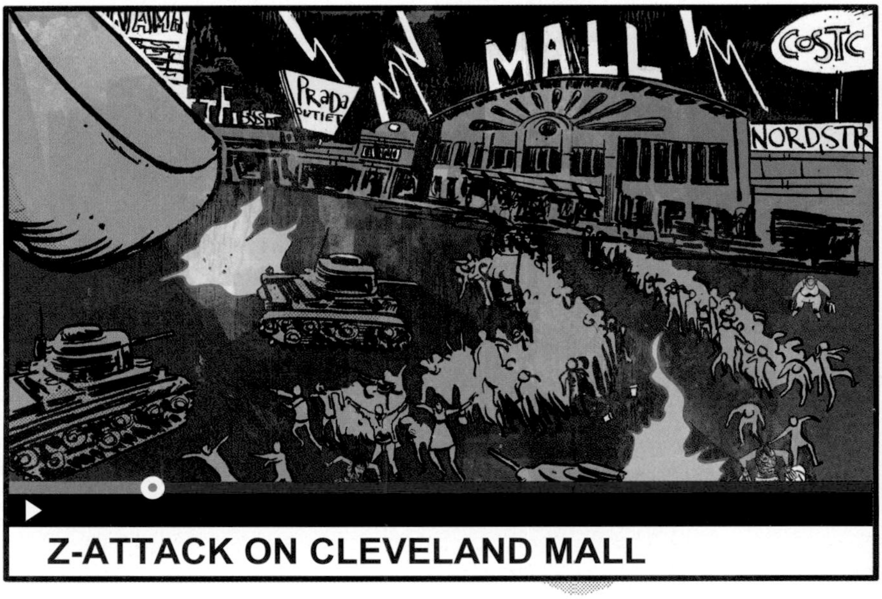
MALL
COSTC
Prada
OUTLET
NORDSTR
Z-ATTACK ON CLEVELAND MALL

VAMPIRES STRIKING OUT FROM THE JUNGLE?

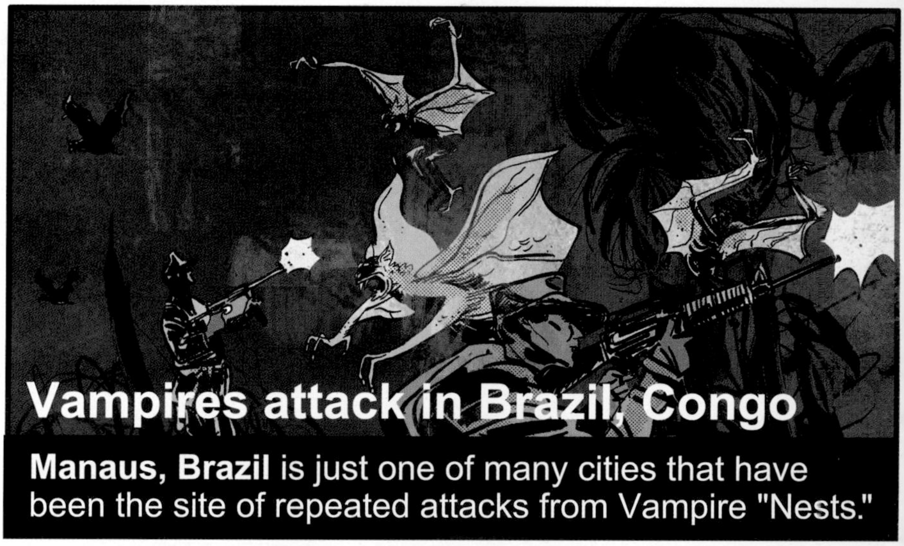
Vampires attack in Brazil, Congo
Manaus, Brazil is just one of many cities that have been the site of repeated attacks from Vampire "Nests."

THE TALKING HEADS DID THEIR USUAL PUPPET SHOW, NOT MUCH TO SEE HERE...

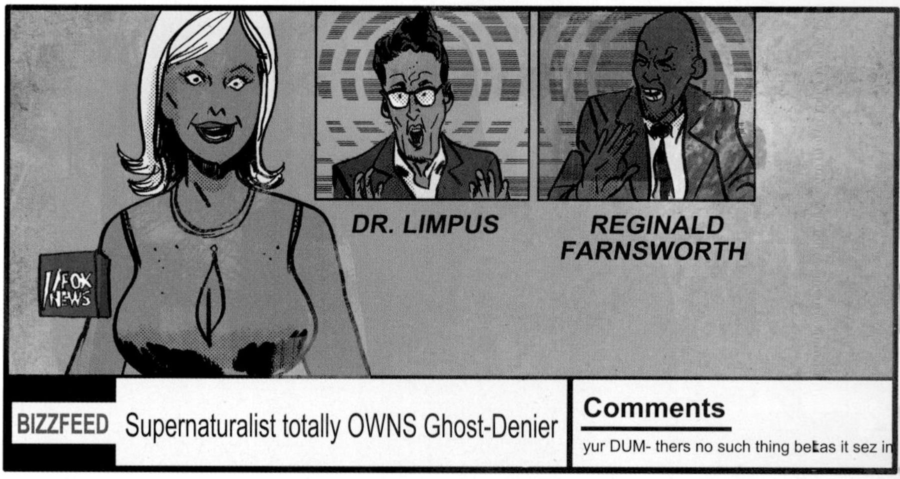
DR. LIMPUS
REGINALD FARNSWORTH
FOX NEWS
BIZZFEED
Supernaturalist totally OWNS Ghost-Denier
Comments
yur DUM- thers no such thing bekas it sez in

AND WHAT DID THE GRAVEDIGGERS UNION HAVE TO SAY?

THOSE TRADITIONAL SLAYERS OF THE UNDEAD?

THE ONES WHO ARE SUPPOSED TO KEEP ALL THAT SHIT IN CHECK?

WELL, PUBLICLY THEY SAID THE SAME THING AS EVERYONE ELSE--

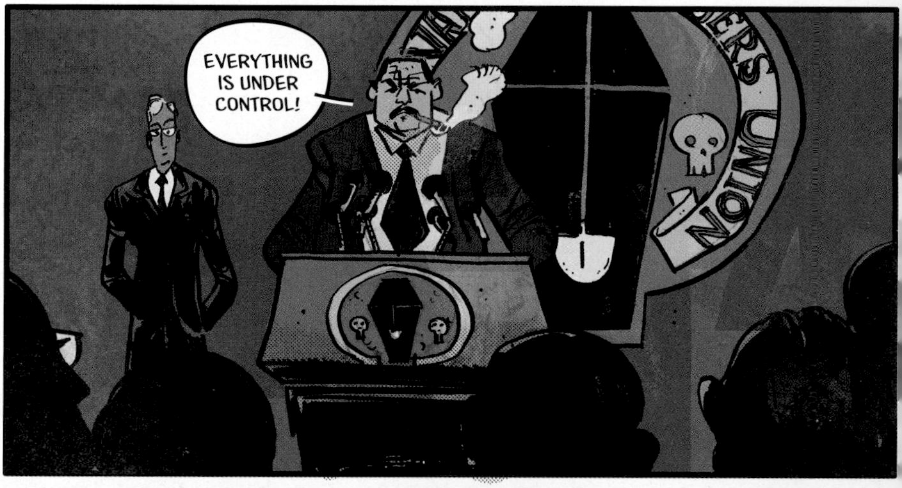
EVERYTHING IS UNDER CONTROL!

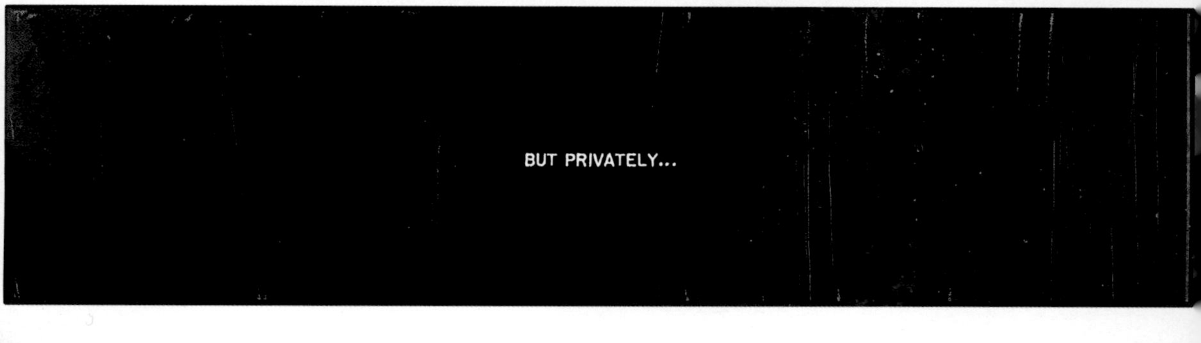
BUT PRIVATELY...

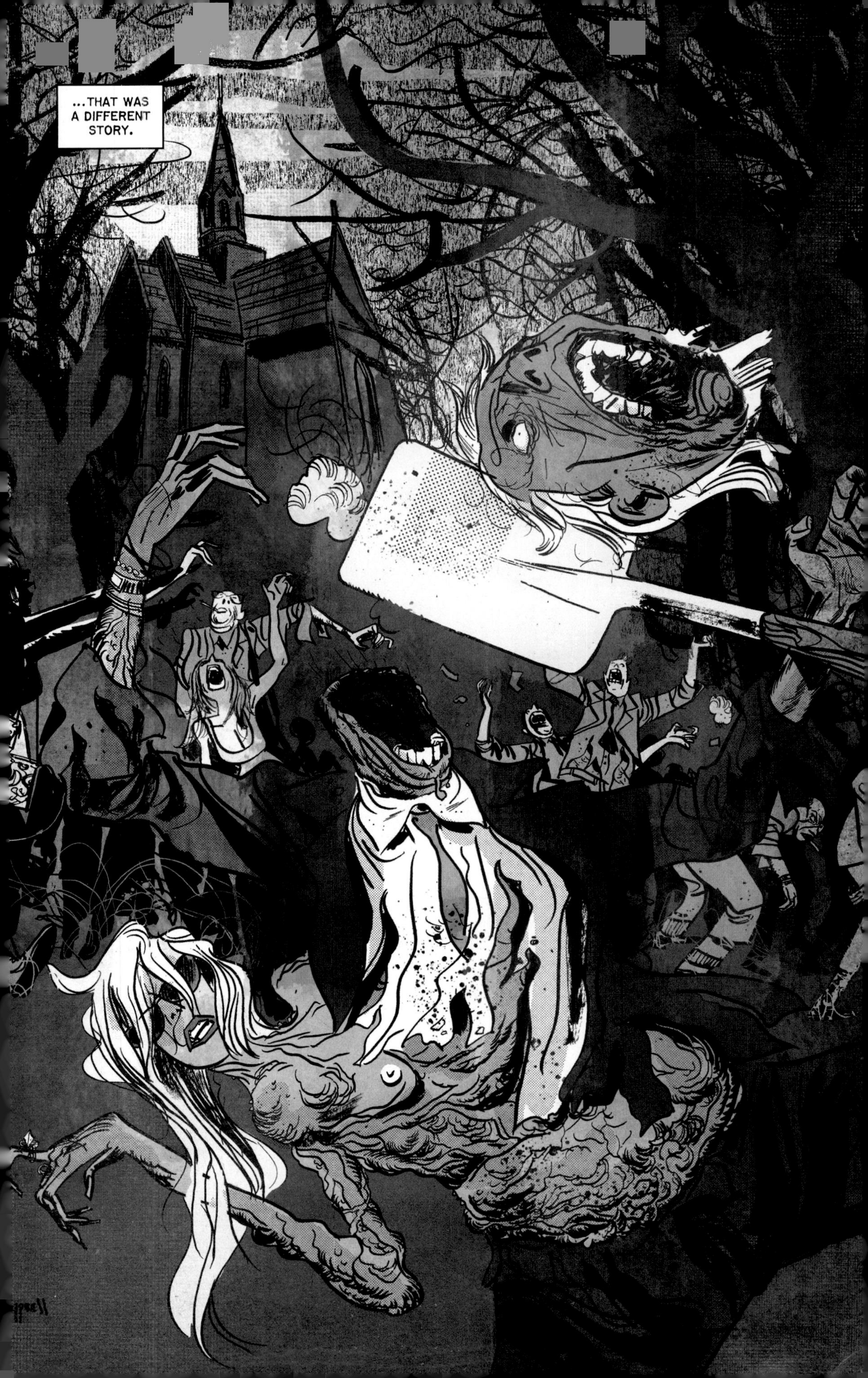
...THAT WAS A DIFFERENT STORY.

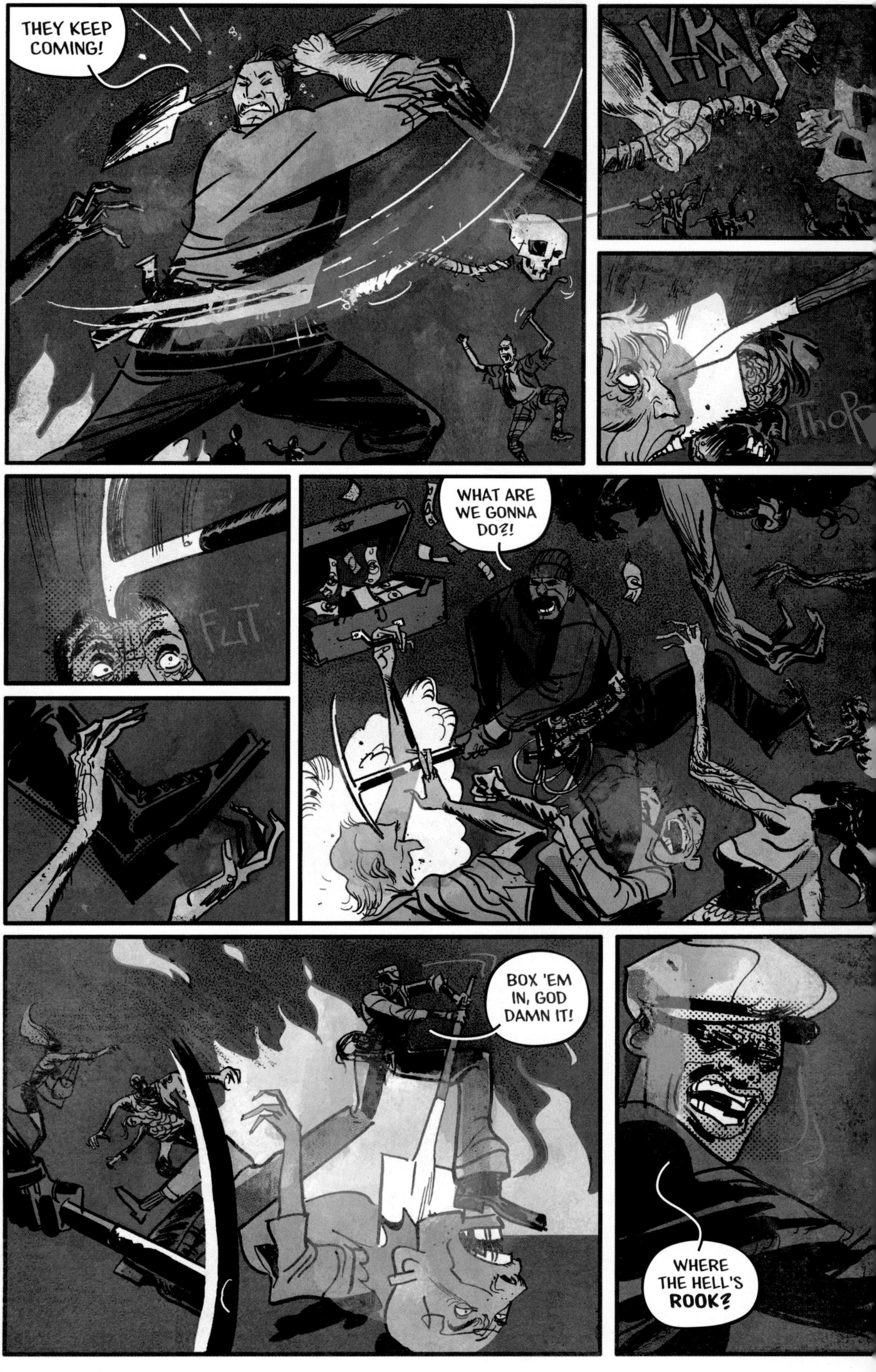
THEY KEEP COMING!
KRAK
THOP
FUT
WHAT ARE WE GONNA DO?!
BOX 'EM IN, GOD DAMN IT!
WHERE THE HELL'S ROOK?

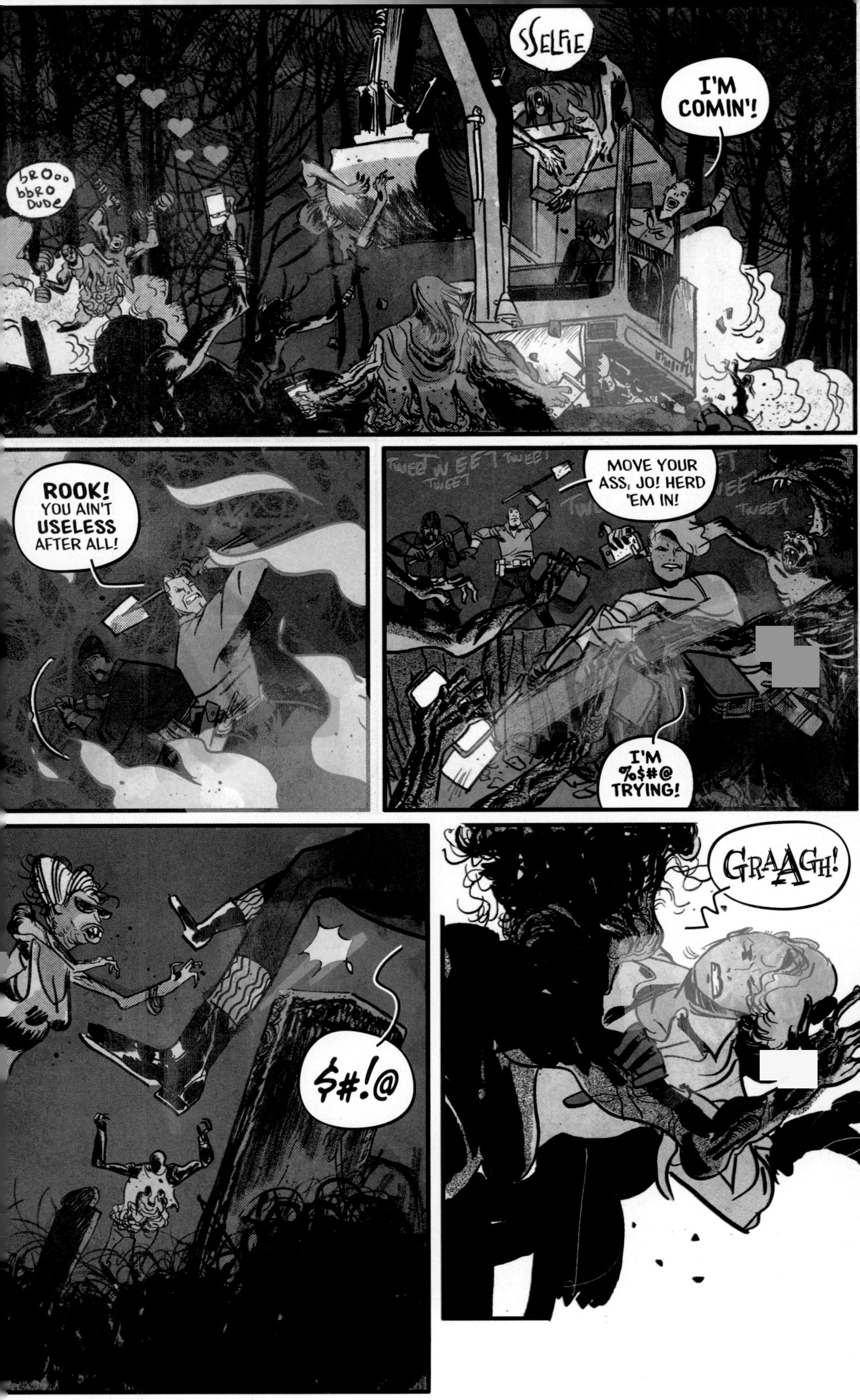

bROoo bbRO DUDE
SSELFIE
I'M COMIN'!
ROOK! YOU AIN'T USELESS AFTER ALL!
MOVE YOUR ASS, JO! HERD 'EM IN!
I'M %$#@ TRYING!
$#!@
GRAAGH!

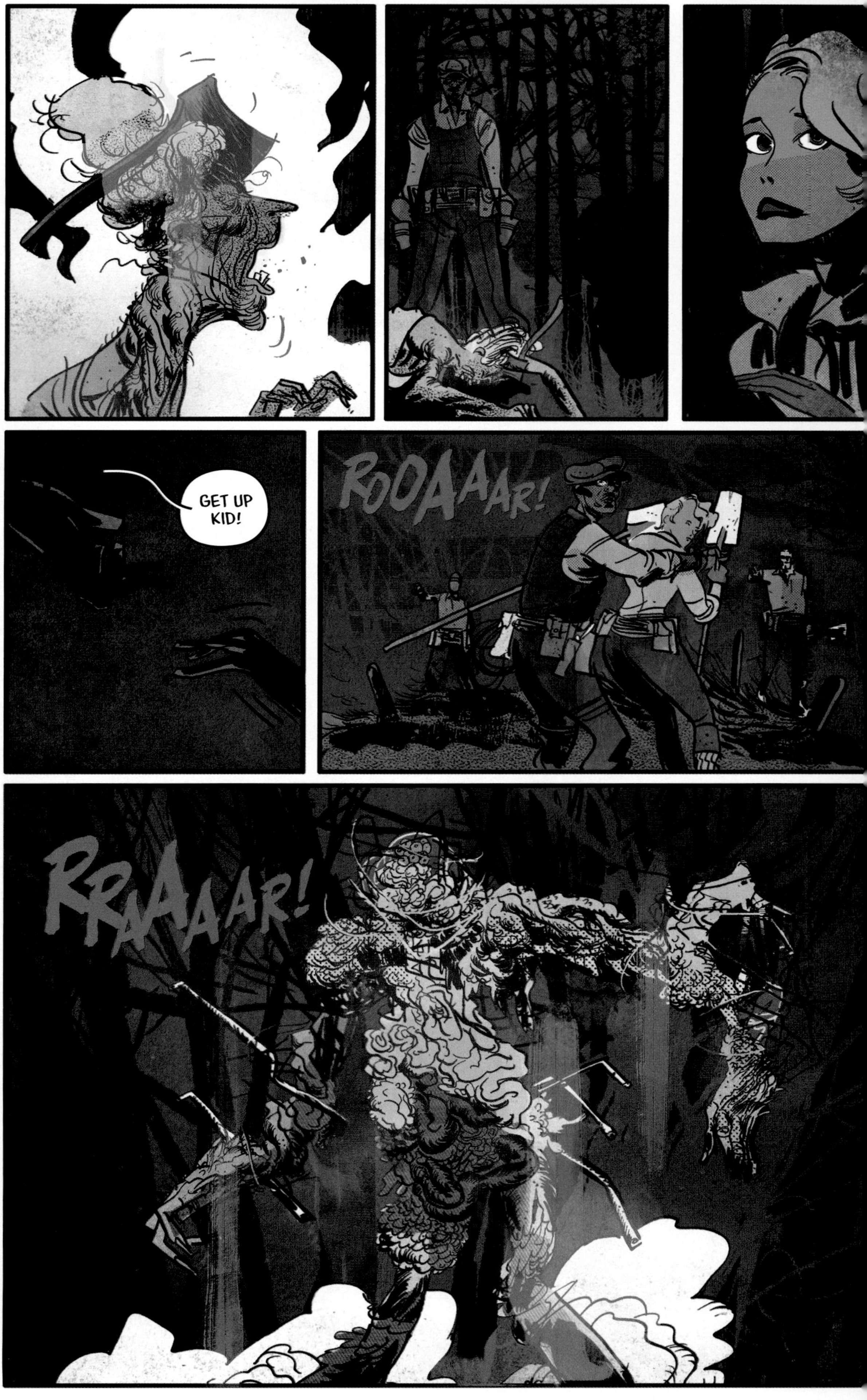
GET UP KID!
ROOAAAR!
RRAAAAR!

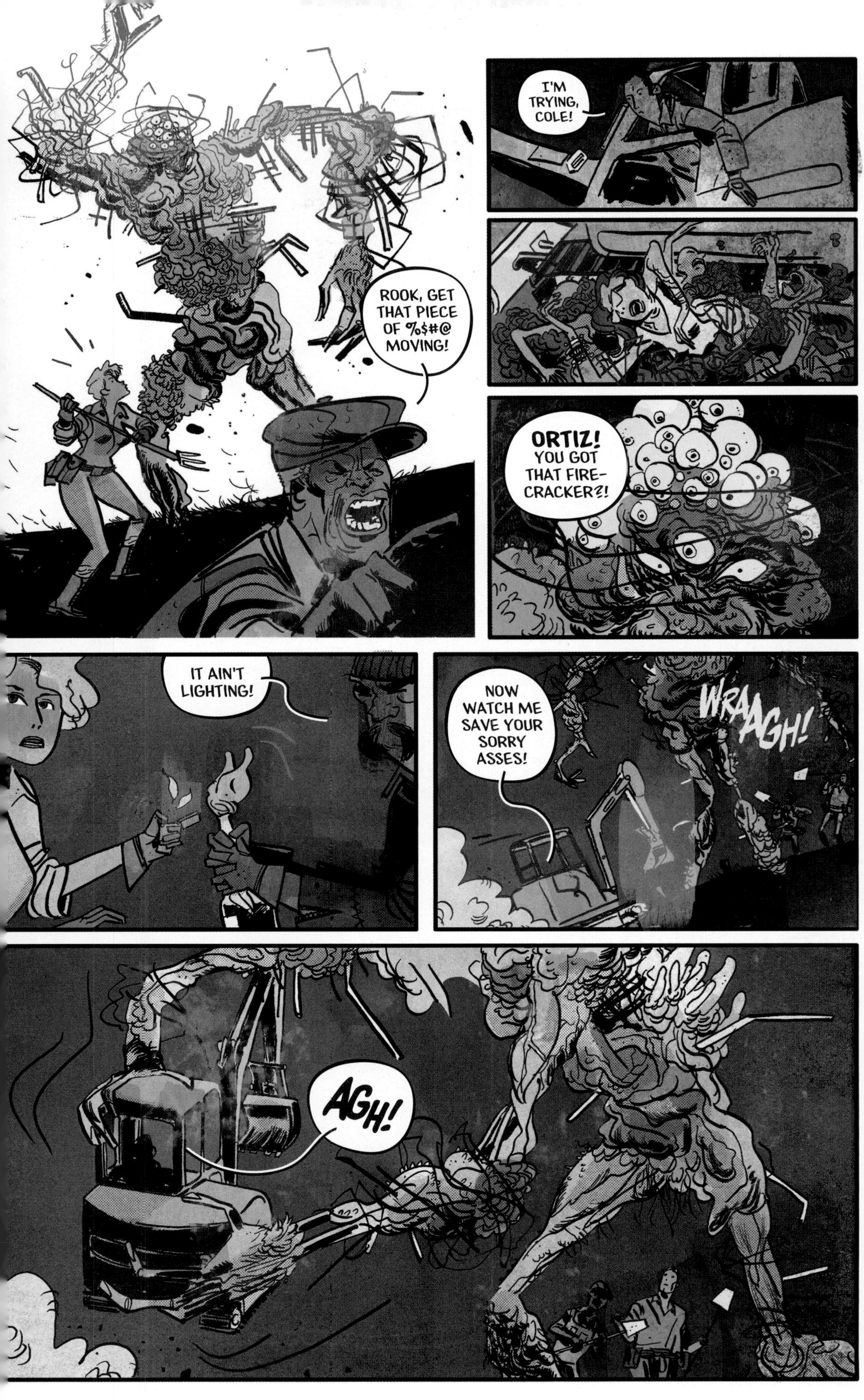
ROOK, GET THAT PIECE OF %$#@ MOVING!
I'M TRYING, COLE!
ORTIZ! YOU GOT THAT FIRE-CRACKER?!
IT AIN'T LIGHTING!
NOW WATCH ME SAVE YOUR SORRY ASSES!
WRAAAGH!
AGH!

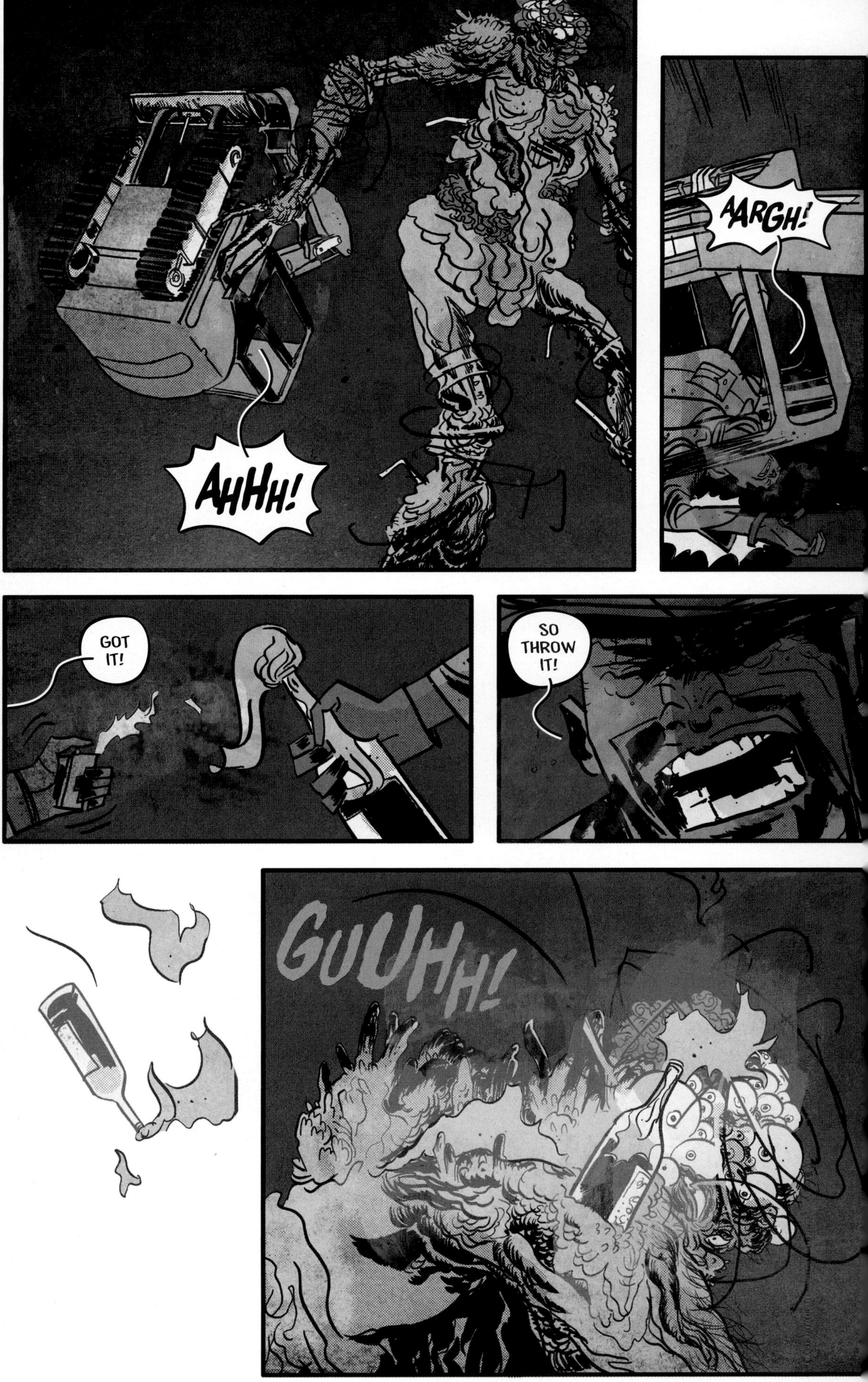
AHHH!
AARGH!
GOT IT!
SO THROW IT!
GUUHH!

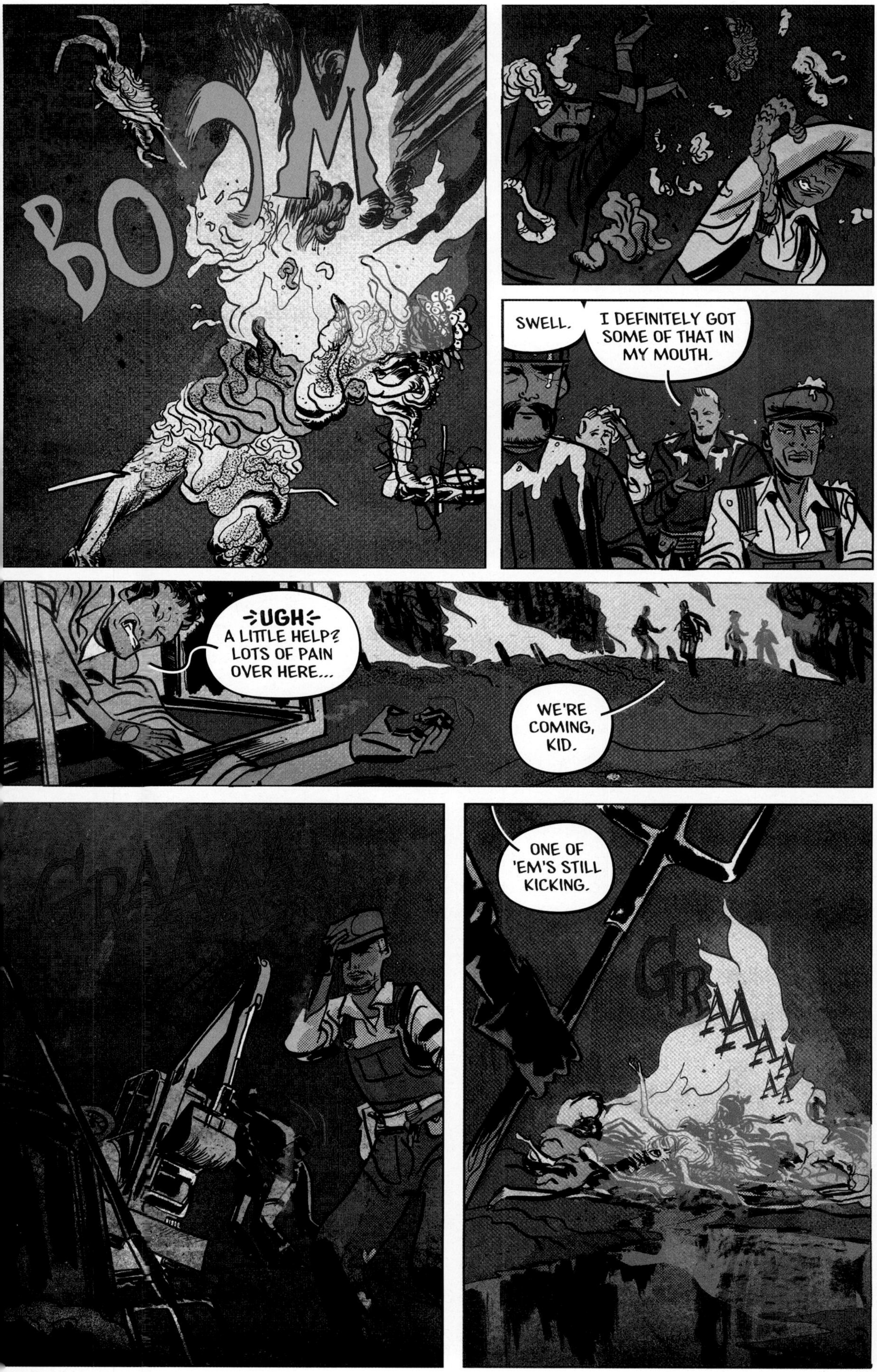
BOOM
SWELL.
I DEFINITELY GOT SOME OF THAT IN MY MOUTH.
UGH
A LITTLE HELP? LOTS OF PAIN OVER HERE...
WE'RE COMING, KID.
GRAAAA
ONE OF 'EM'S STILL KICKING.
GRAAAAAAA

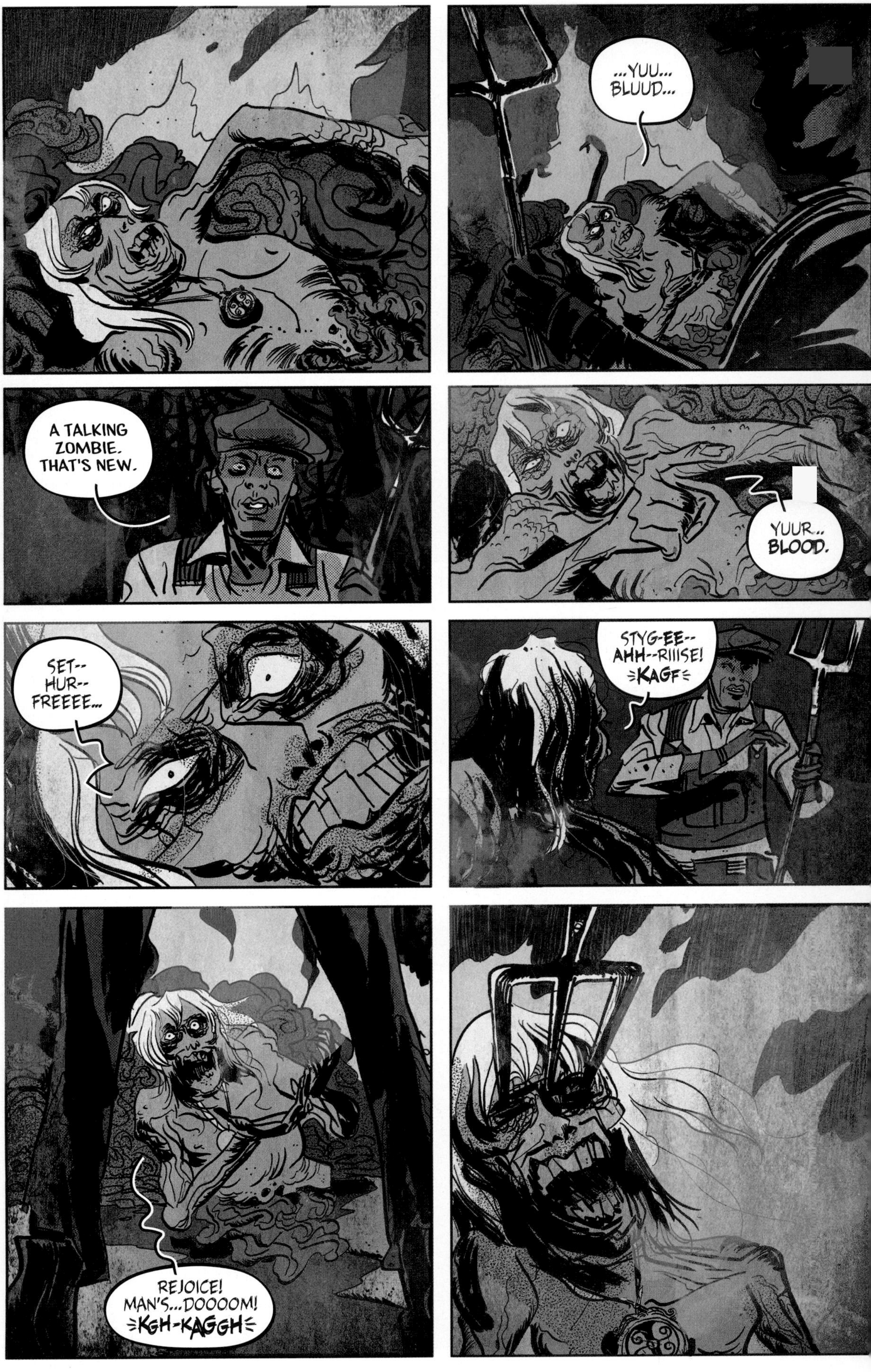
...YUU... BLUUD...
A TALKING ZOMBIE. THAT'S NEW.
YUUR... BLOOD.
SET-- HUR-- FREEEE...
STYG-EE-- AHH--RIIISE!
KAGF
REJOICE! MAN'S...DOOOOM!
KGH-KAGGH

WHAT YOU GOT THERE?

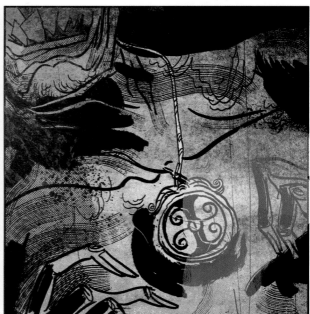

WHAT THE HELL...?

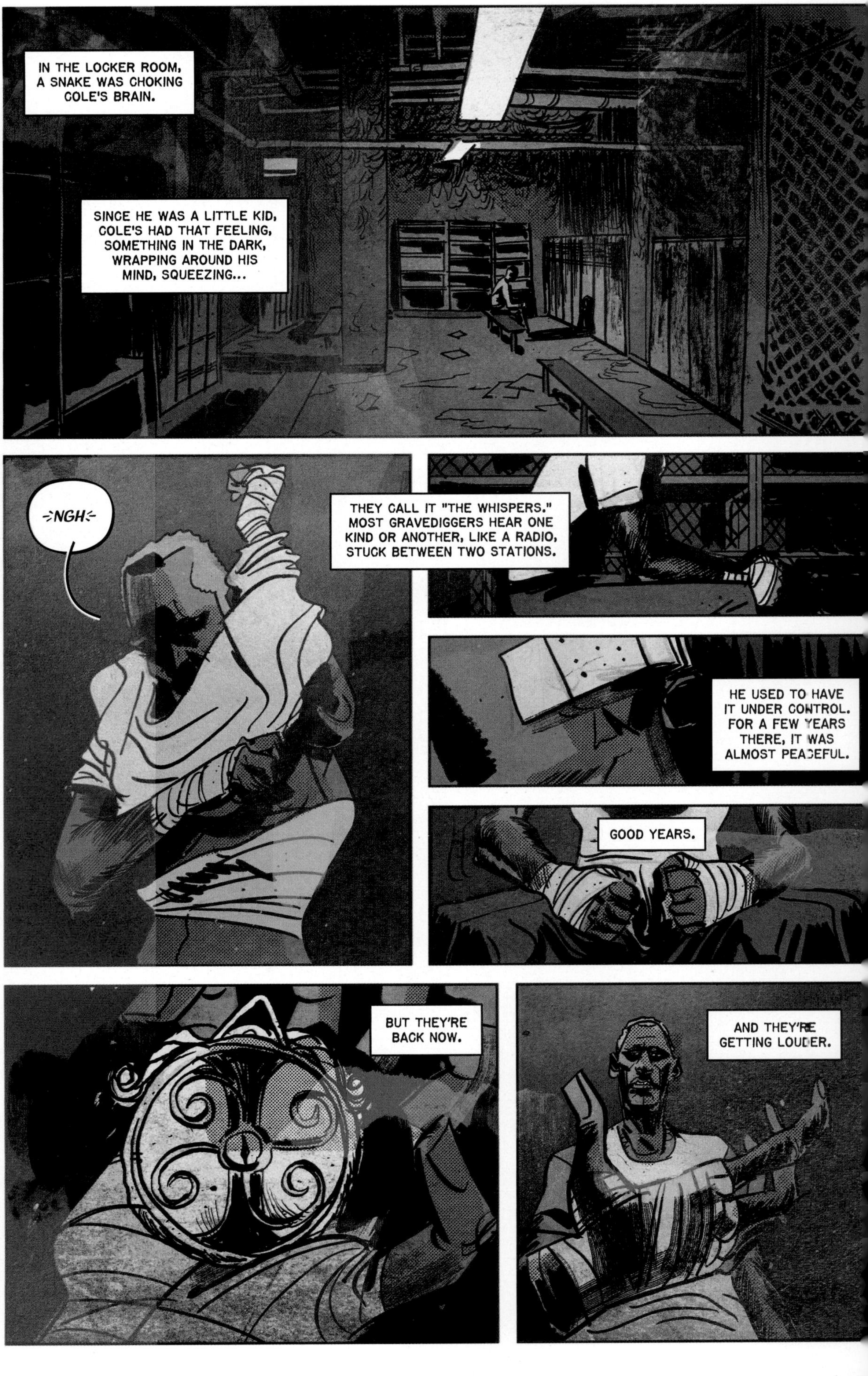
IN THE LOCKER ROOM, A SNAKE WAS CHOKING COLE'S BRAIN.
SINCE HE WAS A LITTLE KID, COLE'S HAD THAT FEELING, SOMETHING IN THE DARK, WRAPPING AROUND HIS MIND, SQUEEZING...
NGH
THEY CALL IT "THE WHISPERS." MOST GRAVEDIGGERS HEAR ONE KIND OR ANOTHER, LIKE A RADIO, STUCK BETWEEN TWO STATIONS.
HE USED TO HAVE IT UNDER CONTROL. FOR A FEW YEARS THERE, IT WAS ALMOST PEACEFUL.
GOOD YEARS.
BUT THEY'RE BACK NOW.
AND THEY'RE GETTING LOUDER.

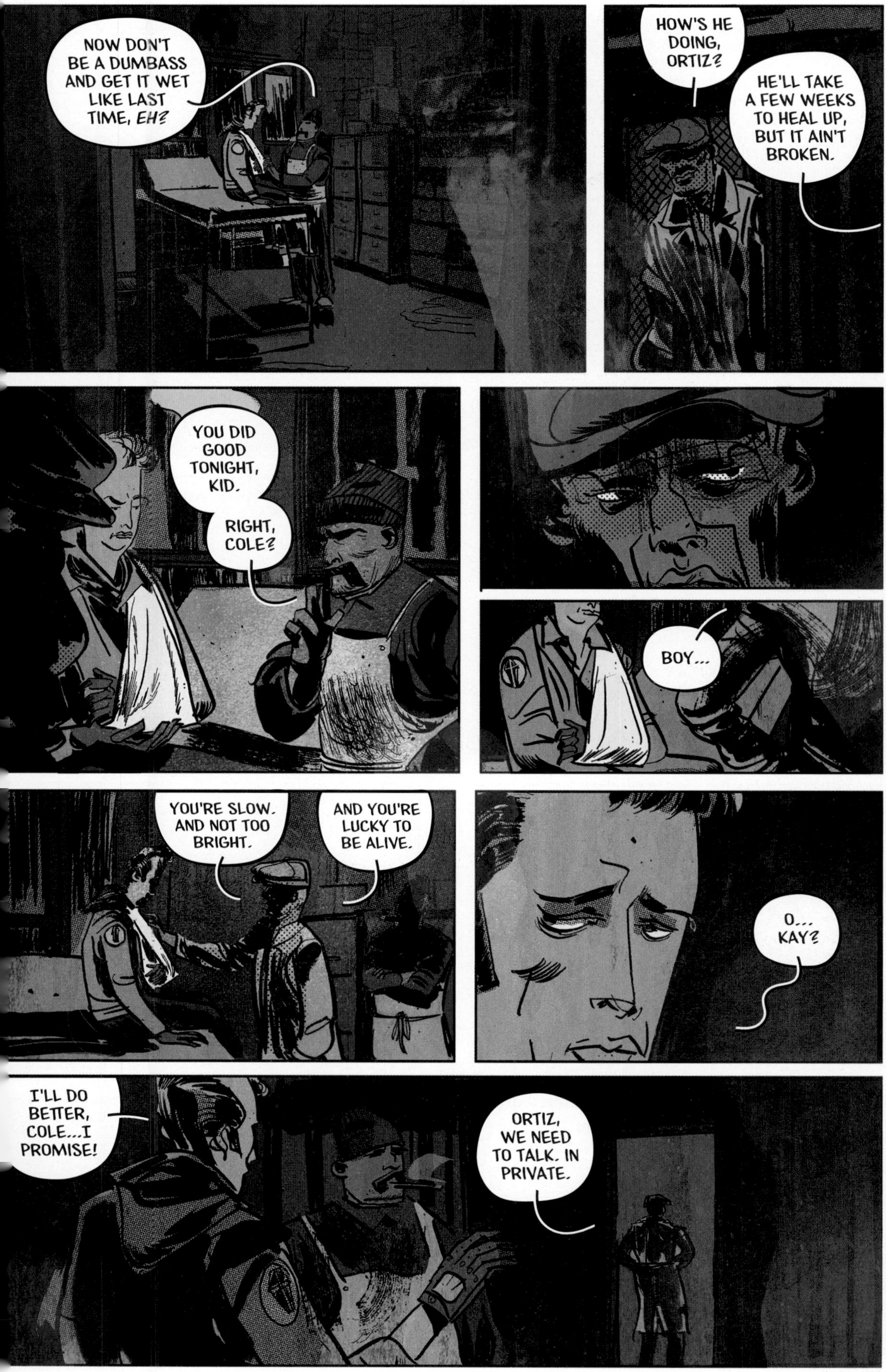
NOW DON'T BE A DUMBASS AND GET IT WET LIKE LAST TIME, *EH?*
HOW'S HE DOING, ORTIZ?
HE'LL TAKE A FEW WEEKS TO HEAL UP, BUT IT AIN'T BROKEN.
YOU DID GOOD TONIGHT, KID.
RIGHT, COLE?
BOY...
YOU'RE SLOW. AND NOT TOO BRIGHT.
AND YOU'RE LUCKY TO BE ALIVE.
O... KAY?
I'LL DO BETTER, COLE...I PROMISE!
ORTIZ, WE NEED TO TALK. IN PRIVATE.

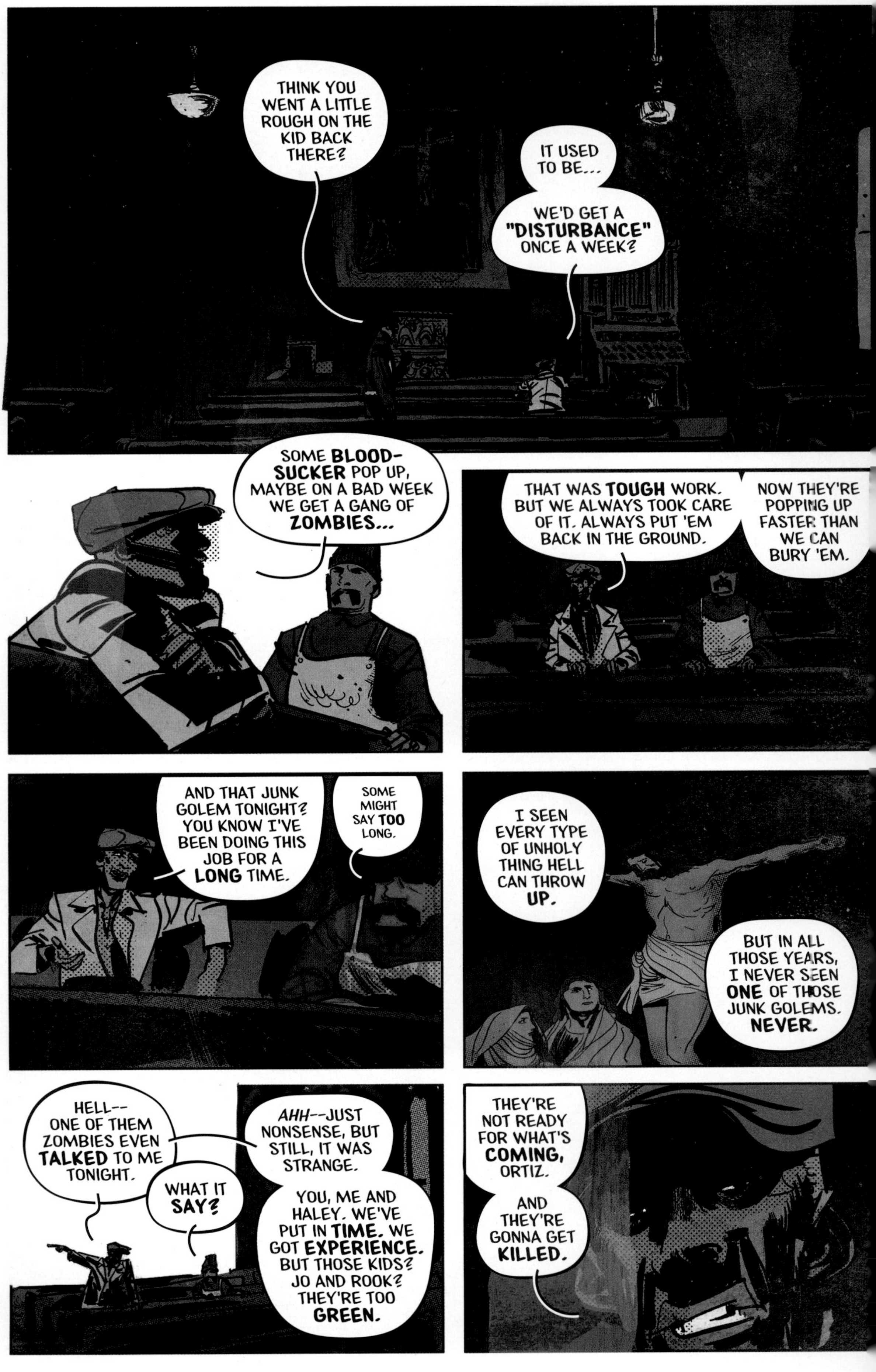
THINK YOU WENT A LITTLE ROUGH ON THE KID BACK THERE?
IT USED TO BE...
WE'D GET A "DISTURBANCE" ONCE A WEEK?
SOME BLOOD-SUCKER POP UP, MAYBE ON A BAD WEEK WE GET A GANG OF ZOMBIES...
THAT WAS TOUGH WORK. BUT WE ALWAYS TOOK CARE OF IT. ALWAYS PUT 'EM BACK IN THE GROUND.
NOW THEY'RE POPPING UP FASTER THAN WE CAN BURY 'EM.
AND THAT JUNK GOLEM TONIGHT? YOU KNOW I'VE BEEN DOING THIS JOB FOR A LONG TIME.
SOME MIGHT SAY TOO LONG.
I SEEN EVERY TYPE OF UNHOLY THING HELL CAN THROW UP.
BUT IN ALL THOSE YEARS, I NEVER SEEN ONE OF THOSE JUNK GOLEMS. NEVER.
HELL-- ONE OF THEM ZOMBIES EVEN TALKED TO ME TONIGHT.
AHH--JUST NONSENSE, BUT STILL, IT WAS STRANGE.
WHAT IT SAY?
YOU, ME AND HALEY. WE'VE PUT IN TIME. WE GOT EXPERIENCE. BUT THOSE KIDS? JO AND ROOK? THEY'RE TOO GREEN.
THEY'RE NOT READY FOR WHAT'S COMING, ORTIZ.
AND THEY'RE GONNA GET KILLED.

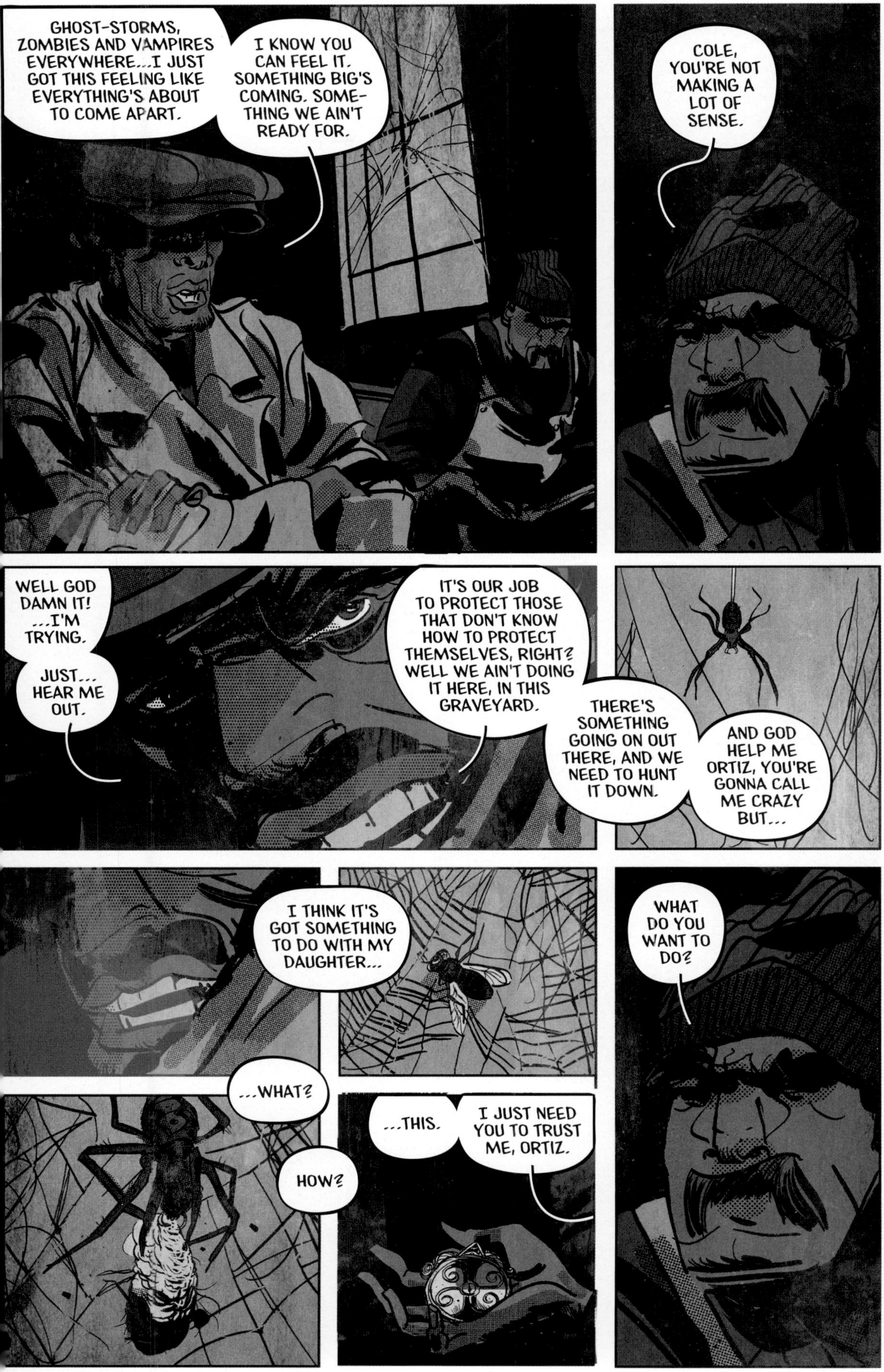
GHOST-STORMS, ZOMBIES AND VAMPIRES EVERYWHERE...I JUST GOT THIS FEELING LIKE EVERYTHING'S ABOUT TO COME APART.
I KNOW YOU CAN FEEL IT. SOMETHING BIG'S COMING. SOME-THING WE AIN'T READY FOR.
COLE, YOU'RE NOT MAKING A LOT OF SENSE.
WELL GOD DAMN IT! ...I'M TRYING.
JUST... HEAR ME OUT.
IT'S OUR JOB TO PROTECT THOSE THAT DON'T KNOW HOW TO PROTECT THEMSELVES, RIGHT? WELL WE AIN'T DOING IT HERE, IN THIS GRAVEYARD.
THERE'S SOMETHING GOING ON OUT THERE, AND WE NEED TO HUNT IT DOWN.
AND GOD HELP ME ORTIZ, YOU'RE GONNA CALL ME CRAZY BUT...
I THINK IT'S GOT SOMETHING TO DO WITH MY DAUGHTER...
WHAT DO YOU WANT TO DO?
...WHAT?
...THIS.
I JUST NEED YOU TO TRUST ME, ORTIZ.
HOW?

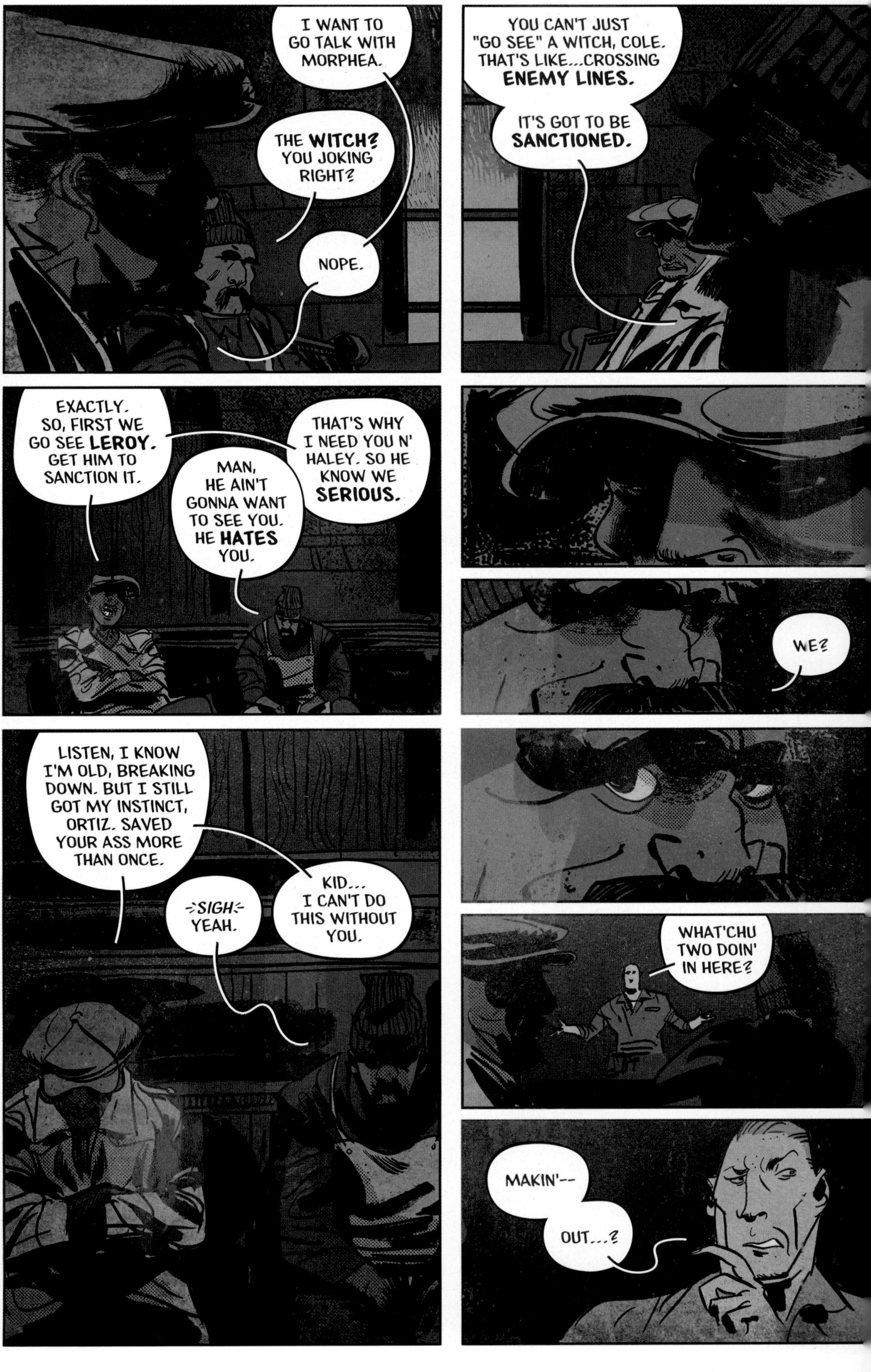
I WANT TO GO TALK WITH MORPHEA.
THE WITCH? YOU JOKING RIGHT?
NOPE.
YOU CAN'T JUST "GO SEE" A WITCH, COLE. THAT'S LIKE...CROSSING ENEMY LINES.
IT'S GOT TO BE SANCTIONED.
EXACTLY. SO, FIRST WE GO SEE LEROY. GET HIM TO SANCTION IT.
MAN, HE AIN'T GONNA WANT TO SEE YOU. HE HATES YOU.
THAT'S WHY I NEED YOU N' HALEY. SO HE KNOW WE SERIOUS.
WE?
LISTEN, I KNOW I'M OLD, BREAKING DOWN. BUT I STILL GOT MY INSTINCT, ORTIZ. SAVED YOUR ASS MORE THAN ONCE.
KID... I CAN'T DO THIS WITHOUT YOU.
-SIGH- YEAH.
WHAT'CHU TWO DOIN' IN HERE?
MAKIN'--
OUT...?

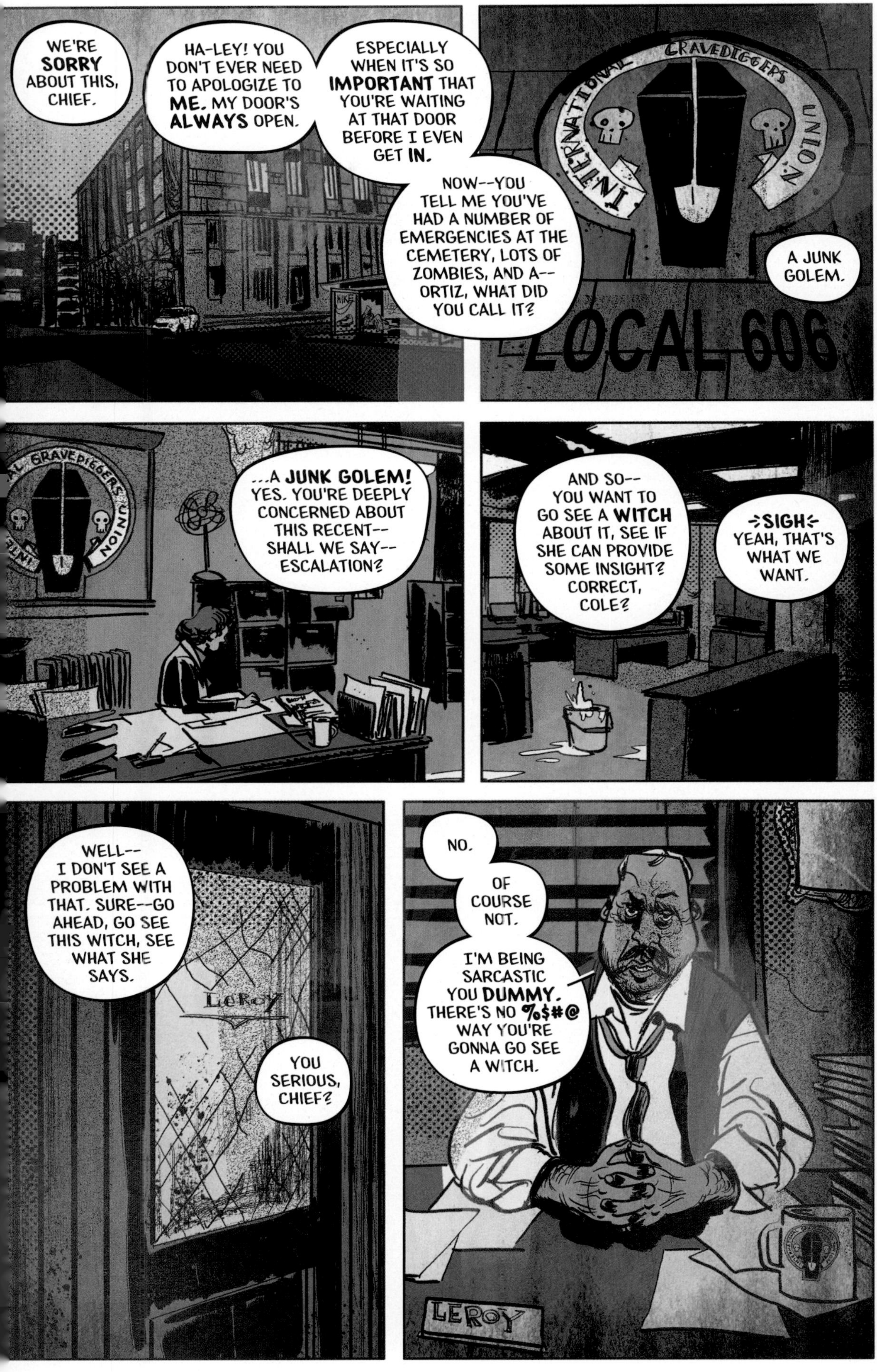
WE'RE SORRY ABOUT THIS, CHIEF.
HA-LEY! YOU DON'T EVER NEED TO APOLOGIZE TO ME. MY DOOR'S ALWAYS OPEN.
ESPECIALLY WHEN IT'S SO IMPORTANT THAT YOU'RE WAITING AT THAT DOOR BEFORE I EVEN GET IN.
NOW--YOU TELL ME YOU'VE HAD A NUMBER OF EMERGENCIES AT THE CEMETERY, LOTS OF ZOMBIES, AND A-- ORTIZ, WHAT DID YOU CALL IT?
INTERNATIONAL GRAVEDIGGERS UNION
A JUNK GOLEM.
LOCAL 606
...A JUNK GOLEM! YES. YOU'RE DEEPLY CONCERNED ABOUT THIS RECENT-- SHALL WE SAY-- ESCALATION?
AND SO-- YOU WANT TO GO SEE A WITCH ABOUT IT, SEE IF SHE CAN PROVIDE SOME INSIGHT? CORRECT, COLE?
SIGH YEAH, THAT'S WHAT WE WANT.
WELL-- I DON'T SEE A PROBLEM WITH THAT. SURE--GO AHEAD, GO SEE THIS WITCH, SEE WHAT SHE SAYS.
LEROY
YOU SERIOUS, CHIEF?
NO.
OF COURSE NOT.
I'M BEING SARCASTIC YOU DUMMY. THERE'S NO %$#@ WAY YOU'RE GONNA GO SEE A WITCH.
LEROY

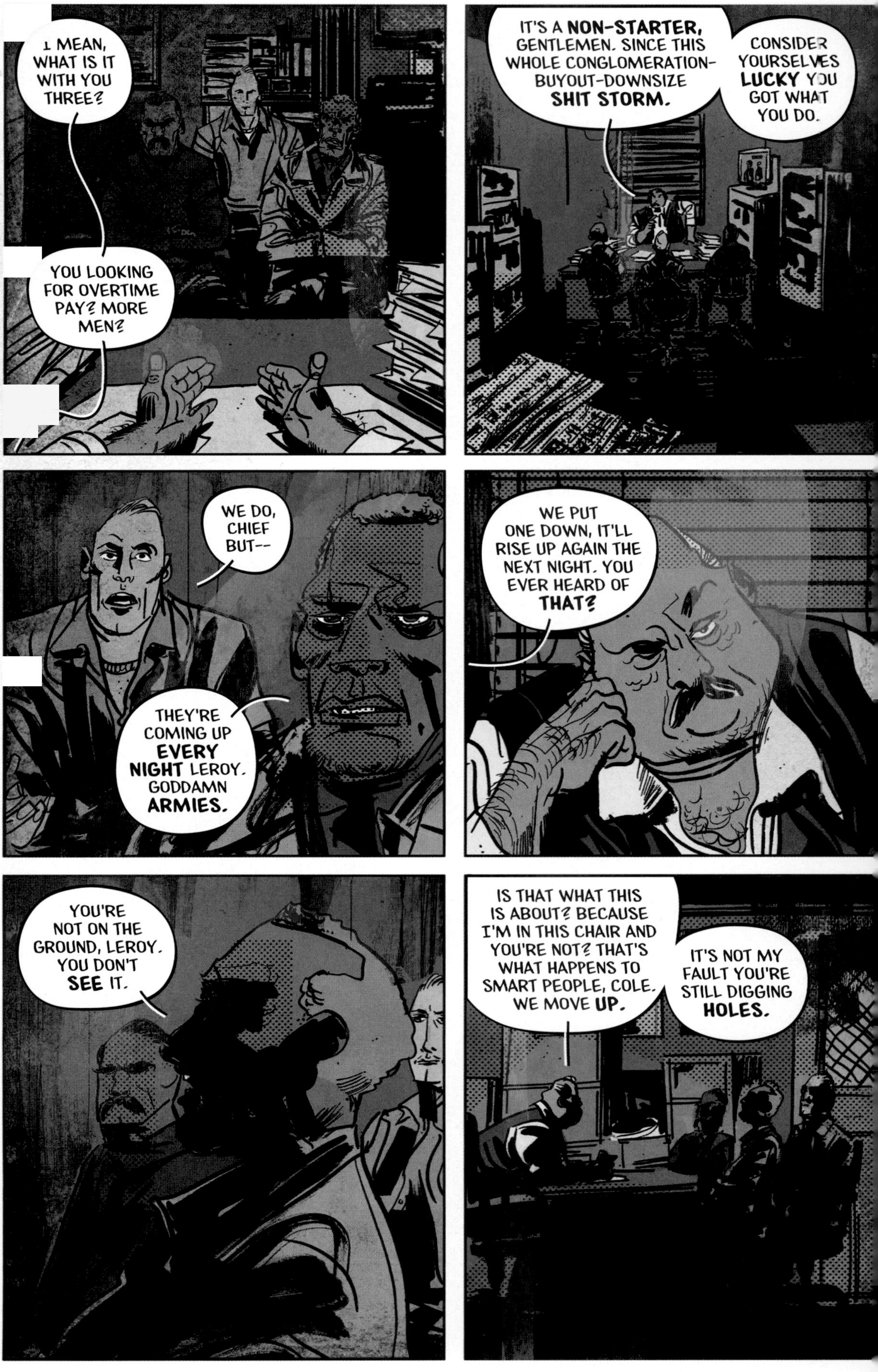
I MEAN, WHAT IS IT WITH YOU THREE?
YOU LOOKING FOR OVERTIME PAY? MORE MEN?
IT'S A NON-STARTER, GENTLEMEN. SINCE THIS WHOLE CONGLOMERATION-BUYOUT-DOWNSIZE SHIT STORM.
CONSIDER YOURSELVES LUCKY YOU GOT WHAT YOU DO.
WE DO, CHIEF BUT--
THEY'RE COMING UP EVERY NIGHT LEROY. GODDAMN ARMIES.
WE PUT ONE DOWN, IT'LL RISE UP AGAIN THE NEXT NIGHT. YOU EVER HEARD OF THAT?
YOU'RE NOT ON THE GROUND, LEROY. YOU DON'T SEE IT.
IS THAT WHAT THIS IS ABOUT? BECAUSE I'M IN THIS CHAIR AND YOU'RE NOT? THAT'S WHAT HAPPENS TO SMART PEOPLE, COLE. WE MOVE UP.
IT'S NOT MY FAULT YOU'RE STILL DIGGING HOLES.

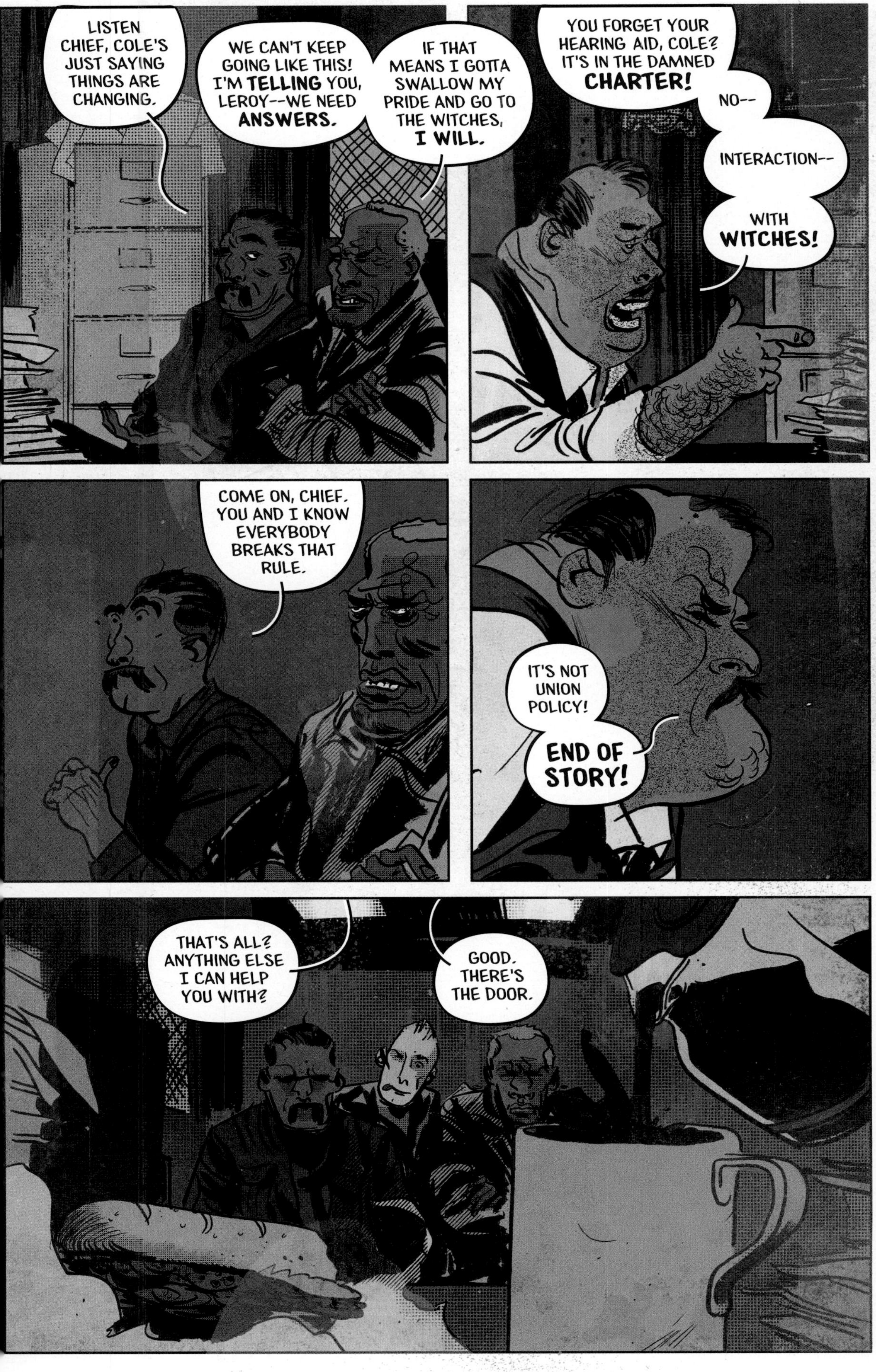
LISTEN CHIEF, COLE'S JUST SAYING THINGS ARE CHANGING.
WE CAN'T KEEP GOING LIKE THIS! I'M TELLING YOU, LEROY--WE NEED ANSWERS.
IF THAT MEANS I GOTTA SWALLOW MY PRIDE AND GO TO THE WITCHES, I WILL.
YOU FORGET YOUR HEARING AID, COLE? IT'S IN THE DAMNED CHARTER!
NO--
INTERACTION--
WITH WITCHES!
COME ON, CHIEF. YOU AND I KNOW EVERYBODY BREAKS THAT RULE.
IT'S NOT UNION POLICY!
END OF STORY!
THAT'S ALL? ANYTHING ELSE I CAN HELP YOU WITH?
GOOD. THERE'S THE DOOR.

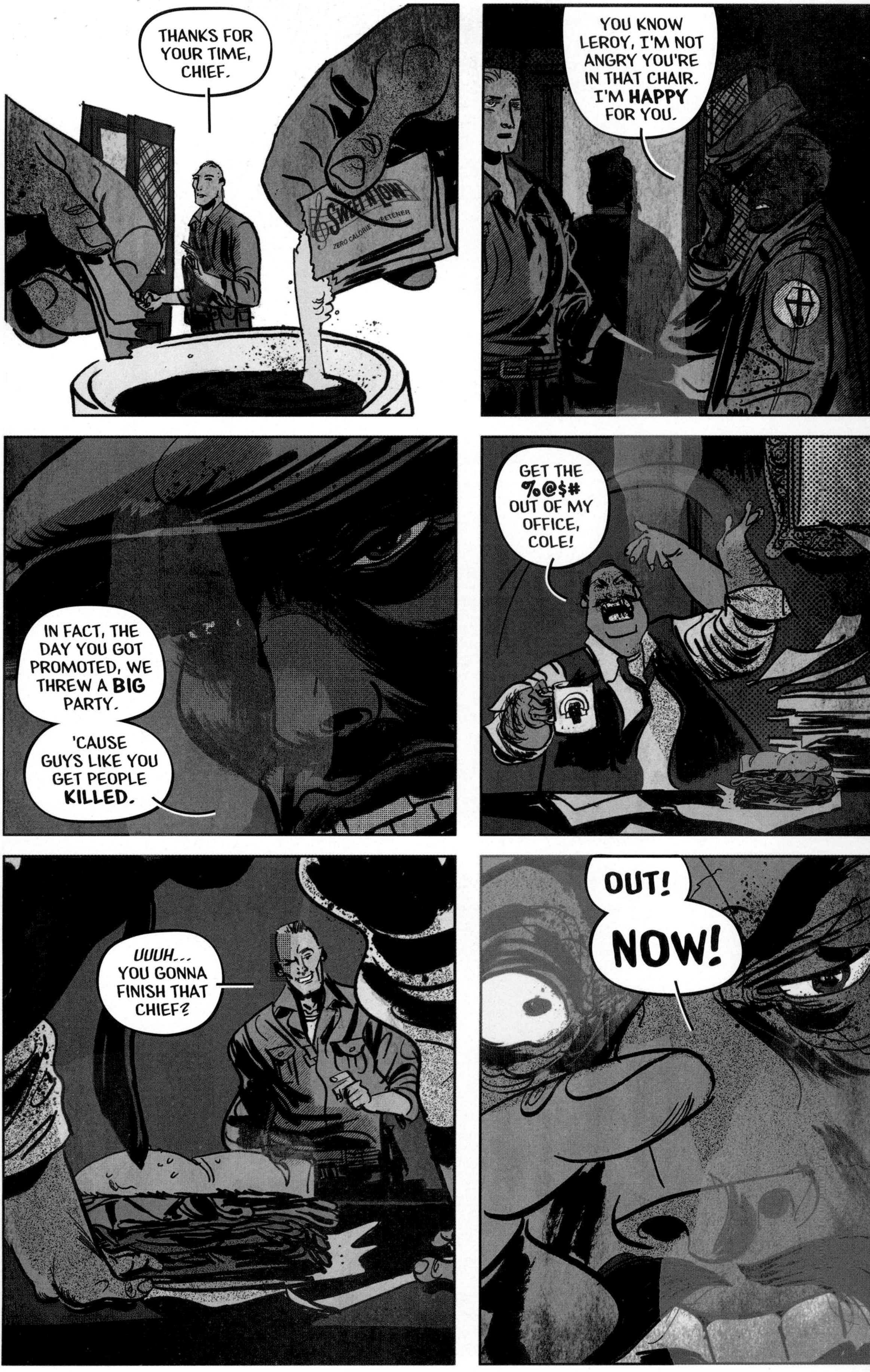
THANKS FOR YOUR TIME, CHIEF.
SWEET'N LOW
ZERO CALORIE SWEETENER
YOU KNOW LEROY, I'M NOT ANGRY YOU'RE IN THAT CHAIR. I'M HAPPY FOR YOU.
IN FACT, THE DAY YOU GOT PROMOTED, WE THREW A BIG PARTY.
'CAUSE GUYS LIKE YOU GET PEOPLE KILLED.
GET THE %@$# OUT OF MY OFFICE, COLE!
UUUH... YOU GONNA FINISH THAT CHIEF?
OUT!
NOW!

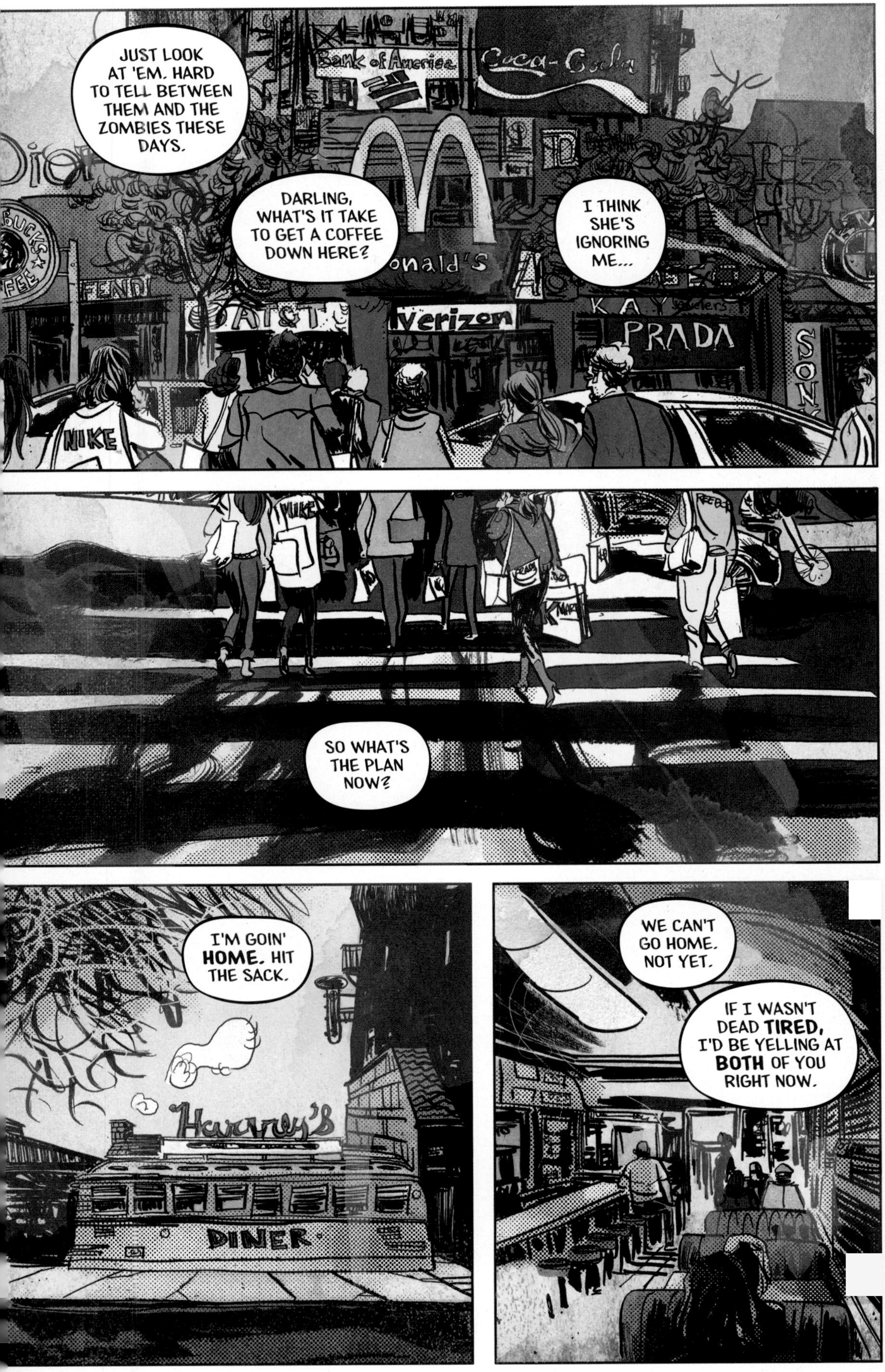
JUST LOOK AT 'EM. HARD TO TELL BETWEEN THEM AND THE ZOMBIES THESE DAYS.
DARLING, WHAT'S IT TAKE TO GET A COFFEE DOWN HERE?
I THINK SHE'S IGNORING ME...
SO WHAT'S THE PLAN NOW?
I'M GOIN' **HOME.** HIT THE SACK.
WE CAN'T GO HOME. NOT YET.
IF I WASN'T DEAD **TIRED,** I'D BE YELLING AT **BOTH** OF YOU RIGHT NOW.
Bank of America
Coca-Cola
verizon
PRADA
NIKE
DINER

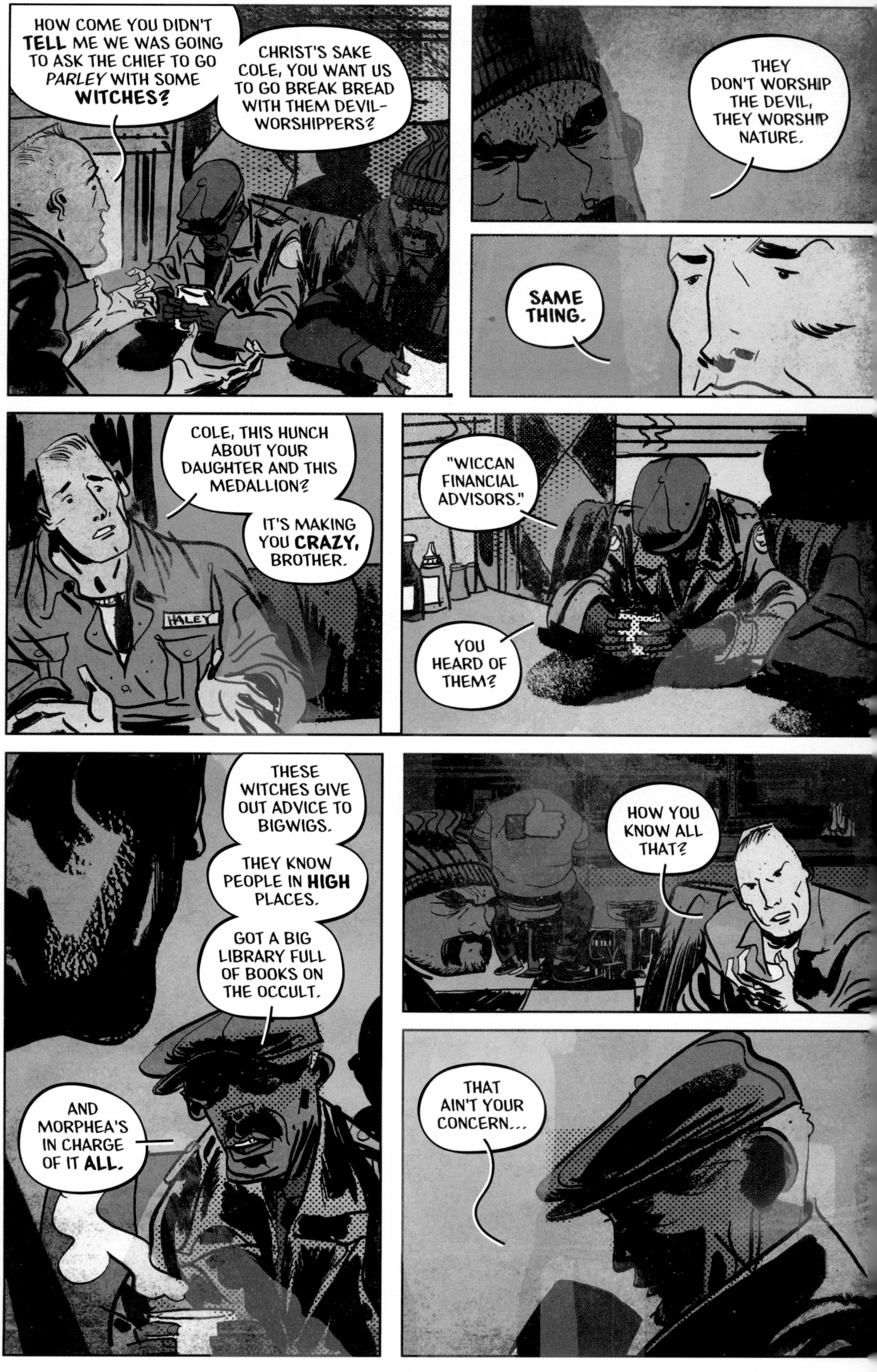

HOW COME YOU DIDN'T TELL ME WE WAS GOING TO ASK THE CHIEF TO GO PARLEY WITH SOME WITCHES?
CHRIST'S SAKE COLE, YOU WANT US TO GO BREAK BREAD WITH THEM DEVIL-WORSHIPPERS?
THEY DON'T WORSHIP THE DEVIL, THEY WORSHIP NATURE.
SAME THING.
COLE, THIS HUNCH ABOUT YOUR DAUGHTER AND THIS MEDALLION?
IT'S MAKING YOU CRAZY, BROTHER.
HALEY
"WICCAN FINANCIAL ADVISORS."
YOU HEARD OF THEM?
THESE WITCHES GIVE OUT ADVICE TO BIGWIGS.
THEY KNOW PEOPLE IN HIGH PLACES.
GOT A BIG LIBRARY FULL OF BOOKS ON THE OCCULT.
AND MORPHEA'S IN CHARGE OF IT ALL.
HOW YOU KNOW ALL THAT?
THAT AIN'T YOUR CONCERN...

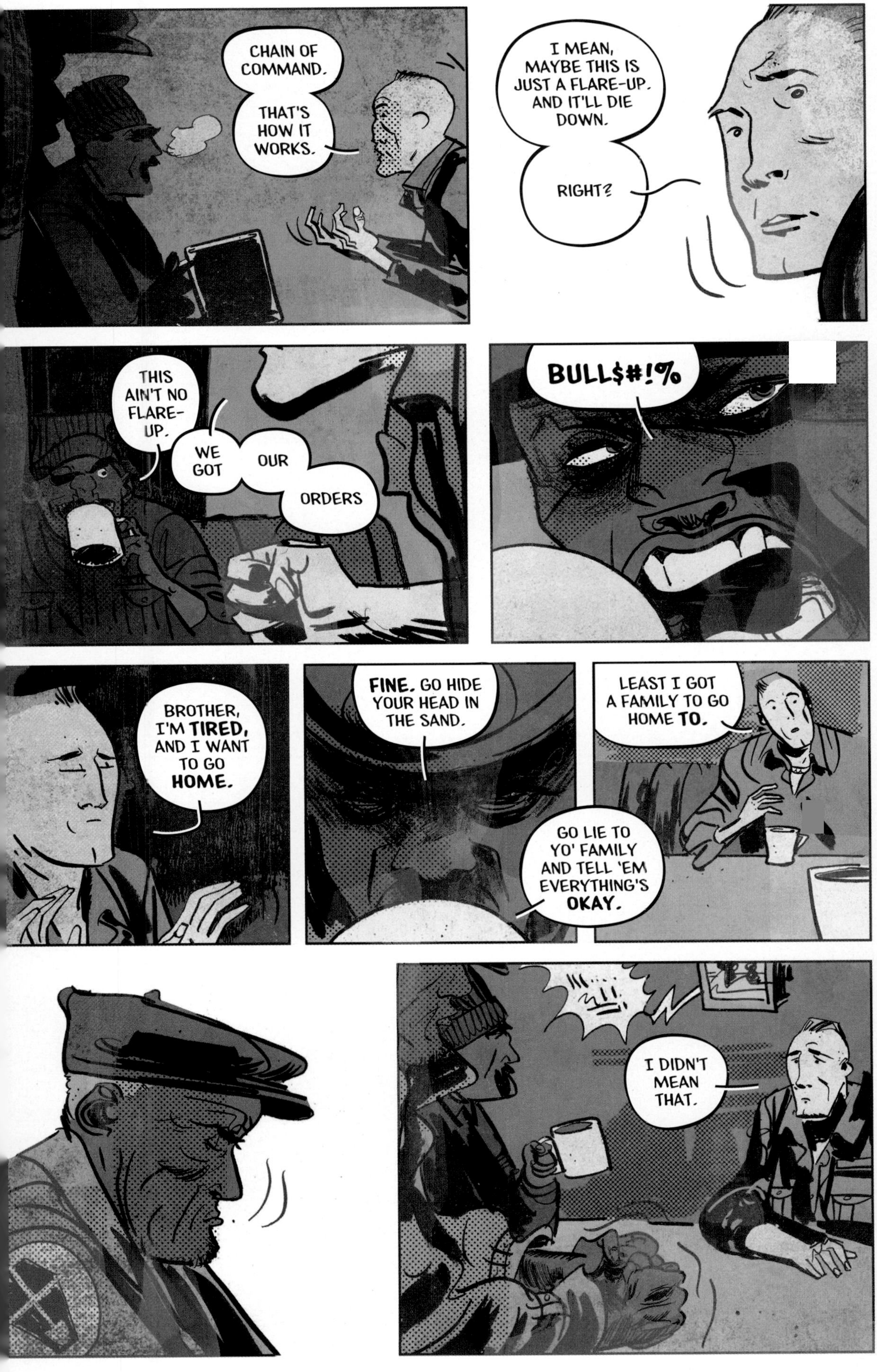
CHAIN OF COMMAND.
THAT'S HOW IT WORKS.
I MEAN, MAYBE THIS IS JUST A FLARE-UP, AND IT'LL DIE DOWN.
RIGHT?
THIS AIN'T NO FLARE-UP.
WE GOT OUR ORDERS
BULL$#!%
BROTHER, I'M **TIRED,** AND I WANT TO GO **HOME.**
FINE. GO HIDE YOUR HEAD IN THE SAND.
LEAST I GOT A FAMILY TO GO HOME **TO.**
GO LIE TO YO' FAMILY AND TELL 'EM EVERYTHING'S **OKAY.**
I DIDN'T MEAN THAT.

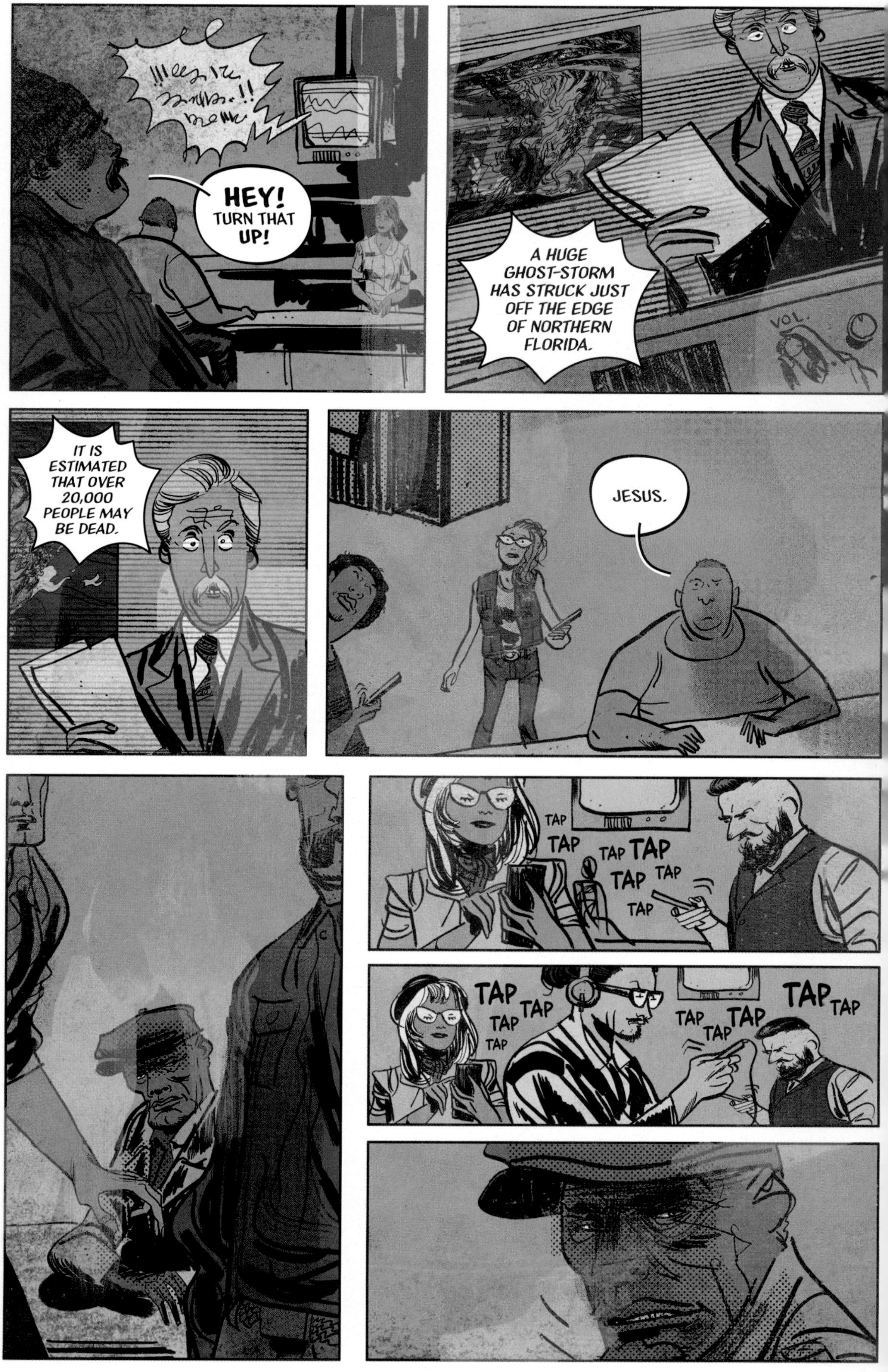
HEY! TURN THAT UP!
A HUGE GHOST-STORM HAS STRUCK JUST OFF THE EDGE OF NORTHERN FLORIDA.
VOL.
IT IS ESTIMATED THAT OVER 20,000 PEOPLE MAY BE DEAD.
JESUS.
TAP TAP TAP TAP TAP TAP TAP
TAP TAP TAP TAP TAP TAP TAP TAP TAP

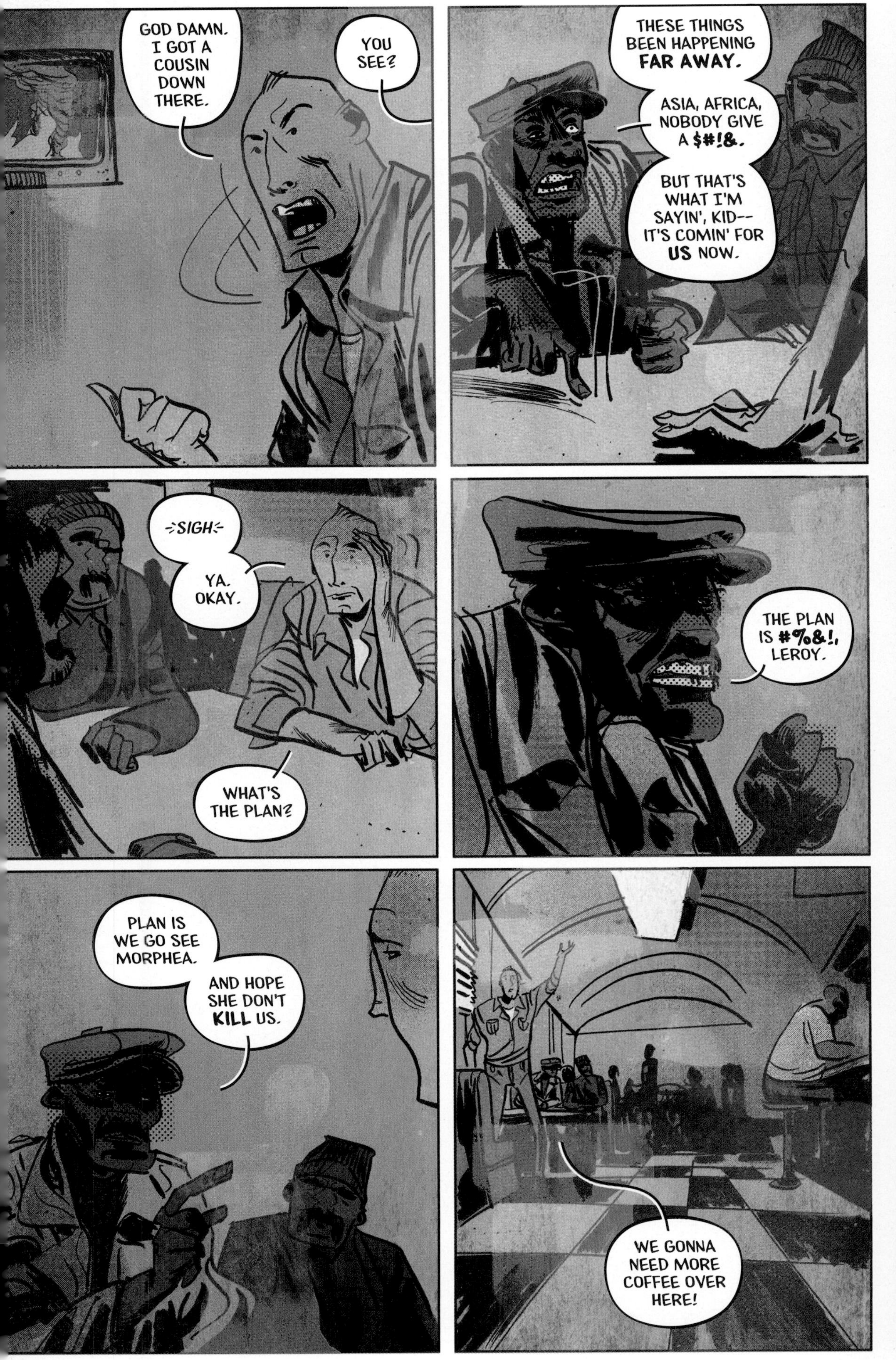
GOD DAMN. I GOT A COUSIN DOWN THERE.
YOU SEE?
THESE THINGS BEEN HAPPENING FAR AWAY.
ASIA, AFRICA, NOBODY GIVE A $#!&.
BUT THAT'S WHAT I'M SAYIN', KID-- IT'S COMIN' FOR US NOW.
SIGH
YA. OKAY.
WHAT'S THE PLAN?
THE PLAN IS #%&!, LEROY.
PLAN IS WE GO SEE MORPHEA.
AND HOPE SHE DON'T KILL US.
WE GONNA NEED MORE COFFEE OVER HERE!

CHAPTER

THE BLACK TEMPLE

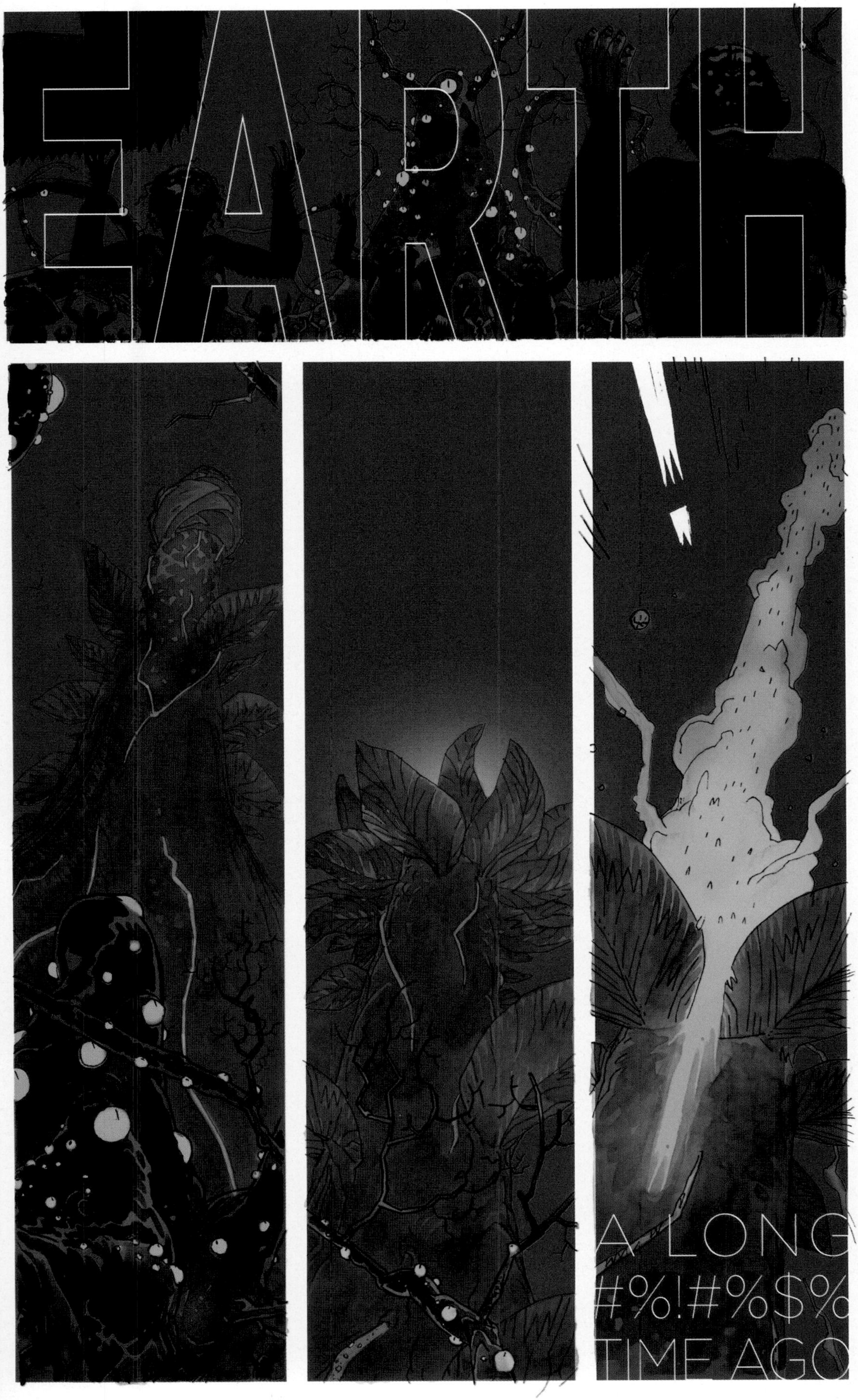
EARTH
A LONG
#%!#%$%
TIME AGO

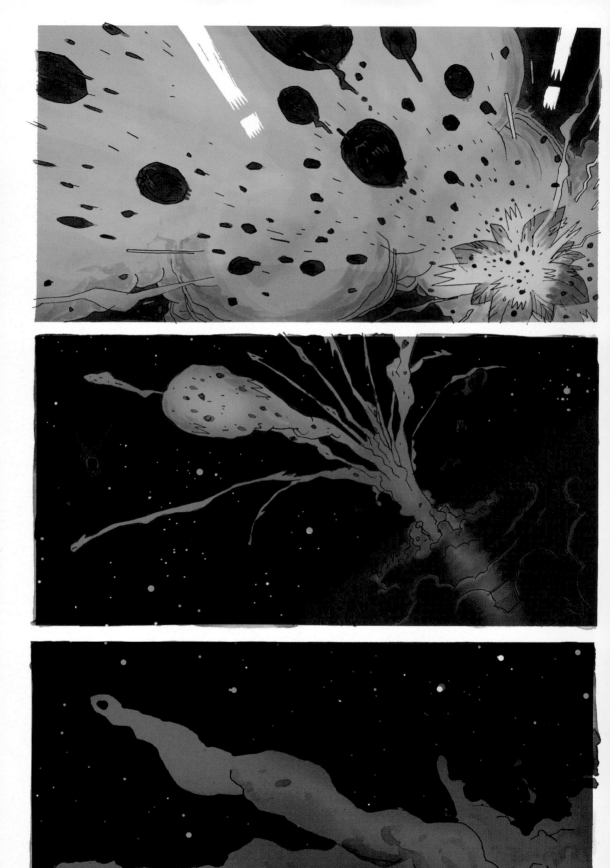

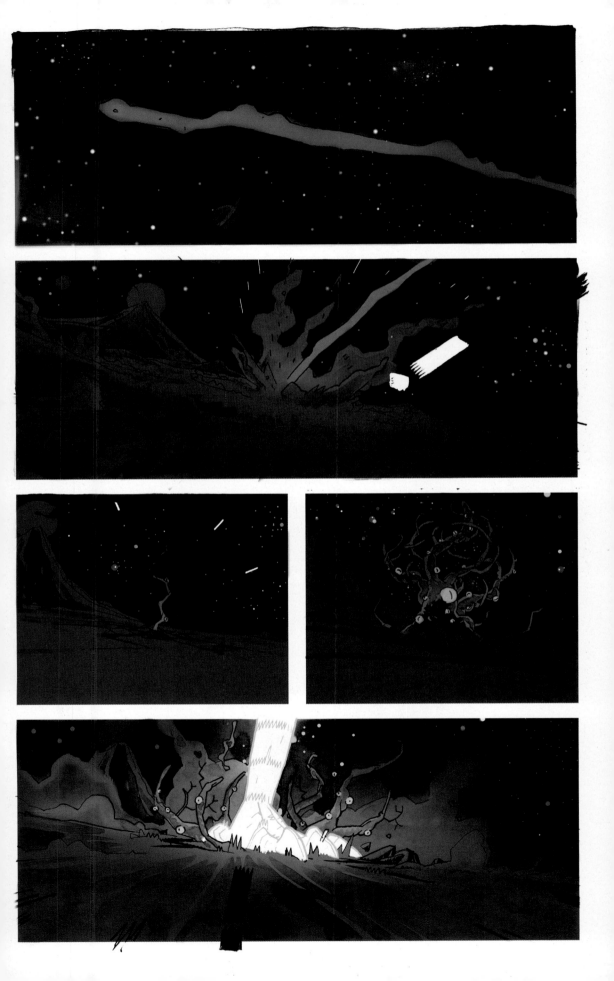

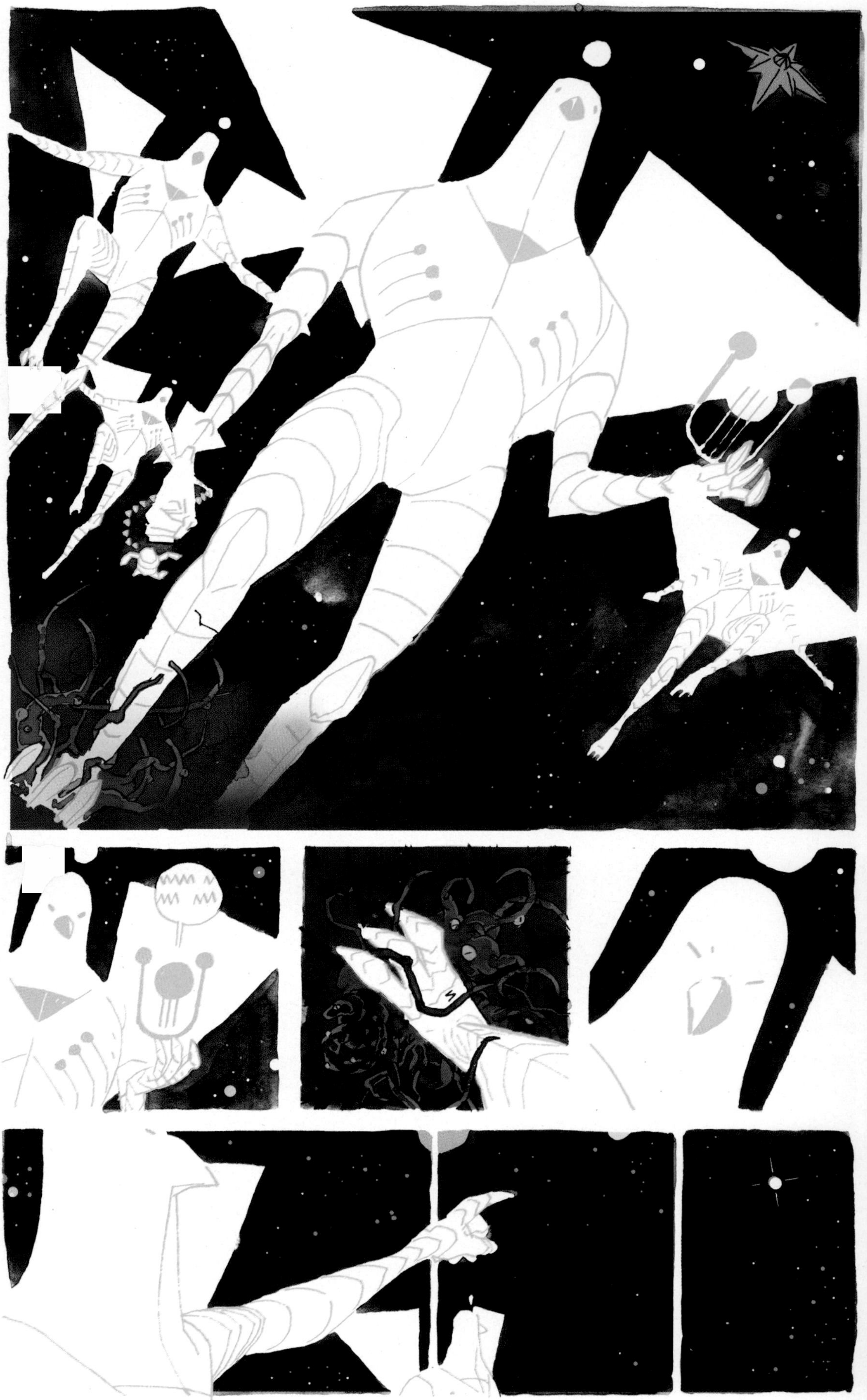

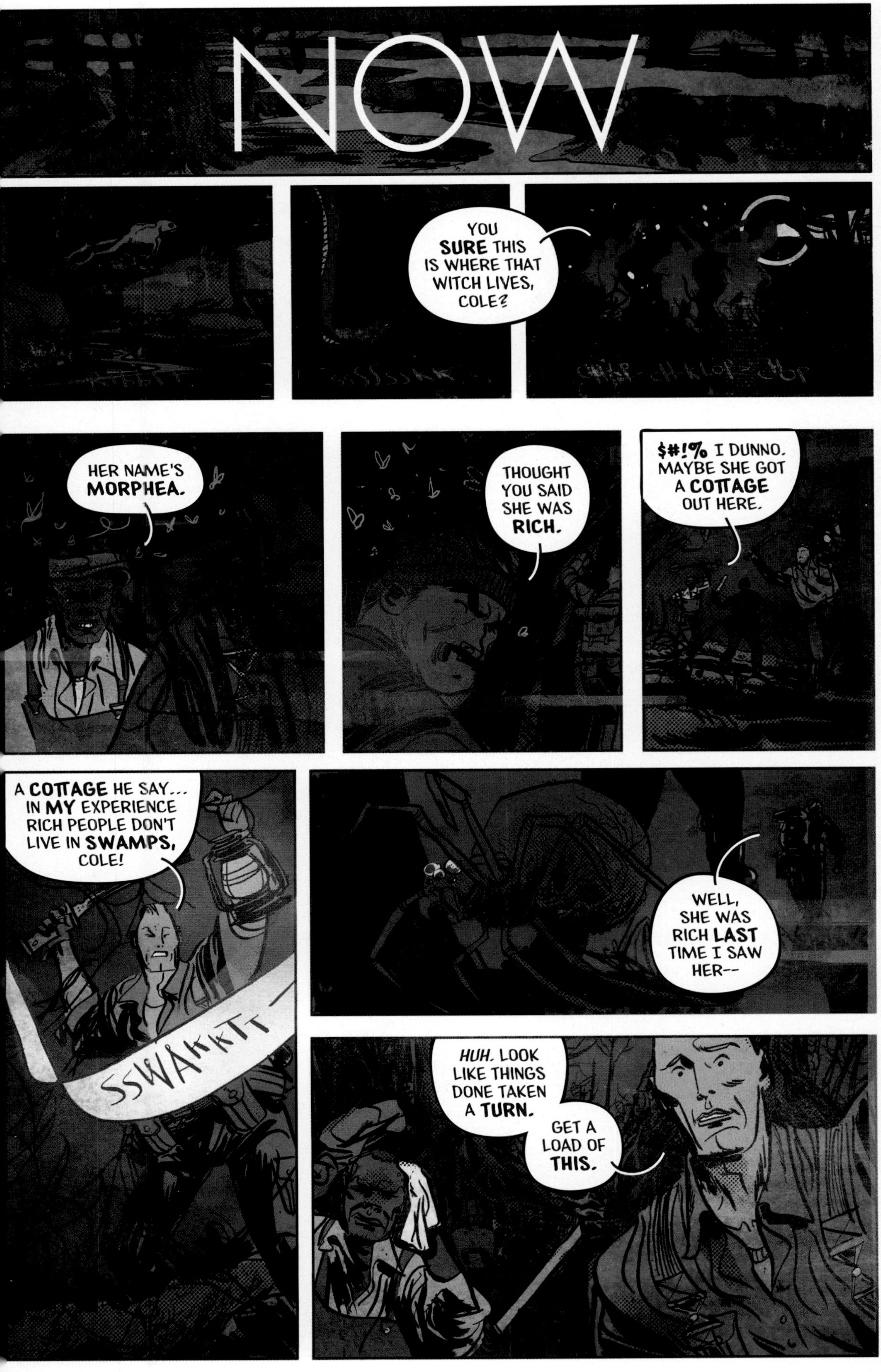
NOW
YOU SURE THIS IS WHERE THAT WITCH LIVES, COLE?
HER NAME'S MORPHEA.
THOUGHT YOU SAID SHE WAS RICH.
$#!% I DUNNO. MAYBE SHE GOT A COTTAGE OUT HERE.
A COTTAGE HE SAY... IN MY EXPERIENCE RICH PEOPLE DON'T LIVE IN SWAMPS, COLE!
SSWAKKTT
WELL, SHE WAS RICH LAST TIME I SAW HER--
HUH. LOOK LIKE THINGS DONE TAKEN A TURN.
GET A LOAD OF THIS.

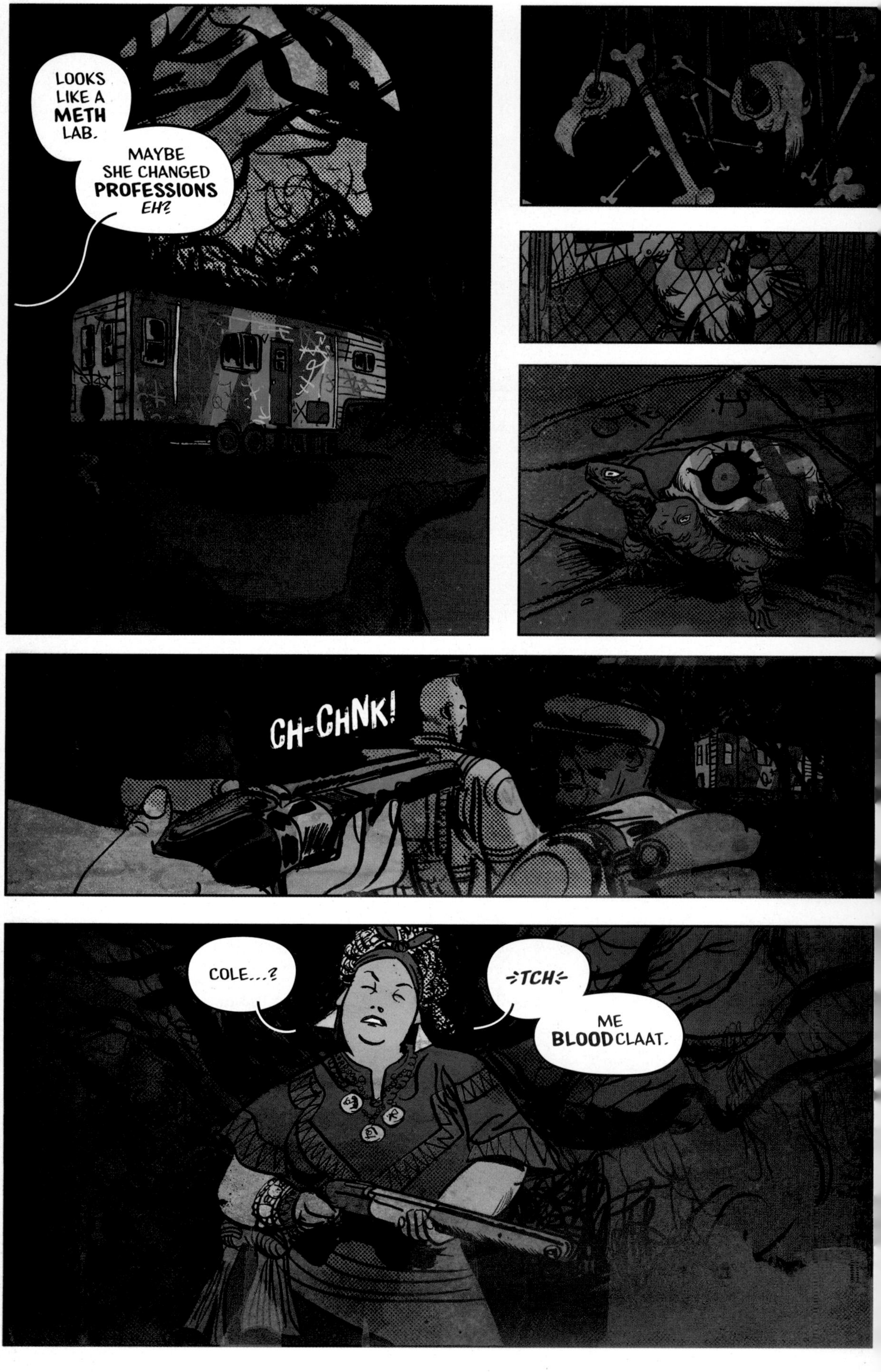
LOOKS LIKE A METH LAB.
MAYBE SHE CHANGED PROFESSIONS EH?
CH-CHNK!
COLE...?
TCH
ME BLOODCLAAT.

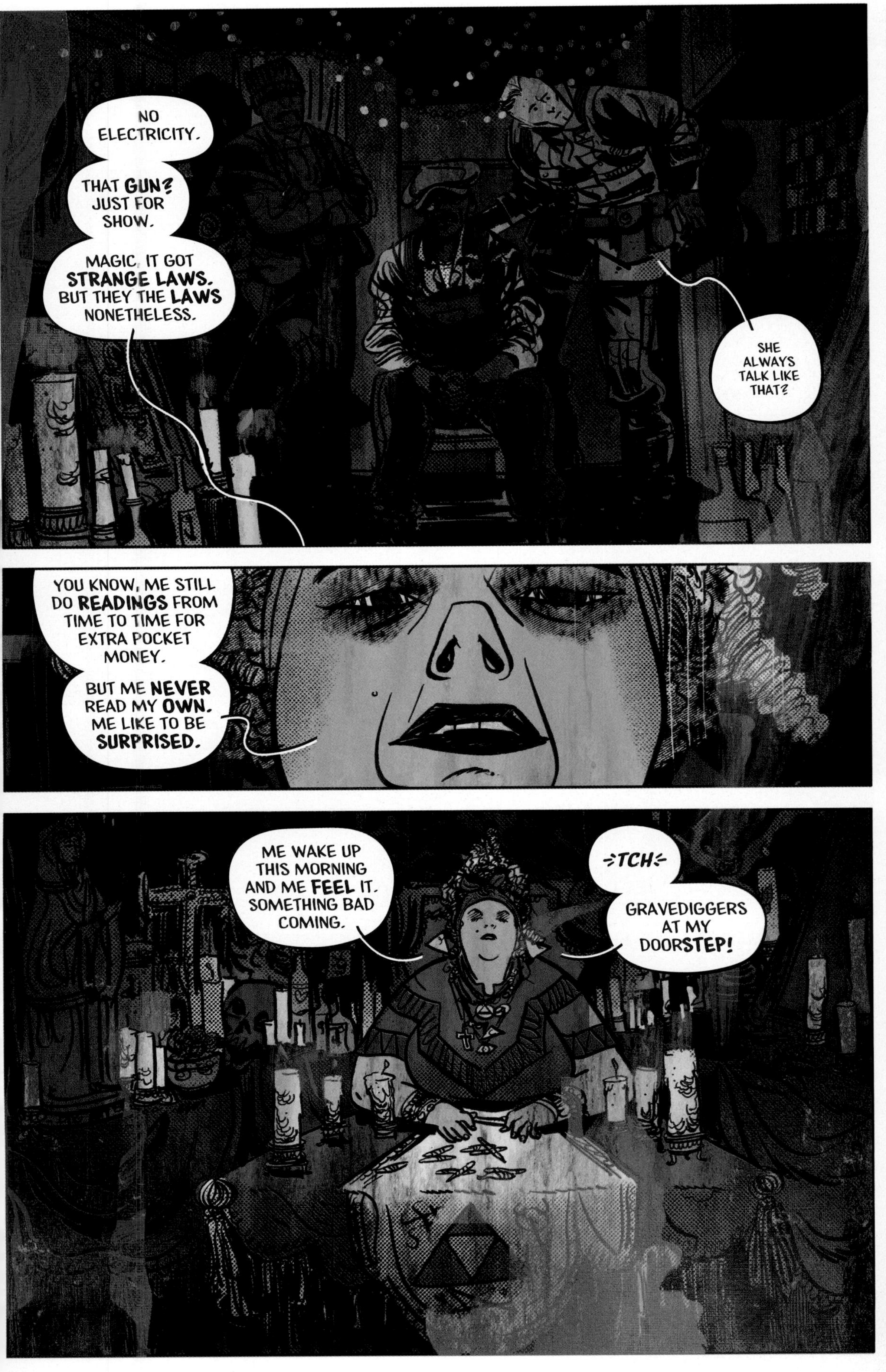
NO ELECTRICITY.
THAT GUN? JUST FOR SHOW.
MAGIC, IT GOT STRANGE LAWS. BUT THEY THE LAWS NONETHELESS.
SHE ALWAYS TALK LIKE THAT?
YOU KNOW, ME STILL DO READINGS FROM TIME TO TIME FOR EXTRA POCKET MONEY.
BUT ME NEVER READ MY OWN. ME LIKE TO BE SURPRISED.
ME WAKE UP THIS MORNING AND ME FEEL IT. SOMETHING BAD COMING.
TCH
GRAVEDIGGERS AT MY DOORSTEP!

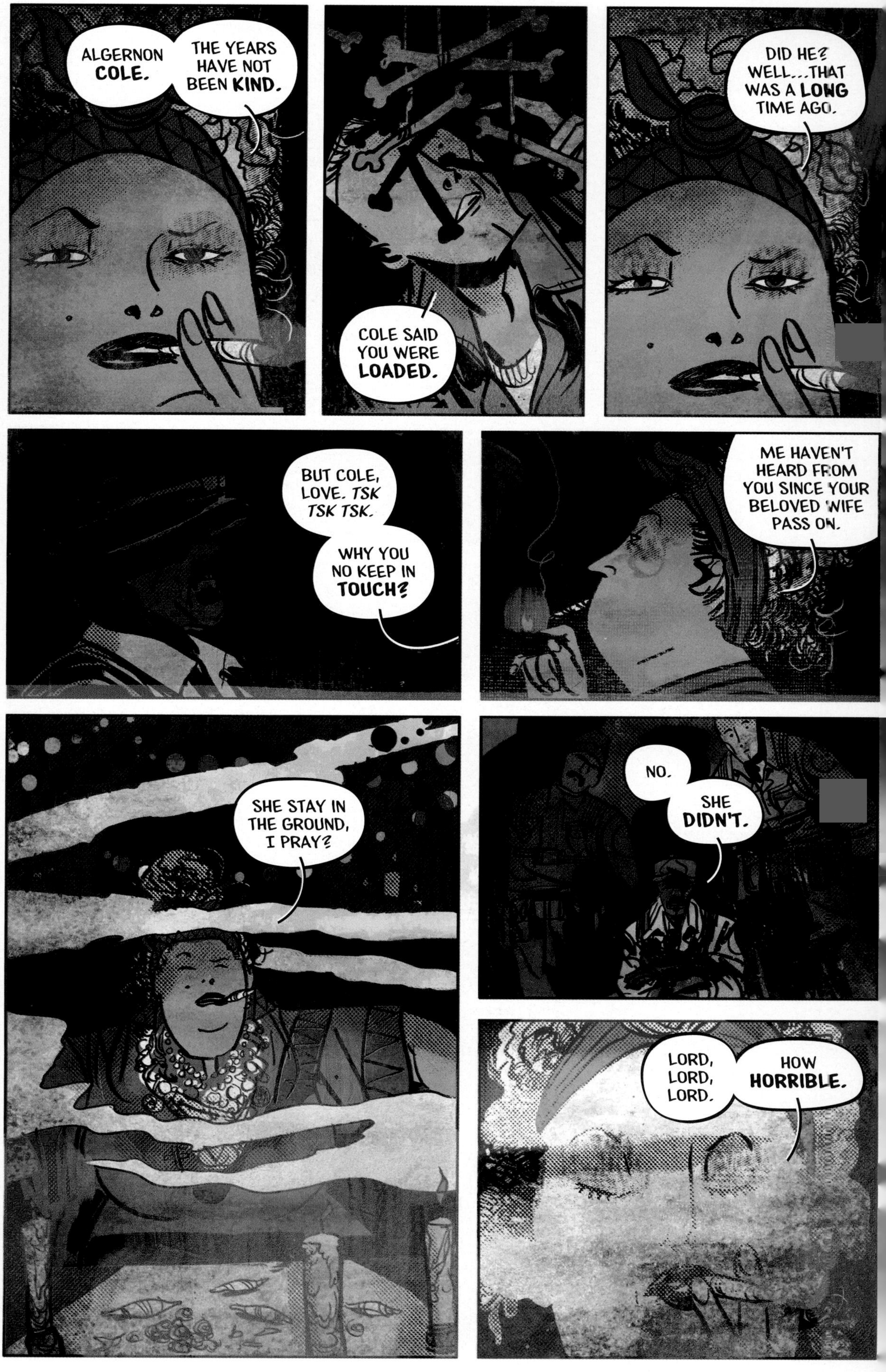
ALGERNON COLE.
THE YEARS HAVE NOT BEEN KIND.
COLE SAID YOU WERE LOADED.
DID HE? WELL...THAT WAS A LONG TIME AGO.
BUT COLE, LOVE. TSK TSK TSK.
WHY YOU NO KEEP IN TOUCH?
ME HAVEN'T HEARD FROM YOU SINCE YOUR BELOVED WIFE PASS ON.
SHE STAY IN THE GROUND, I PRAY?
NO.
SHE DIDN'T.
LORD, LORD, LORD.
HOW HORRIBLE.

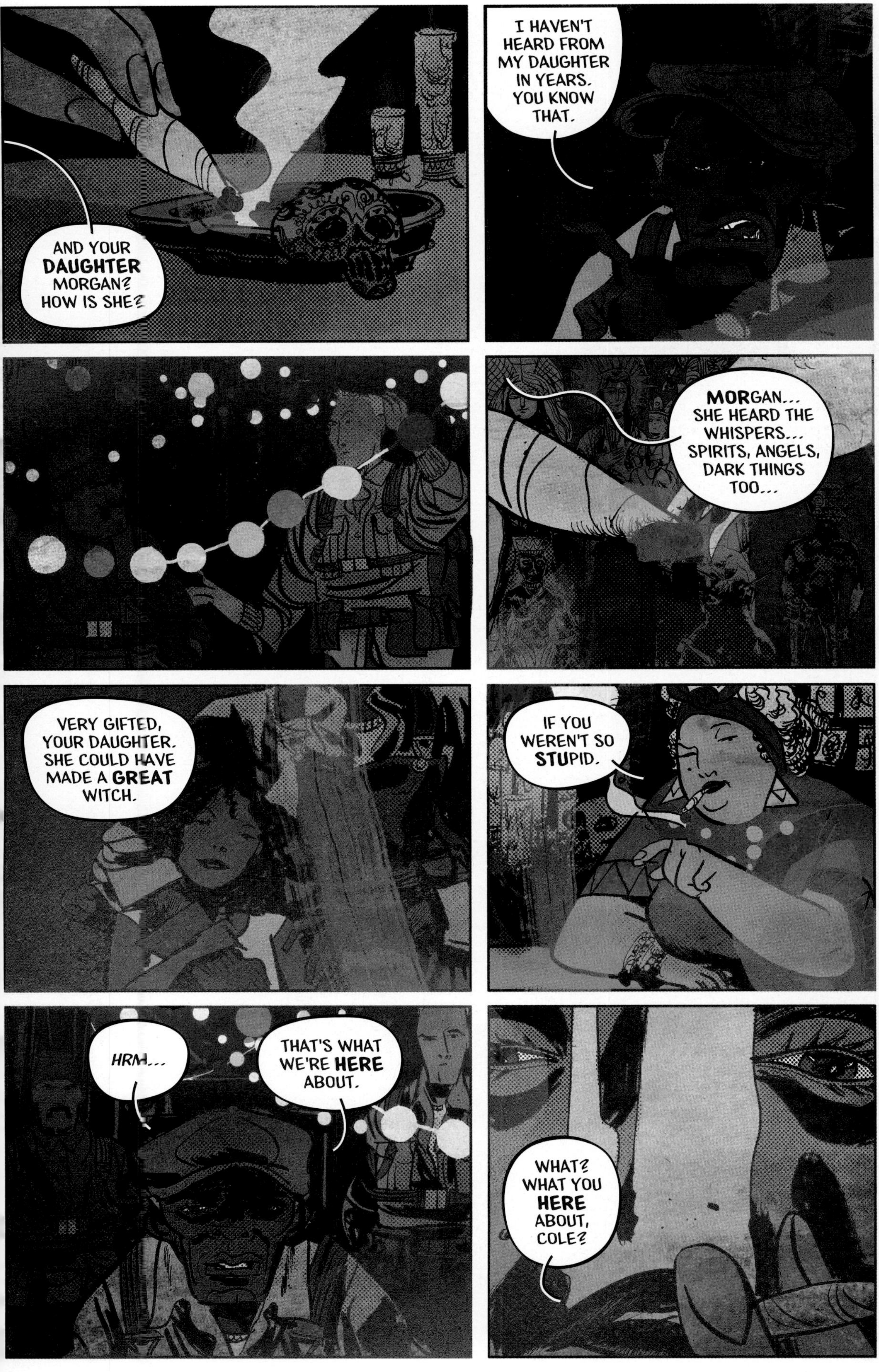
AND YOUR **DAUGHTER** MORGAN? HOW IS SHE?
I HAVEN'T HEARD FROM MY DAUGHTER IN YEARS. YOU KNOW THAT.
MORGAN... SHE HEARD THE WHISPERS... SPIRITS, ANGELS, DARK THINGS TOO...
VERY GIFTED, YOUR DAUGHTER. SHE COULD HAVE MADE A **GREAT** WITCH.
IF YOU WEREN'T SO **STU**PID.
HRM...
THAT'S WHAT WE'RE **HERE** ABOUT.
WHAT? WHAT YOU **HERE** ABOUT, COLE?

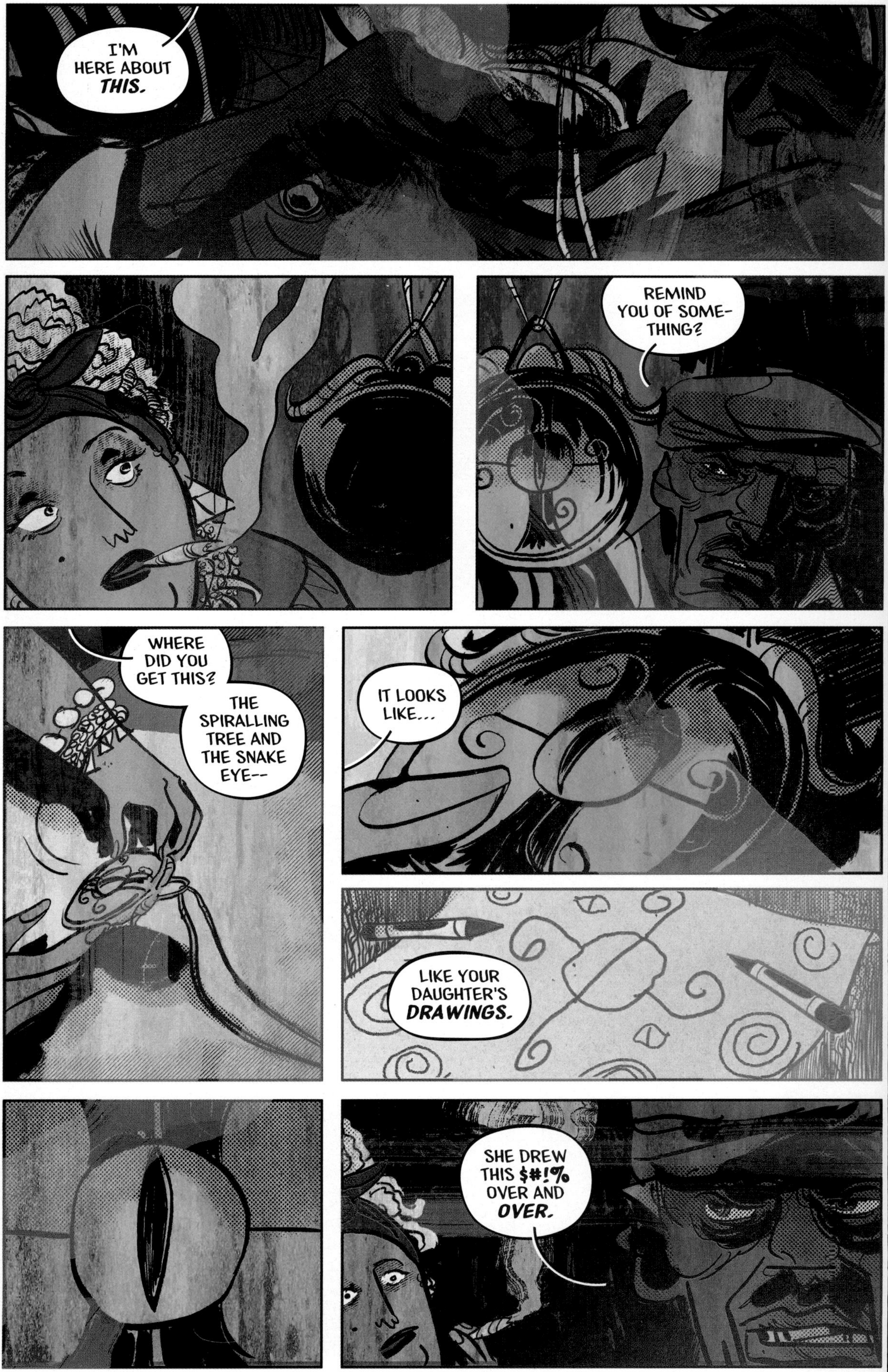
I'M HERE ABOUT THIS.
REMIND YOU OF SOME-THING?
WHERE DID YOU GET THIS?
THE SPIRALLING TREE AND THE SNAKE EYE--
IT LOOKS LIKE...
LIKE YOUR DAUGHTER'S DRAWINGS.
SHE DREW THIS $#!% OVER AND OVER.

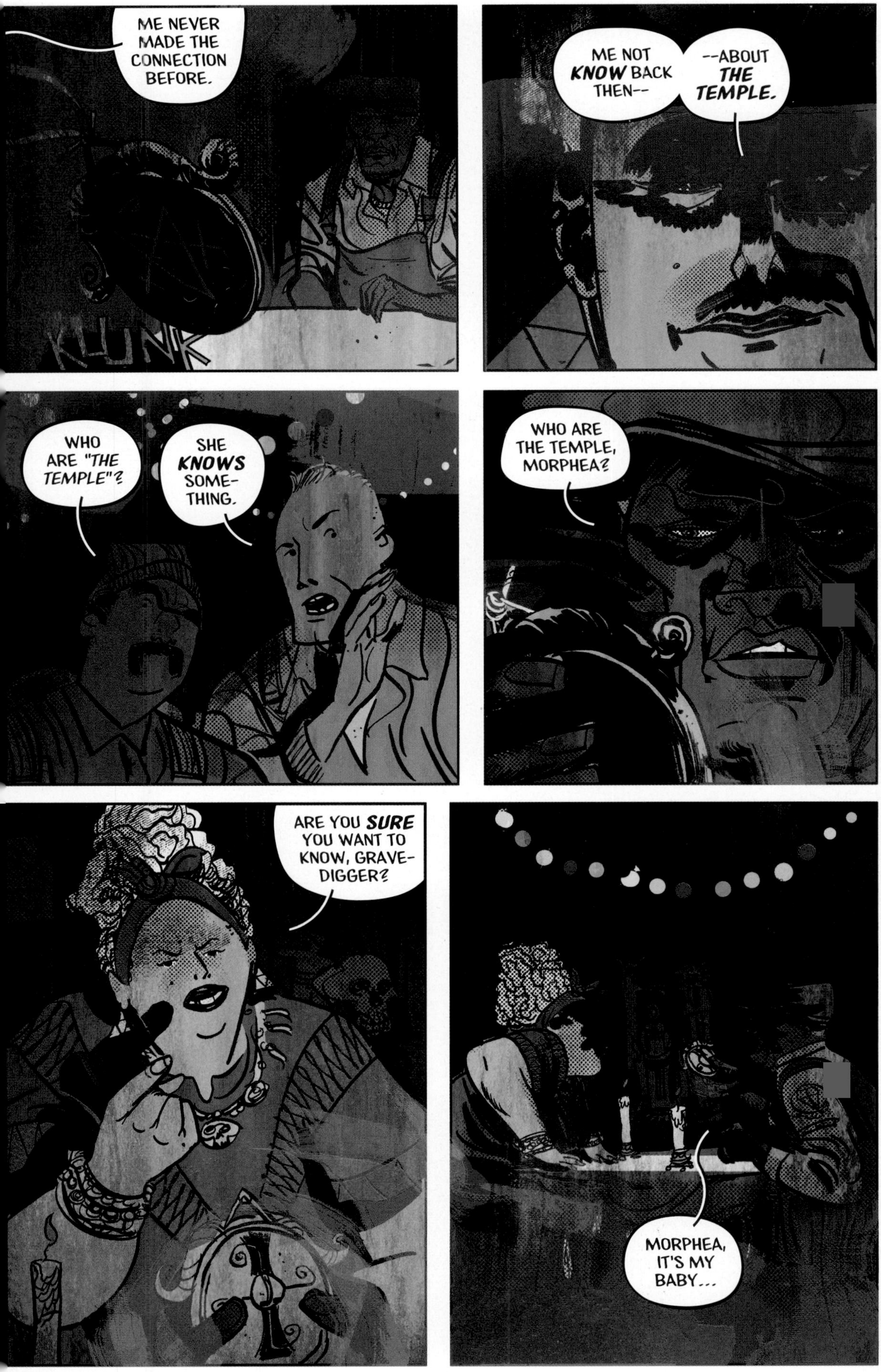

ME NEVER MADE THE CONNECTION BEFORE.
KLUNK
ME NOT KNOW BACK THEN--
--ABOUT THE TEMPLE.
WHO ARE "THE TEMPLE"?
SHE KNOWS SOME-THING.
WHO ARE THE TEMPLE, MORPHEA?
ARE YOU SURE YOU WANT TO KNOW, GRAVE-DIGGER?
MORPHEA, IT'S MY BABY...

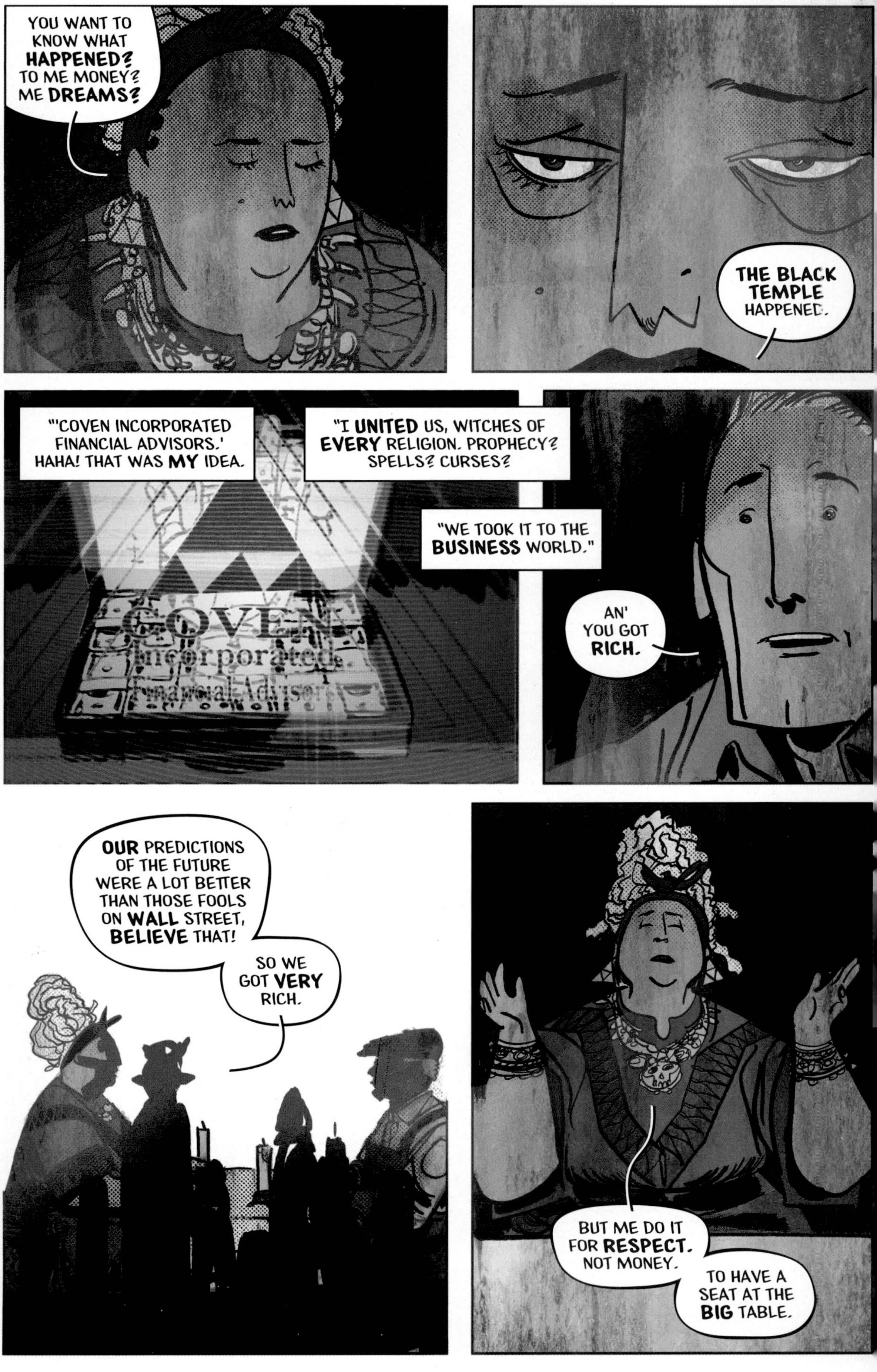
YOU WANT TO KNOW WHAT HAPPENED? TO ME MONEY? ME DREAMS?
THE BLACK TEMPLE HAPPENED.
"'COVEN INCORPORATED FINANCIAL ADVISORS.' HAHA! THAT WAS MY IDEA.
"I UNITED US, WITCHES OF EVERY RELIGION. PROPHECY? SPELLS? CURSES?
"WE TOOK IT TO THE BUSINESS WORLD."
COVEN
AN' YOU GOT RICH.
OUR PREDICTIONS OF THE FUTURE WERE A LOT BETTER THAN THOSE FOOLS ON WALL STREET, BELIEVE THAT!
SO WE GOT VERY RICH.
BUT ME DO IT FOR RESPECT. NOT MONEY.
TO HAVE A SEAT AT THE BIG TABLE.

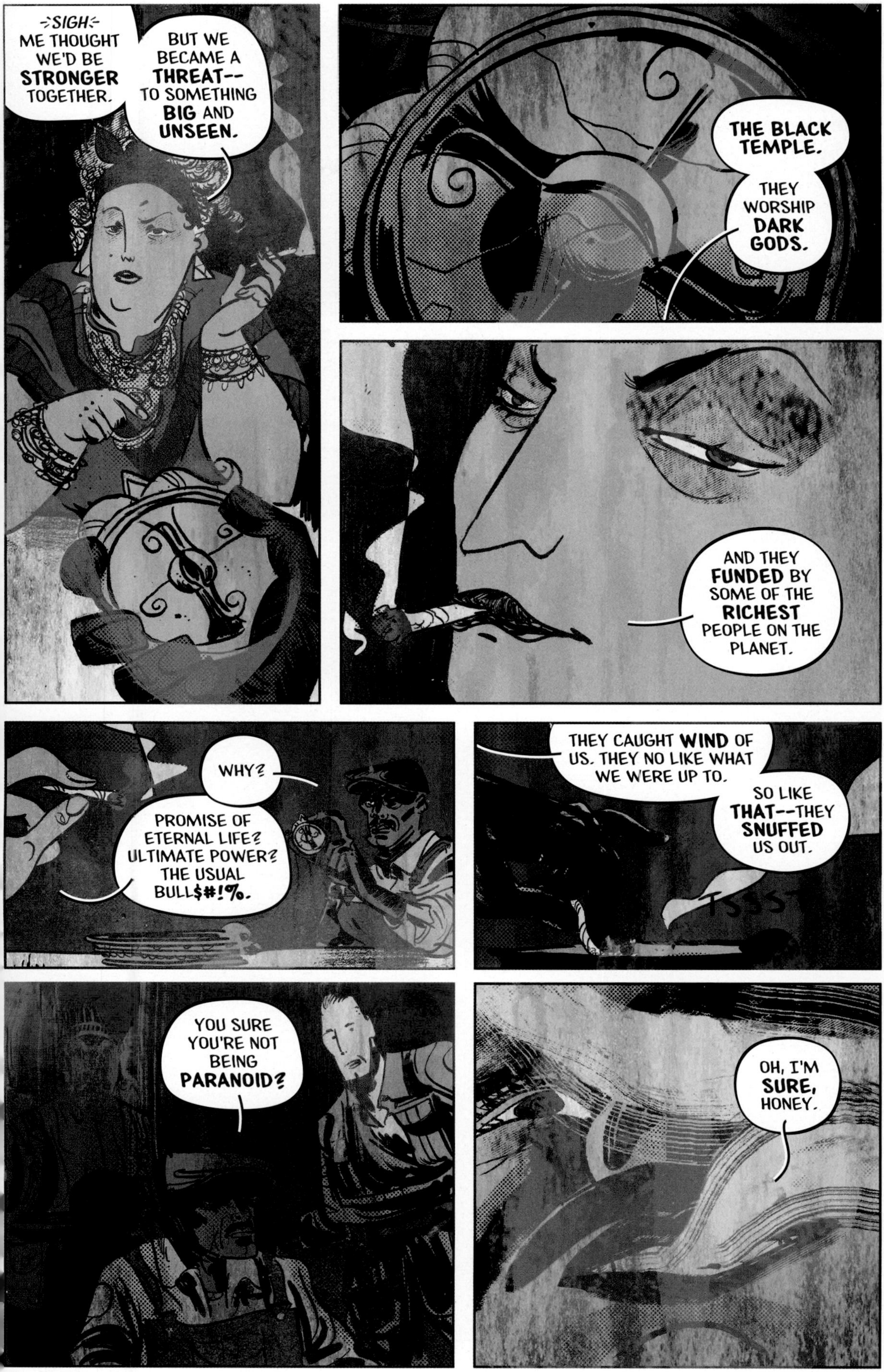

SIGH
ME THOUGHT WE'D BE STRONGER TOGETHER.
BUT WE BECAME A THREAT-- TO SOMETHING BIG AND UNSEEN.
THE BLACK TEMPLE.
THEY WORSHIP DARK GODS.
AND THEY FUNDED BY SOME OF THE RICHEST PEOPLE ON THE PLANET.
WHY?
PROMISE OF ETERNAL LIFE? ULTIMATE POWER? THE USUAL BULL$#!%.
THEY CAUGHT WIND OF US. THEY NO LIKE WHAT WE WERE UP TO.
SO LIKE THAT--THEY SNUFFED US OUT.
TSSST
YOU SURE YOU'RE NOT BEING PARANOID?
OH, I'M SURE, HONEY.

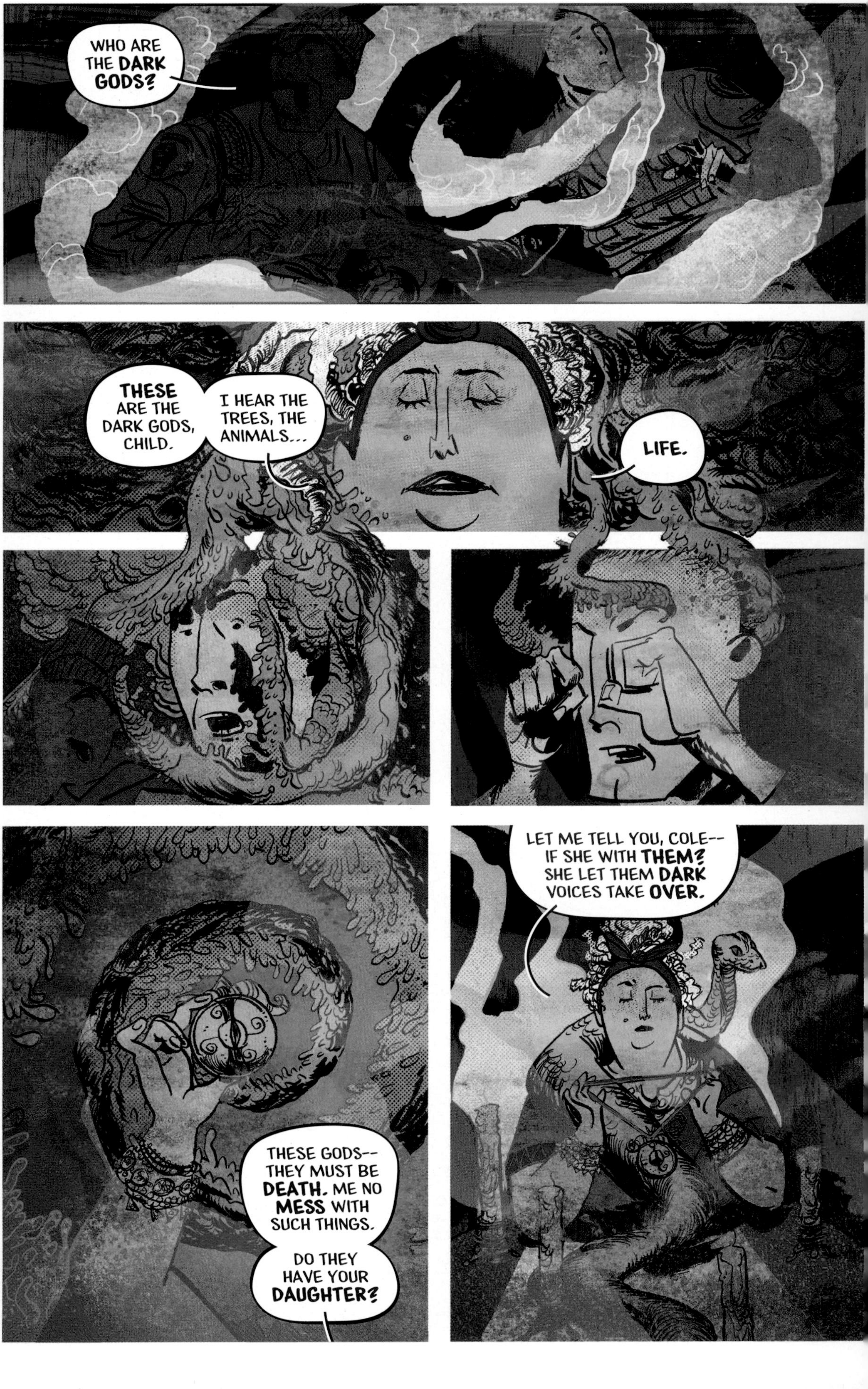
WHO ARE THE DARK GODS?
THESE ARE THE DARK GODS, CHILD.
I HEAR THE TREES, THE ANIMALS...
LIFE.
THESE GODS-- THEY MUST BE DEATH. ME NO MESS WITH SUCH THINGS.
DO THEY HAVE YOUR DAUGHTER?
LET ME TELL YOU, COLE-- IF SHE WITH THEM? SHE LET THEM DARK VOICES TAKE OVER.

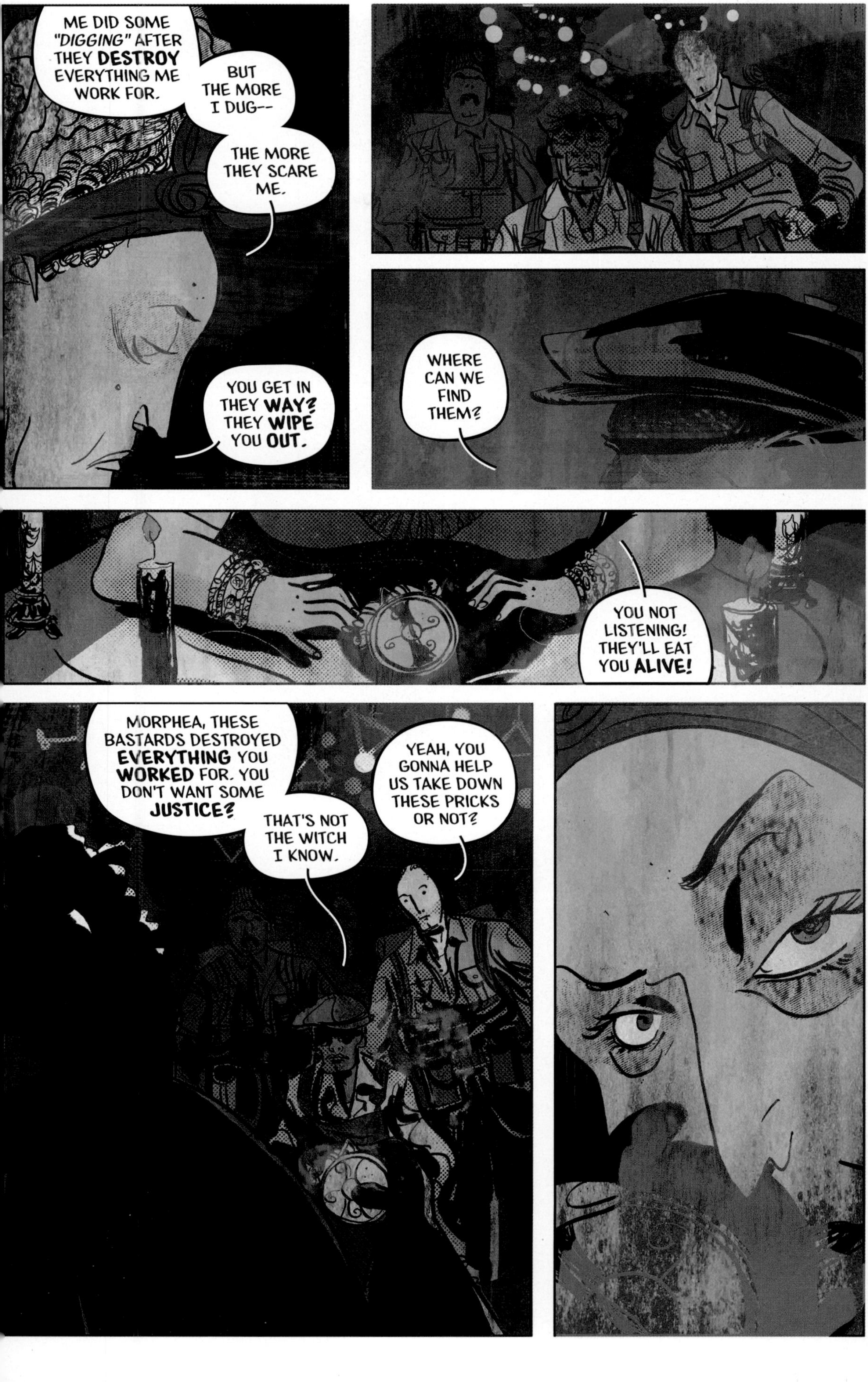
ME DID SOME "DIGGING" AFTER THEY **DESTROY** EVERYTHING ME WORK FOR.
BUT THE MORE I DUG--
THE MORE THEY SCARE ME.
YOU GET IN THEY **WAY?** THEY **WIPE** YOU **OUT.**
WHERE CAN WE FIND THEM?
YOU NOT LISTENING! THEY'LL EAT YOU **ALIVE!**
MORPHEA, THESE BASTARDS DESTROYED **EVERYTHING** YOU **WORKED** FOR. YOU DON'T WANT SOME **JUSTICE?**
THAT'S NOT THE WITCH I KNOW.
YEAH, YOU GONNA HELP US TAKE DOWN THESE PRICKS OR NOT?

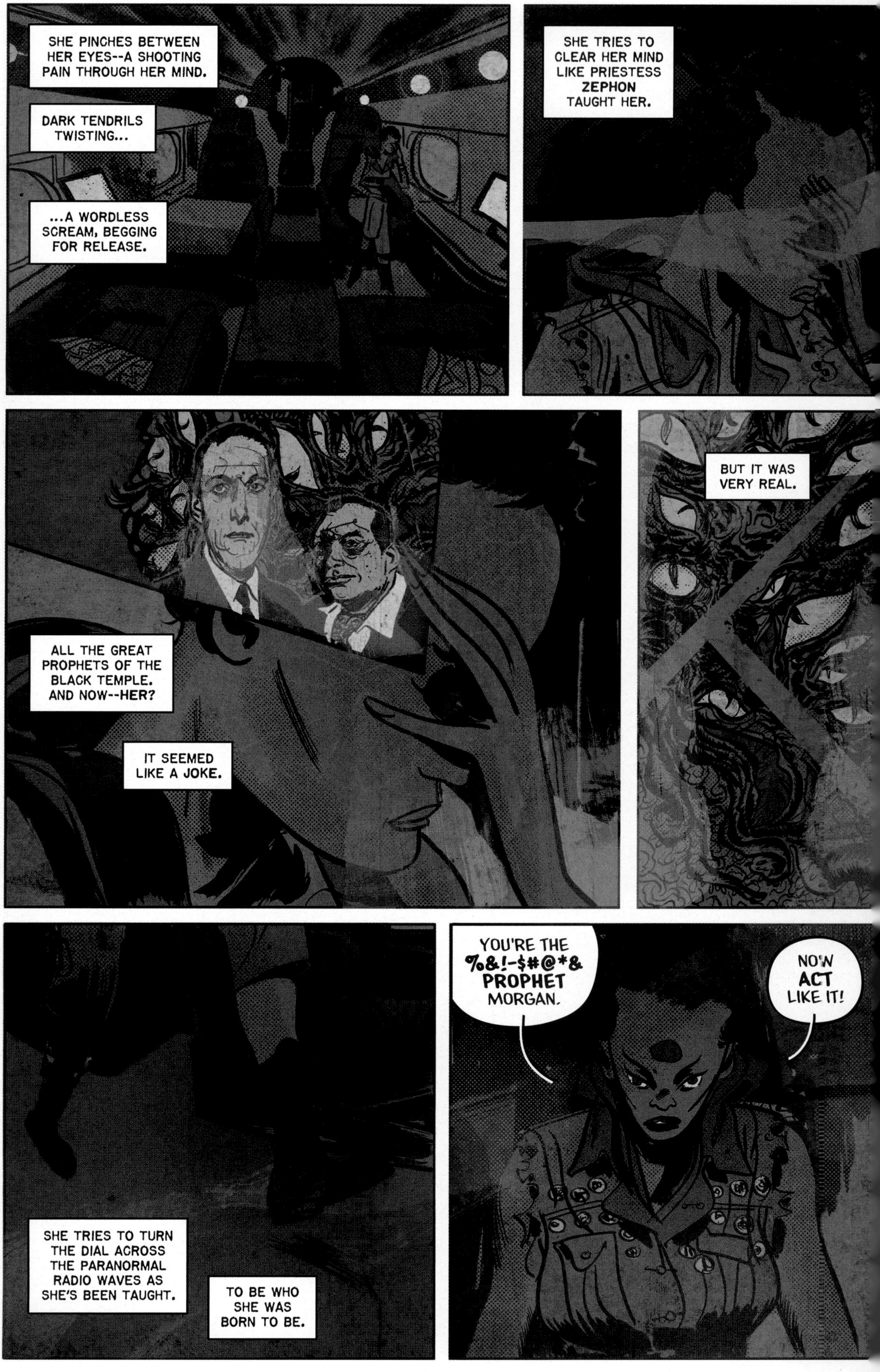
SHE PINCHES BETWEEN HER EYES--A SHOOTING PAIN THROUGH HER MIND.
DARK TENDRILS TWISTING...
...A WORDLESS SCREAM, BEGGING FOR RELEASE.
SHE TRIES TO CLEAR HER MIND LIKE PRIESTESS **ZEPHON** TAUGHT HER.
ALL THE GREAT PROPHETS OF THE BLACK TEMPLE. AND NOW--**HER**?
IT SEEMED LIKE A **JOKE**.
BUT IT WAS VERY REAL.
SHE TRIES TO TURN THE DIAL ACROSS THE PARANORMAL RADIO WAVES AS SHE'S BEEN TAUGHT.
TO BE WHO SHE WAS BORN TO BE.
YOU'RE THE %&!-$#@*& **PROPHET** MORGAN.
NOW **ACT** LIKE IT!

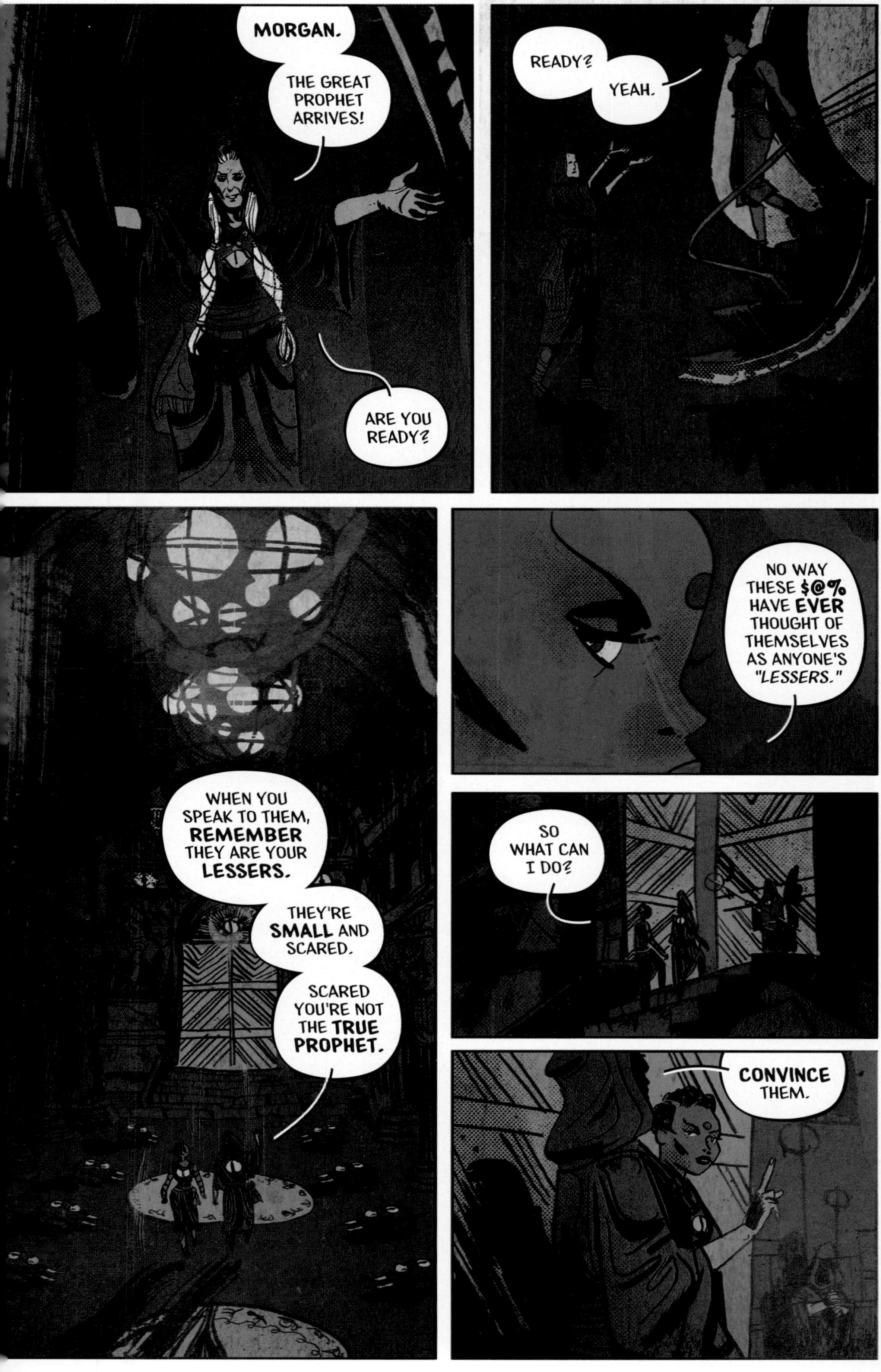
MORGAN.
THE GREAT PROPHET ARRIVES!
ARE YOU READY?
READY?
YEAH.
WHEN YOU SPEAK TO THEM, REMEMBER THEY ARE YOUR LESSERS.
THEY'RE SMALL AND SCARED.
SCARED YOU'RE NOT THE TRUE PROPHET.
NO WAY THESE $@% HAVE EVER THOUGHT OF THEMSELVES AS ANYONE'S "LESSERS."
SO WHAT CAN I DO?
CONVINCE THEM.

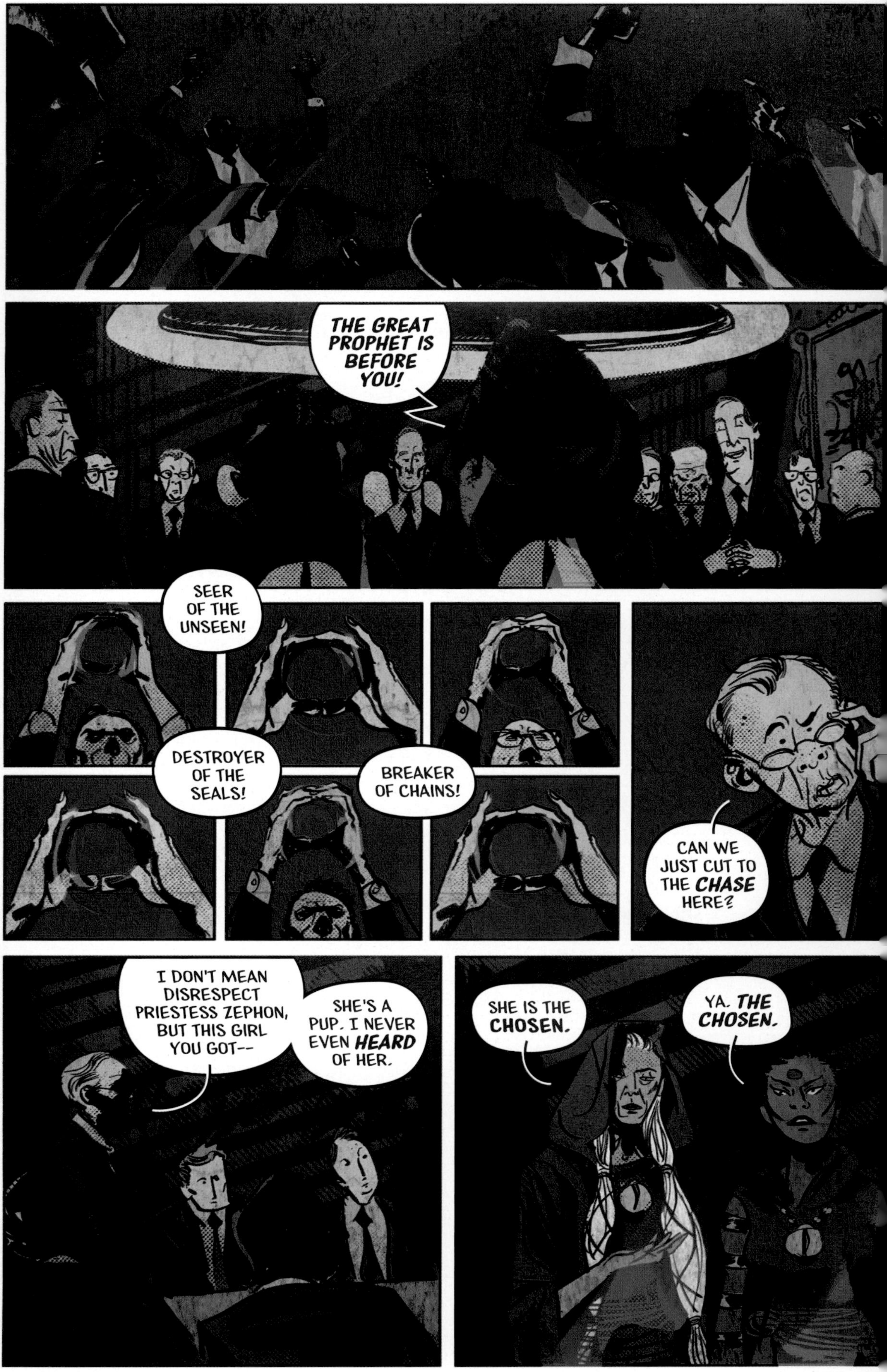
THE GREAT PROPHET IS BEFORE YOU!
SEER OF THE UNSEEN!
DESTROYER OF THE SEALS!
BREAKER OF CHAINS!
CAN WE JUST CUT TO THE CHASE HERE?
I DON'T MEAN DISRESPECT PRIESTESS ZEPHON, BUT THIS GIRL YOU GOT--
SHE'S A PUP. I NEVER EVEN HEARD OF HER.
SHE IS THE CHOSEN.
YA. THE CHOSEN.

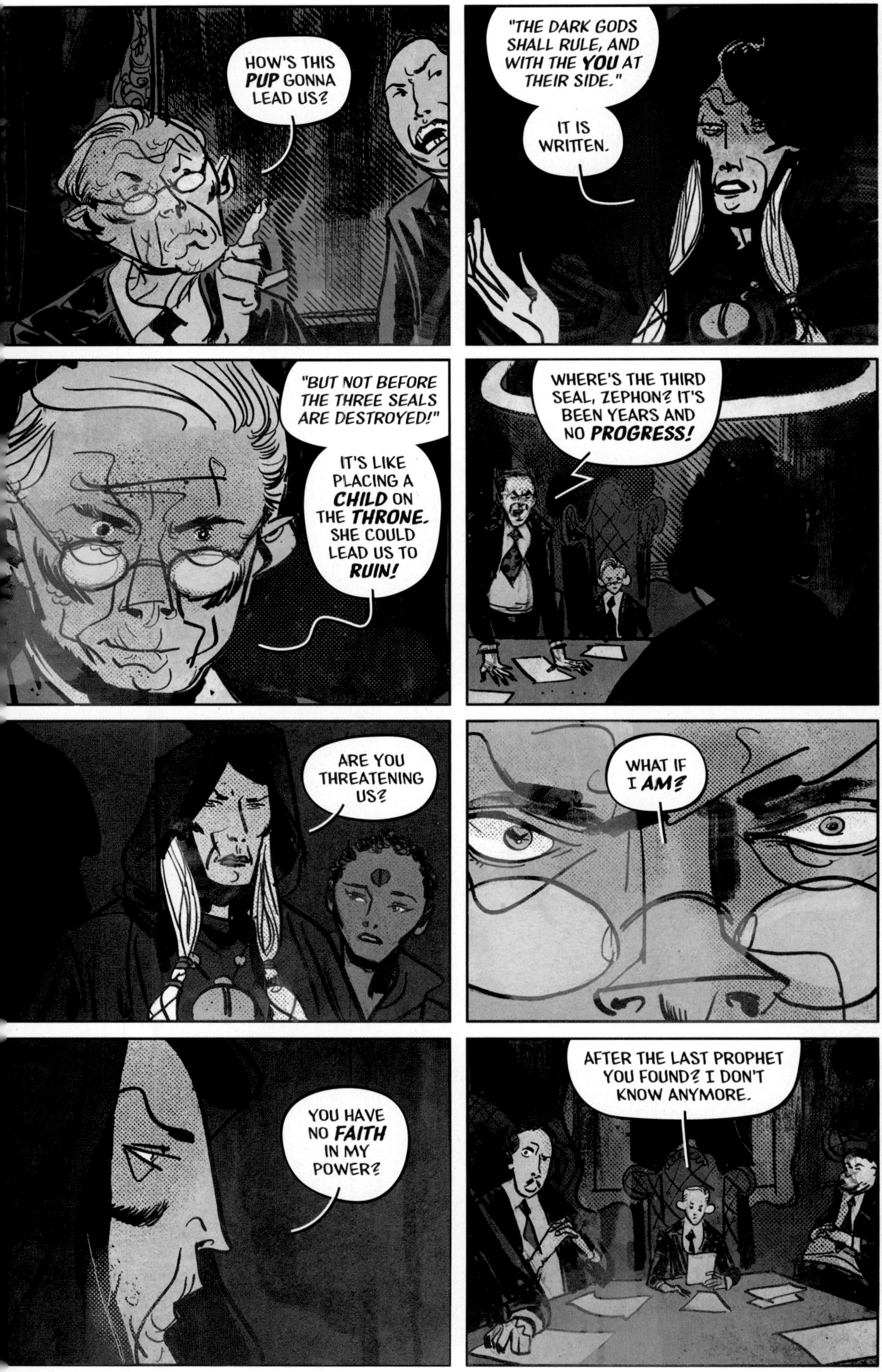
HOW'S THIS PUP GONNA LEAD US?
"THE DARK GODS SHALL RULE, AND WITH THE YOU AT THEIR SIDE."
IT IS WRITTEN.
"BUT NOT BEFORE THE THREE SEALS ARE DESTROYED!"
IT'S LIKE PLACING A CHILD ON THE THRONE. SHE COULD LEAD US TO RUIN!
WHERE'S THE THIRD SEAL, ZEPHON? IT'S BEEN YEARS AND NO PROGRESS!
ARE YOU THREATENING US?
WHAT IF I AM?
YOU HAVE NO FAITH IN MY POWER?
AFTER THE LAST PROPHET YOU FOUND? I DON'T KNOW ANYMORE.

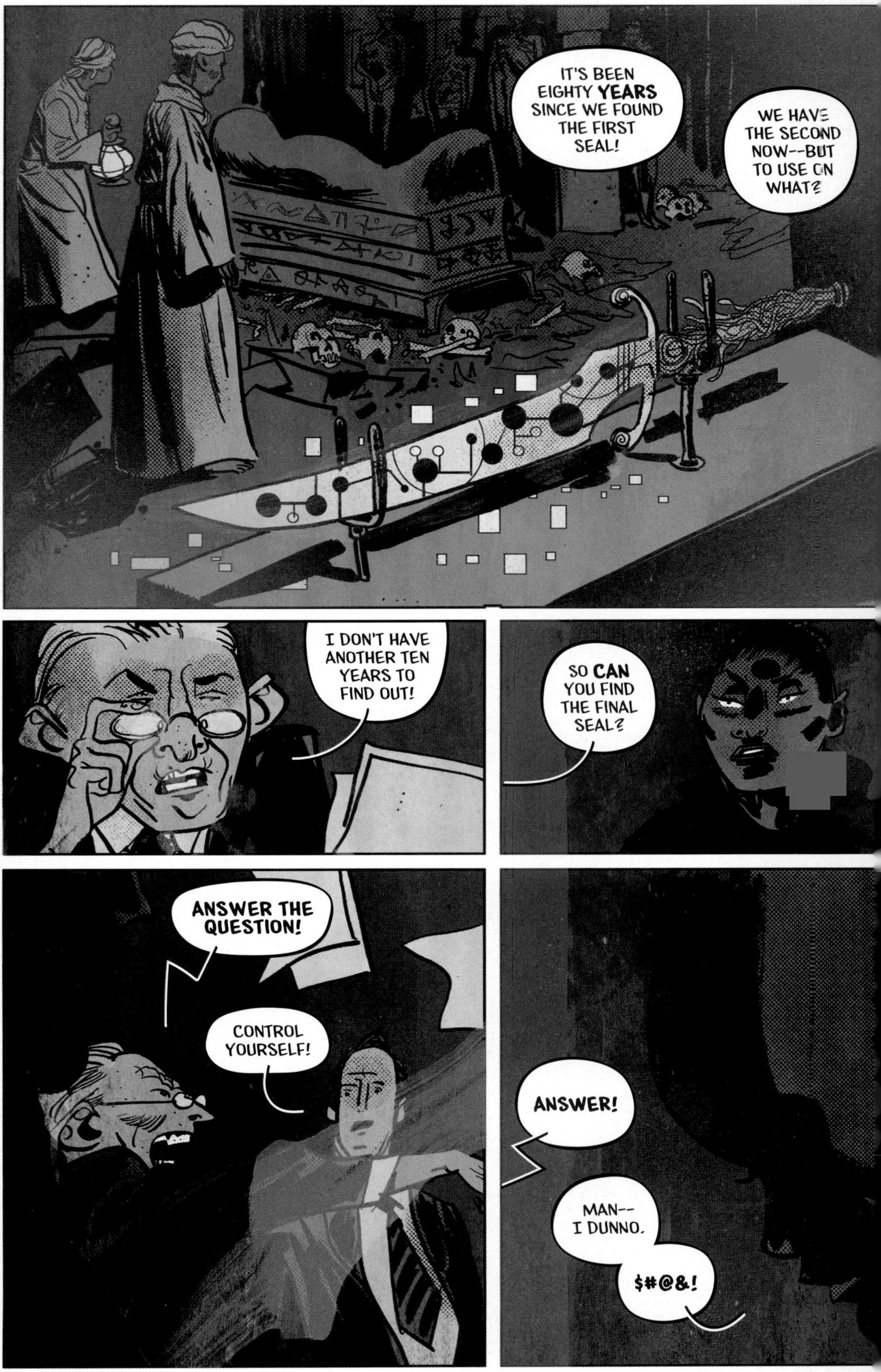
IT'S BEEN EIGHTY YEARS SINCE WE FOUND THE FIRST SEAL!
WE HAVE THE SECOND NOW--BUT TO USE ON WHAT?
I DON'T HAVE ANOTHER TEN YEARS TO FIND OUT!
SO CAN YOU FIND THE FINAL SEAL?
ANSWER THE QUESTION!
CONTROL YOURSELF!
ANSWER!
MAN-- I DUNNO.
$#@&!

SLAM!

SHE IS THE VOICE NOW! SHE HEARS THE CALL OF OUR DARK LORDS!

SHE WILL DESTROY THE FINAL SEAL! I SWEAR MY LIFE ON IT!

WE ARE SO CLOSE.

TOO CLOSE FOR DISSENSION IN OUR RANKS.

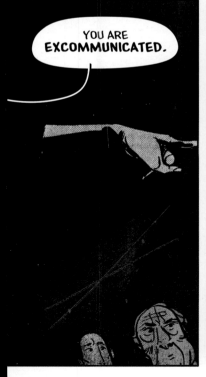

YOU ARE EXCOMMUNICATED.

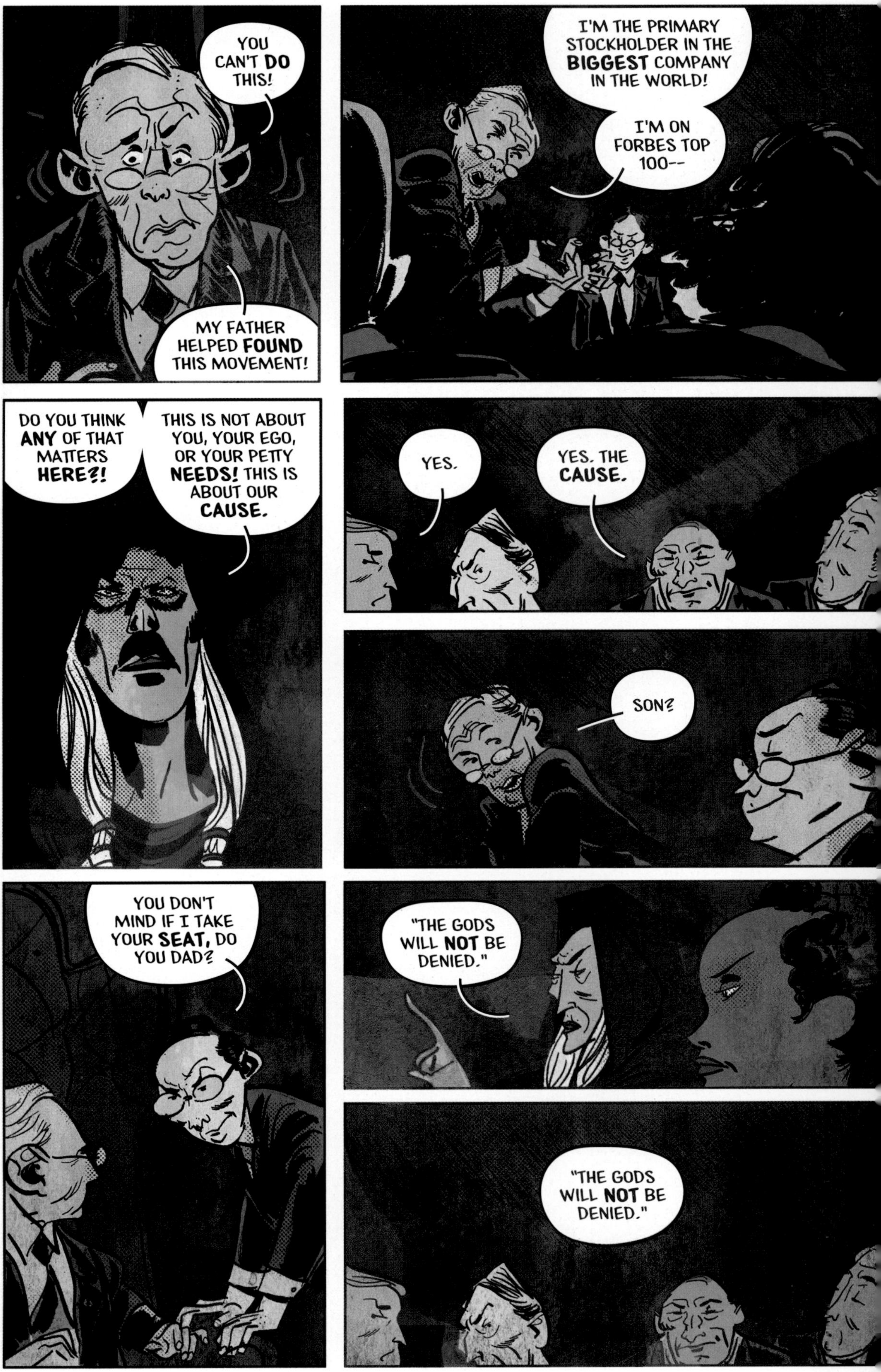
YOU CAN'T DO THIS!
MY FATHER HELPED FOUND THIS MOVEMENT!
I'M THE PRIMARY STOCKHOLDER IN THE BIGGEST COMPANY IN THE WORLD!
I'M ON FORBES TOP 100--
DO YOU THINK ANY OF THAT MATTERS HERE?!
THIS IS NOT ABOUT YOU, YOUR EGO, OR YOUR PETTY NEEDS! THIS IS ABOUT OUR CAUSE.
YES.
YES. THE CAUSE.
SON?
YOU DON'T MIND IF I TAKE YOUR SEAT, DO YOU DAD?
"THE GODS WILL NOT BE DENIED."
"THE GODS WILL NOT BE DENIED."

HOW MUCH DID **THAT** COST US?

HE WAS A MAJOR CONTRIBUTOR. BUT IT'S BEEN **DWINDLING** IN RECENT YEARS.

I'LL DO BETTER.

DON'T APOLOGIZE.

THOSE **PEOPLE?** POLLUTERS? WAR PROFITEERS? THEY ARE MANKIND AT ITS **WORST.**

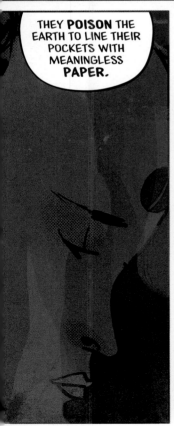

THEY **POISON** THE EARTH TO LINE THEIR POCKETS WITH MEANINGLESS **PAPER.**

THAT'S WHY THE FOUNDER'S PLAN WAS SO **INGENIOUS.**

WE USE THESE PEOPLE TO OUR ENDS, AND WHEN WE'VE **WON,** WE DISCARD THEM.

THEY'RE A **RESOURCE** TO BE EXPLOITED.

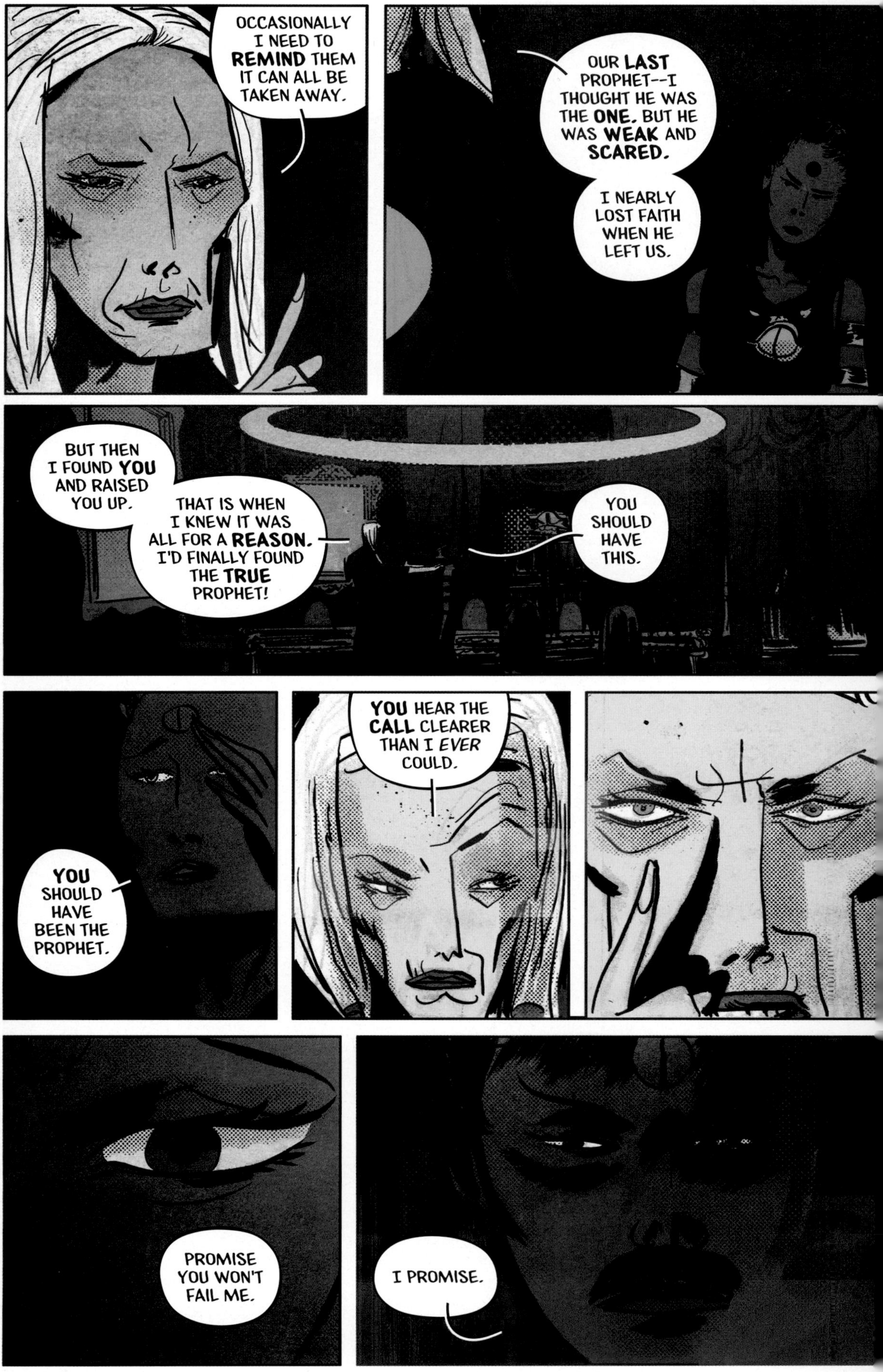
OCCASIONALLY I NEED TO REMIND THEM IT CAN ALL BE TAKEN AWAY.
OUR LAST PROPHET--I THOUGHT HE WAS THE ONE. BUT HE WAS WEAK AND SCARED.
I NEARLY LOST FAITH WHEN HE LEFT US.
BUT THEN I FOUND YOU AND RAISED YOU UP.
THAT IS WHEN I KNEW IT WAS ALL FOR A REASON. I'D FINALLY FOUND THE TRUE PROPHET!
YOU SHOULD HAVE THIS.
YOU SHOULD HAVE BEEN THE PROPHET.
YOU HEAR THE CALL CLEARER THAN I EVER COULD.
PROMISE YOU WON'T FAIL ME.
I PROMISE.

THE YUPPIE VAMPIRE

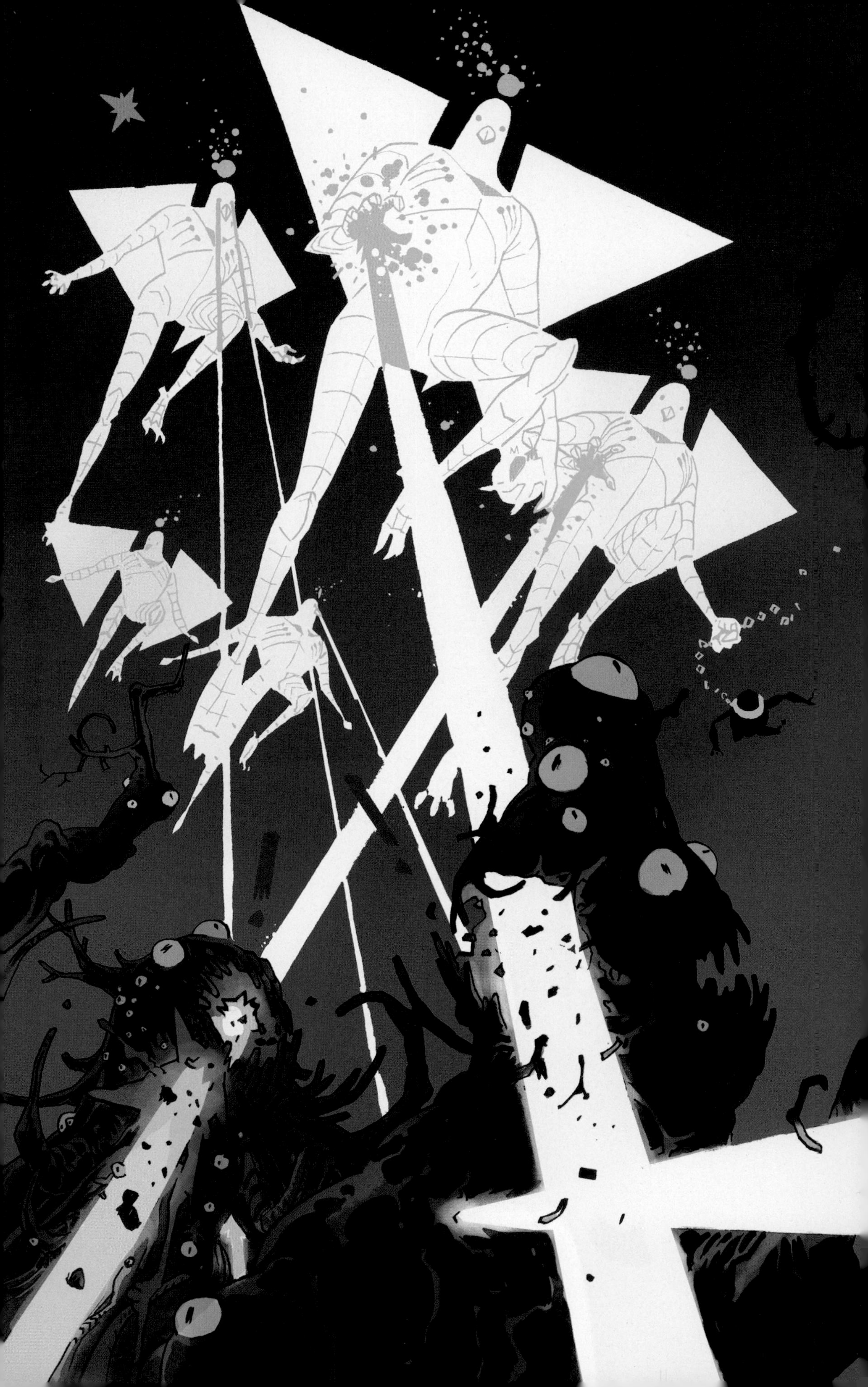

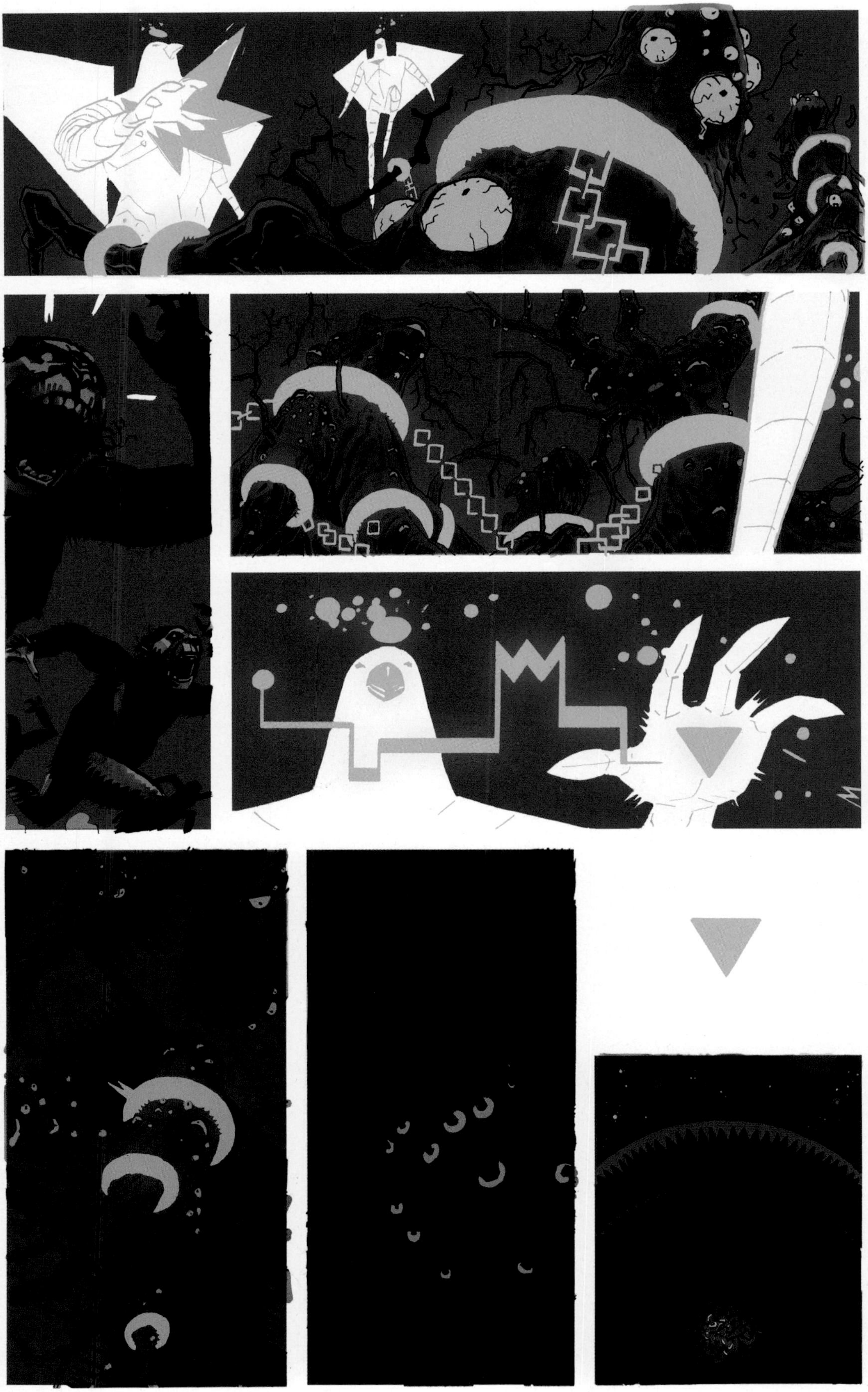

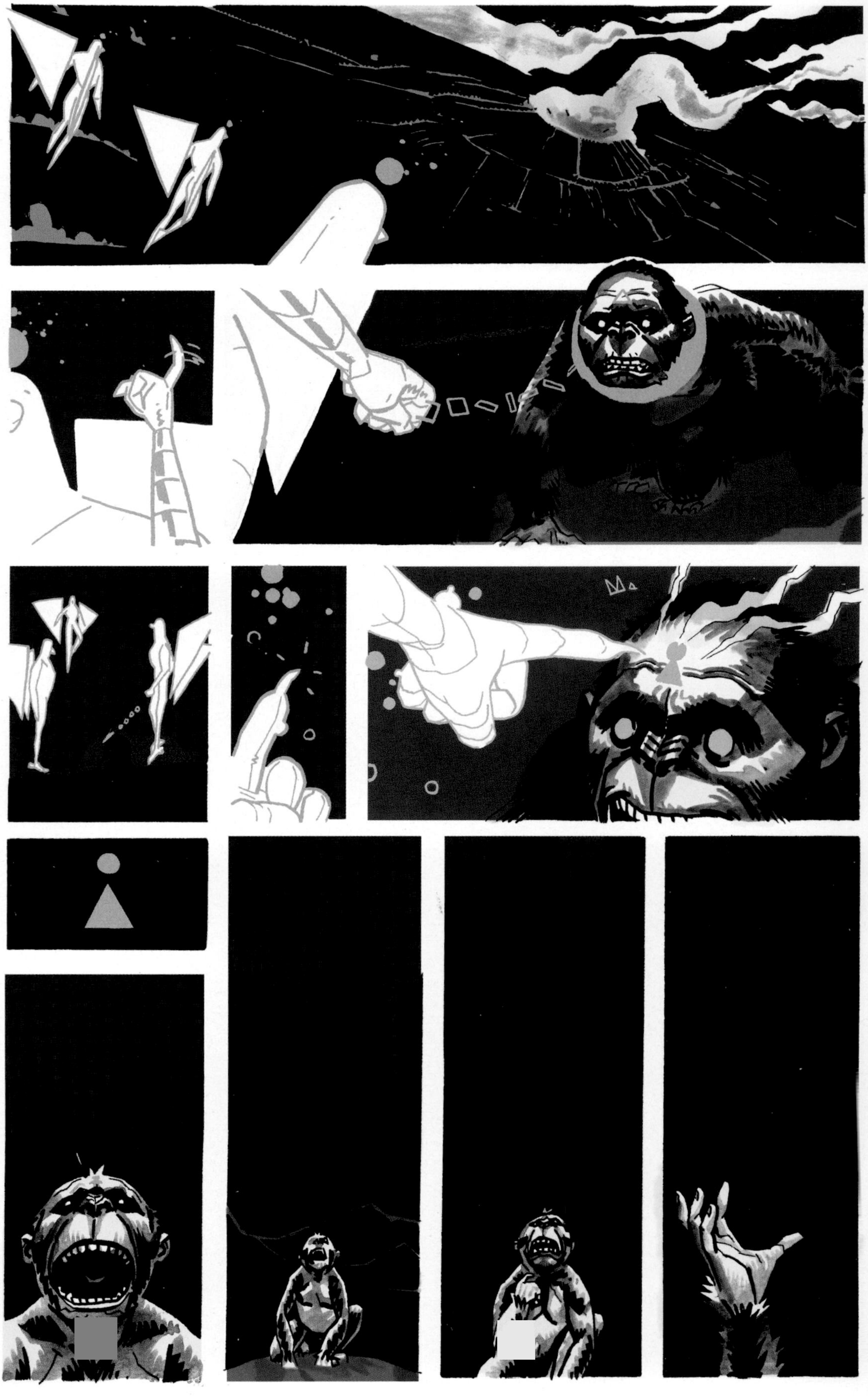

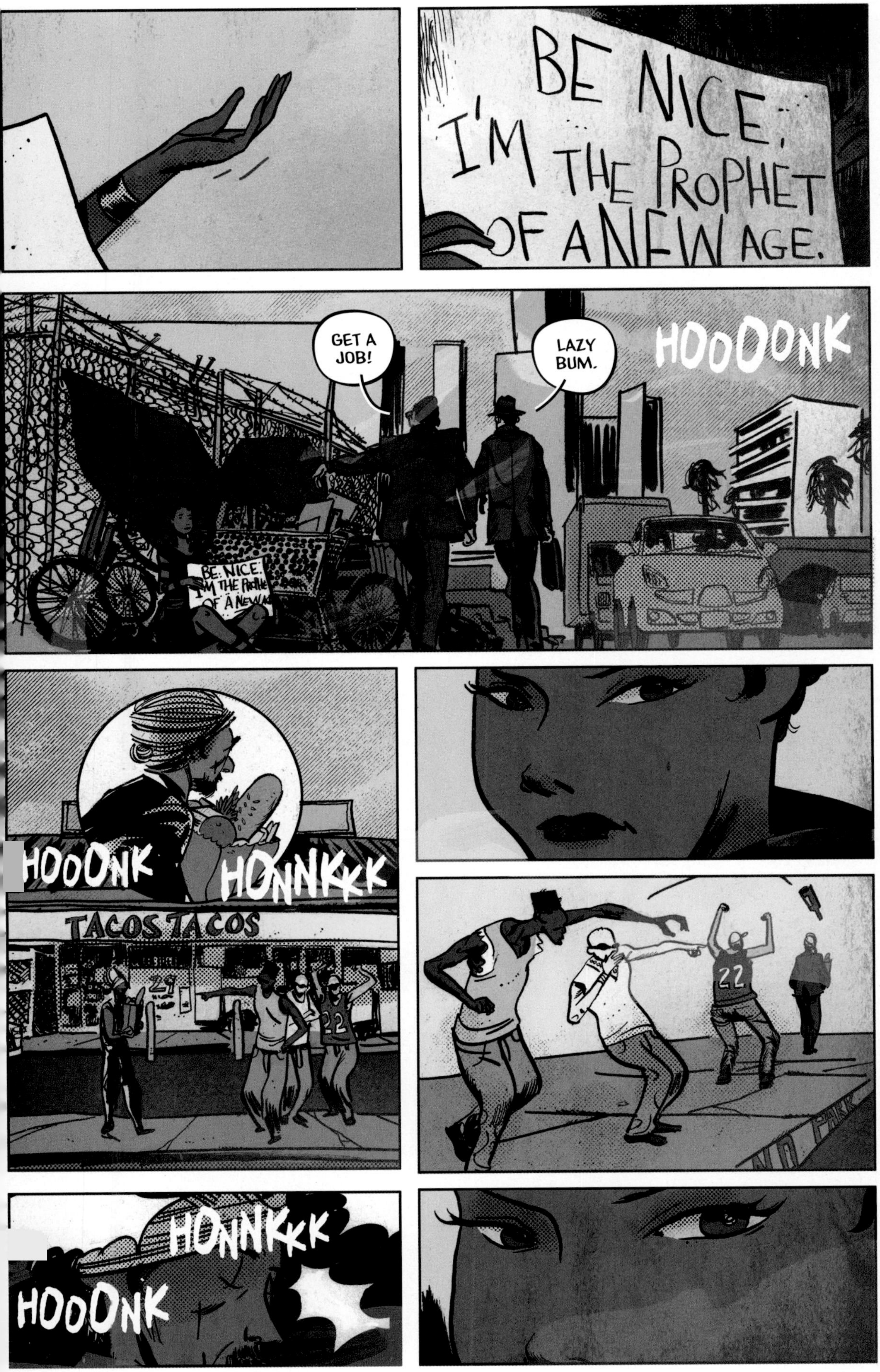
BE NICE; I'M THE PROPHET OF A NEW AGE.
GET A JOB!
LAZY BUM.
HOOOONK
BE NICE. I'M THE PROPHET OF A NEW AGE
HOOONK
HONNKKK
TACOS TACOS
22
NO PARK
HONNKKK
HOOONK

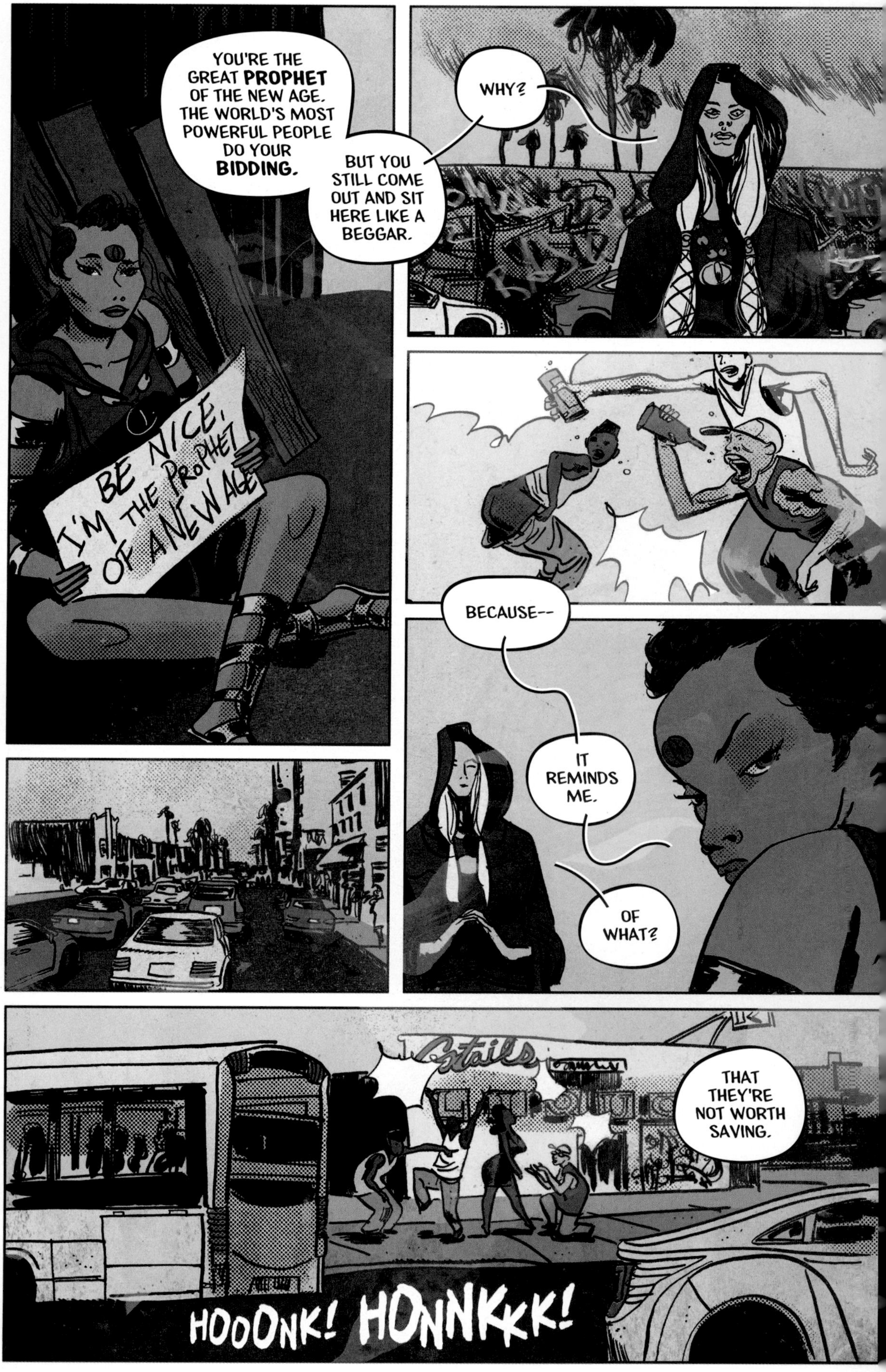
YOU'RE THE GREAT **PROPHET** OF THE NEW AGE. THE WORLD'S MOST POWERFUL PEOPLE DO YOUR **BIDDING.**
BE NICE, I'M THE PROPHET OF A NEW AGE
WHY?
BUT YOU STILL COME OUT AND SIT HERE LIKE A BEGGAR.
BECAUSE--
IT REMINDS ME.
OF WHAT?
THAT THEY'RE NOT WORTH SAVING.
HOOONK! HONNKKK!

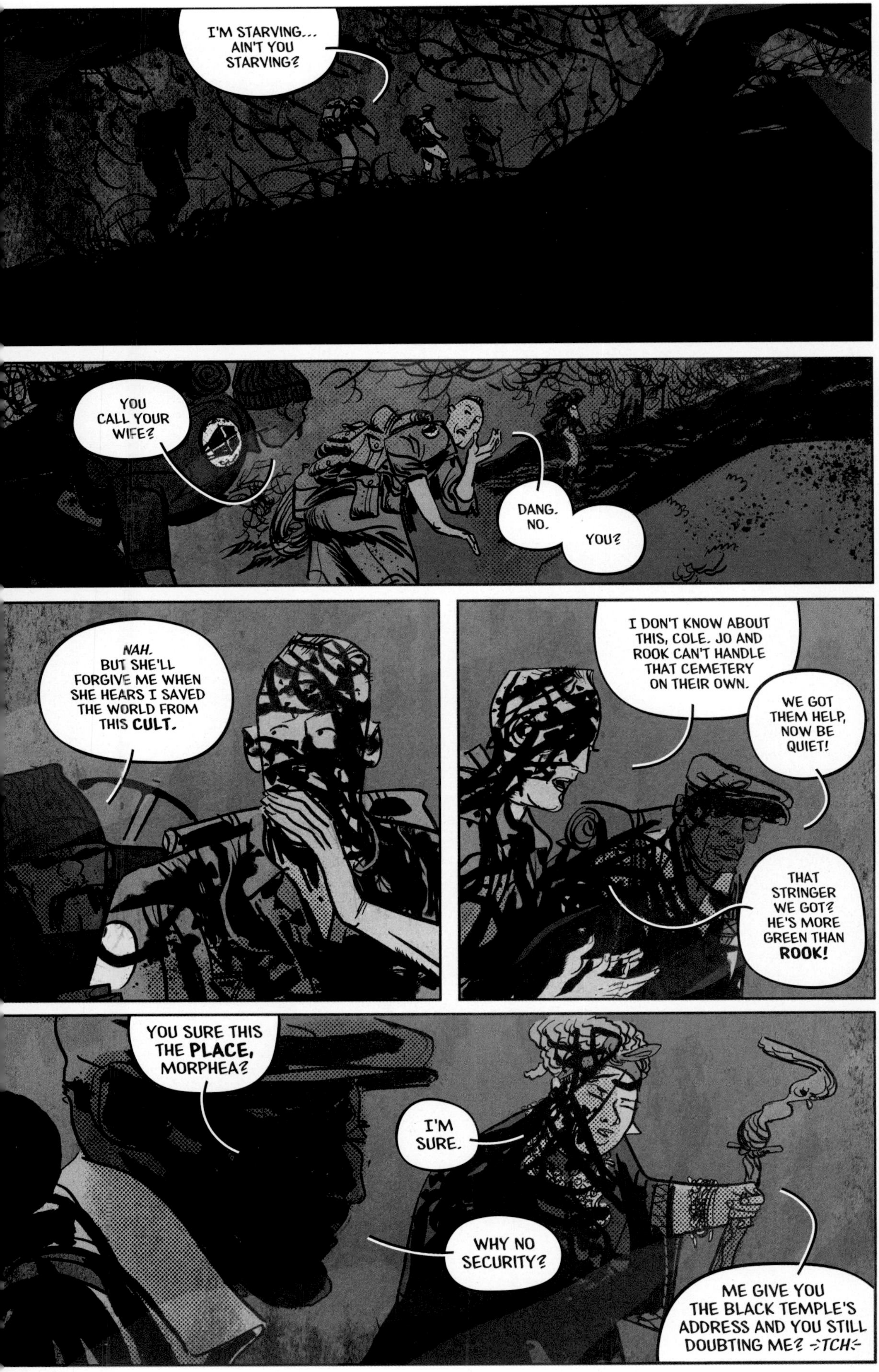
I'M STARVING... AIN'T YOU STARVING?
YOU CALL YOUR WIFE?
DANG. NO.
YOU?
NAH. BUT SHE'LL FORGIVE ME WHEN SHE HEARS I SAVED THE WORLD FROM THIS CULT.
I DON'T KNOW ABOUT THIS, COLE. JO AND ROOK CAN'T HANDLE THAT CEMETERY ON THEIR OWN.
WE GOT THEM HELP, NOW BE QUIET!
THAT STRINGER WE GOT? HE'S MORE GREEN THAN ROOK!
YOU SURE THIS THE PLACE, MORPHEA?
I'M SURE.
WHY NO SECURITY?
ME GIVE YOU THE BLACK TEMPLE'S ADDRESS AND YOU STILL DOUBTING ME? TCH

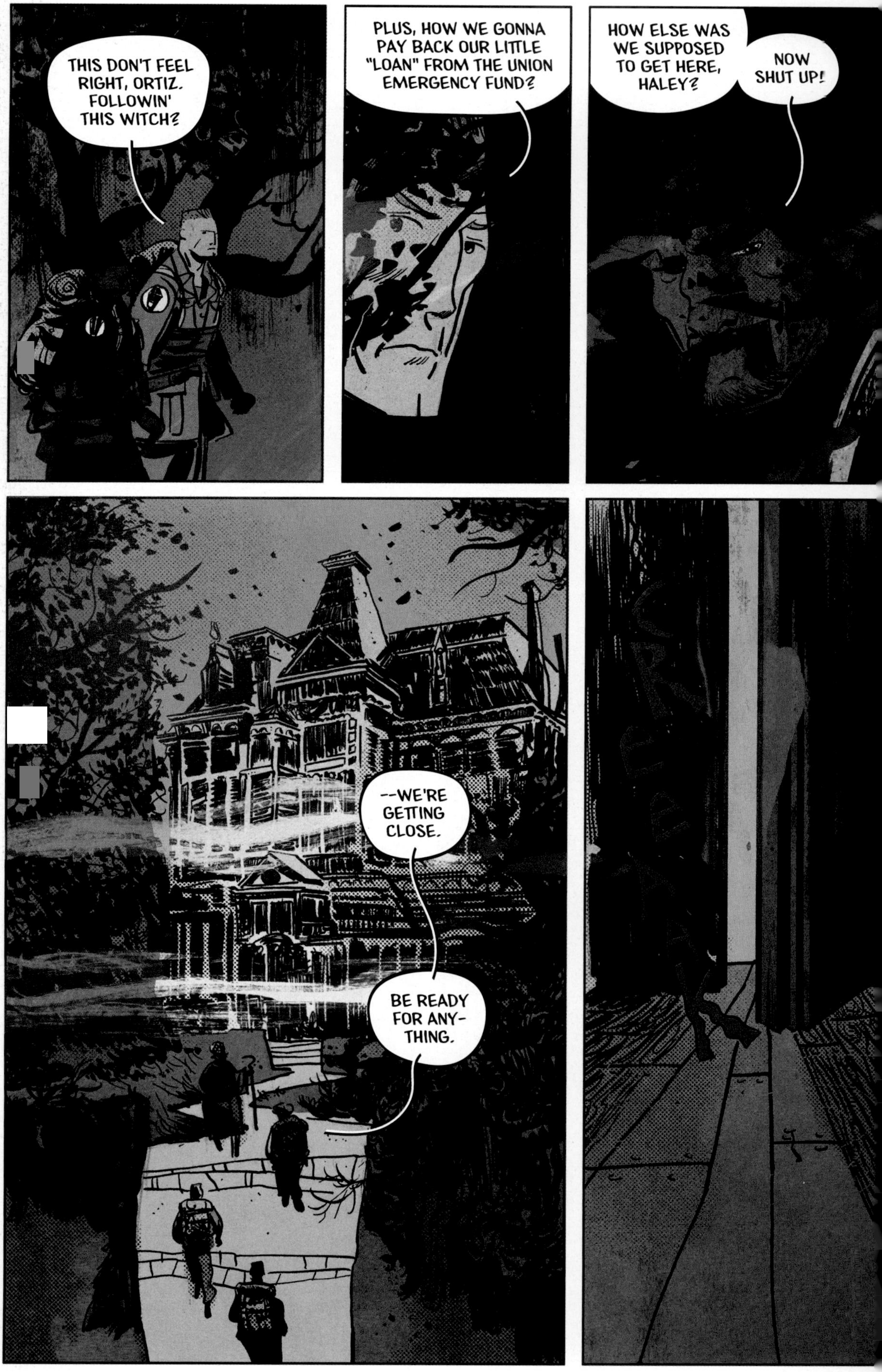
THIS DON'T FEEL RIGHT, ORTIZ. FOLLOWIN' THIS WITCH?
PLUS, HOW WE GONNA PAY BACK OUR LITTLE "LOAN" FROM THE UNION EMERGENCY FUND?
HOW ELSE WAS WE SUPPOSED TO GET HERE, HALEY?
NOW SHUT UP!
--WE'RE GETTING CLOSE.
BE READY FOR ANY-THING.

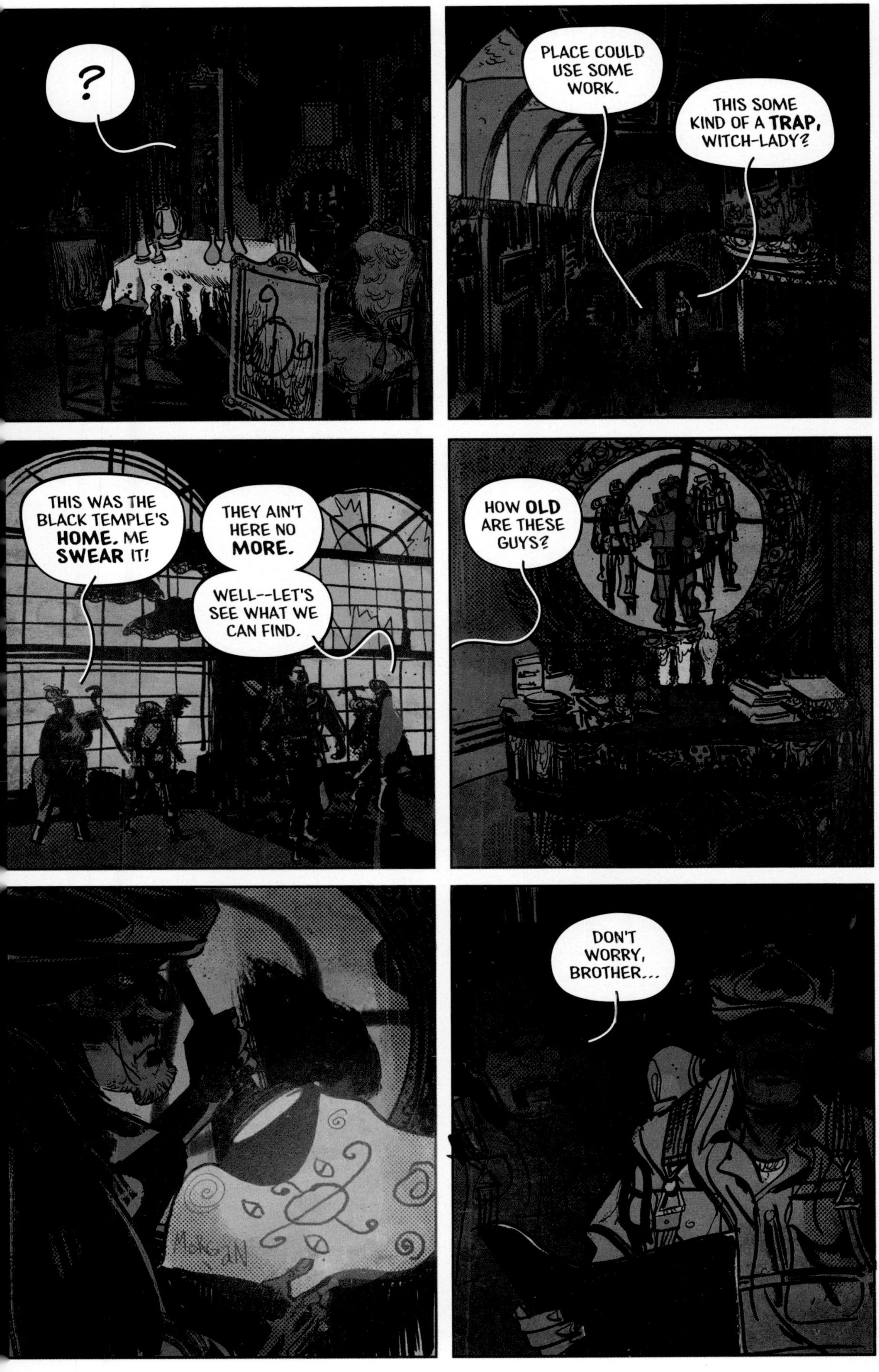
?
PLACE COULD USE SOME WORK.
THIS SOME KIND OF A TRAP, WITCH-LADY?
THIS WAS THE BLACK TEMPLE'S HOME. ME SWEAR IT!
THEY AIN'T HERE NO MORE.
WELL--LET'S SEE WHAT WE CAN FIND.
HOW OLD ARE THESE GUYS?
MORGAN
DON'T WORRY, BROTHER...

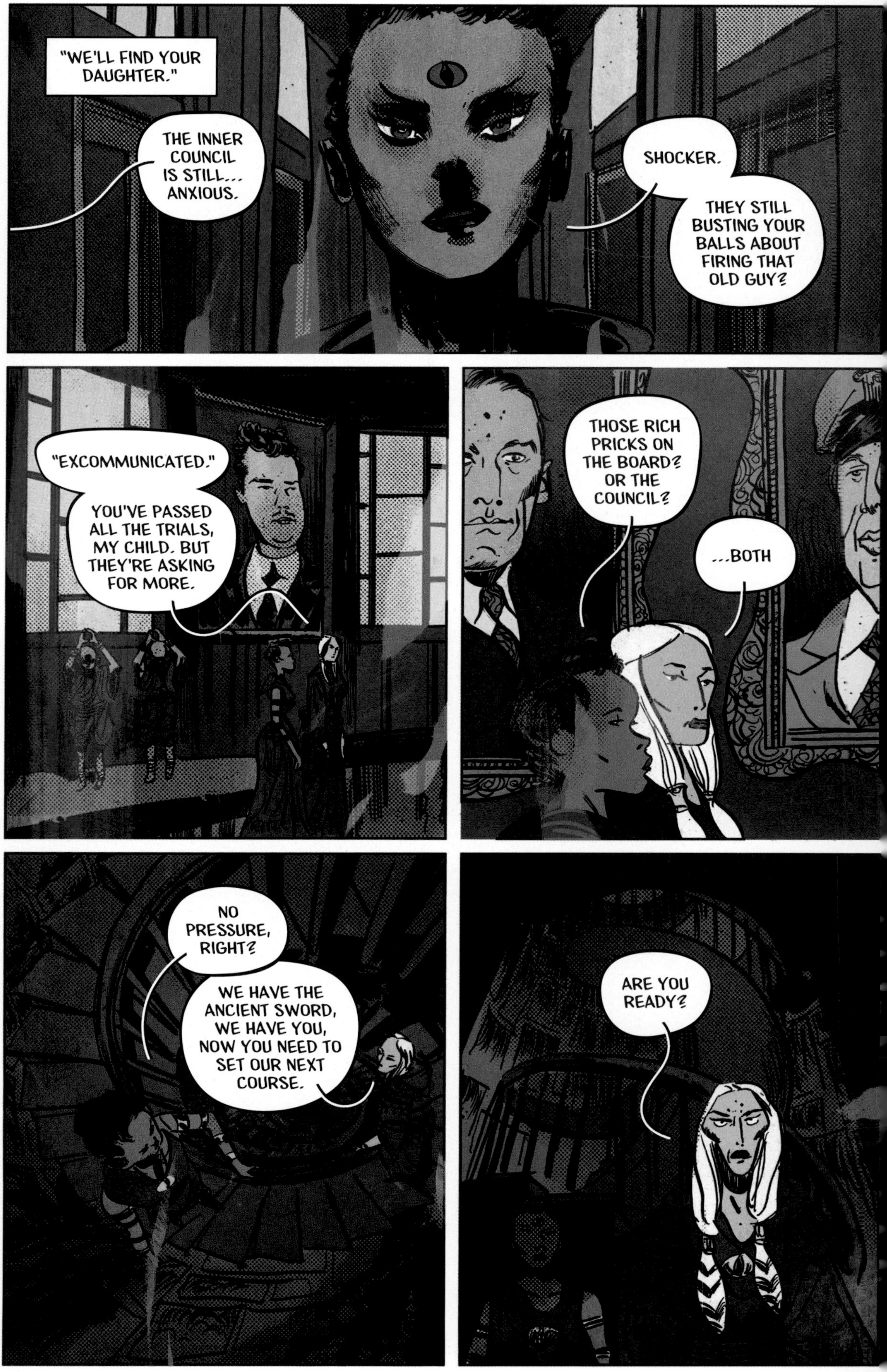
"WE'LL FIND YOUR DAUGHTER."
THE INNER COUNCIL IS STILL... ANXIOUS.
SHOCKER.
THEY STILL BUSTING YOUR BALLS ABOUT FIRING THAT OLD GUY?
"EXCOMMUNICATED."
YOU'VE PASSED ALL THE TRIALS, MY CHILD. BUT THEY'RE ASKING FOR MORE.
THOSE RICH PRICKS ON THE BOARD? OR THE COUNCIL?
...BOTH
NO PRESSURE, RIGHT?
WE HAVE THE ANCIENT SWORD, WE HAVE YOU, NOW YOU NEED TO SET OUR NEXT COURSE.
ARE YOU READY?

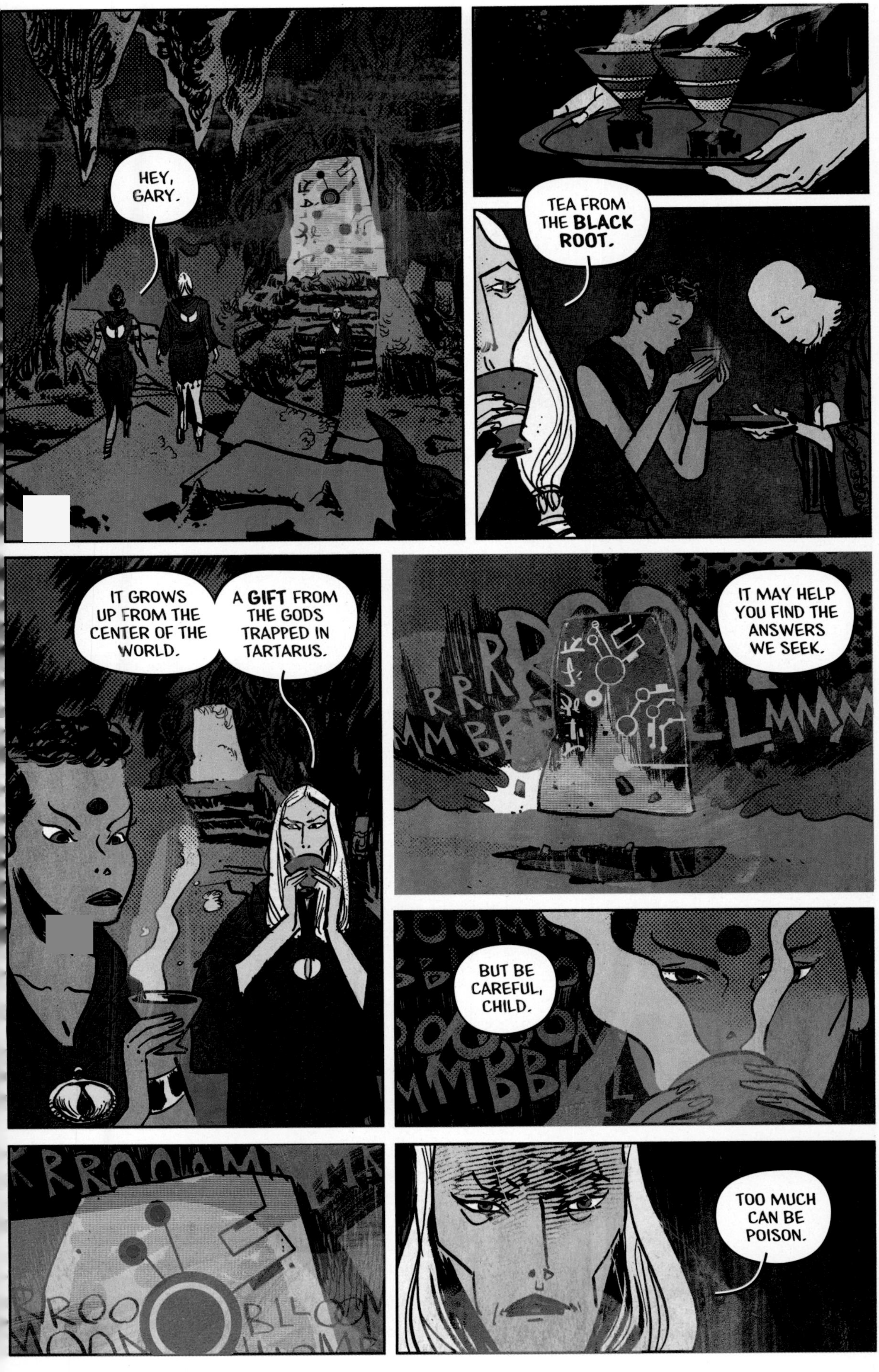
HEY, GARY.
TEA FROM THE BLACK ROOT.
IT GROWS UP FROM THE CENTER OF THE WORLD.
A GIFT FROM THE GODS TRAPPED IN TARTARUS.
IT MAY HELP YOU FIND THE ANSWERS WE SEEK.
BUT BE CAREFUL, CHILD.
TOO MUCH CAN BE POISON.

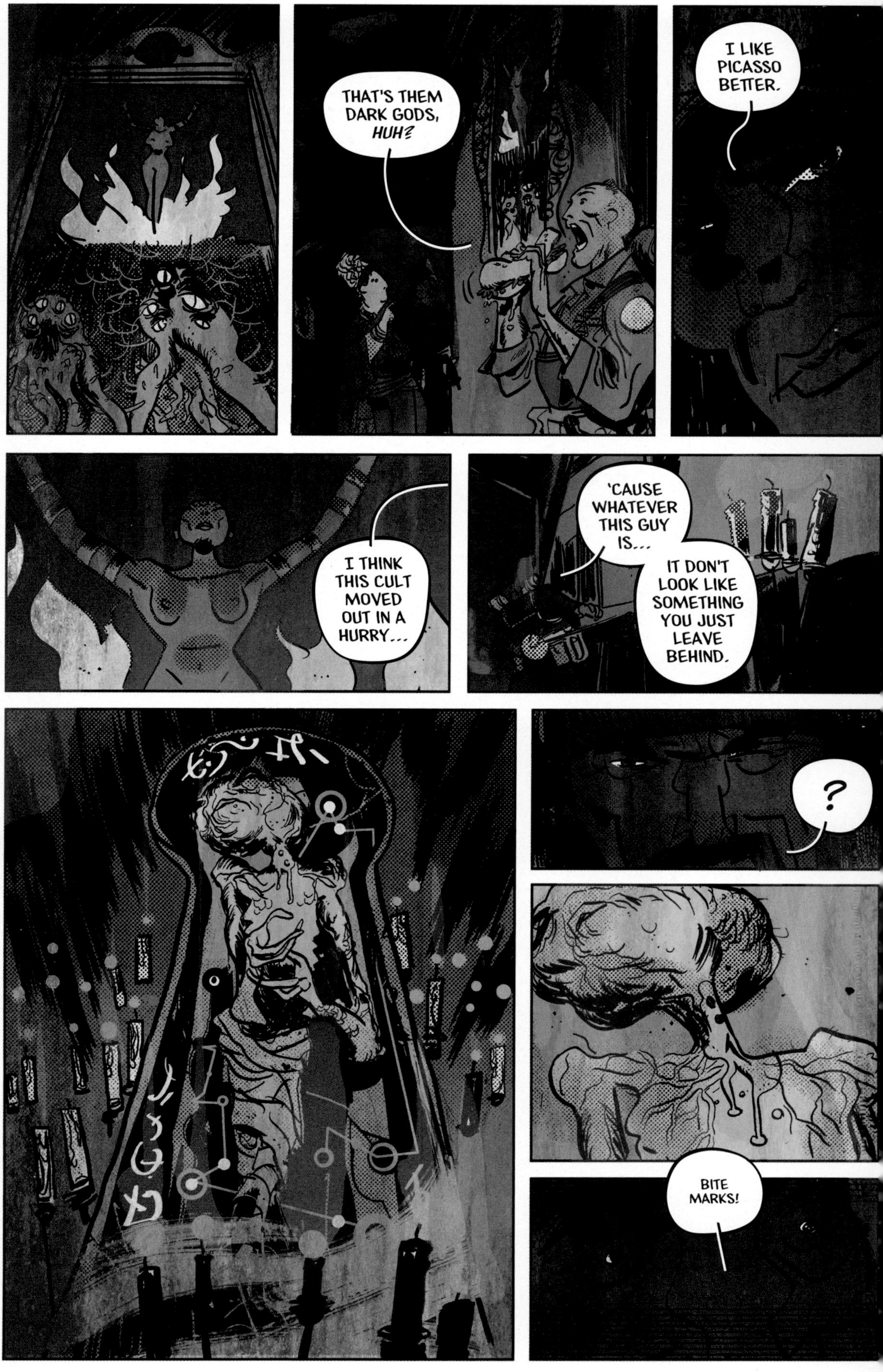
THAT'S THEM DARK GODS, *HUH?*
I LIKE PICASSO BETTER.
I THINK THIS CULT MOVED OUT IN A HURRY...
'CAUSE WHATEVER THIS GUY IS...
IT DON'T LOOK LIKE SOMETHING YOU JUST LEAVE BEHIND.
?
BITE MARKS!

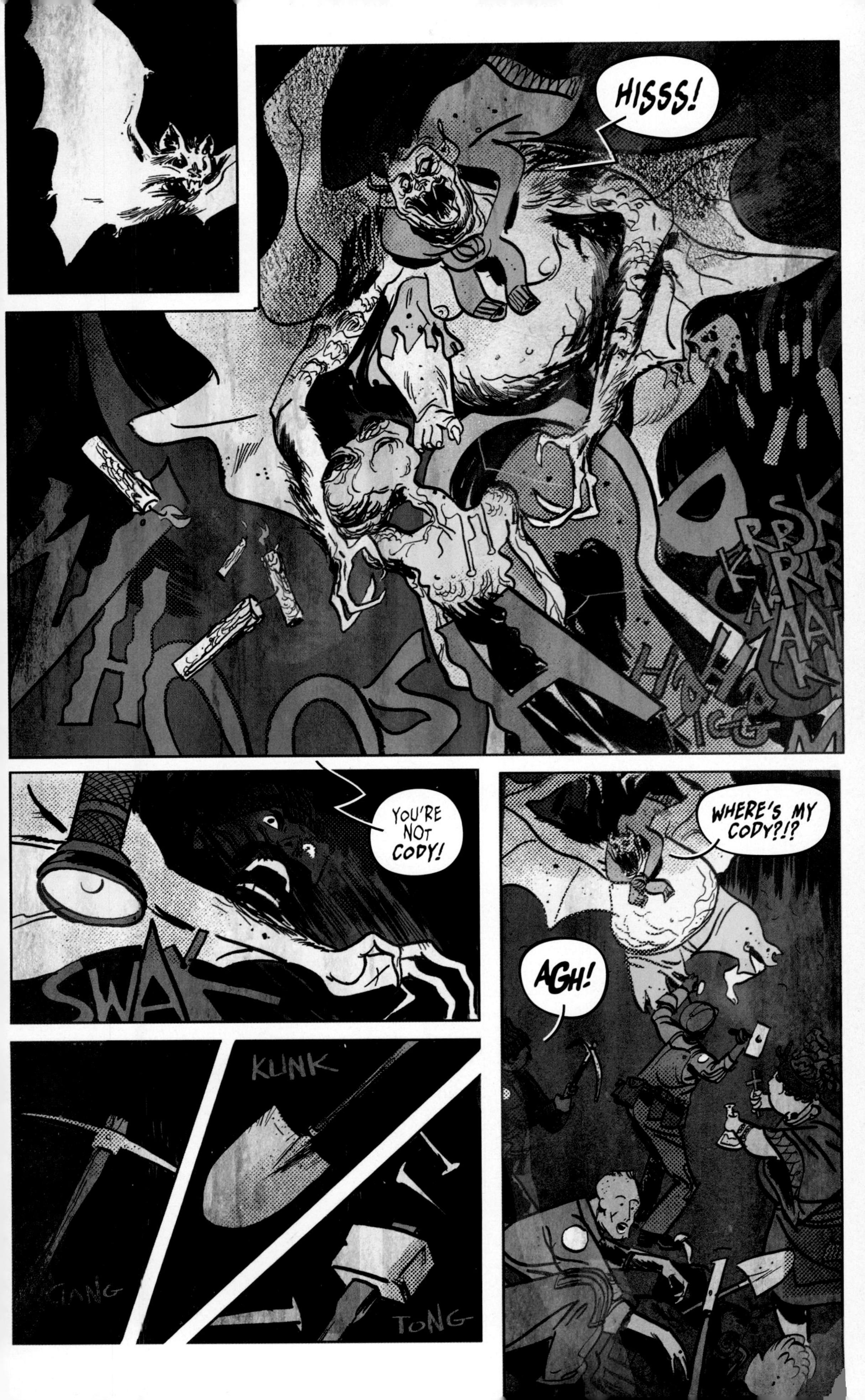

HISSS!
YOU'RE NOT CODY!
WHERE'S MY CODY?!?
AGH!
KUNK
TONG

ROOMMBLE
ROOMMBLE
MMBLE
MMBLE
ROMM
OMBLE
I THINK I TOOK TOO MUCH...

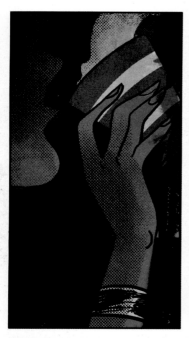

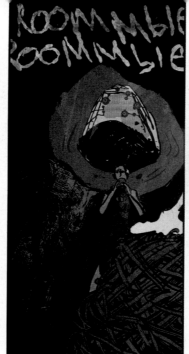

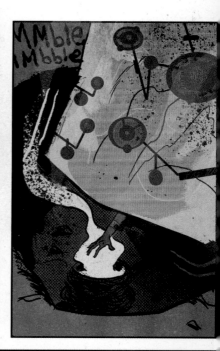

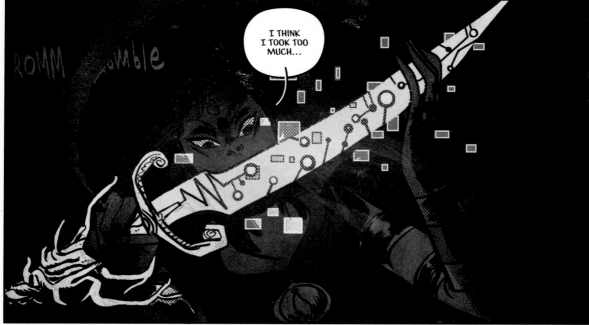

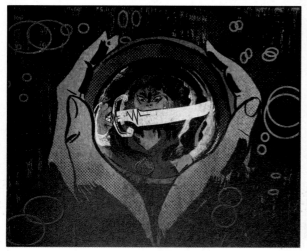

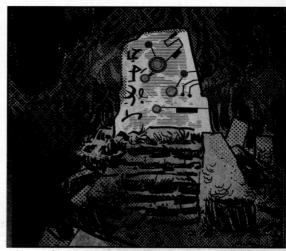

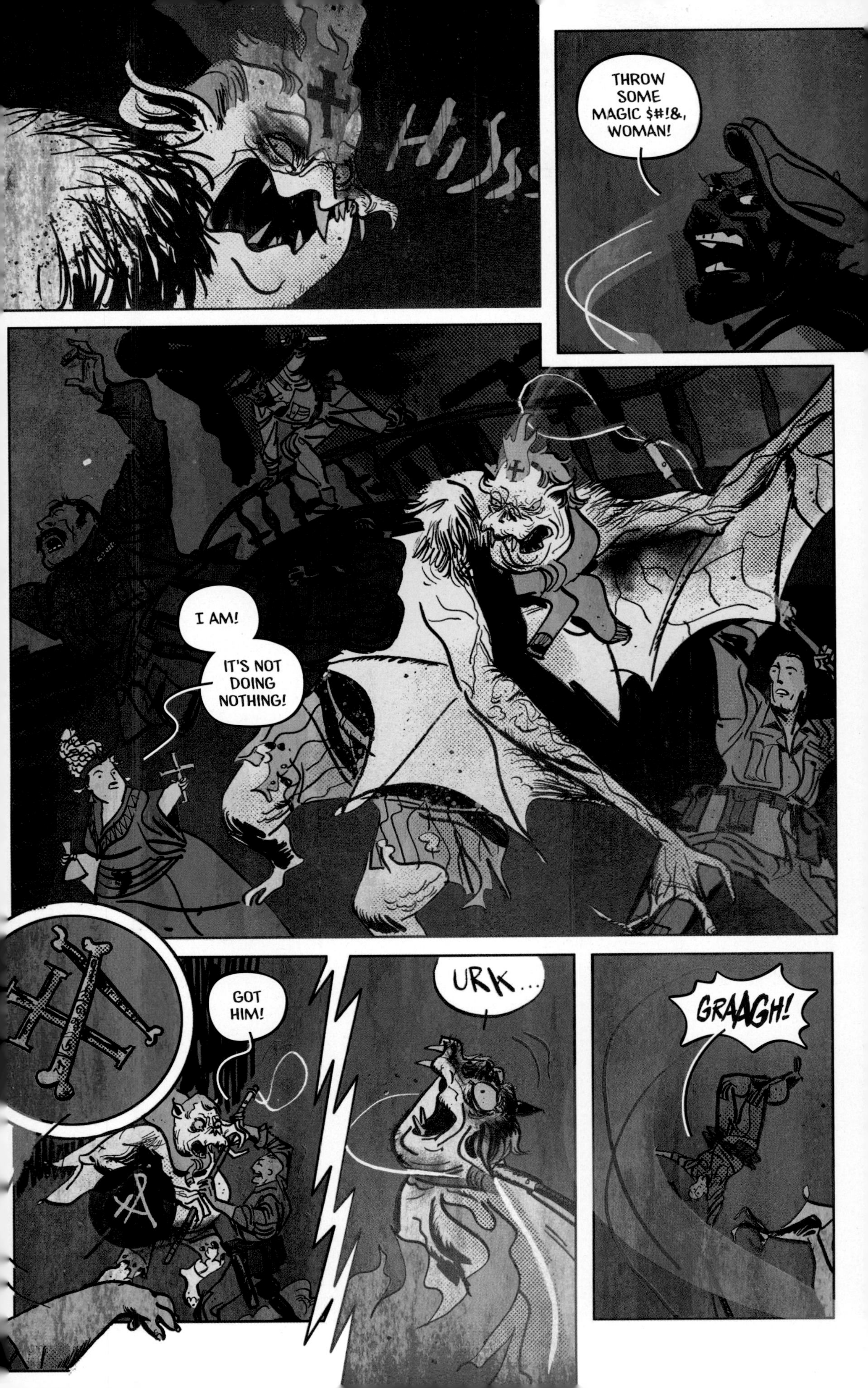
HISS
THROW SOME MAGIC $#!&, WOMAN!
I AM!
IT'S NOT DOING NOTHING!
GOT HIM!
URK...
GRAAGH!

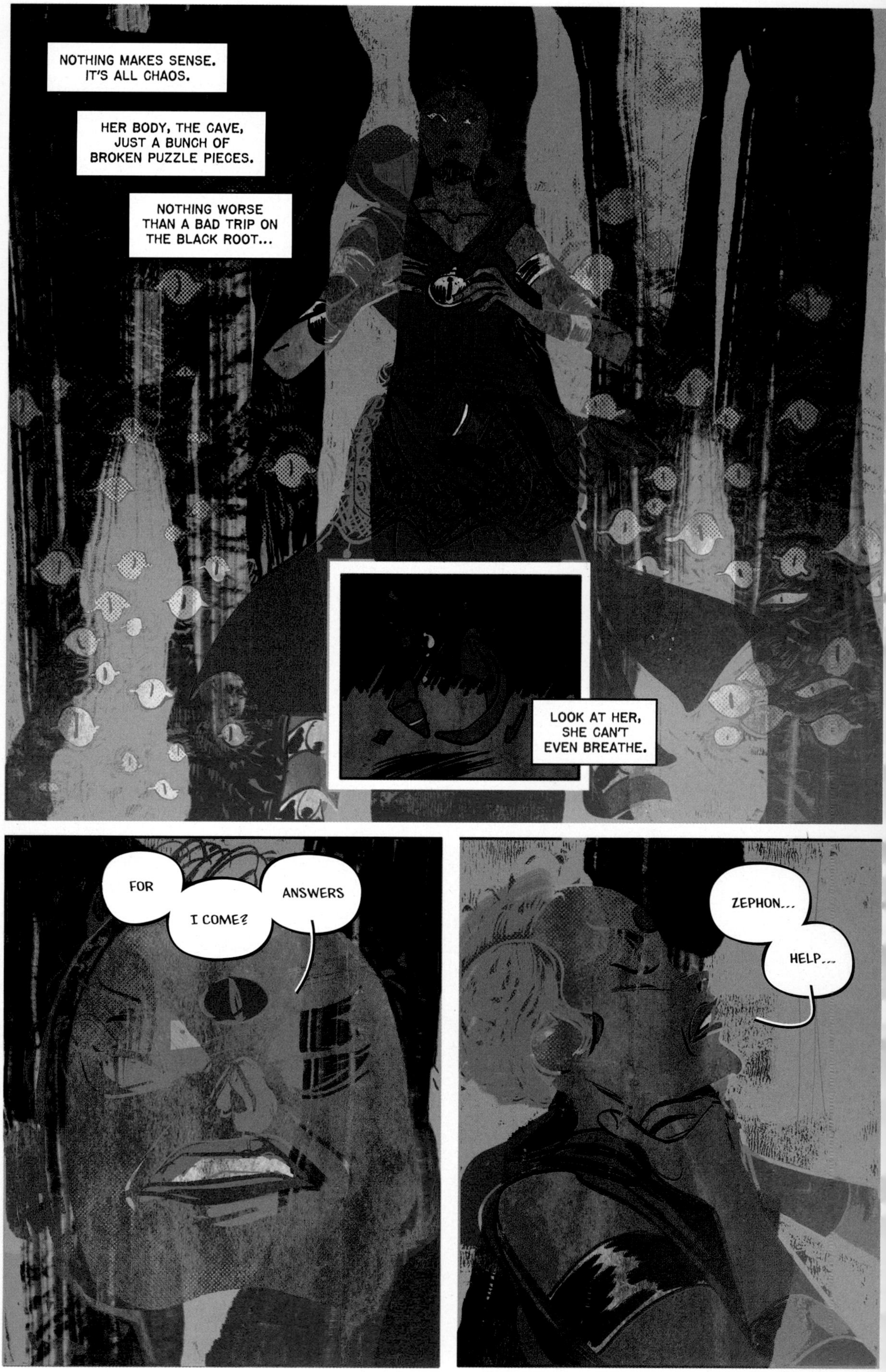
NOTHING MAKES SENSE. IT'S ALL CHAOS.
HER BODY, THE CAVE, JUST A BUNCH OF BROKEN PUZZLE PIECES.
NOTHING WORSE THAN A BAD TRIP ON THE BLACK ROOT...
LOOK AT HER, SHE CAN'T EVEN BREATHE.
FOR
I COME?
ANSWERS
ZEPHON...
HELP...

PANIC THAT LASTS AN ETERNITY.

BUT EVENTUALLY...

SHE FITS THE PIECES BACK TOGETHER.

AND SUDDENLY, EVERYTHING'S CONNECTED...

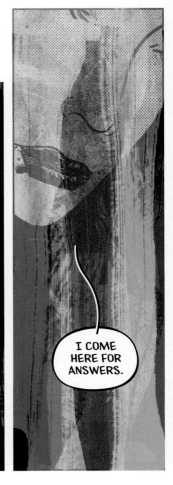

I COME HERE FOR ANSWERS.

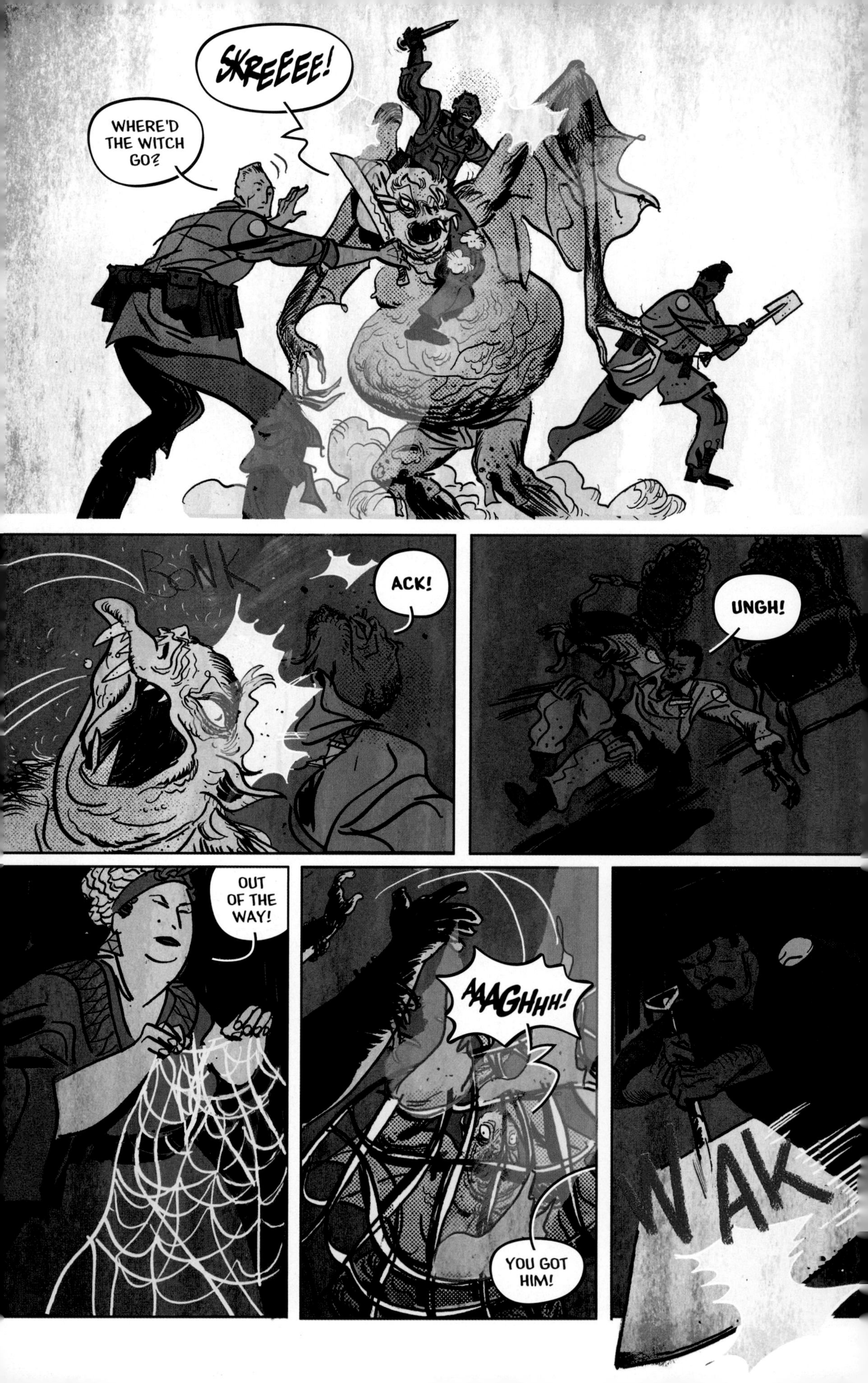
SKREEEEE!
WHERE'D THE WITCH GO?
BONK
ACK!
UNGH!
OUT OF THE WAY!
AAAGHHH!
YOU GOT HIM!
WAK

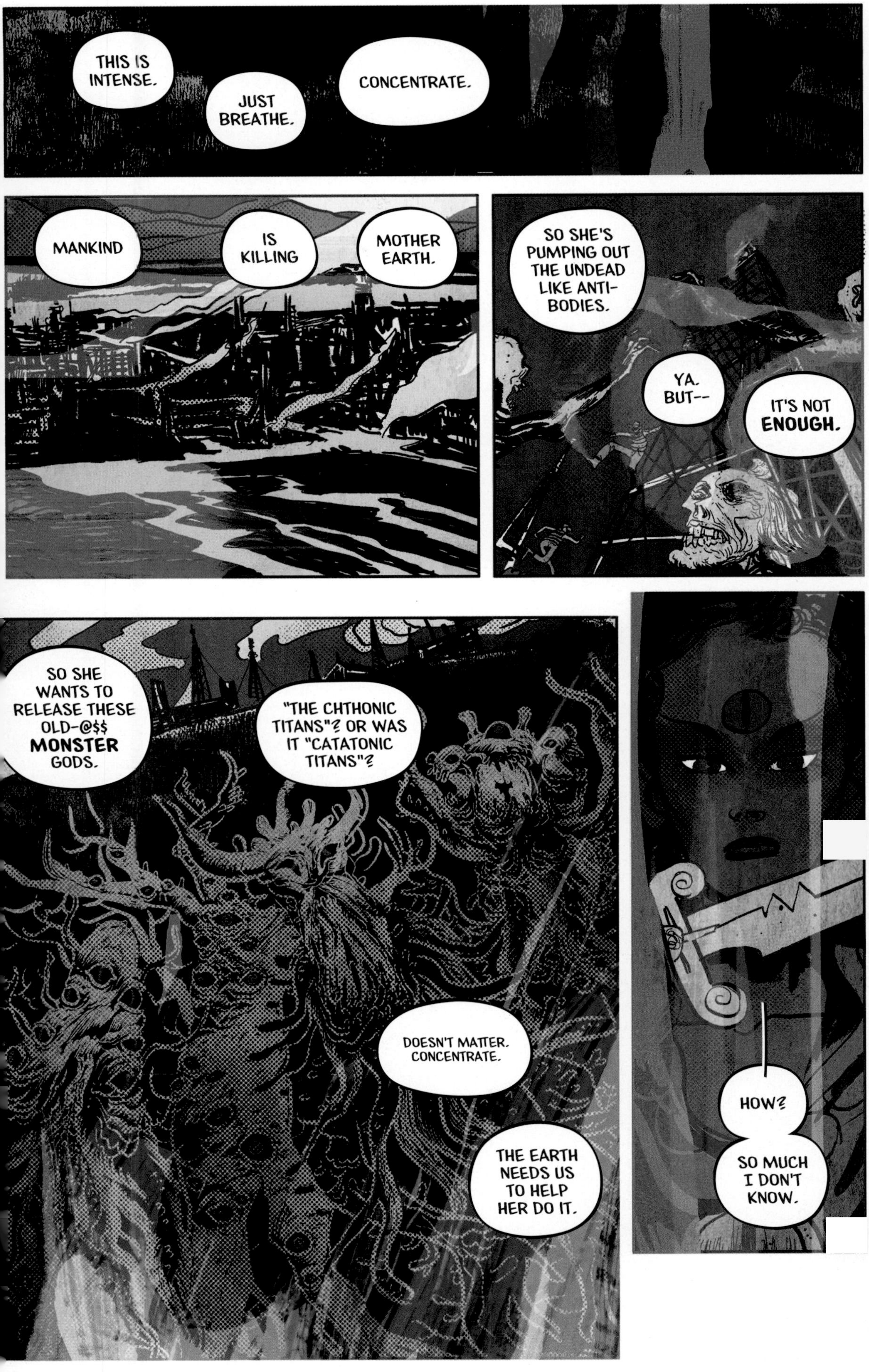
THIS IS INTENSE.
JUST BREATHE.
CONCENTRATE.
MANKIND
IS KILLING
MOTHER EARTH.
SO SHE'S PUMPING OUT THE UNDEAD LIKE ANTI-BODIES.
YA. BUT--
IT'S NOT **ENOUGH.**
SO SHE WANTS TO RELEASE THESE OLD-@$$ **MONSTER** GODS.
"THE CHTHONIC TITANS"? OR WAS IT "CATATONIC TITANS"?
DOESN'T MATTER. CONCENTRATE.
THE EARTH NEEDS US TO HELP HER DO IT.
HOW?
SO MUCH I DON'T KNOW.

THE UNDEAD.
MAYBE THEY KNOW STUFF, RIGHT?
WHOA.
BUT ZOMBIES? &*%$#& BRAIN DEAD.
VAMPIRES? NO. &*%$#& CRAZY.
BUT--
THE GHOSTS...
YES!
THE GHOSTS!

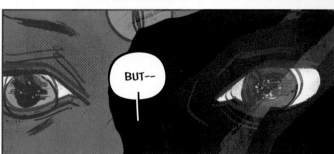

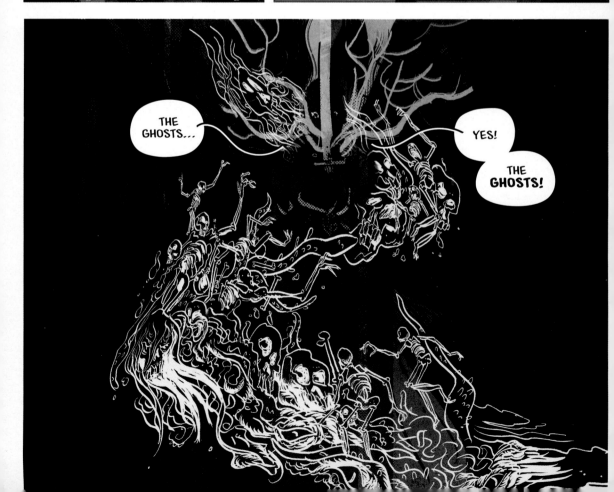

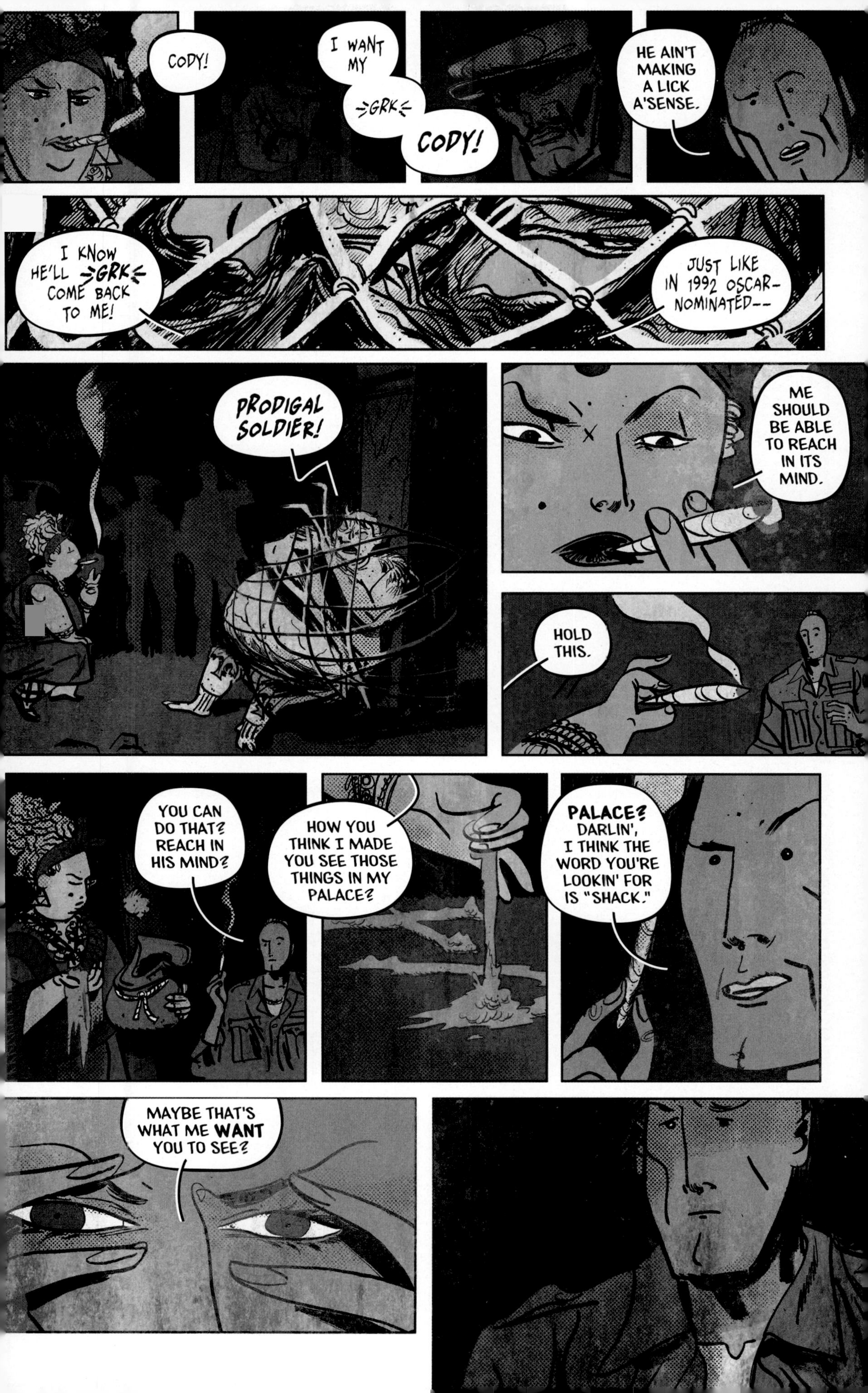
CODY!
I WANT MY
GRK
CODY!
HE AIN'T MAKING A LICK A'SENSE.
I KNOW HE'LL GRK COME BACK TO ME!
JUST LIKE IN 1992 OSCAR-NOMINATED--
PRODIGAL SOLDIER!
ME SHOULD BE ABLE TO REACH IN ITS MIND.
HOLD THIS.
YOU CAN DO THAT? REACH IN HIS MIND?
HOW YOU THINK I MADE YOU SEE THOSE THINGS IN MY PALACE?
PALACE? DARLIN', I THINK THE WORD YOU'RE LOOKIN' FOR IS "SHACK."
MAYBE THAT'S WHAT ME WANT YOU TO SEE?

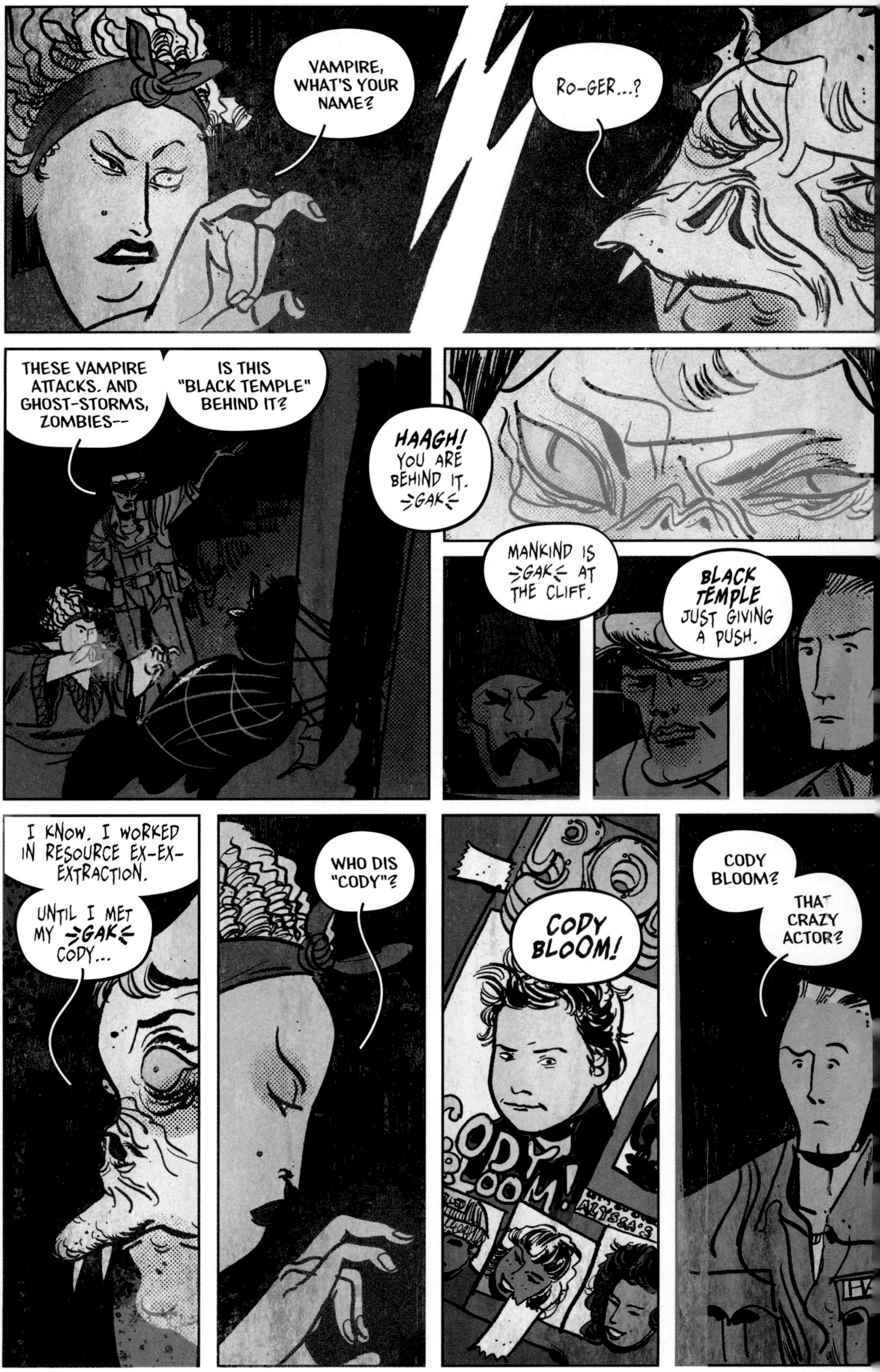
VAMPIRE, WHAT'S YOUR NAME?
RO-GER...?
THESE VAMPIRE ATTACKS. AND GHOST-STORMS, ZOMBIES--
IS THIS "BLACK TEMPLE" BEHIND IT?
HAAGH! YOU ARE BEHIND IT. GAK
MANKIND IS GAK AT THE CLIFF.
BLACK TEMPLE JUST GIVING A PUSH.
I KNOW. I WORKED IN RESOURCE EX-EX-EXTRACTION.
UNTIL I MET MY GAK CODY...
WHO DIS "CODY"?
CODY BLOOM!
CODY BLOOM!
ALYSSA'S
CODY BLOOM?
THAT CRAZY ACTOR?

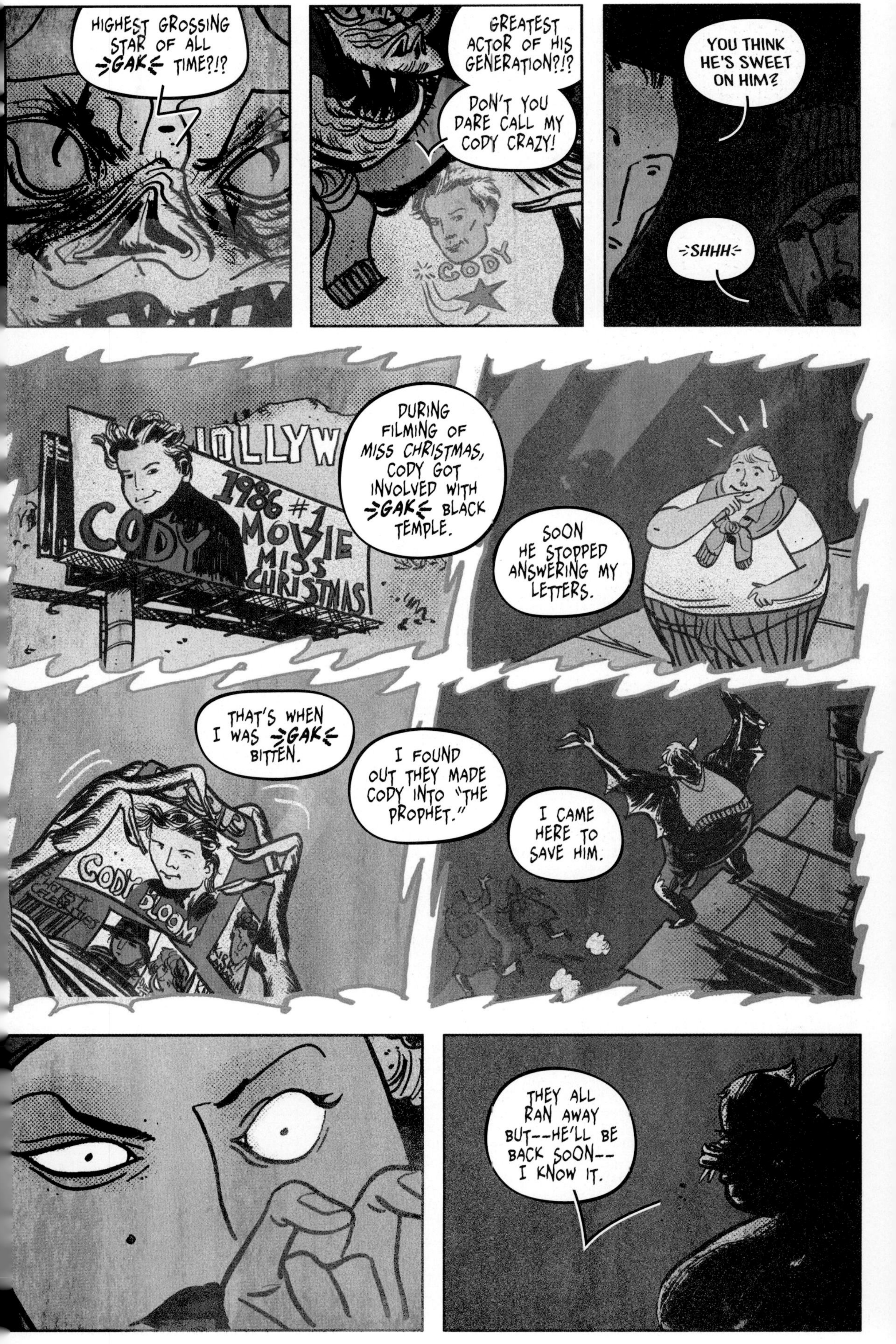
HIGHEST GROSSING STAR OF ALL -GAK- TIME?!?
GREATEST ACTOR OF HIS GENERATION?!?
DON'T YOU DARE CALL MY CODY CRAZY!
CODY
YOU THINK HE'S SWEET ON HIM?
-SHHH-
HOLLYW
CODY
1986 #1 MOVIE MISS CHRISTMAS
DURING FILMING OF MISS CHRISTMAS, CODY GOT INVOLVED WITH -GAK- BLACK TEMPLE.
SOON HE STOPPED ANSWERING MY LETTERS.
THAT'S WHEN I WAS -GAK- BITTEN.
CODY BLOOM
I FOUND OUT THEY MADE CODY INTO "THE PROPHET."
I CAME HERE TO SAVE HIM.
THEY ALL RAN AWAY BUT--HE'LL BE BACK SOON--I KNOW IT.

AND WHAT ABOUT THAT BIG %#$&*% ALIEN-LOOKING THING?

IT KEEPS ME FED.

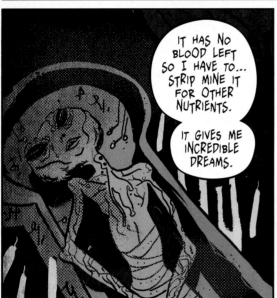

IT HAS NO BLOOD LEFT SO I HAVE TO... STRIP MINE IT FOR OTHER NUTRIENTS.

IT GIVES ME INCREDIBLE DREAMS.

MONSTERS WITH MILLIONS OF EYES.

GIANT BIRD PEOPLE...

SO CODY BLOOM'S THE PROPHET FOR THIS CULT?

MAYBE HE'LL HAVE ANSWERS.

THINK THIS ONE'S GIVEN US AS MUCH AS HE'S GONNA.

YOU'RE GOING TO FIND MY CODY?

WILL YOU TAKE ME WITH YOU?

'FRAID NOT, PARTNER.

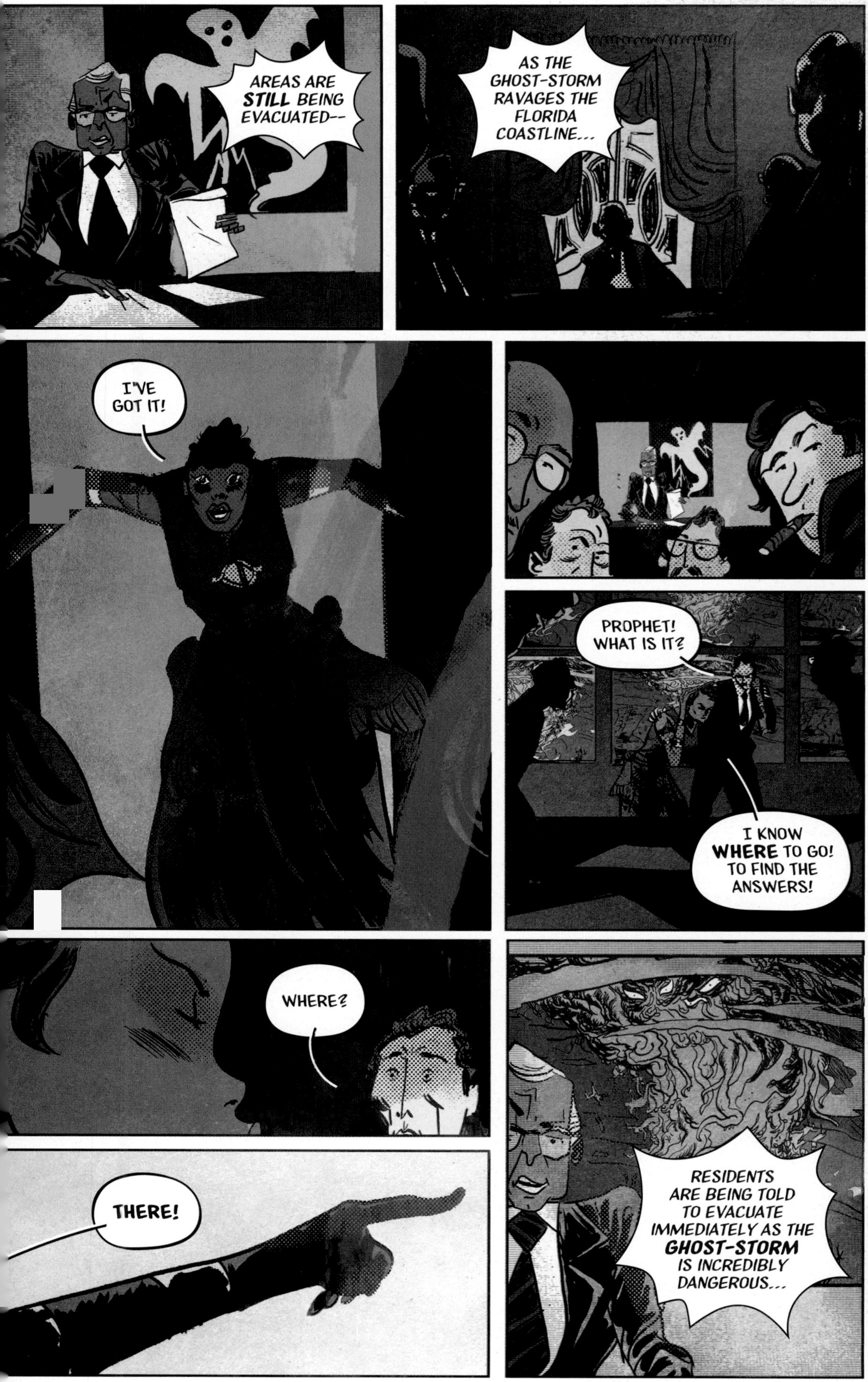
AREAS ARE STILL BEING EVACUATED--
AS THE GHOST-STORM RAVAGES THE FLORIDA COASTLINE...
I'VE GOT IT!
PROPHET! WHAT IS IT?
I KNOW WHERE TO GO! TO FIND THE ANSWERS!
WHERE?
THERE!
RESIDENTS ARE BEING TOLD TO EVACUATE IMMEDIATELY AS THE GHOST-STORM IS INCREDIBLY DANGEROUS...

CHAPTER

GHOST-STORM

EARTH
6000 YEARS AGO

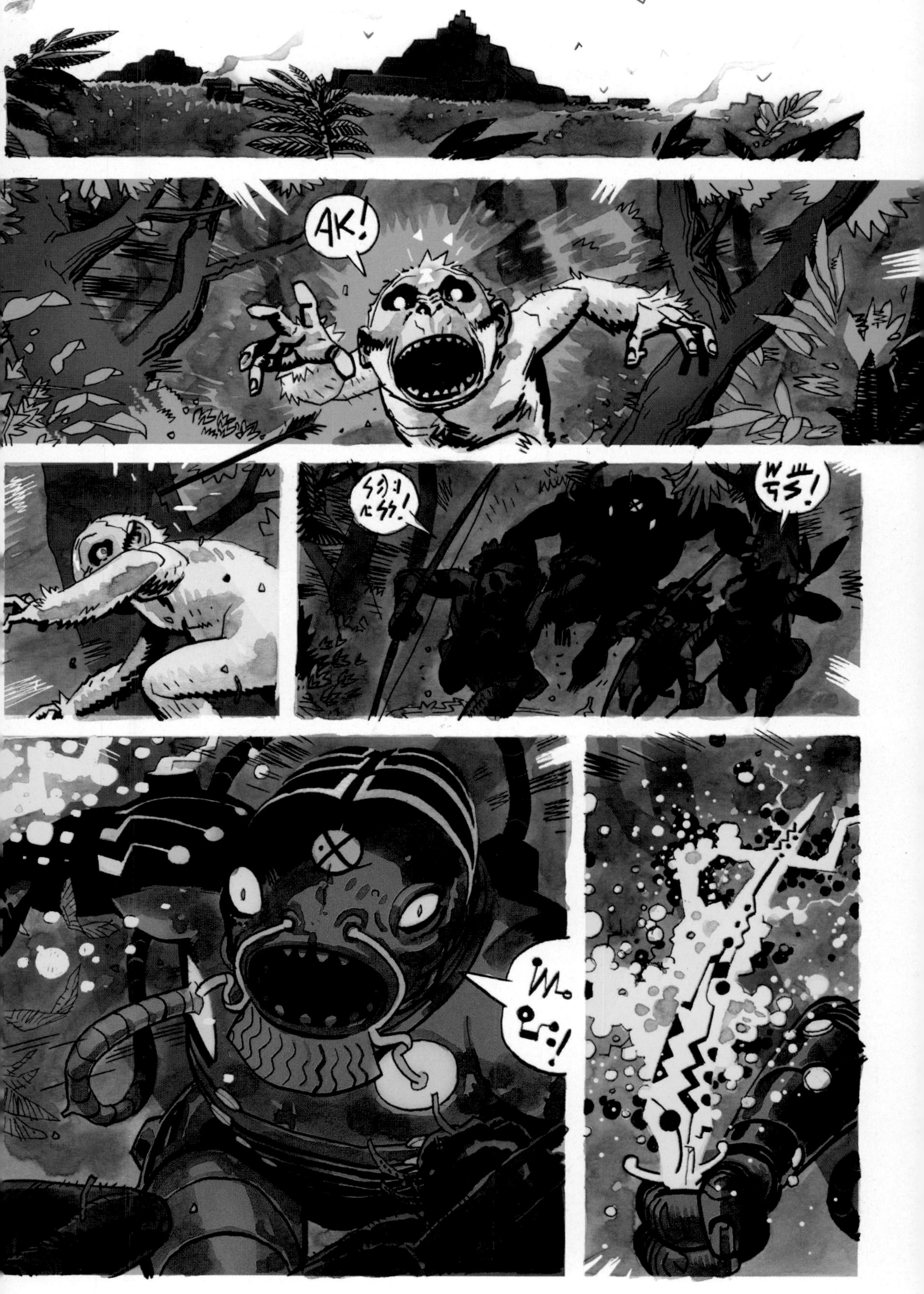
AK!

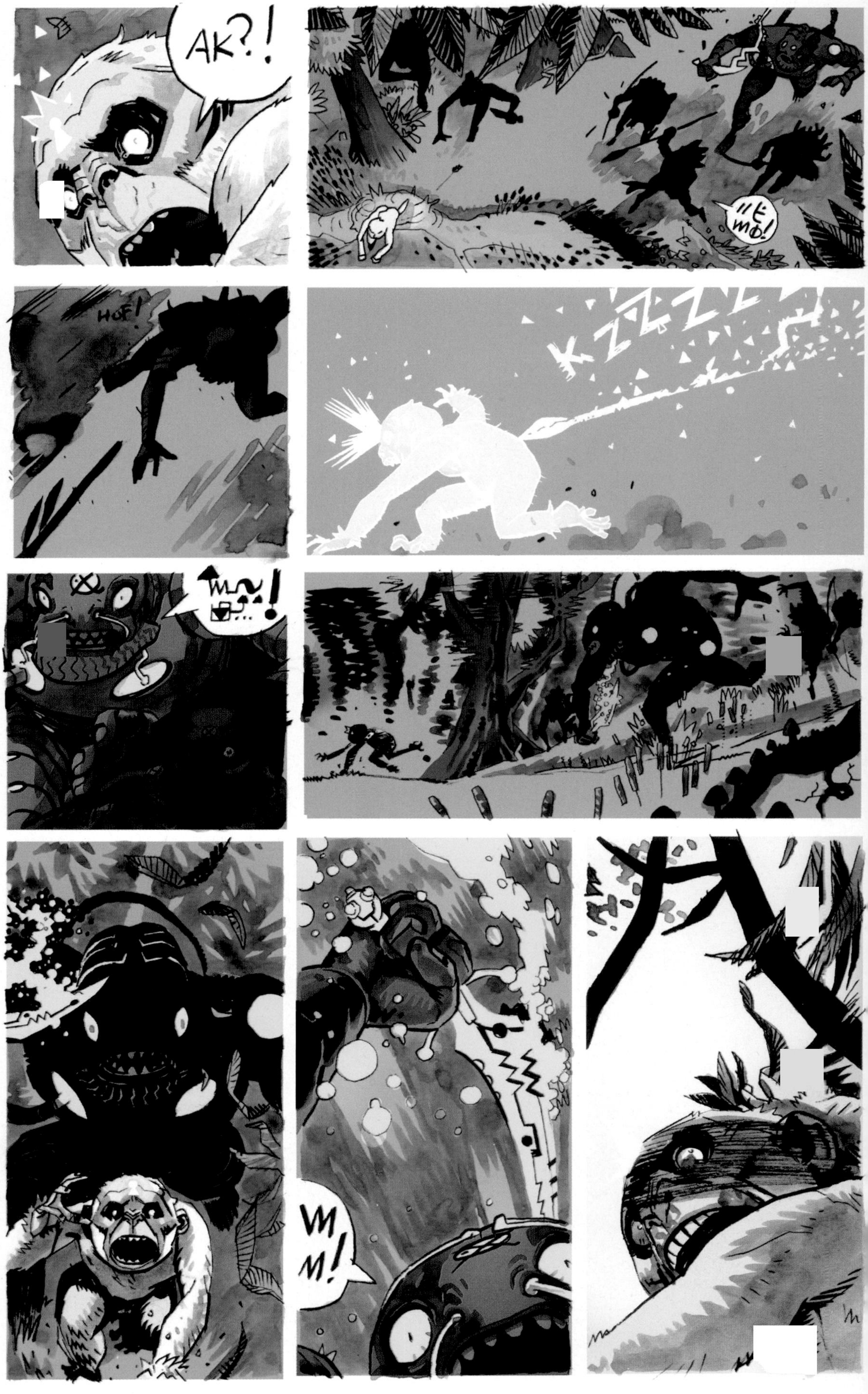
AK?!
HOF!
KZZZ

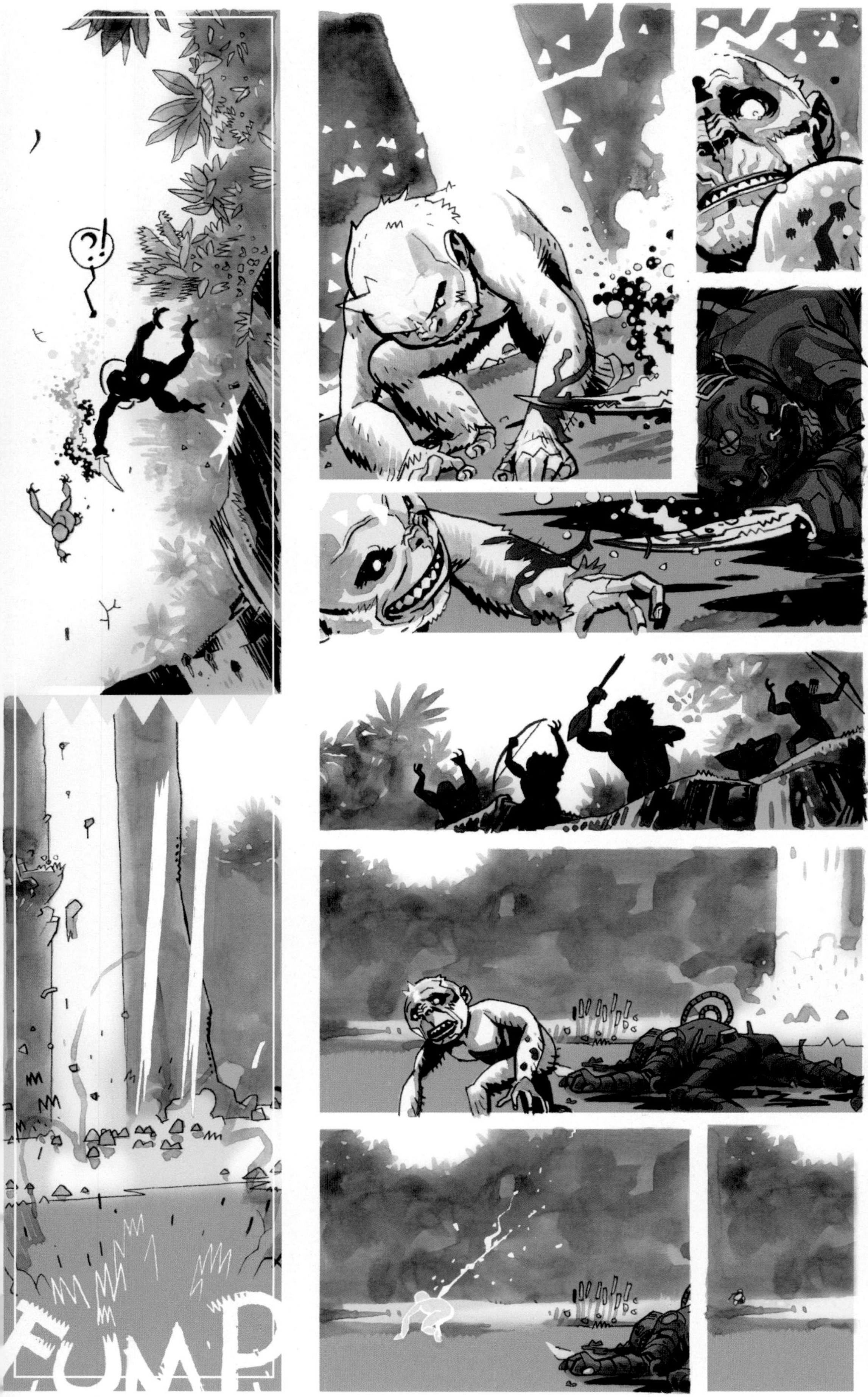
?!
FUMP

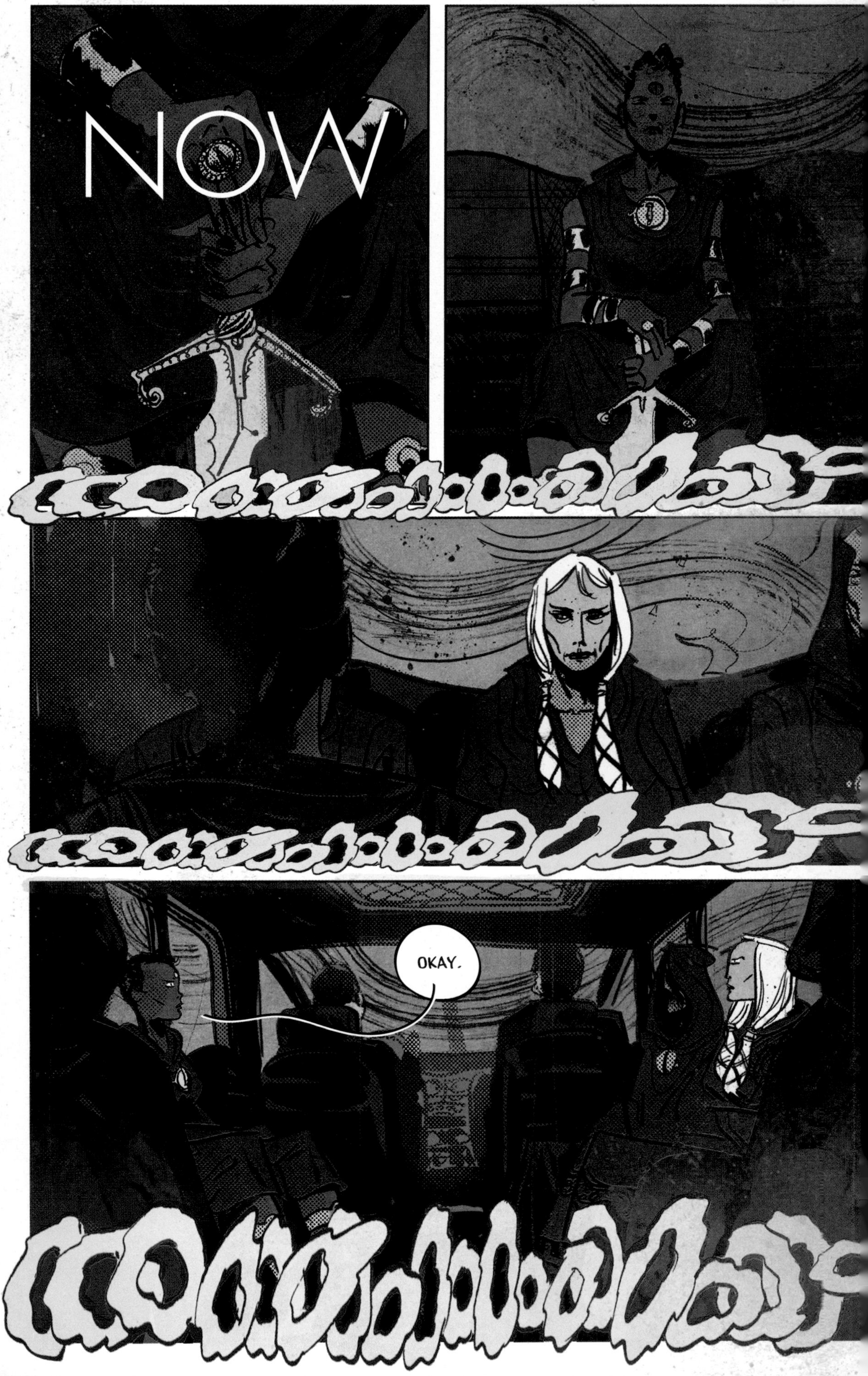
NOW
OKAY.

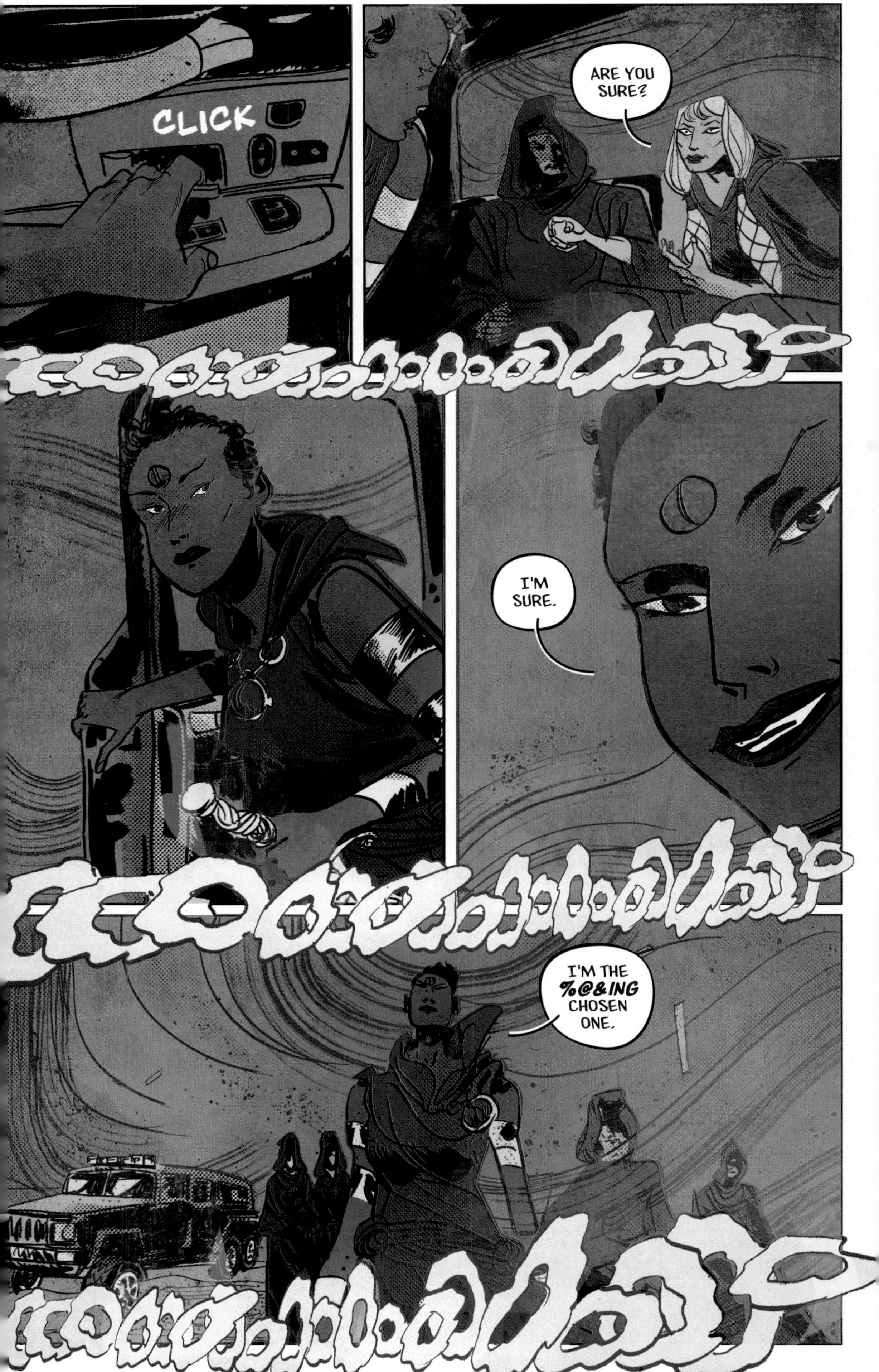
CLICK
ARE YOU SURE?
I'M SURE.
I'M THE %@&ING CHOSEN ONE.

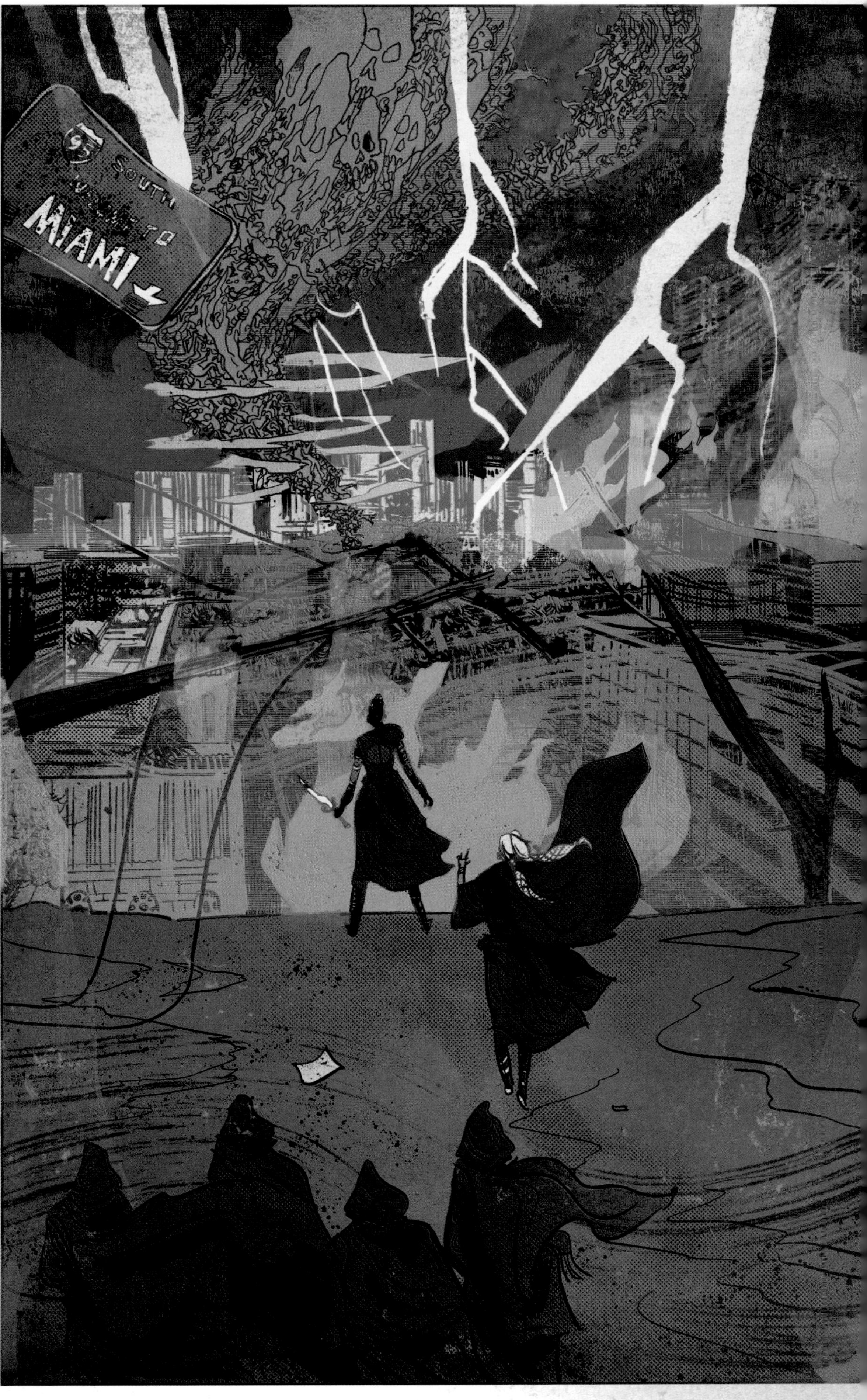

95
SOUTH
MIAMI

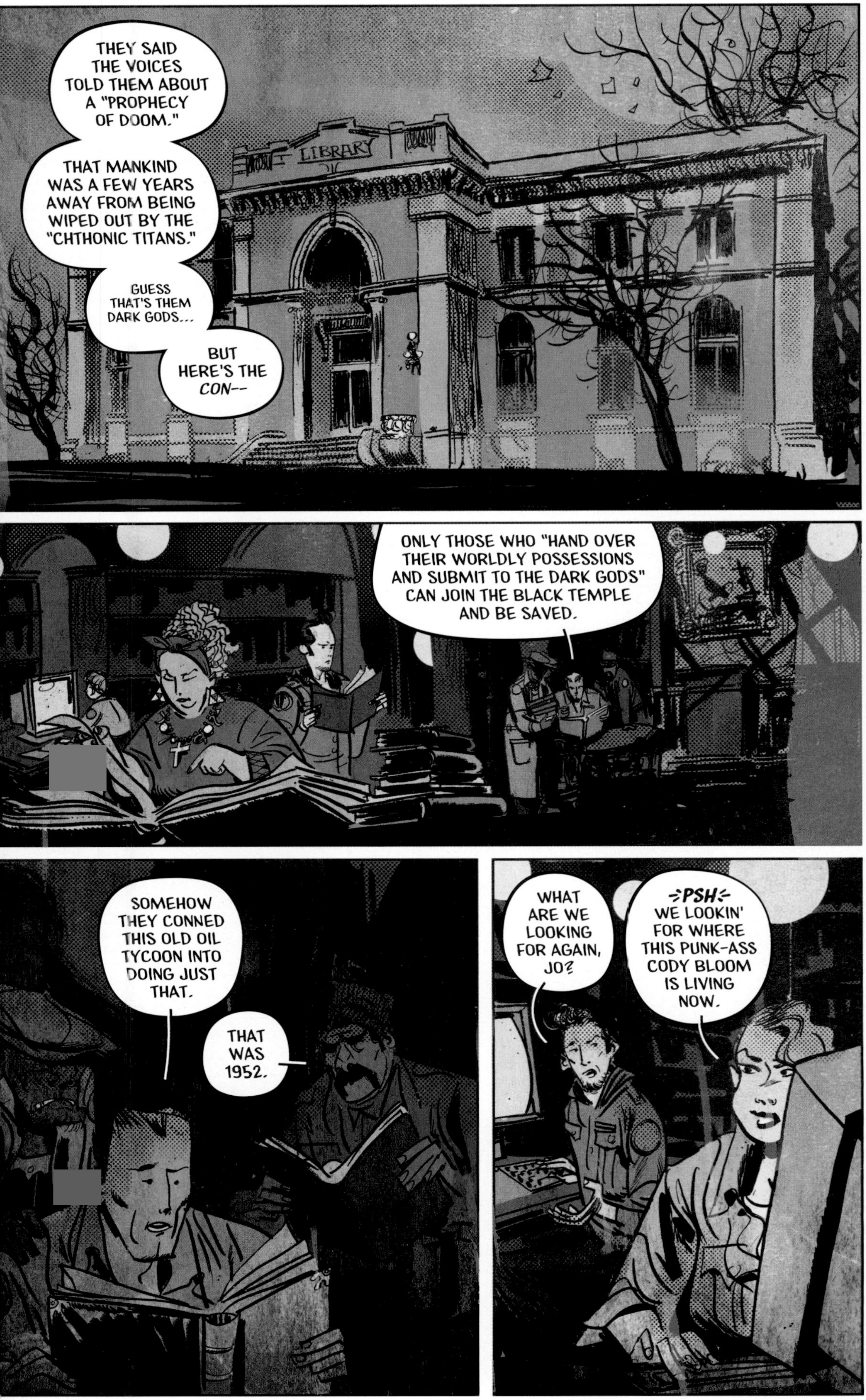
THEY SAID THE VOICES TOLD THEM ABOUT A "PROPHECY OF DOOM."
THAT MANKIND WAS A FEW YEARS AWAY FROM BEING WIPED OUT BY THE "CHTHONIC TITANS."
GUESS THAT'S THEM DARK GODS...
BUT HERE'S THE *CON--*
LIBRARY
ONLY THOSE WHO "HAND OVER THEIR WORLDLY POSSESSIONS AND SUBMIT TO THE DARK GODS" CAN JOIN THE BLACK TEMPLE AND BE SAVED.
SOMEHOW THEY CONNED THIS OLD OIL TYCOON INTO DOING JUST THAT.
THAT WAS 1952.
WHAT ARE WE LOOKING FOR AGAIN, JO?
PSH
WE LOOKIN' FOR WHERE THIS PUNK-ASS CODY BLOOM IS LIVING NOW.

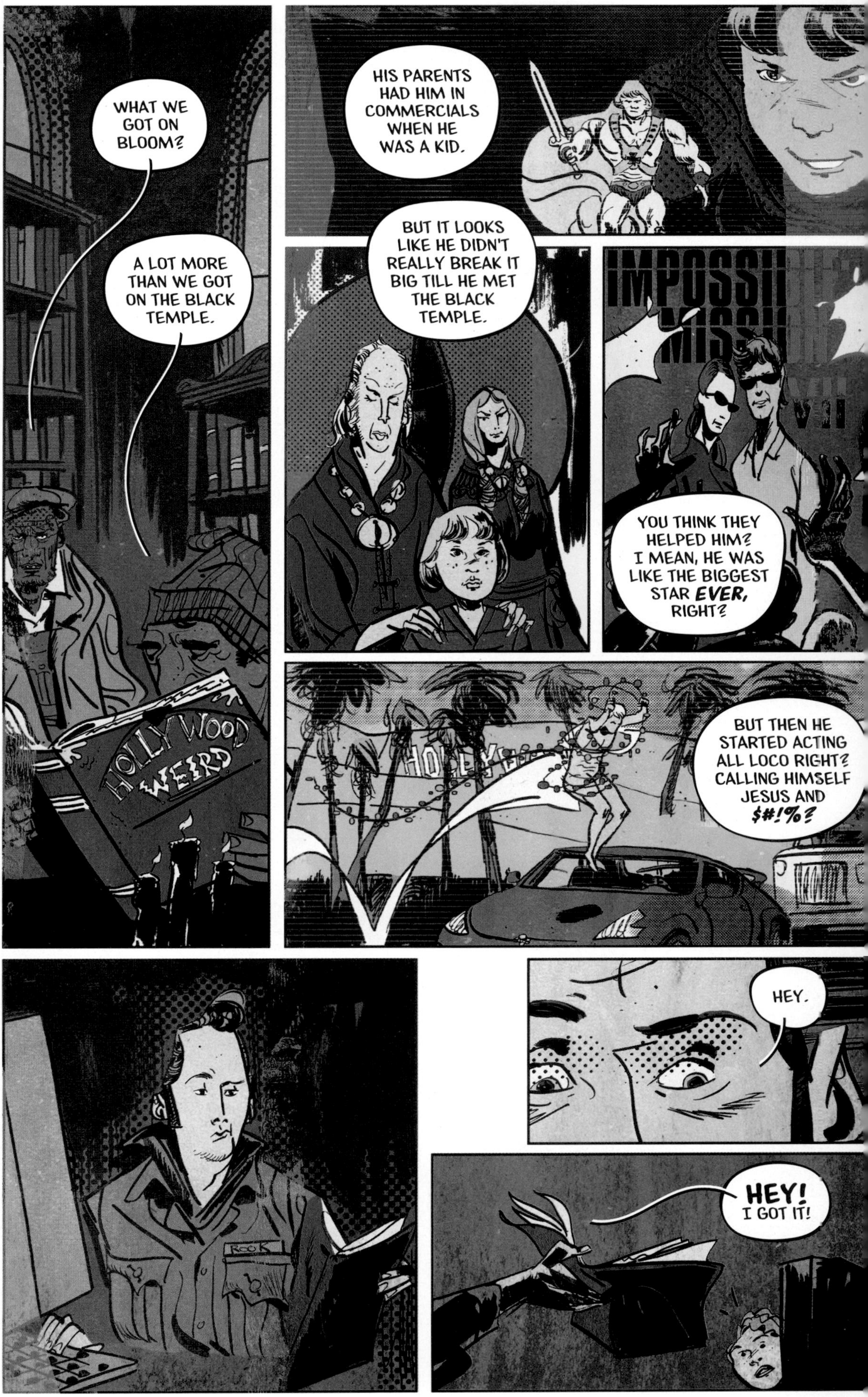
WHAT WE GOT ON BLOOM?
A LOT MORE THAN WE GOT ON THE BLACK TEMPLE.
HIS PARENTS HAD HIM IN COMMERCIALS WHEN HE WAS A KID.
BUT IT LOOKS LIKE HE DIDN'T REALLY BREAK IT BIG TILL HE MET THE BLACK TEMPLE.
YOU THINK THEY HELPED HIM? I MEAN, HE WAS LIKE THE BIGGEST STAR EVER, RIGHT?
BUT THEN HE STARTED ACTING ALL LOCO RIGHT? CALLING HIMSELF JESUS AND $#!%?
HOLLYWOOD WEIRD
ROOK
HEY.
HEY! I GOT IT!

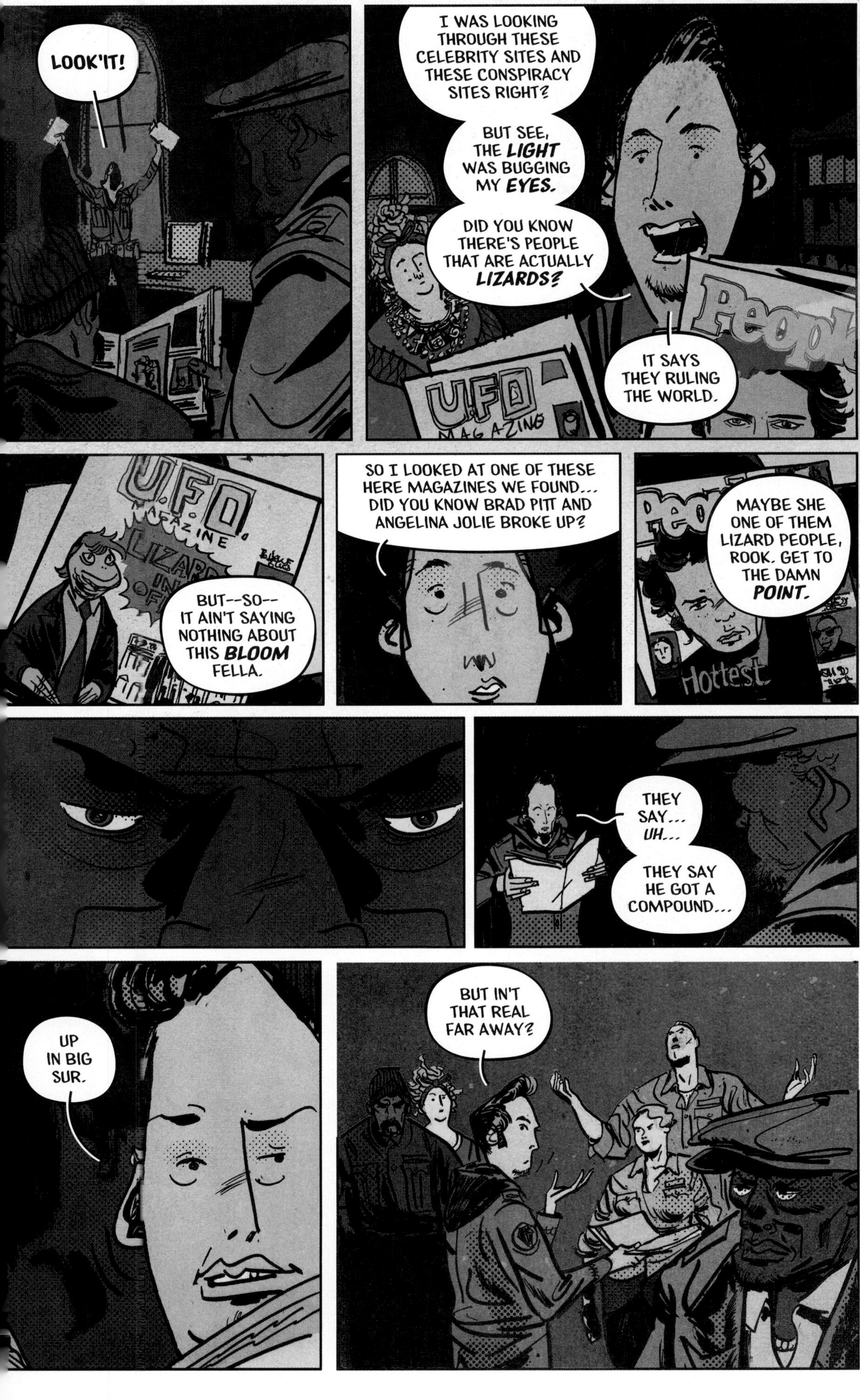

LOOK'IT!
I WAS LOOKING THROUGH THESE CELEBRITY SITES AND THESE CONSPIRACY SITES RIGHT?
BUT SEE, THE LIGHT WAS BUGGING MY EYES.
DID YOU KNOW THERE'S PEOPLE THAT ARE ACTUALLY LIZARDS?
IT SAYS THEY RULING THE WORLD.
People
U.F.O MAGAZINE
U.F.O. MAGAZINE
LIZARD
BUT--SO-- IT AIN'T SAYING NOTHING ABOUT THIS BLOOM FELLA.
SO I LOOKED AT ONE OF THESE HERE MAGAZINES WE FOUND... DID YOU KNOW BRAD PITT AND ANGELINA JOLIE BROKE UP?
MAYBE SHE ONE OF THEM LIZARD PEOPLE, ROOK. GET TO THE DAMN POINT.
Hottest
THEY SAY... UH...
THEY SAY HE GOT A COMPOUND...
UP IN BIG SUR.
BUT IN'T THAT REAL FAR AWAY?

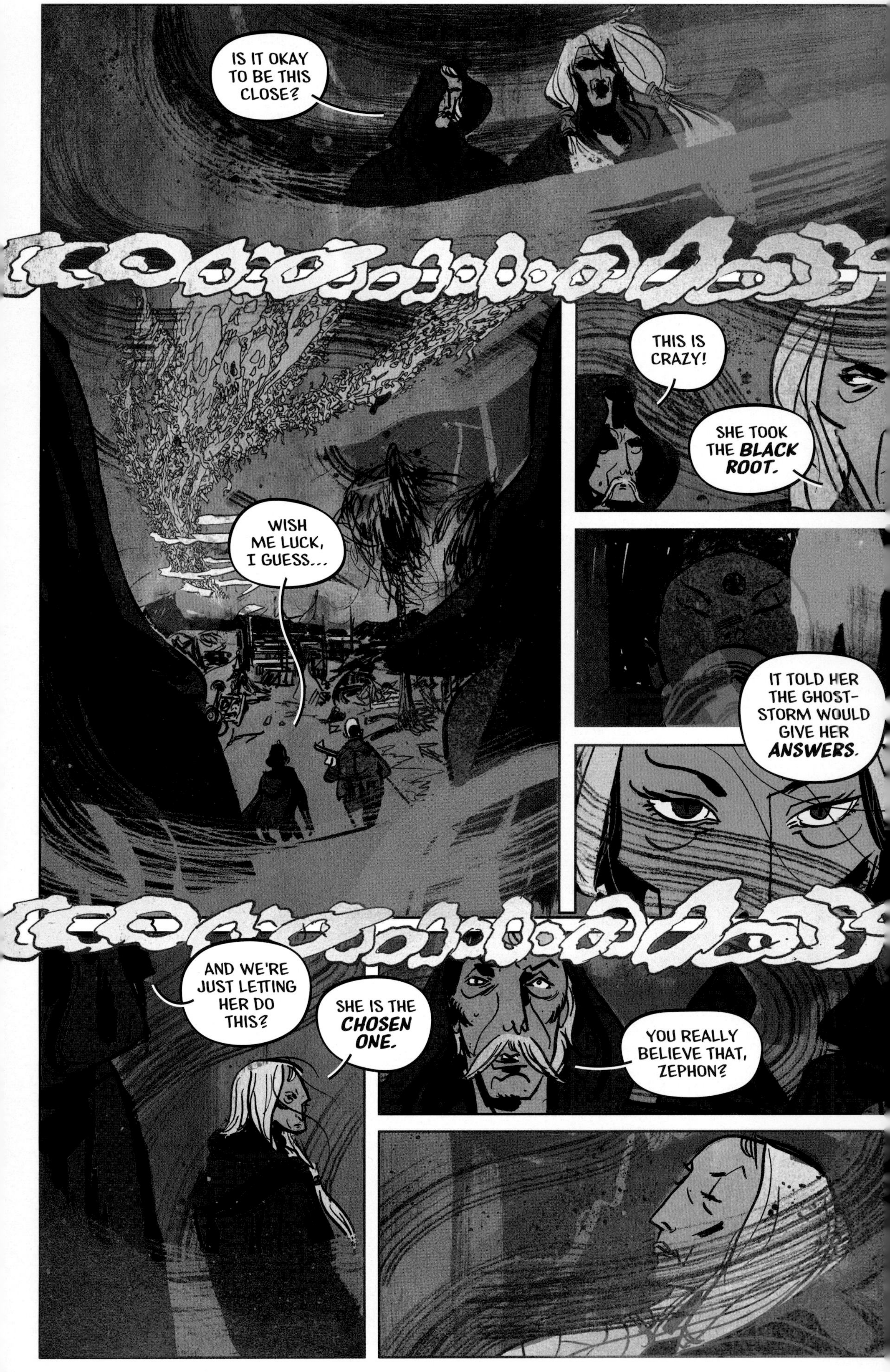
IS IT OKAY TO BE THIS CLOSE?
WISH ME LUCK, I GUESS...
THIS IS CRAZY!
SHE TOOK THE BLACK ROOT.
IT TOLD HER THE GHOST-STORM WOULD GIVE HER ANSWERS.
AND WE'RE JUST LETTING HER DO THIS?
SHE IS THE CHOSEN ONE.
YOU REALLY BELIEVE THAT, ZEPHON?

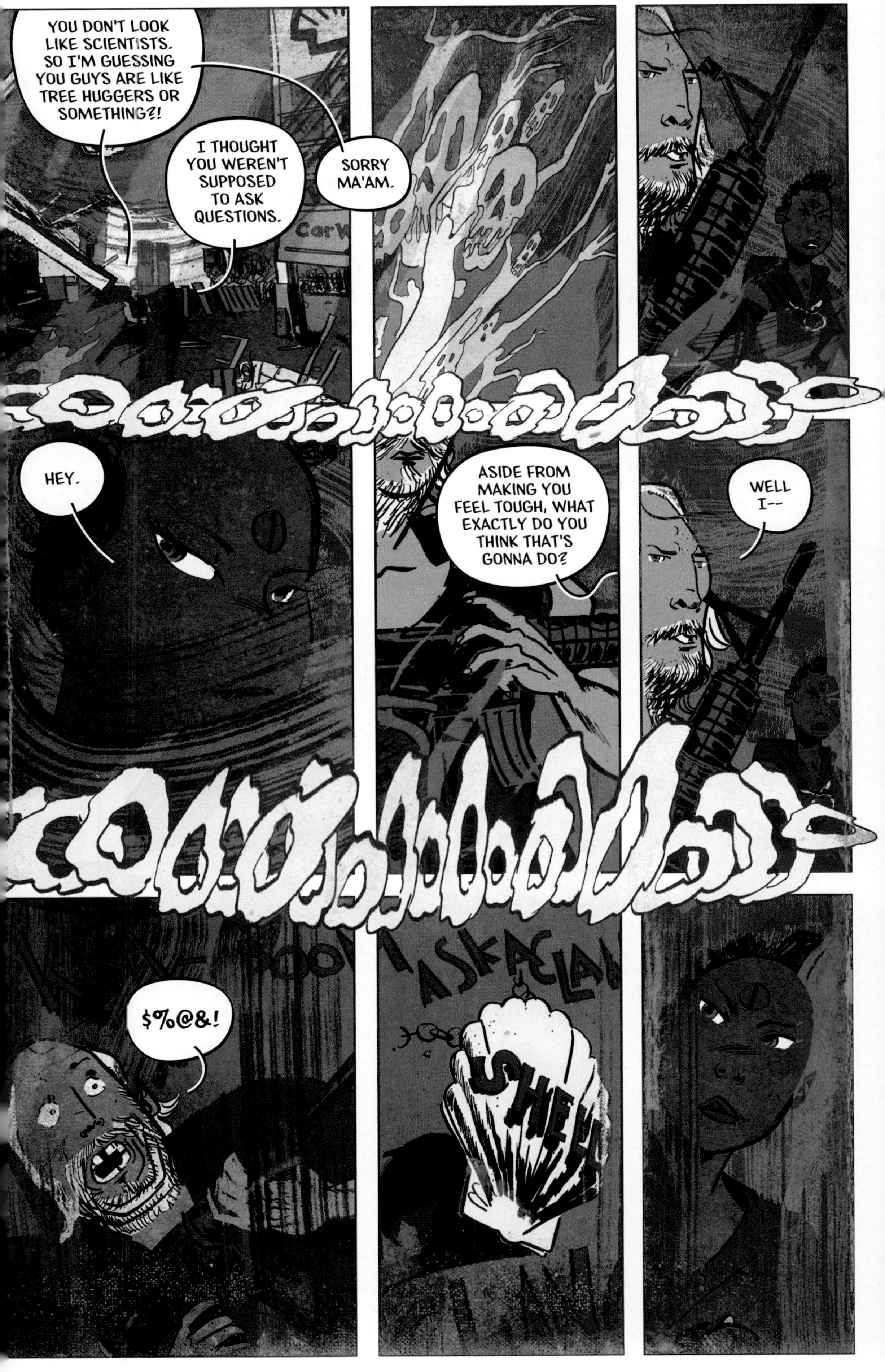
YOU DON'T LOOK LIKE SCIENTISTS. SO I'M GUESSING YOU GUYS ARE LIKE TREE HUGGERS OR SOMETHING?!
I THOUGHT YOU WEREN'T SUPPOSED TO ASK QUESTIONS.
SORRY MA'AM.
HEY.
ASIDE FROM MAKING YOU FEEL TOUGH, WHAT EXACTLY DO YOU THINK THAT'S GONNA DO?
WELL I--
$%@&!
SHELL

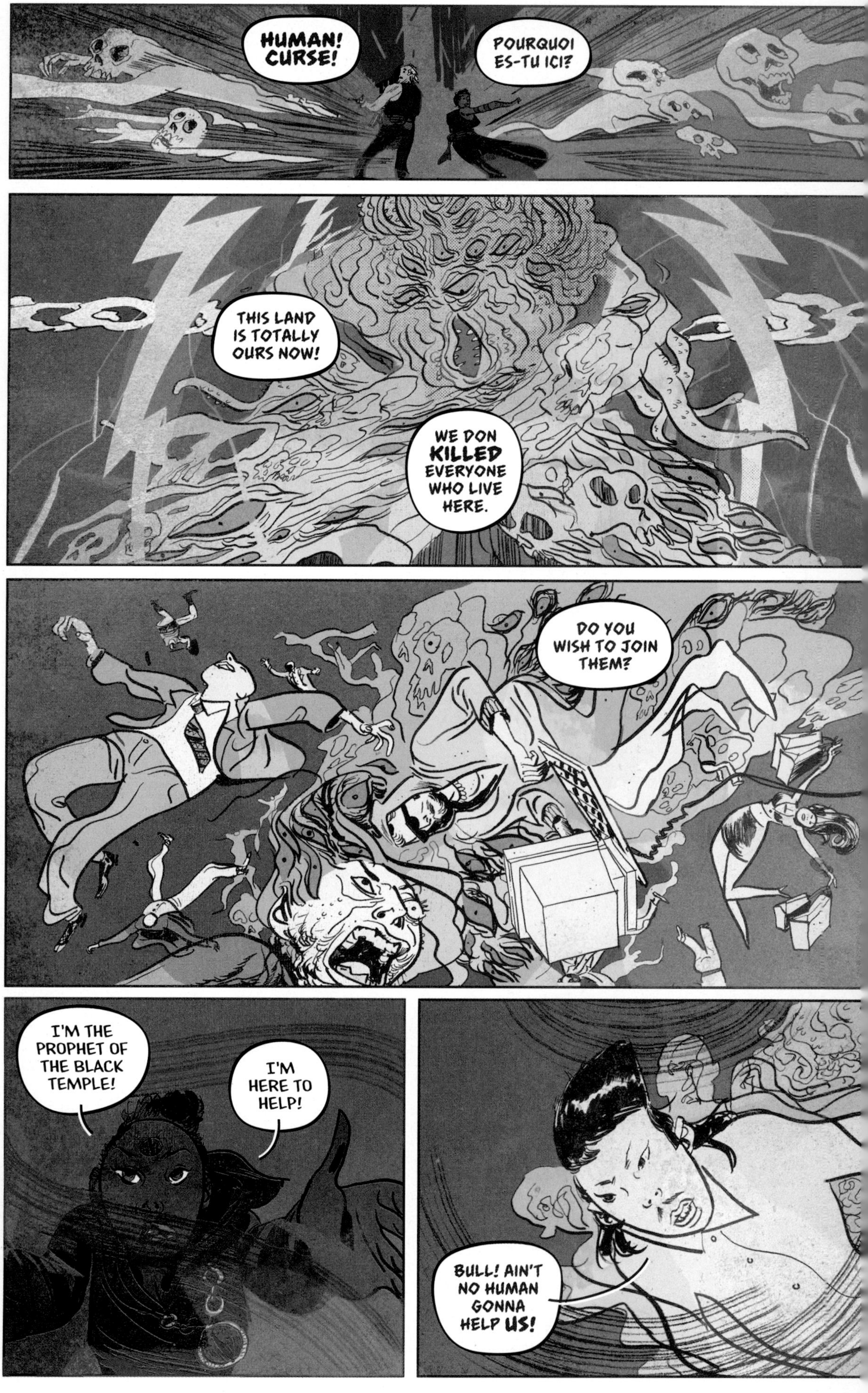
HUMAN! CURSE!
POURQUOI ES-TU ICI?
THIS LAND IS TOTALLY OURS NOW!
WE DON KILLED EVERYONE WHO LIVE HERE.
DO YOU WISH TO JOIN THEM?
I'M THE PROPHET OF THE BLACK TEMPLE!
I'M HERE TO HELP!
BULL! AIN'T NO HUMAN GONNA HELP US!

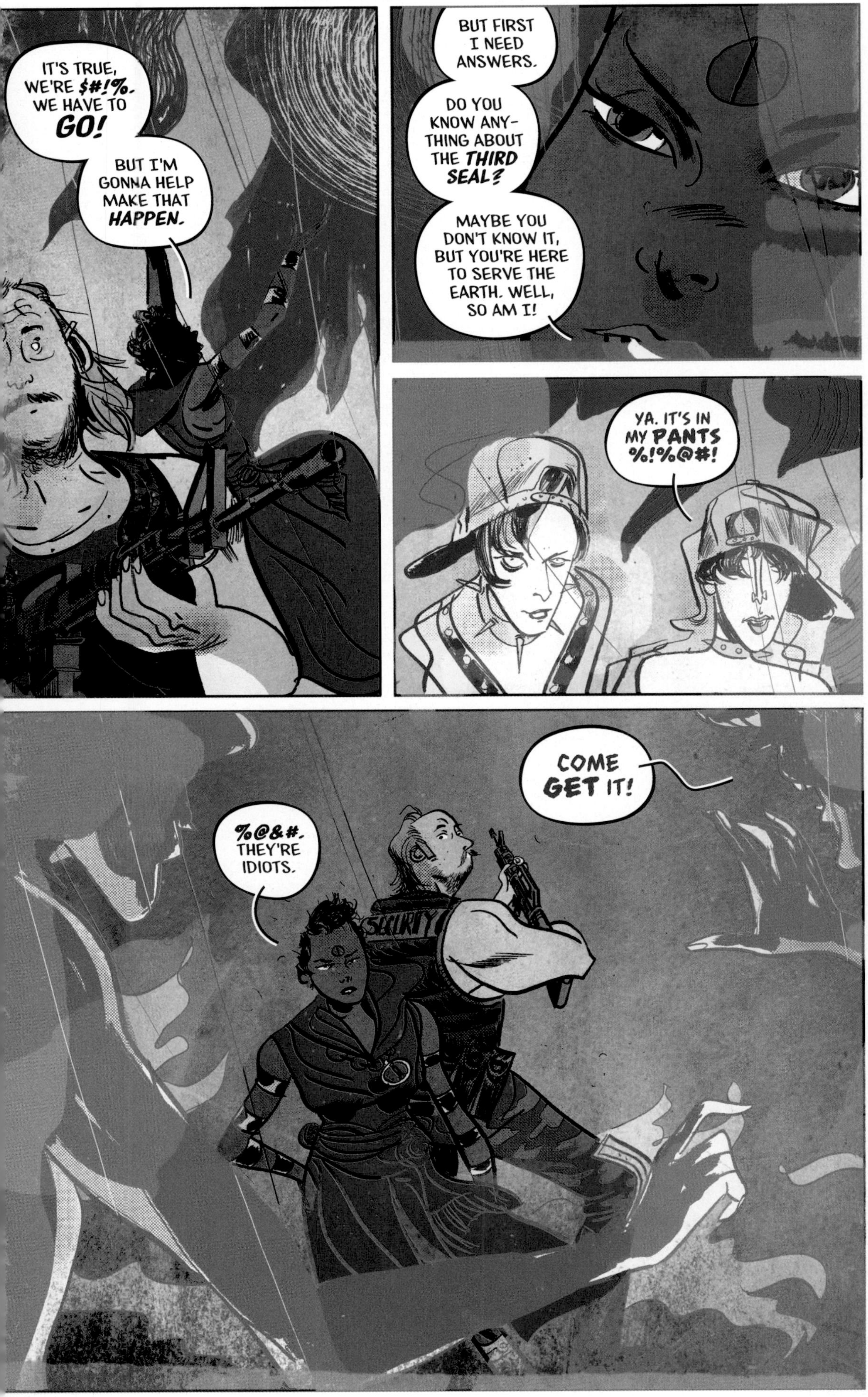
IT'S TRUE, WE'RE $#!%. WE HAVE TO GO!
BUT I'M GONNA HELP MAKE THAT HAPPEN.
BUT FIRST I NEED ANSWERS.
DO YOU KNOW ANY-THING ABOUT THE THIRD SEAL?
MAYBE YOU DON'T KNOW IT, BUT YOU'RE HERE TO SERVE THE EARTH. WELL, SO AM I!
YA. IT'S IN MY PANTS %!%@#!
COME GET IT!
%@&#. THEY'RE IDIOTS.
SECURITY

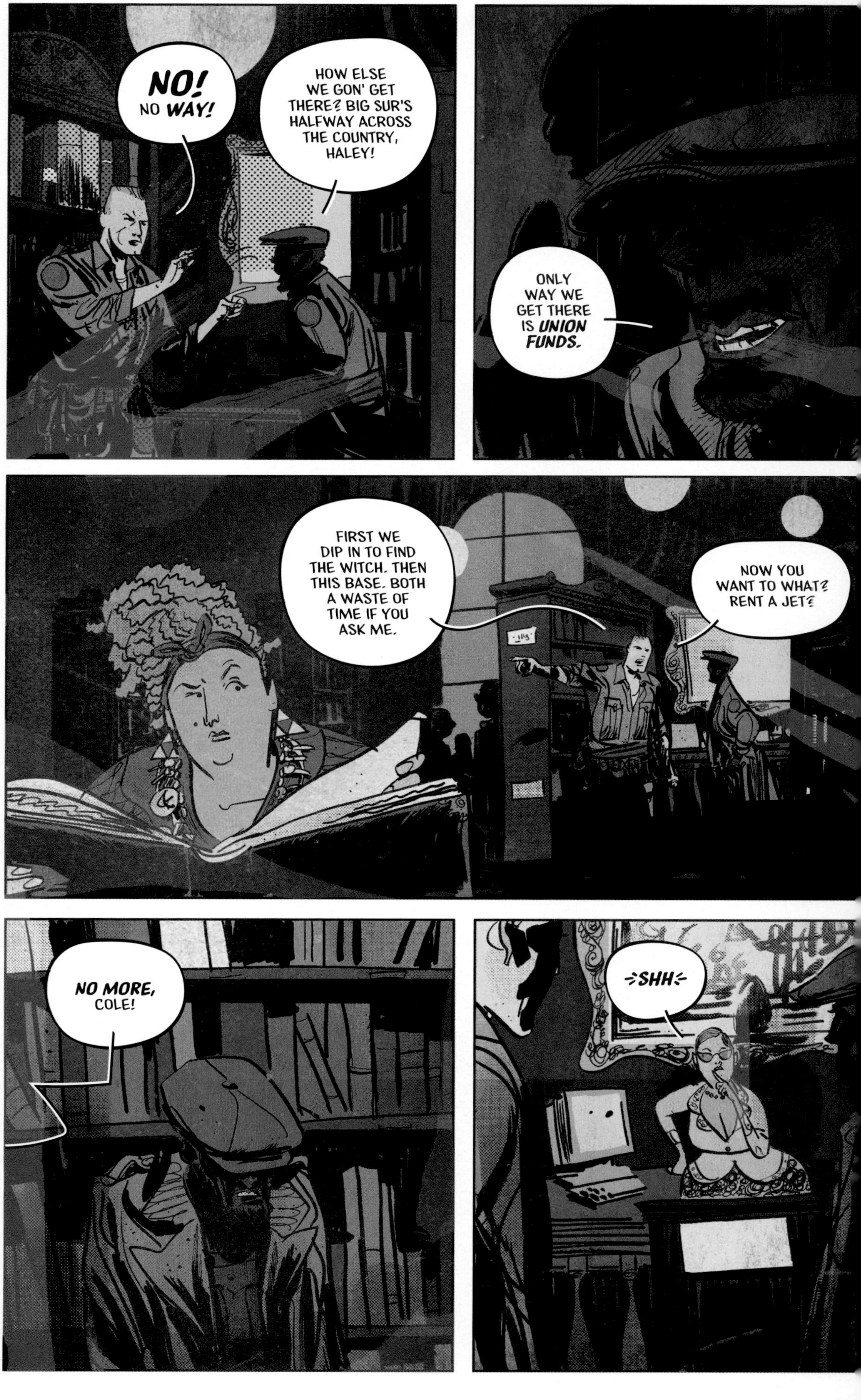
NO! NO WAY!
HOW ELSE WE GON' GET THERE? BIG SUR'S HALFWAY ACROSS THE COUNTRY, HALEY!
ONLY WAY WE GET THERE IS UNION FUNDS.
FIRST WE DIP IN TO FIND THE WITCH. THEN THIS BASE. BOTH A WASTE OF TIME IF YOU ASK ME.
NOW YOU WANT TO WHAT? RENT A JET?
NO MORE, COLE!
SHH

NONE OF THAT GONNA *MATTER* IF THE DAMNED WORLD *ENDS!*

WE DON'T EVEN KNOW IF THIS WITCH IS TELLIN' THE TRUTH!

YOU DO WHAT YOU WANT BUT I'M DONE!

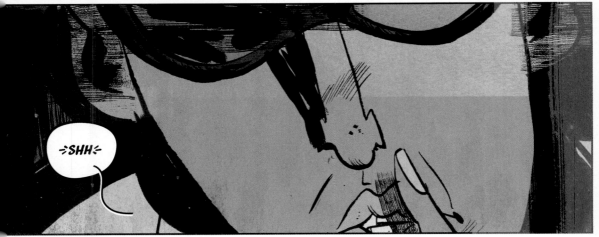

÷SHH÷

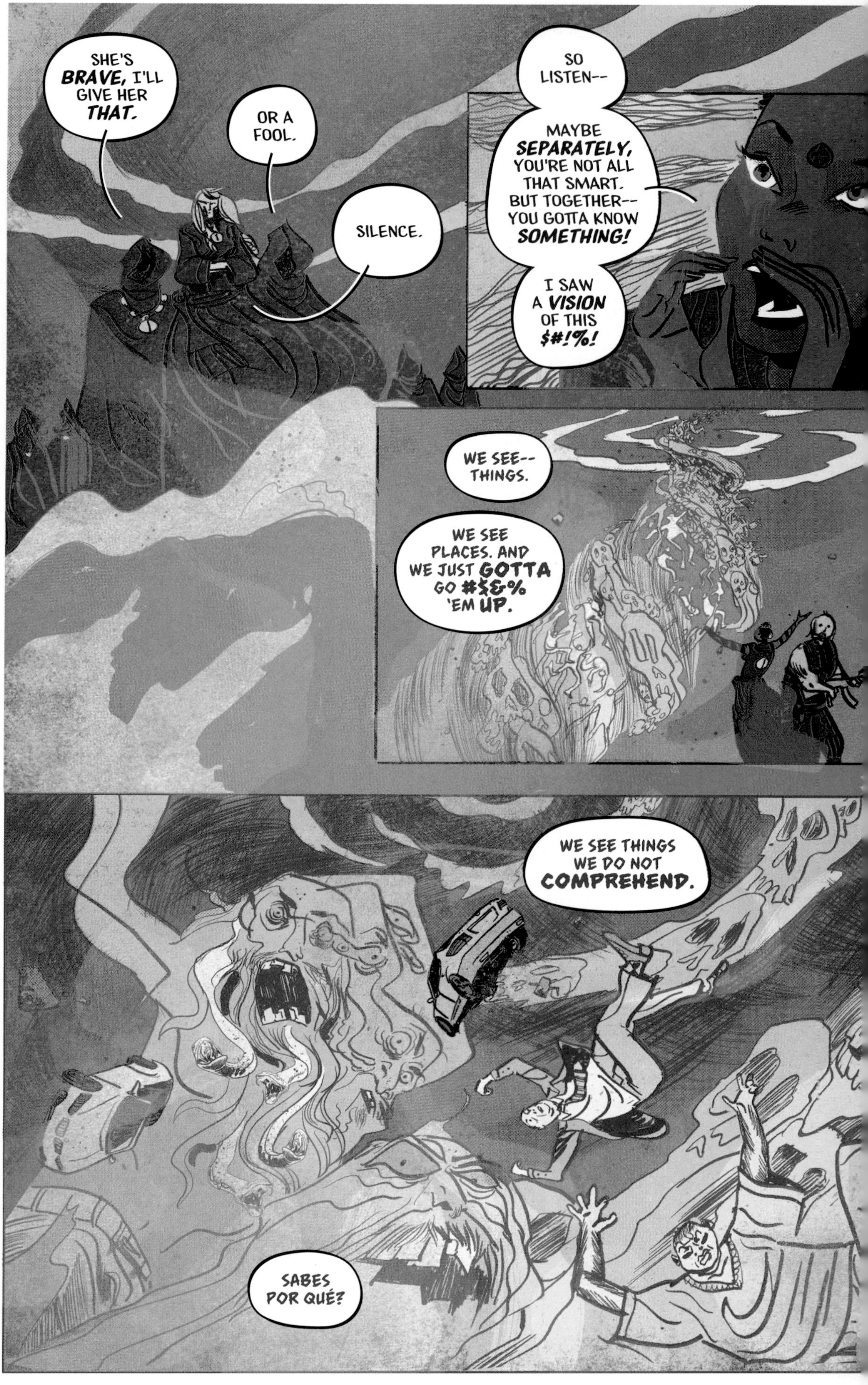
SHE'S BRAVE, I'LL GIVE HER THAT.
OR A FOOL.
SILENCE.
SO LISTEN--
MAYBE SEPARATELY, YOU'RE NOT ALL THAT SMART. BUT TOGETHER-- YOU GOTTA KNOW SOMETHING!
I SAW A VISION OF THIS $#!%!
WE SEE-- THINGS.
WE SEE PLACES. AND WE JUST GOTTA GO #$&% 'EM UP.
WE SEE THINGS WE DO NOT COMPREHEND.
SABES POR QUÉ?

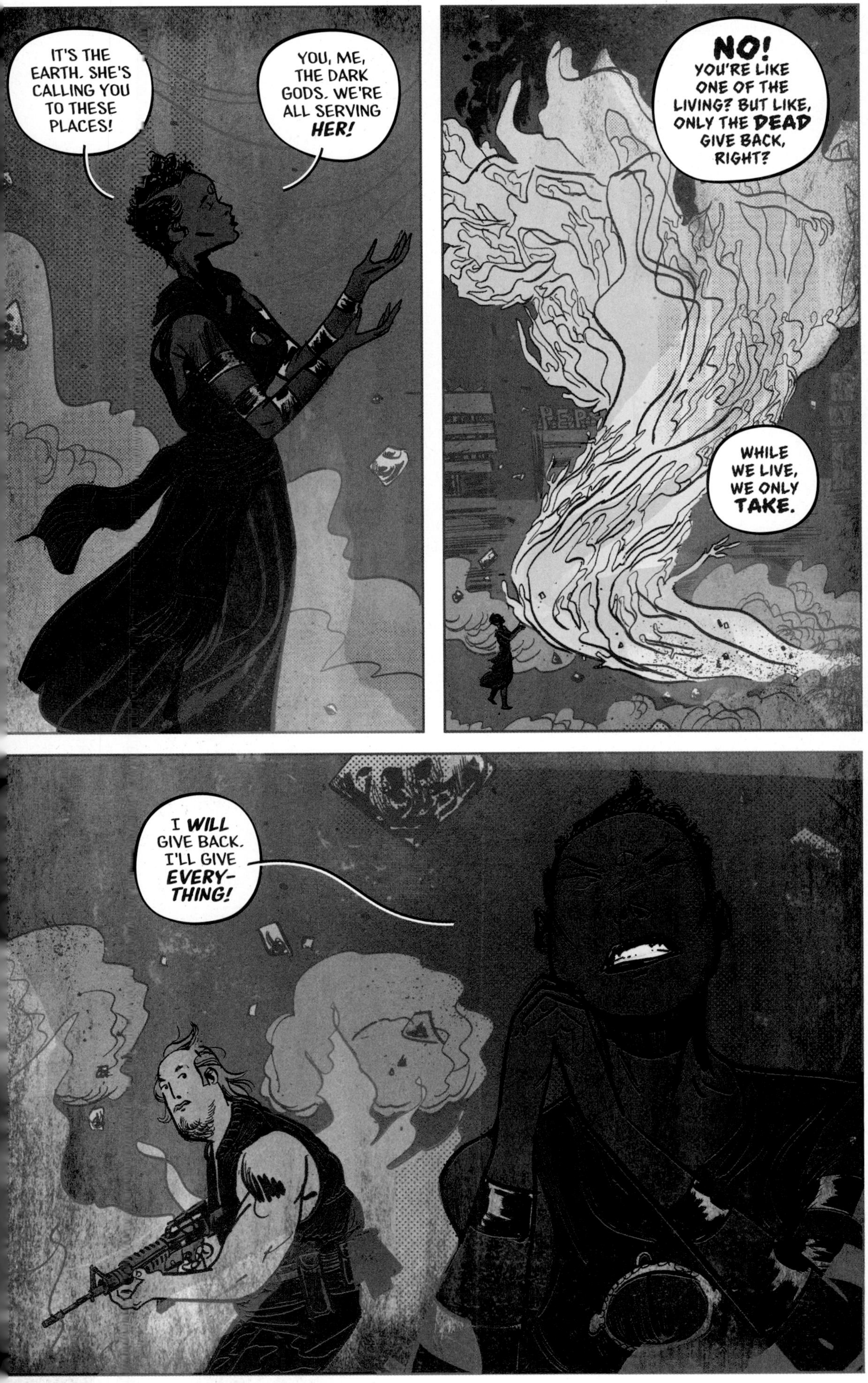
IT'S THE EARTH. SHE'S CALLING YOU TO THESE PLACES!
YOU, ME, THE DARK GODS. WE'RE ALL SERVING HER!
NO! YOU'RE LIKE ONE OF THE LIVING? BUT LIKE, ONLY THE DEAD GIVE BACK, RIGHT?
WHILE WE LIVE, WE ONLY TAKE.
I WILL GIVE BACK. I'LL GIVE EVERYTHING!

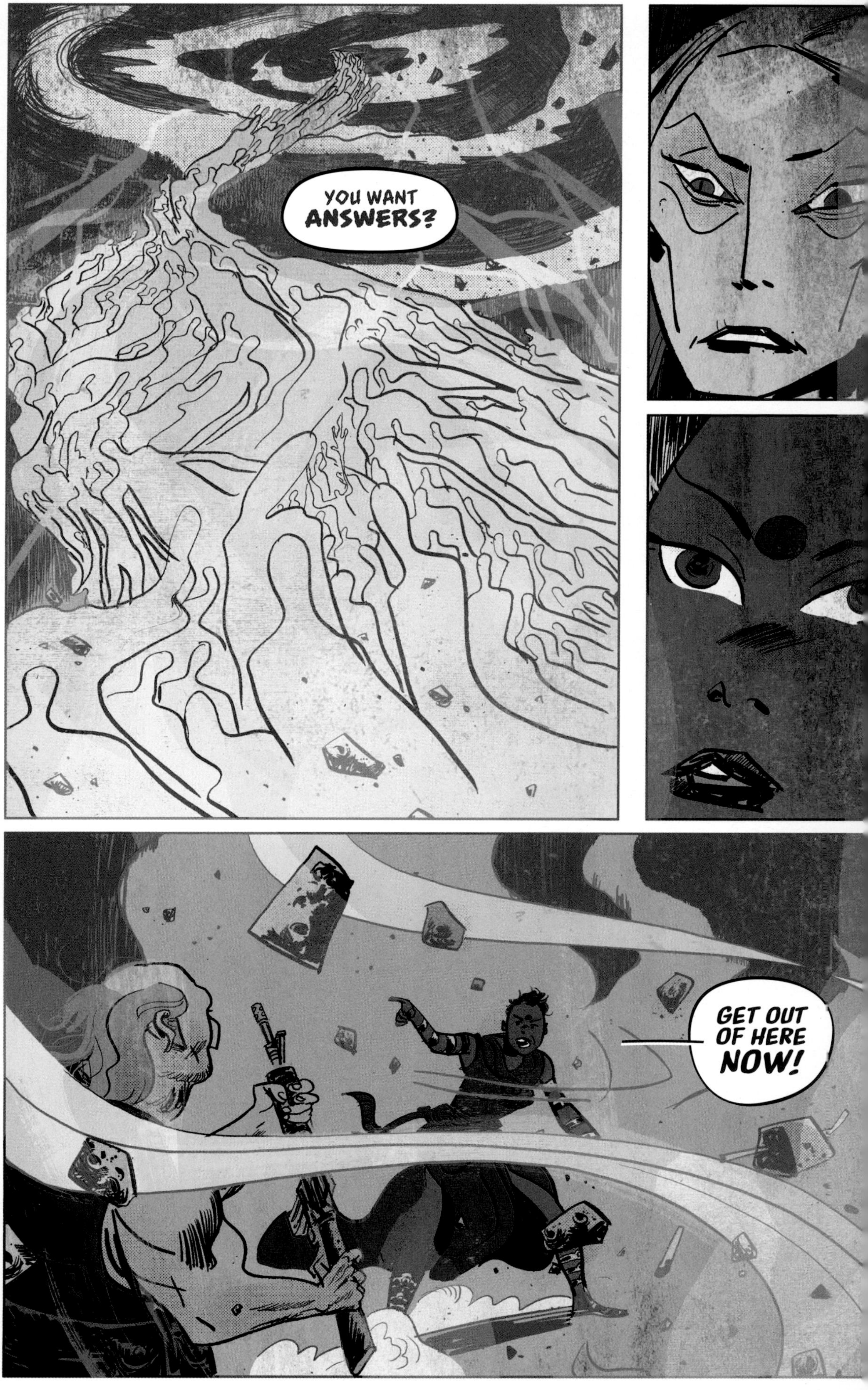
YOU WANT ANSWERS?
GET OUT OF HERE NOW!

ALL THE EYES!

SHOW US--

WE BUILD A--

IT WAS A CANNON.

SOMETHING.

WHAT ARE THESE BIRD THINGS?

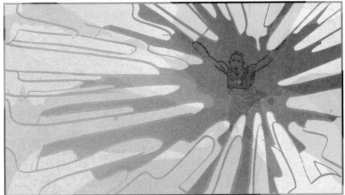

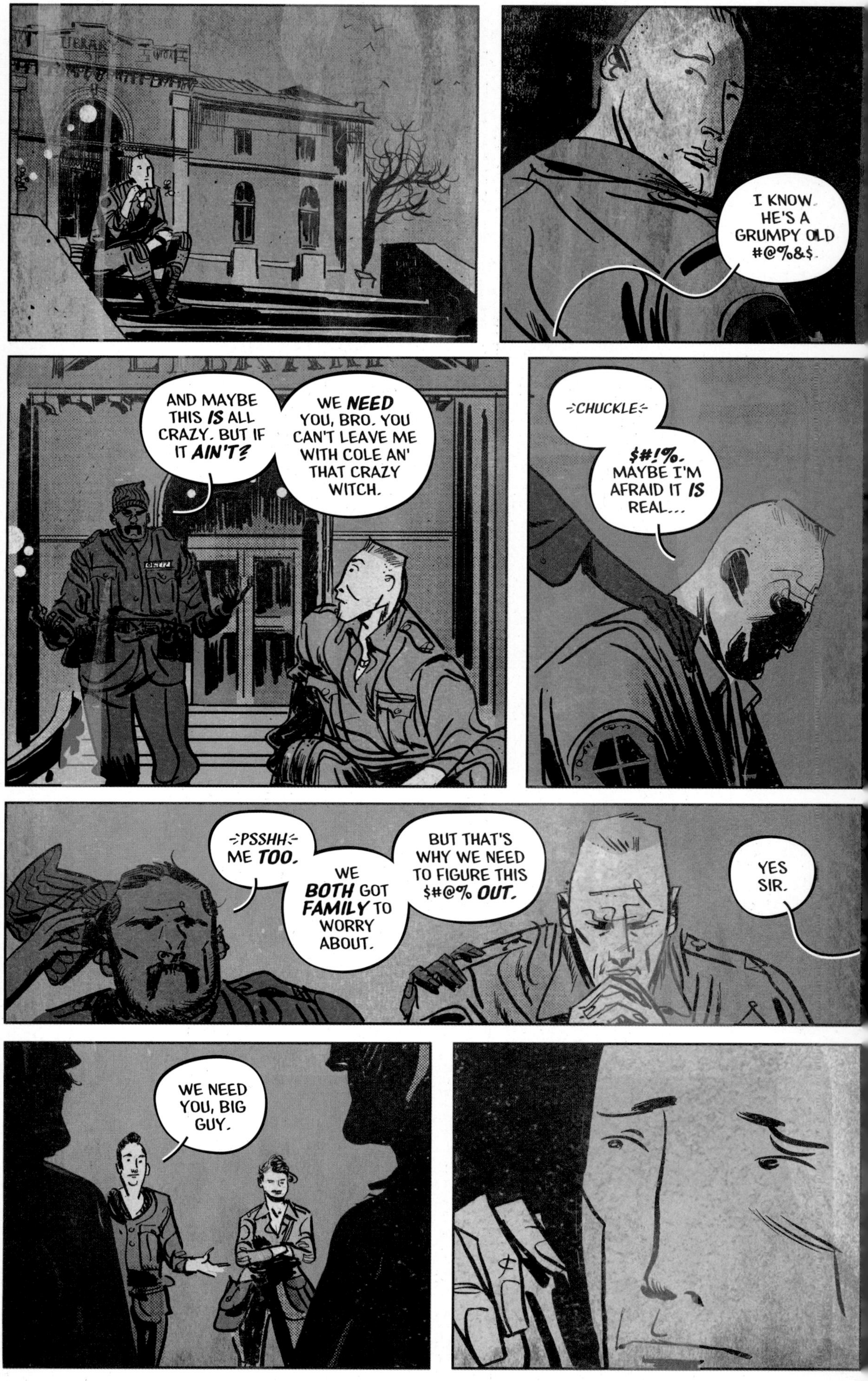
I KNOW HE'S A GRUMPY OLD #@%&$.
AND MAYBE THIS IS ALL CRAZY. BUT IF IT AIN'T?
WE NEED YOU, BRO. YOU CAN'T LEAVE ME WITH COLE AN' THAT CRAZY WITCH.
CHUCKLE
$#!%. MAYBE I'M AFRAID IT IS REAL...
PSSHH ME TOO.
WE BOTH GOT FAMILY TO WORRY ABOUT.
BUT THAT'S WHY WE NEED TO FIGURE THIS $#@% OUT.
YES SIR.
WE NEED YOU, BIG GUY.

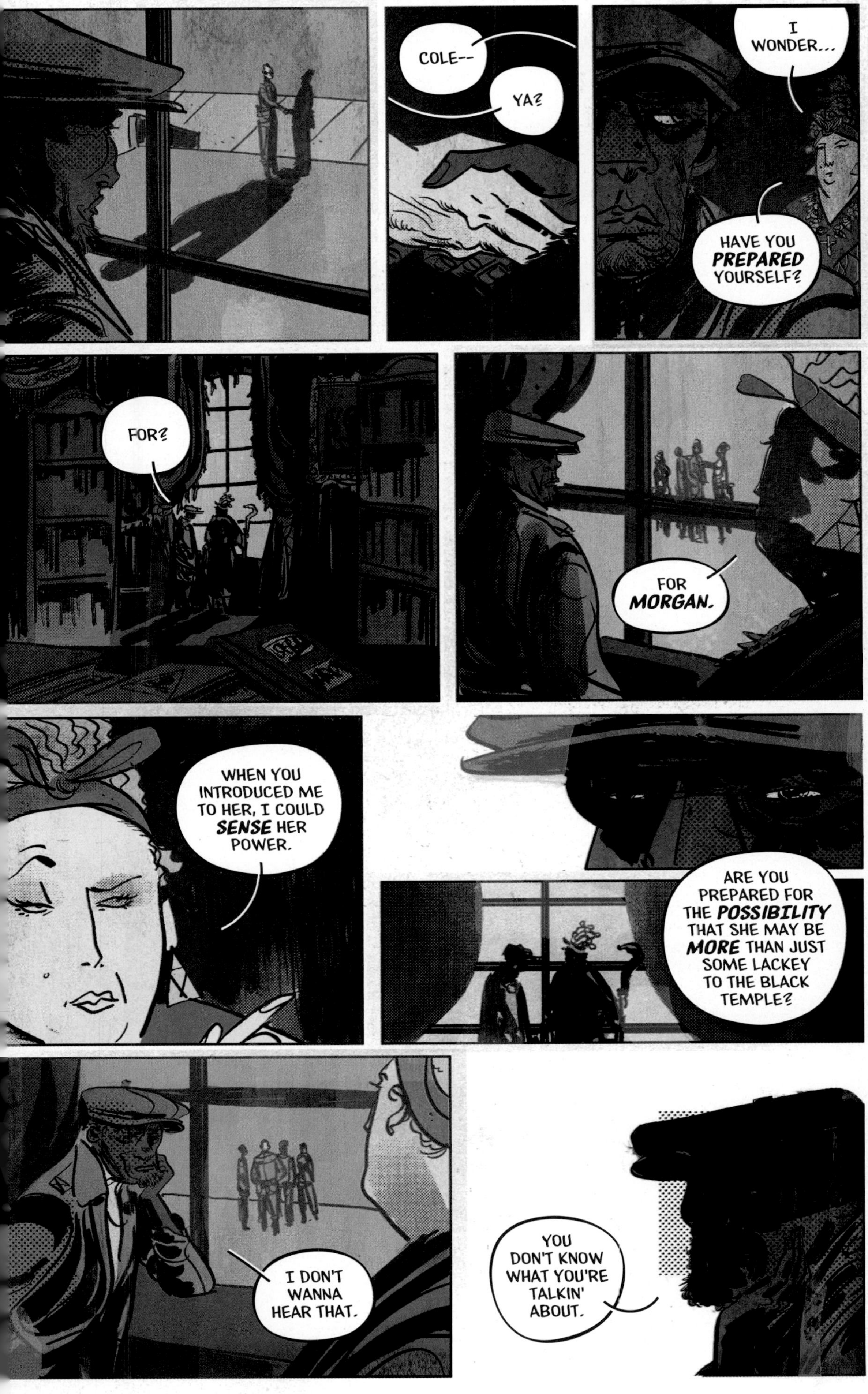
COLE--
YA?
I WONDER...
HAVE YOU PREPARED YOURSELF?
FOR?
FOR MORGAN.
WHEN YOU INTRODUCED ME TO HER, I COULD SENSE HER POWER.
ARE YOU PREPARED FOR THE POSSIBILITY THAT SHE MAY BE MORE THAN JUST SOME LACKEY TO THE BLACK TEMPLE?
I DON'T WANNA HEAR THAT.
YOU DON'T KNOW WHAT YOU'RE TALKIN' ABOUT.

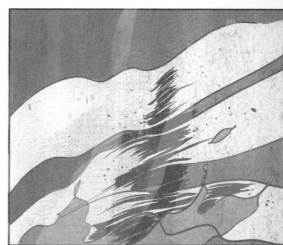

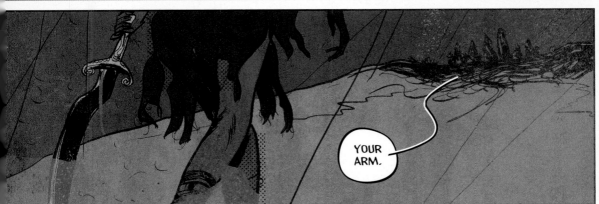

YOUR ARM.

I THINK THEY TRIED TO TAKE IT FROM ME.

BUT I WOULDN'T LET--

÷UGH÷

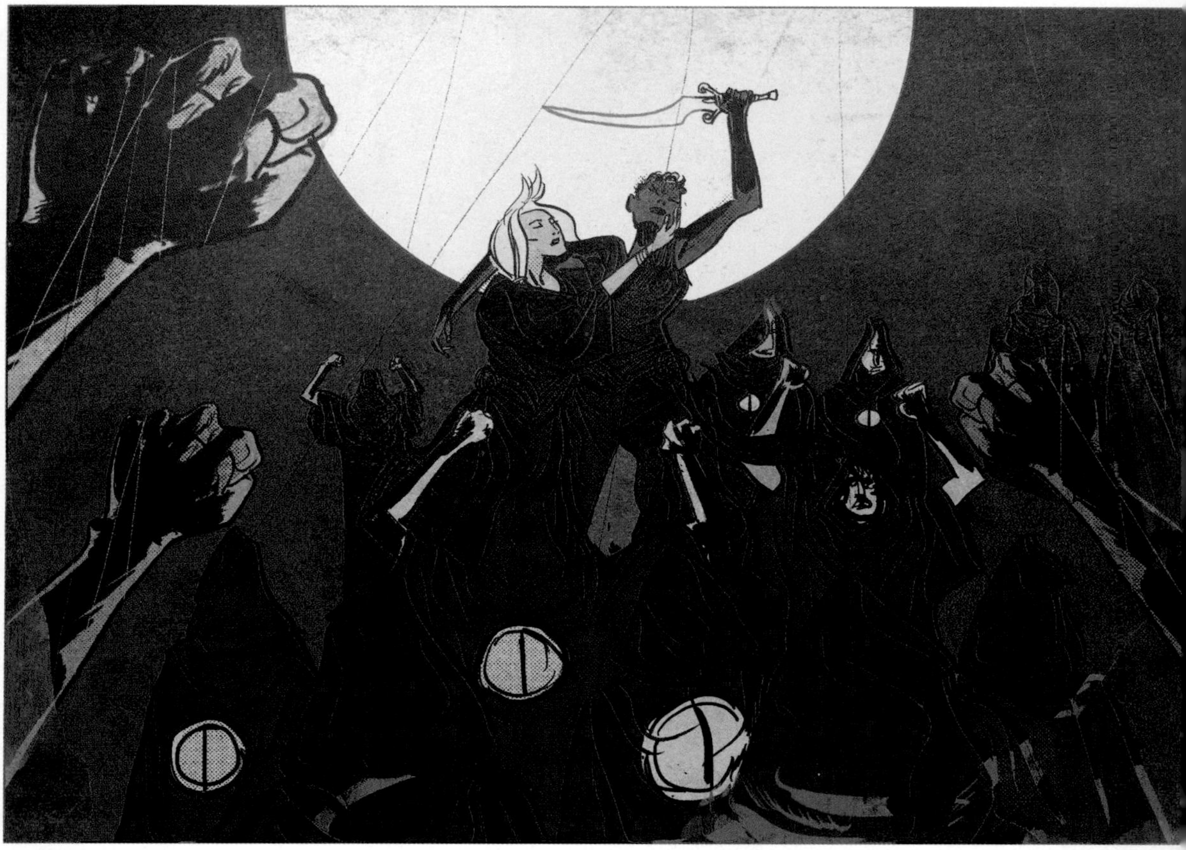

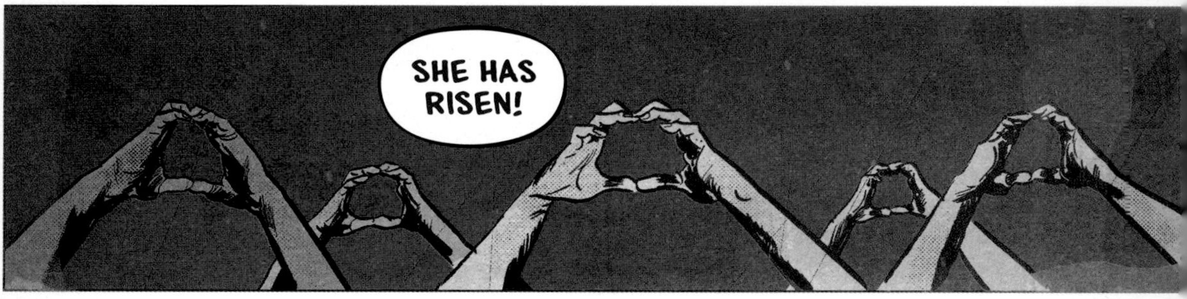
SHE HAS RISEN!

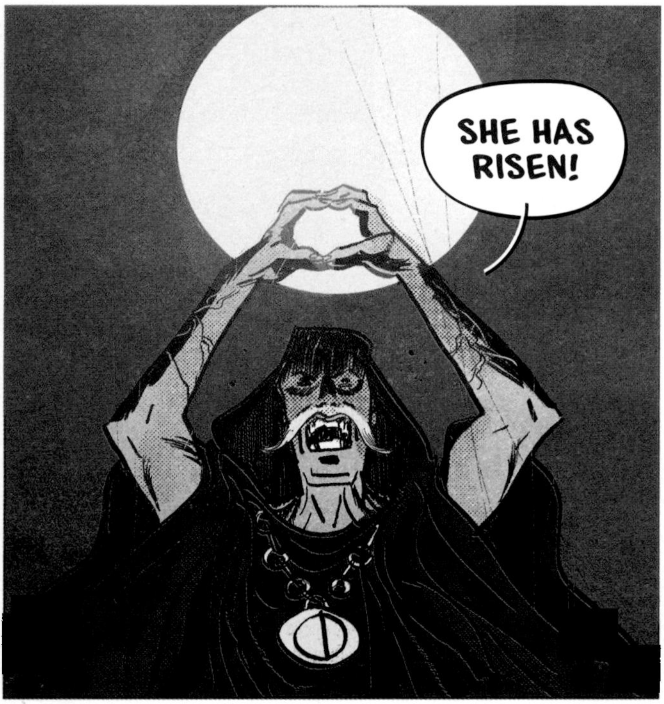
SHE HAS RISEN!

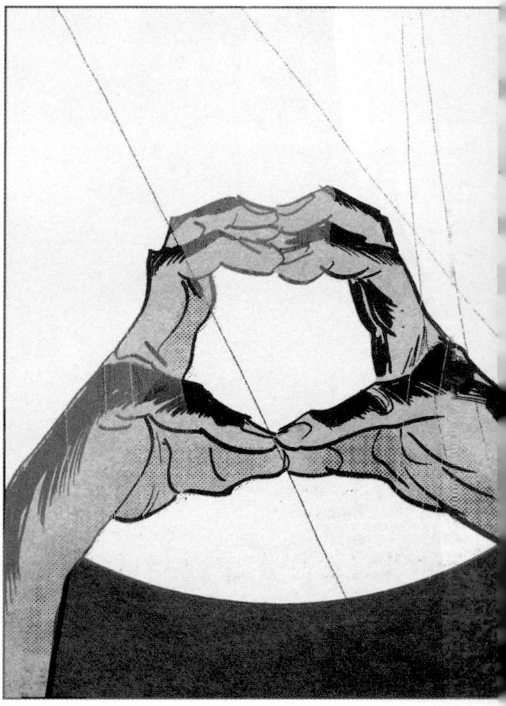

CHAPTER

SPACE MONKEY

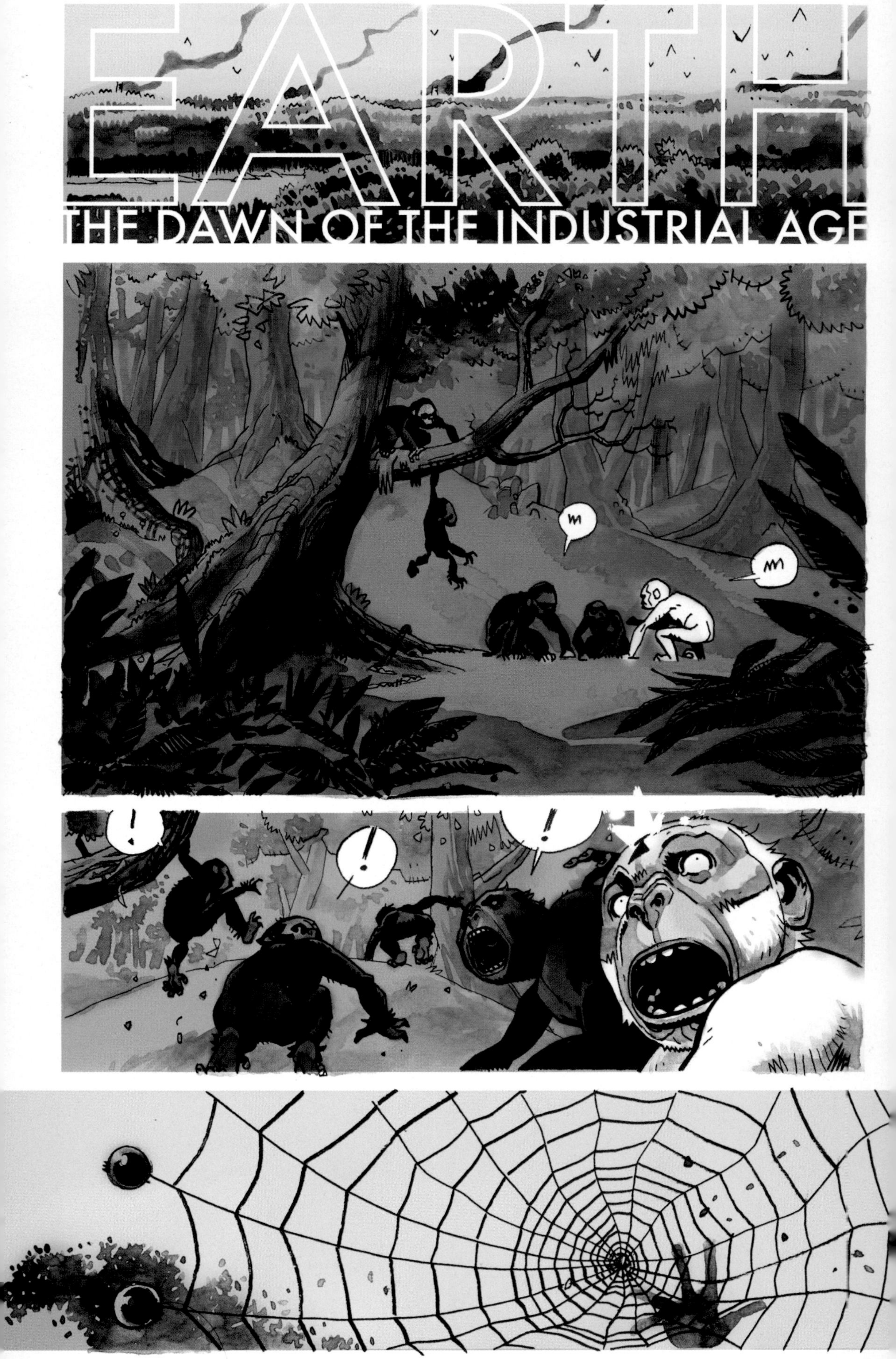
EARTH
THE DAWN OF THE INDUSTRIAL AGE
!
!
!

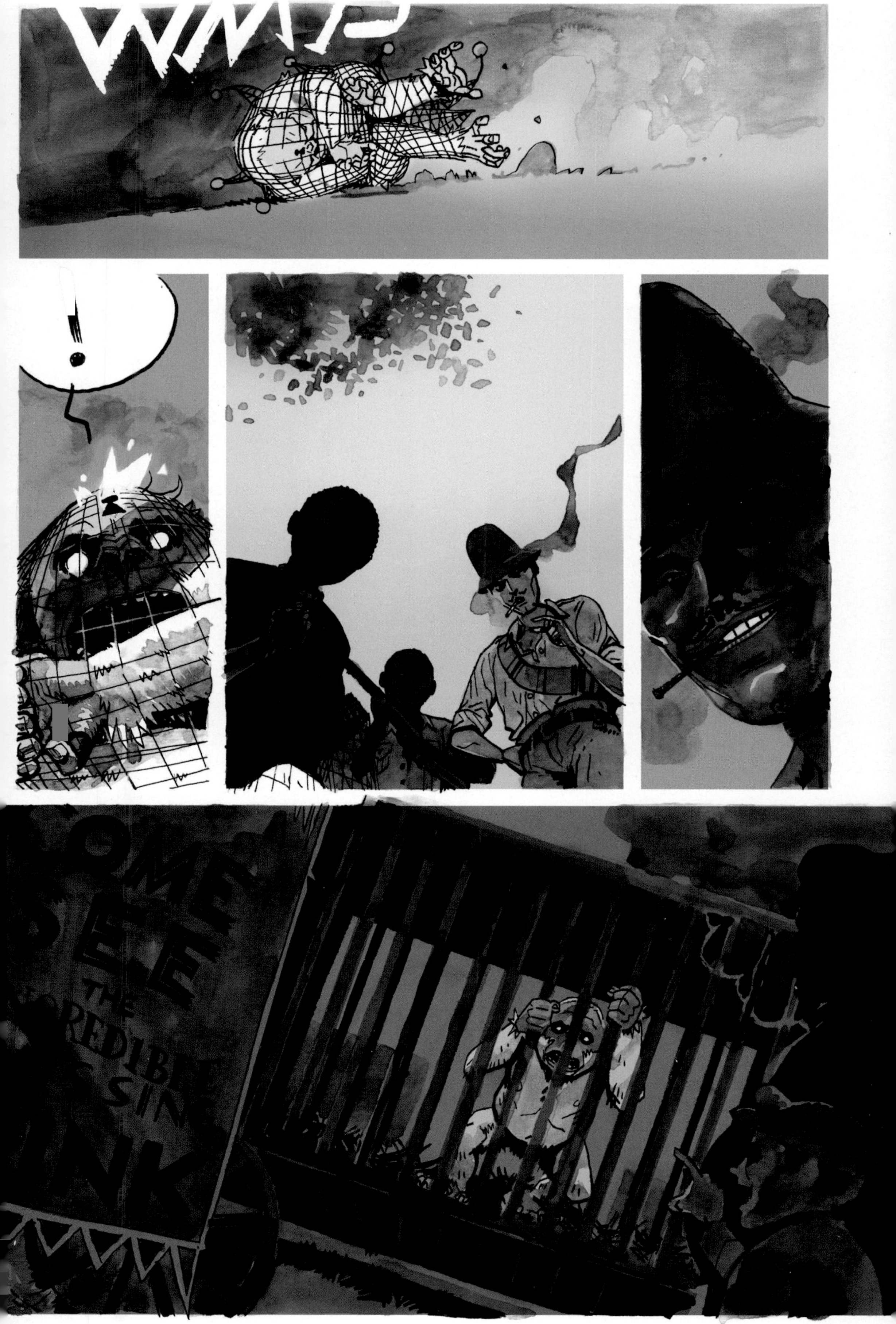
!
SEE
THE

I'LL ADMIT-- I HAD MY DOUBTS ABOUT YOU.

BUT WHEN ME AND THE WIFE SAW YOU MARCH OUT OF THAT GHOST-STORM?

WELL, WE KNEW YOU WERE THE **REAL DEAL.**

bbZZZZz

BOOM-b-a-BOOM ROOM-b-a-BOOM

MY HUSBAND AND I ARE SO HONORED TO BE ALIVE AT THE PROPHET'S ASCENSION.

BOOM-b BOOM-b b-BOOM b-BOOM

THEY SAY THE SPIRITS SHOWED YOU A VISION! WHEN WE GONNA HEAR ABOUT IT?

HENRY!

GREAT PROPHET, WE'RE JUST SO **EXCITED!**

WE PRAY FOR THE COMING OF THE GODS OF ACHERON AND OUR REBIRTH.

YOU SUFFER FOR OUR SINS, AND WE'RE GRATEFUL.

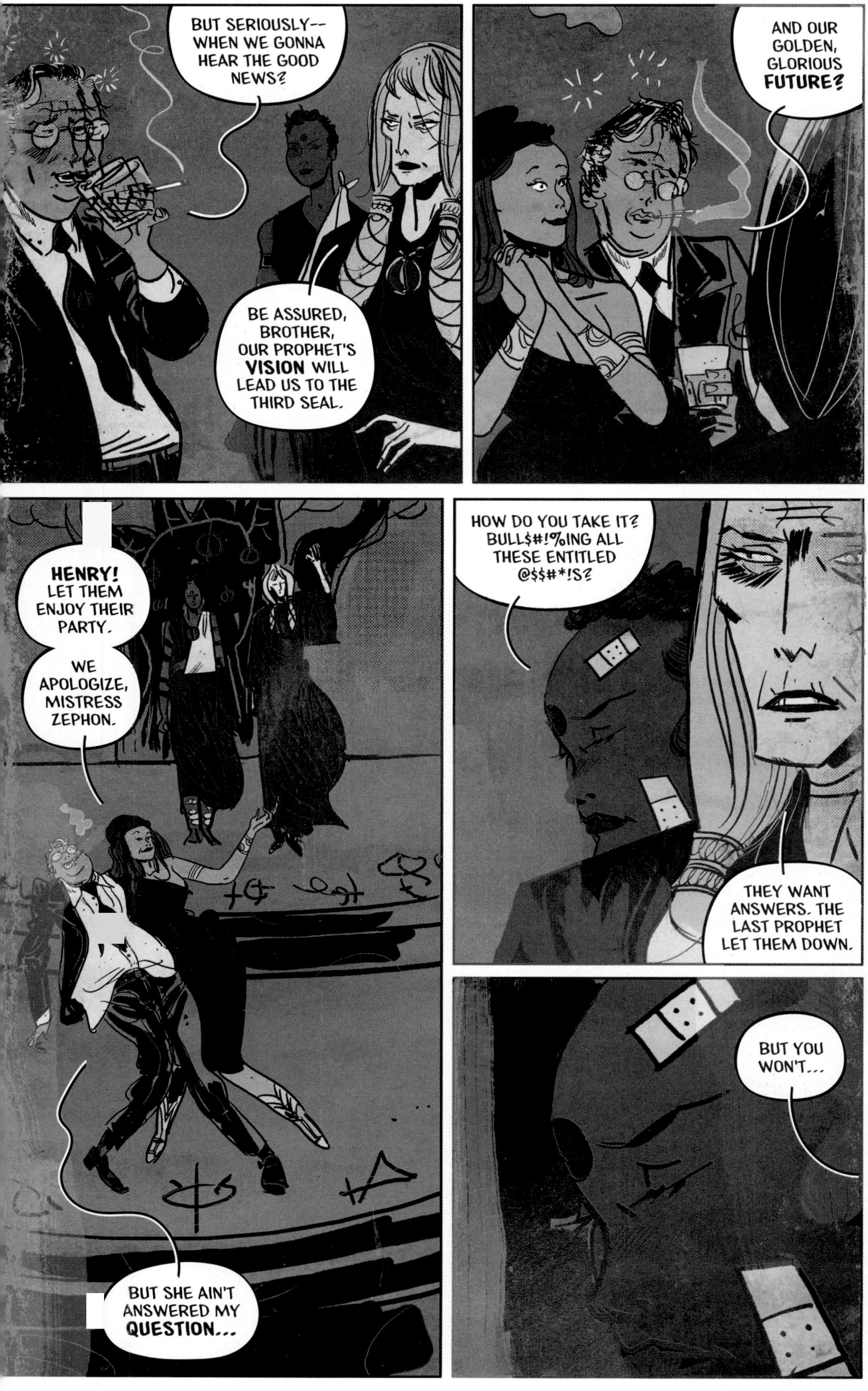
BUT SERIOUSLY-- WHEN WE GONNA HEAR THE GOOD NEWS?
BE ASSURED, BROTHER, OUR PROPHET'S VISION WILL LEAD US TO THE THIRD SEAL.
AND OUR GOLDEN, GLORIOUS FUTURE?
HENRY! LET THEM ENJOY THEIR PARTY.
WE APOLOGIZE, MISTRESS ZEPHON.
BUT SHE AIN'T ANSWERED MY QUESTION...
HOW DO YOU TAKE IT? BULL$#!%ING ALL THESE ENTITLED @$$#*!S?
THEY WANT ANSWERS. THE LAST PROPHET LET THEM DOWN.
BUT YOU WON'T...

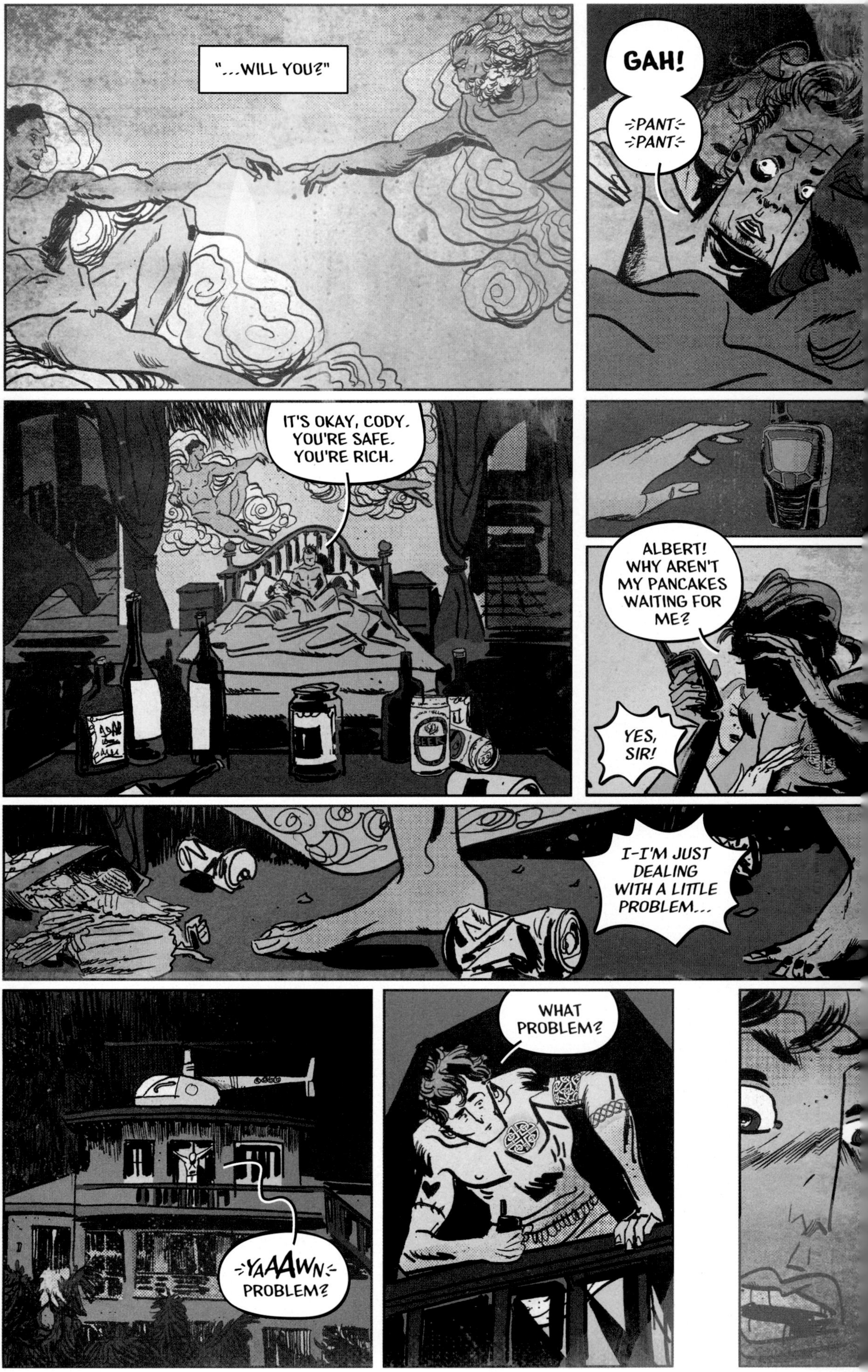
"...WILL YOU?"
GAH!
PANT PANT
IT'S OKAY, CODY. YOU'RE SAFE. YOU'RE RICH.
ALBERT! WHY AREN'T MY PANCAKES WAITING FOR ME?
YES, SIR!
I-I'M JUST DEALING WITH A LITTLE PROBLEM...
YAAAWN PROBLEM?
WHAT PROBLEM?

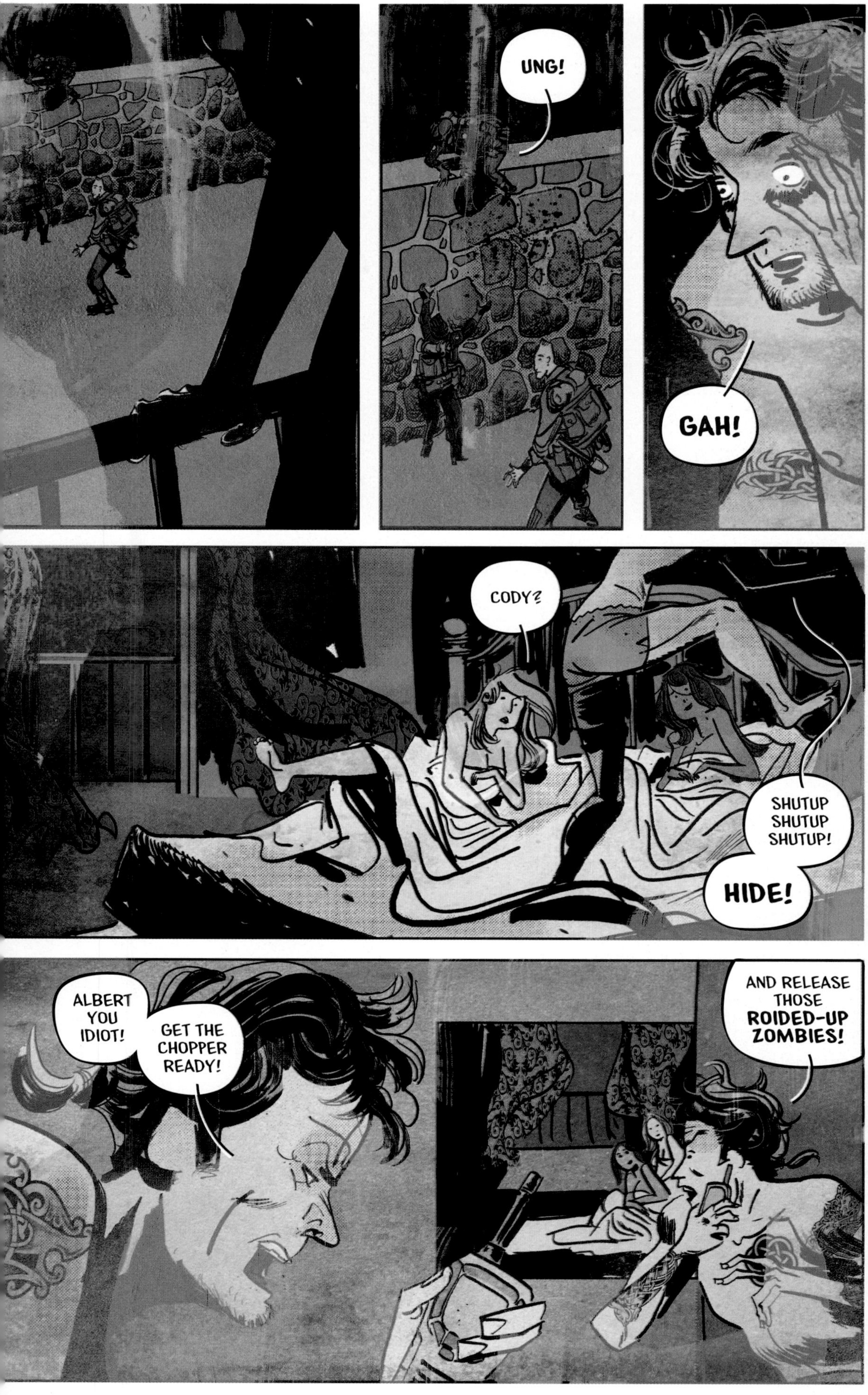
UNG!
GAH!
CODY?
SHUTUP SHUTUP SHUTUP!
HIDE!
ALBERT YOU IDIOT!
GET THE CHOPPER READY!
AND RELEASE THOSE ROIDED-UP ZOMBIES!

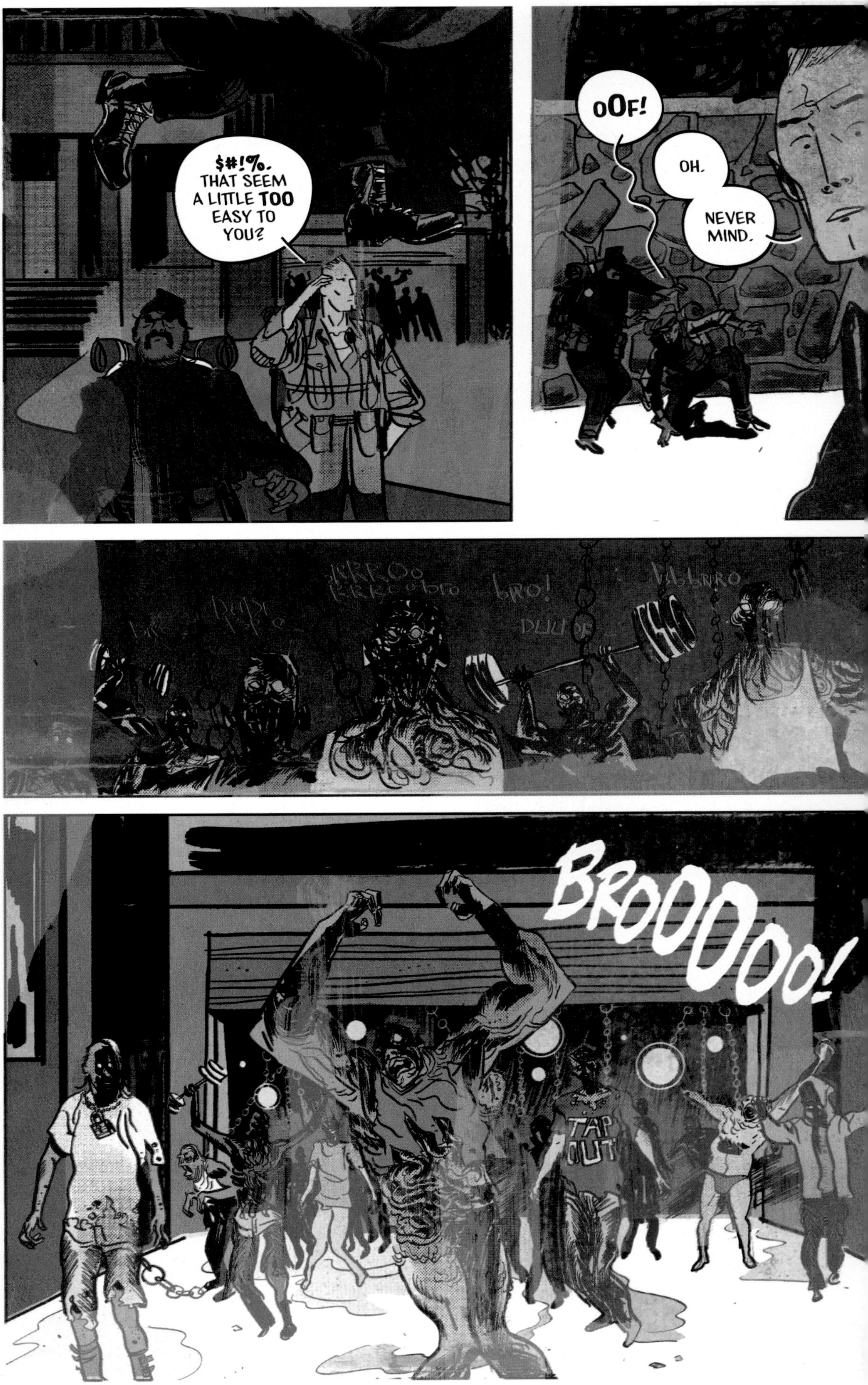
$#!%. THAT SEEM A LITTLE TOO EASY TO YOU?
OOF!
OH.
NEVER MIND.
BROOOOOO!
TAP OUT

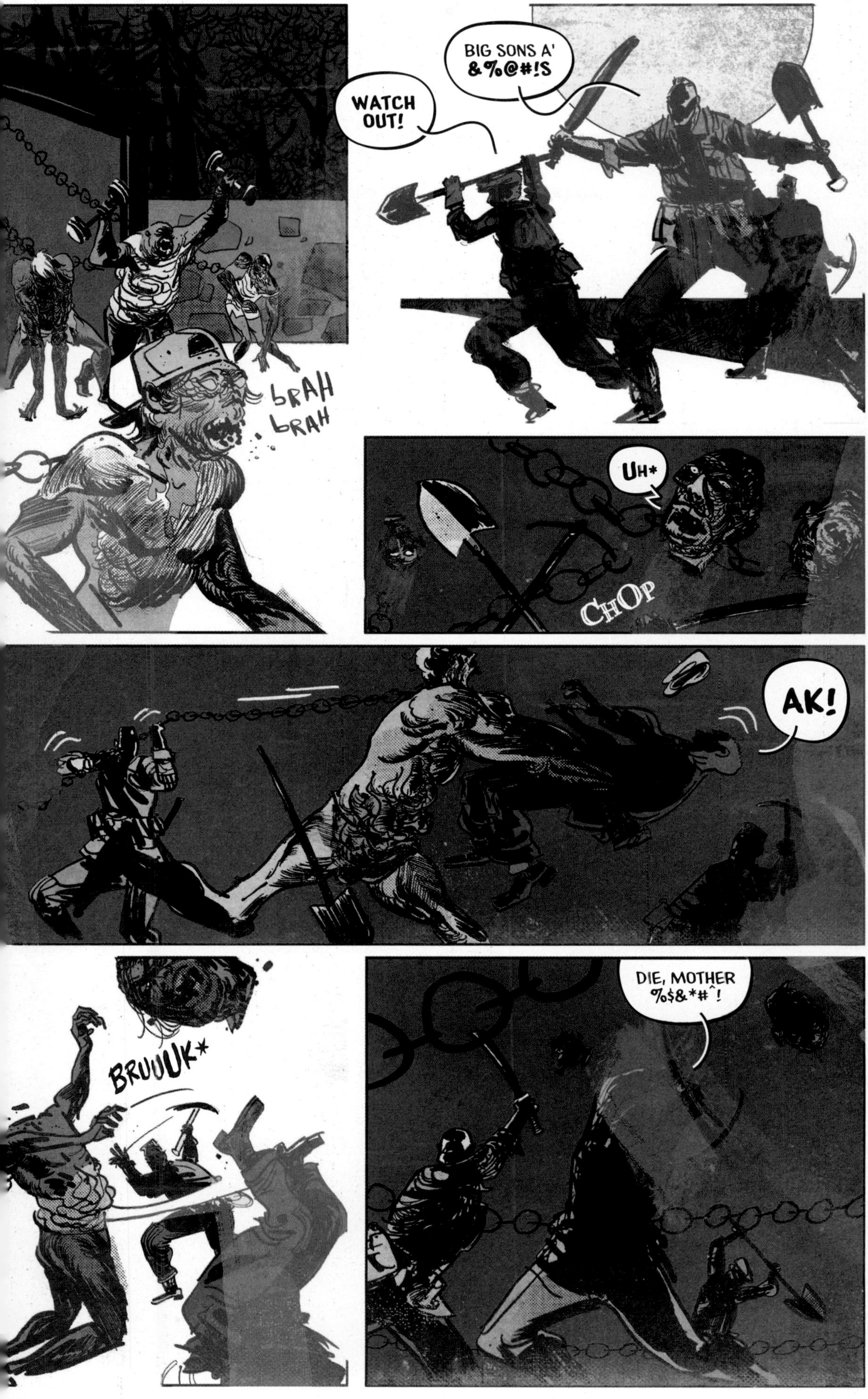
brAH
brAH
WATCH OUT!
BIG SONS A' &%@#!S
UH*
CHOP
AK!
BRUUUK*
DIE, MOTHER %$&*#^!

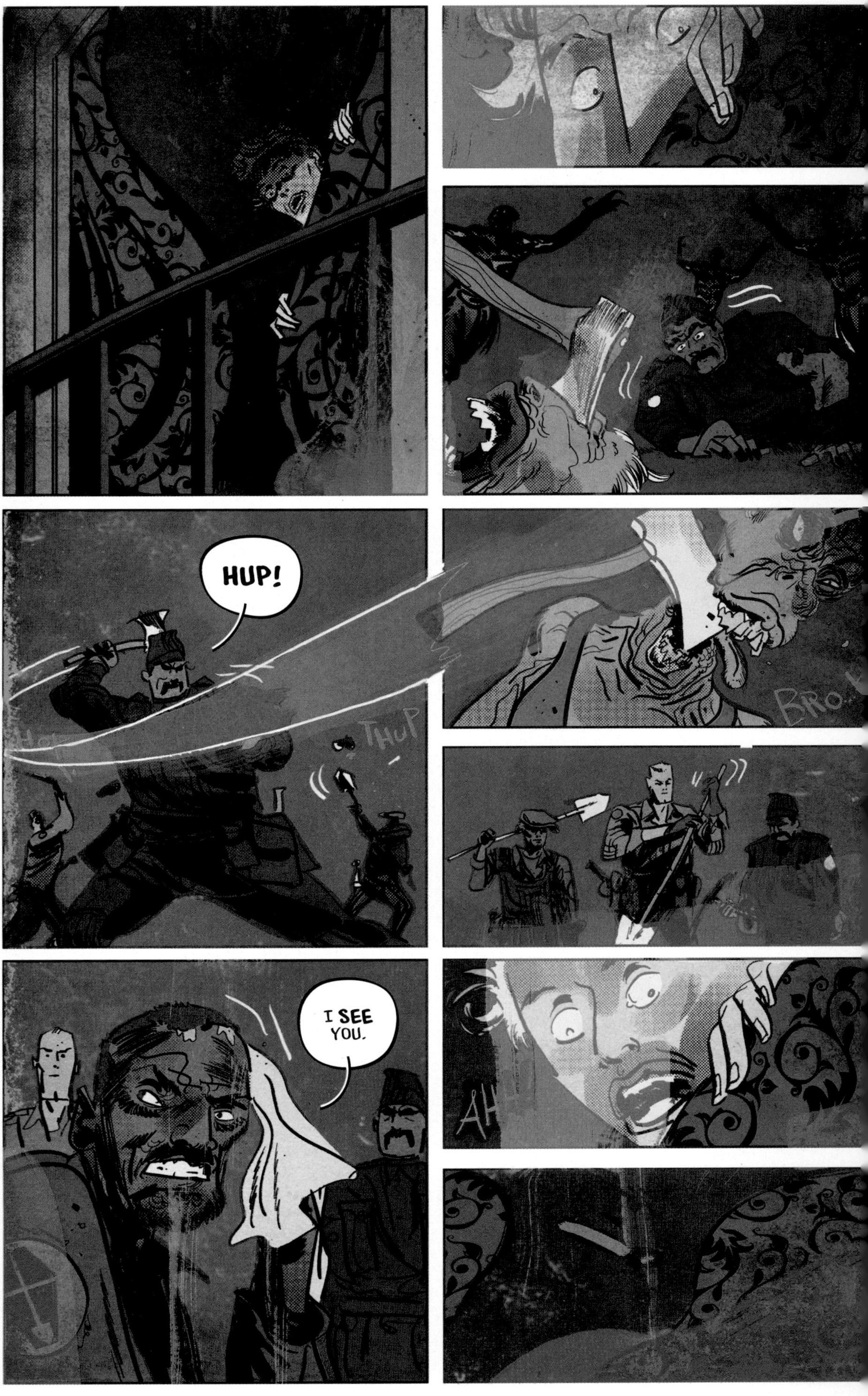
HUP!
THUP
BRO
I SEE YOU.
AH

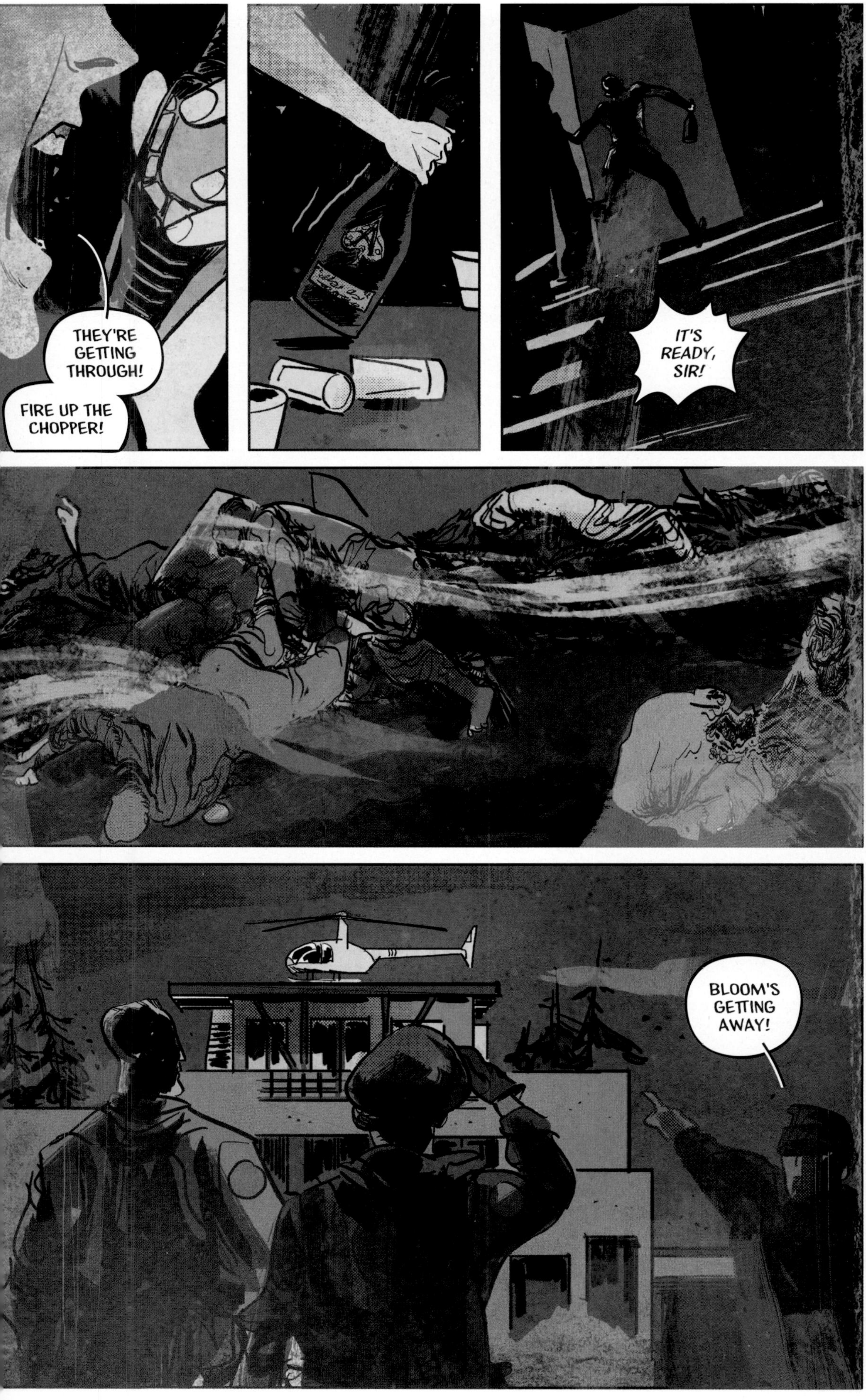
THEY'RE GETTING THROUGH!
FIRE UP THE CHOPPER!
IT'S READY, SIR!
BLOOM'S GETTING AWAY!

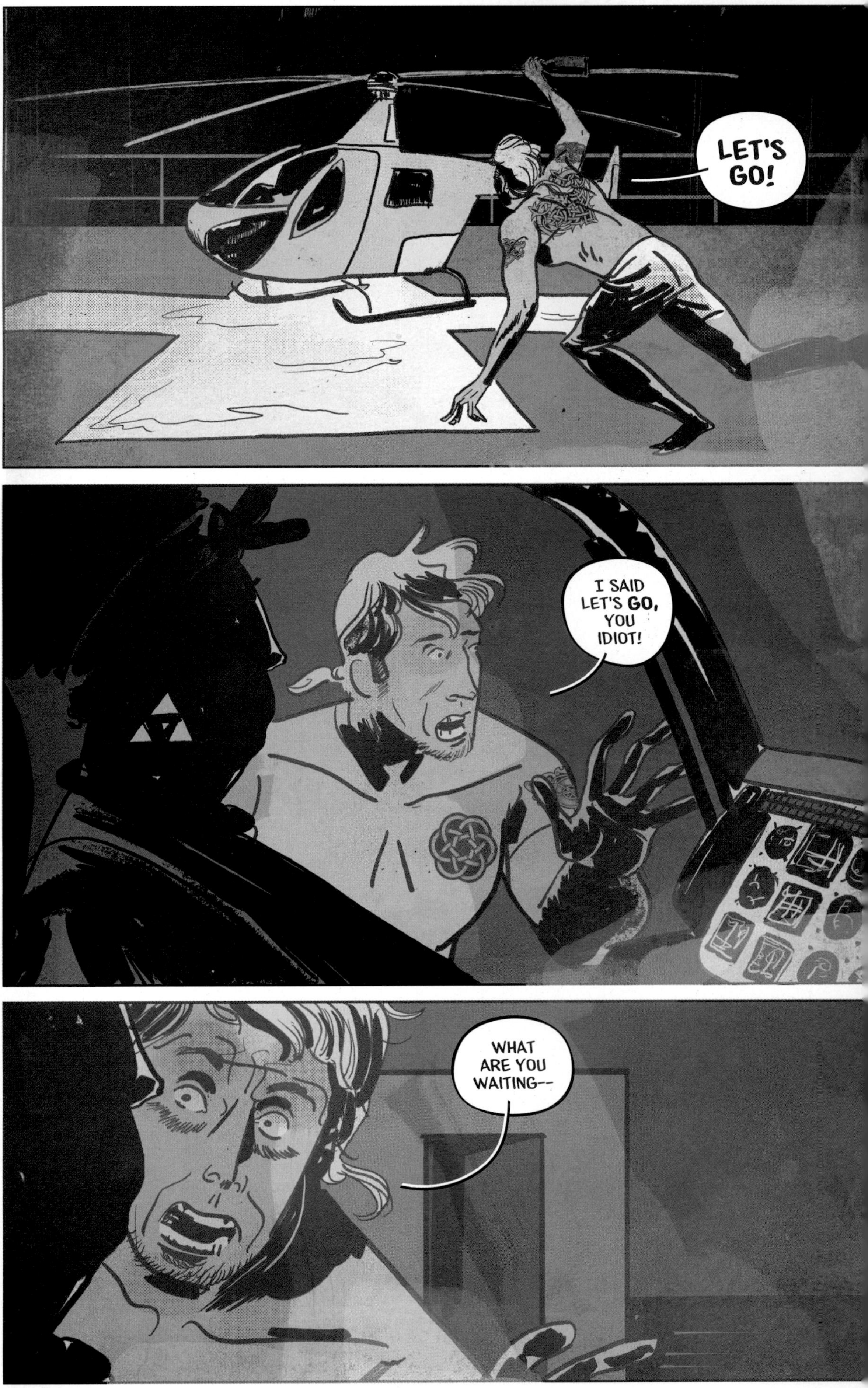
LET'S GO!
I SAID LET'S GO, YOU IDIOT!
WHAT ARE YOU WAITING--

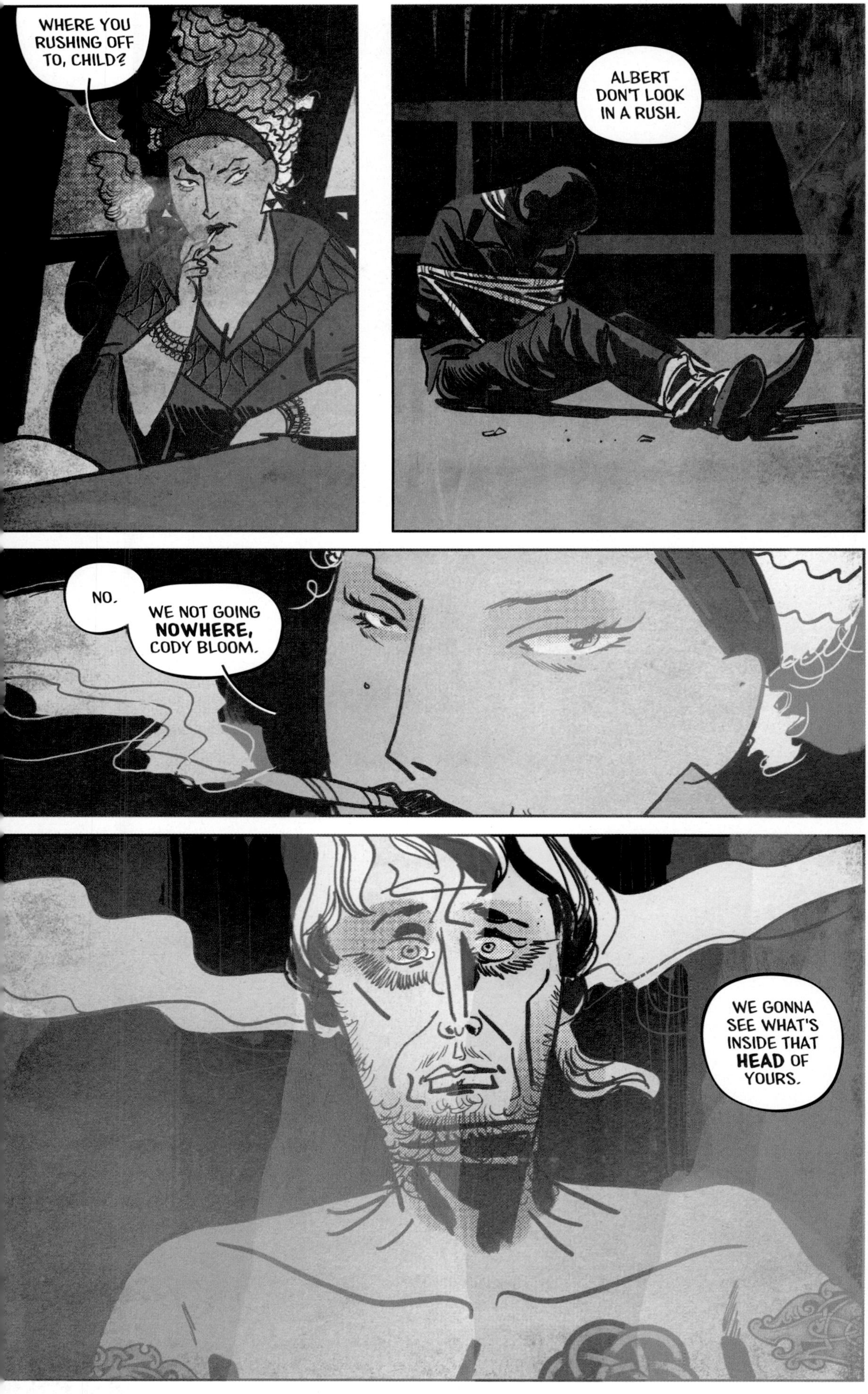
WHERE YOU RUSHING OFF TO, CHILD?
ALBERT DON'T LOOK IN A RUSH.
NO.
WE NOT GOING **NOWHERE,** CODY BLOOM.
WE GONNA SEE WHAT'S INSIDE THAT **HEAD** OF YOURS.

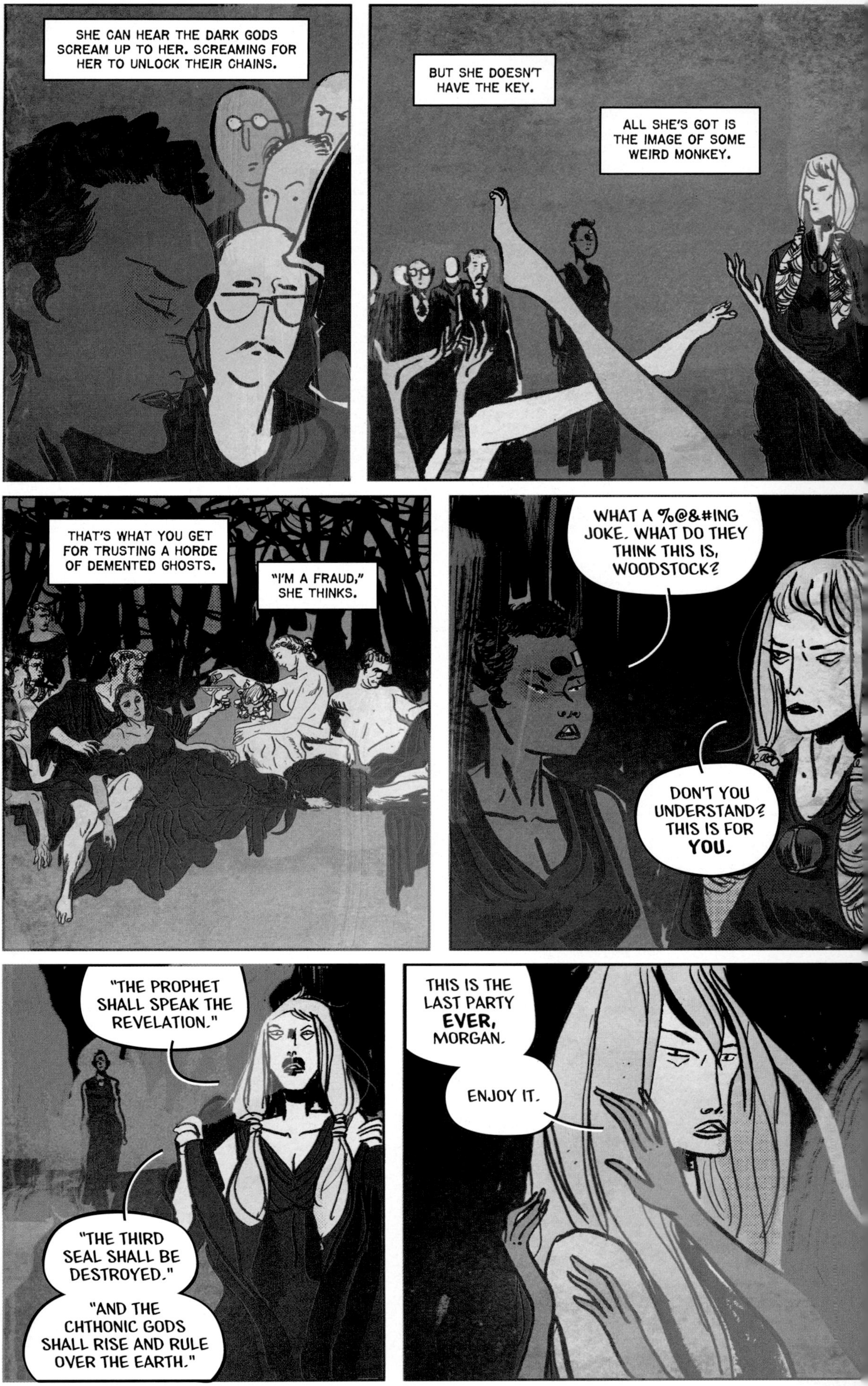

SHE CAN HEAR THE DARK GODS SCREAM UP TO HER. SCREAMING FOR HER TO UNLOCK THEIR CHAINS.
BUT SHE DOESN'T HAVE THE KEY.
ALL SHE'S GOT IS THE IMAGE OF SOME WEIRD MONKEY.
THAT'S WHAT YOU GET FOR TRUSTING A HORDE OF DEMENTED GHOSTS.
"I'M A FRAUD," SHE THINKS.
WHAT A %@&#ING JOKE. WHAT DO THEY THINK THIS IS, WOODSTOCK?
DON'T YOU UNDERSTAND? THIS IS FOR YOU.
"THE PROPHET SHALL SPEAK THE REVELATION."
"THE THIRD SEAL SHALL BE DESTROYED."
"AND THE CHTHONIC GODS SHALL RISE AND RULE OVER THE EARTH."
THIS IS THE LAST PARTY EVER, MORGAN.
ENJOY IT.

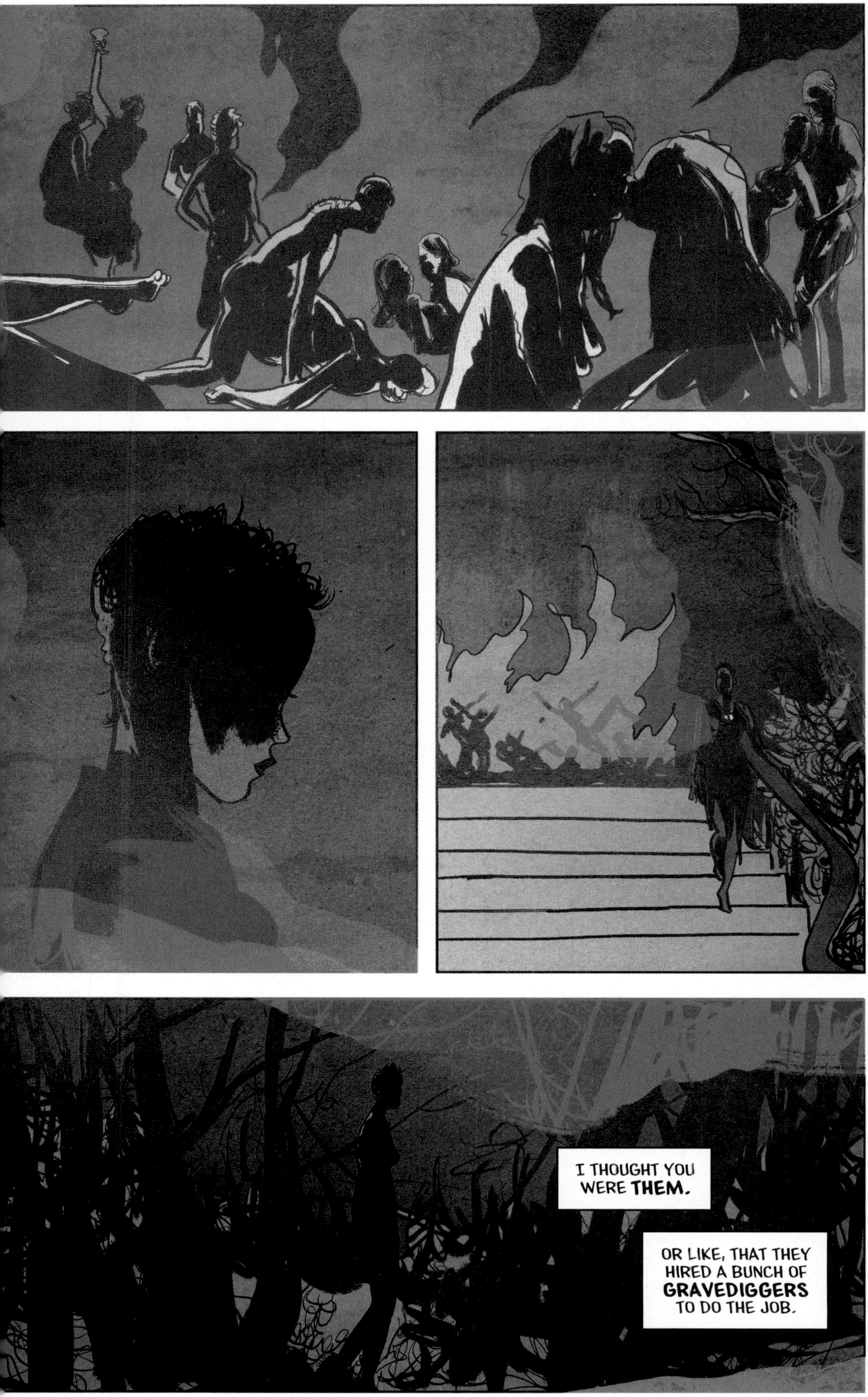
I THOUGHT YOU WERE **THEM.**
OR LIKE, THAT THEY HIRED A BUNCH OF **GRAVEDIGGERS** TO DO THE JOB.

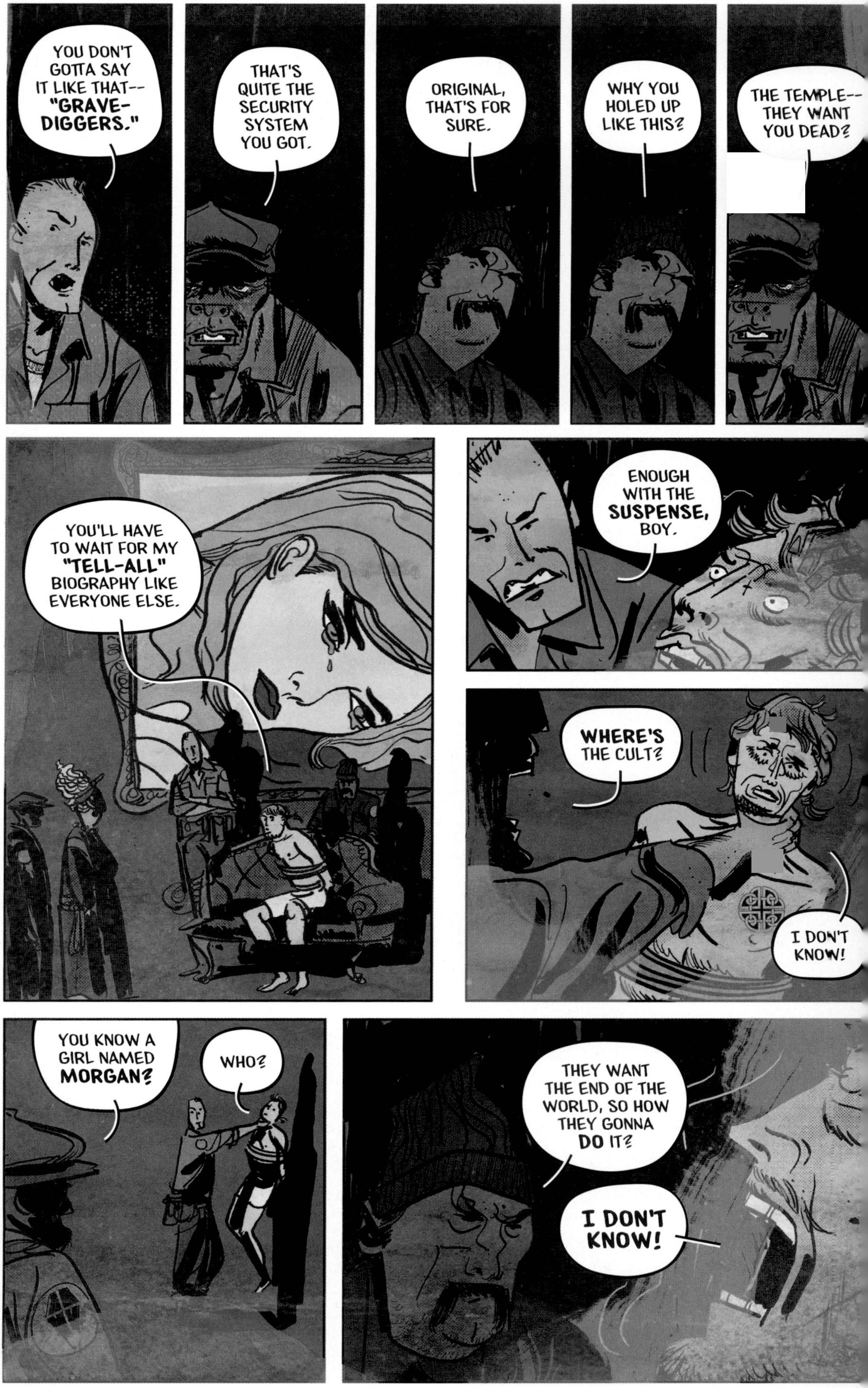
YOU DON'T GOTTA SAY IT LIKE THAT-- "GRAVE-DIGGERS."
THAT'S QUITE THE SECURITY SYSTEM YOU GOT.
ORIGINAL, THAT'S FOR SURE.
WHY YOU HOLED UP LIKE THIS?
THE TEMPLE-- THEY WANT YOU DEAD?
YOU'LL HAVE TO WAIT FOR MY "TELL-ALL" BIOGRAPHY LIKE EVERYONE ELSE.
ENOUGH WITH THE SUSPENSE, BOY.
WHERE'S THE CULT?
I DON'T KNOW!
YOU KNOW A GIRL NAMED MORGAN?
WHO?
THEY WANT THE END OF THE WORLD, SO HOW THEY GONNA DO IT?
I DON'T KNOW!

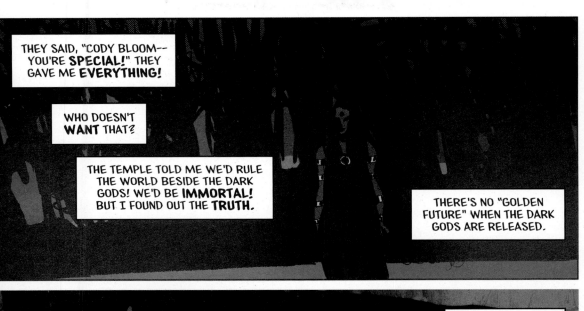

THEY SAID, "CODY BLOOM-- YOU'RE **SPECIAL!**" THEY GAVE ME **EVERYTHING!**

WHO DOESN'T **WANT** THAT?

THE TEMPLE TOLD ME WE'D RULE THE WORLD BESIDE THE DARK GODS! WE'D BE **IMMORTAL!** BUT I FOUND OUT THE **TRUTH.**

THERE'S NO "GOLDEN FUTURE" WHEN THE DARK GODS ARE RELEASED.

EVERYONE DIES. ALL MANKIND. EVEN THE TEMPLE.

EVEN ME.

HOW?

THEY SAID THE ANSWER WAS IN MY HEAD. THAT'S WHY I WAS THEIR PROPHET.

THEY TOLD ME I WAS **SO** CLOSE TO FINDING THE "THIRD SEAL."

IF YOU CAN'T FIND THE ANSWER...

YOU CAN JUST DRIFT AWAY...

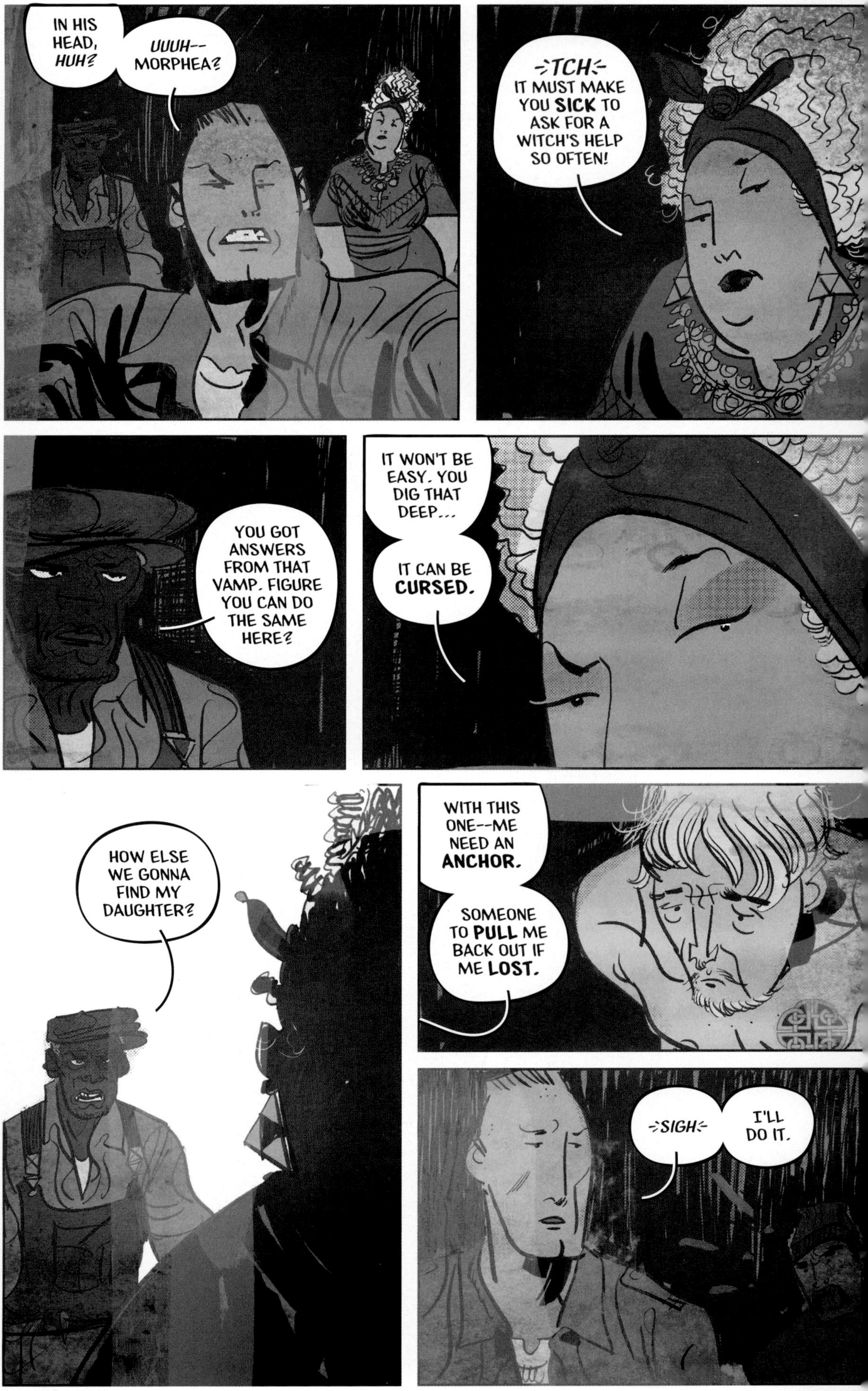
IN HIS HEAD, HUH?
UUUH-- MORPHEA?
=TCH= IT MUST MAKE YOU SICK TO ASK FOR A WITCH'S HELP SO OFTEN!
YOU GOT ANSWERS FROM THAT VAMP. FIGURE YOU CAN DO THE SAME HERE?
IT WON'T BE EASY. YOU DIG THAT DEEP...
IT CAN BE CURSED.
HOW ELSE WE GONNA FIND MY DAUGHTER?
WITH THIS ONE--ME NEED AN ANCHOR.
SOMEONE TO PULL ME BACK OUT IF ME LOST.
=SIGH=
I'LL DO IT.

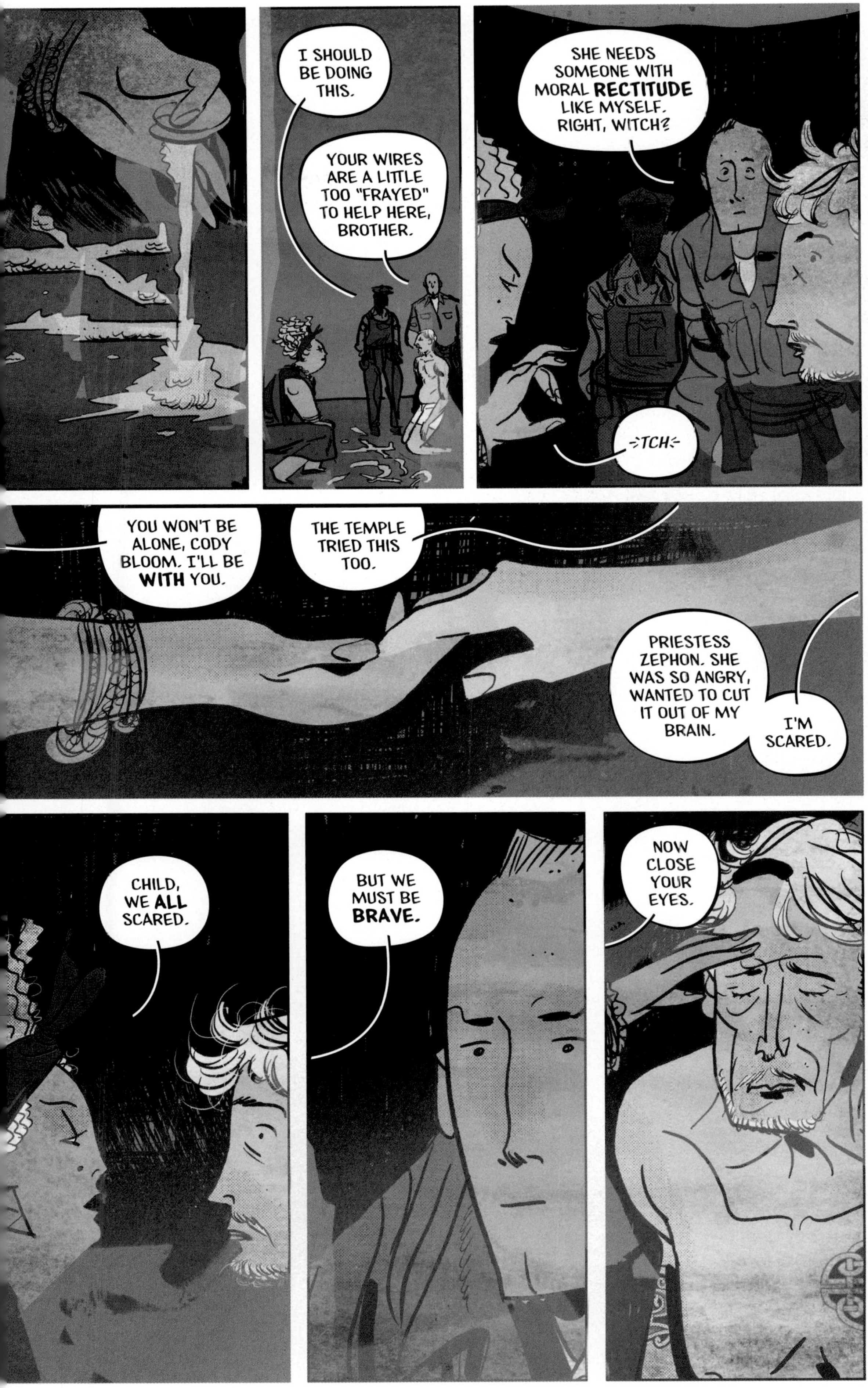
I SHOULD BE DOING THIS.
YOUR WIRES ARE A LITTLE TOO "FRAYED" TO HELP HERE, BROTHER.
SHE NEEDS SOMEONE WITH MORAL RECTITUDE LIKE MYSELF. RIGHT, WITCH?
TCH
YOU WON'T BE ALONE, CODY BLOOM. I'LL BE WITH YOU.
THE TEMPLE TRIED THIS TOO.
PRIESTESS ZEPHON. SHE WAS SO ANGRY, WANTED TO CUT IT OUT OF MY BRAIN.
I'M SCARED.
CHILD, WE ALL SCARED.
BUT WE MUST BE BRAVE.
NOW CLOSE YOUR EYES.

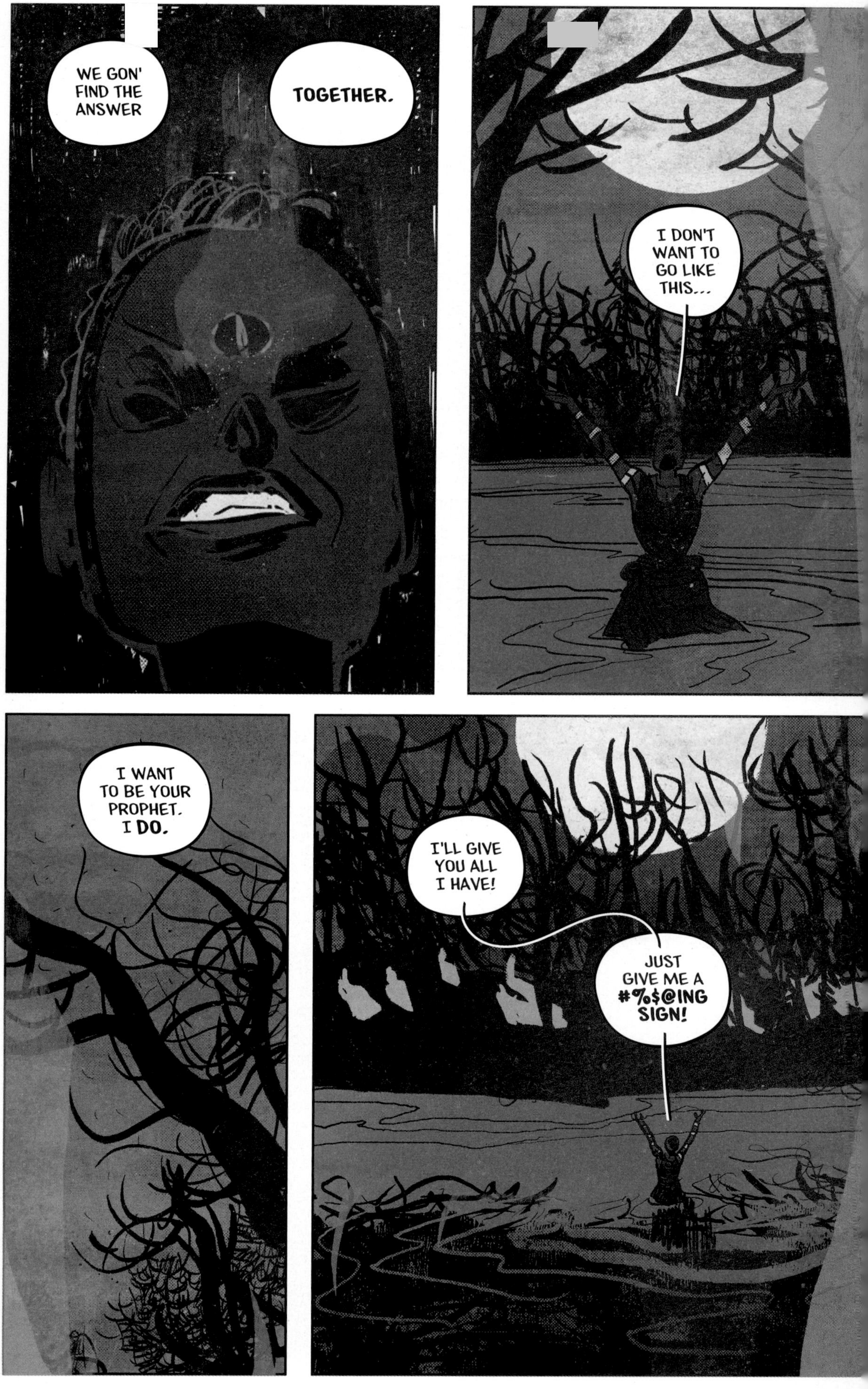
WE GON' FIND THE ANSWER
TOGETHER.
I DON'T WANT TO GO LIKE THIS...
I WANT TO BE YOUR PROPHET. I DO.
I'LL GIVE YOU ALL I HAVE!
JUST GIVE ME A #%$@ING SIGN!

I'M GOING TO FAIL AND YOU'RE GONNA BE **MAD**.

DEMANDING PARENTS, DEMANDING DIRECTORS, DEMANDING GOD-DAMNED **WITCHES**.

I WON'T BE MAD, CODY. WHAT'S YOUR FAVORITE MOVIE... THAT YOU WEREN'T IN?

ST-STAR WARS.

AH--WELL...ME LIKE THAT LITTLE **GREEN** THING, AND YOU THE CHOSEN ONE.

I'M LUKE?

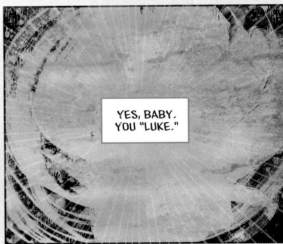

YES, BABY. YOU "LUKE."

I THINK WE **IN**.

IN WHAT?

WHAT DO I SEE, CODY BLOOM? TELL ME.

WEIRD.

YUP.

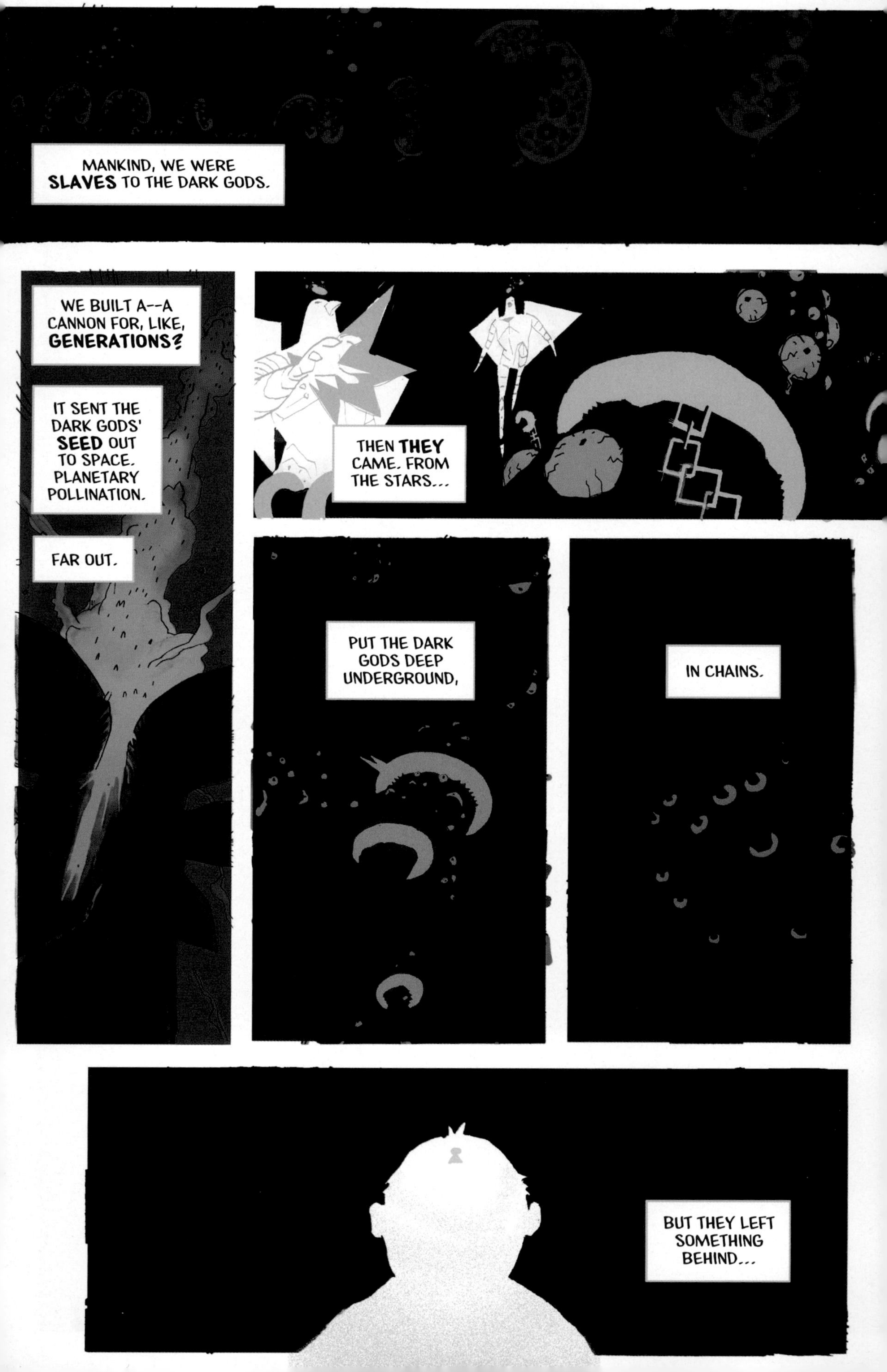
MANKIND, WE WERE SLAVES TO THE DARK GODS.
WE BUILT A--A CANNON FOR, LIKE, GENERATIONS?
IT SENT THE DARK GODS' SEED OUT TO SPACE. PLANETARY POLLINATION.
FAR OUT.
THEN THEY CAME. FROM THE STARS...
PUT THE DARK GODS DEEP UNDERGROUND,
IN CHAINS.
BUT THEY LEFT SOMETHING BEHIND...

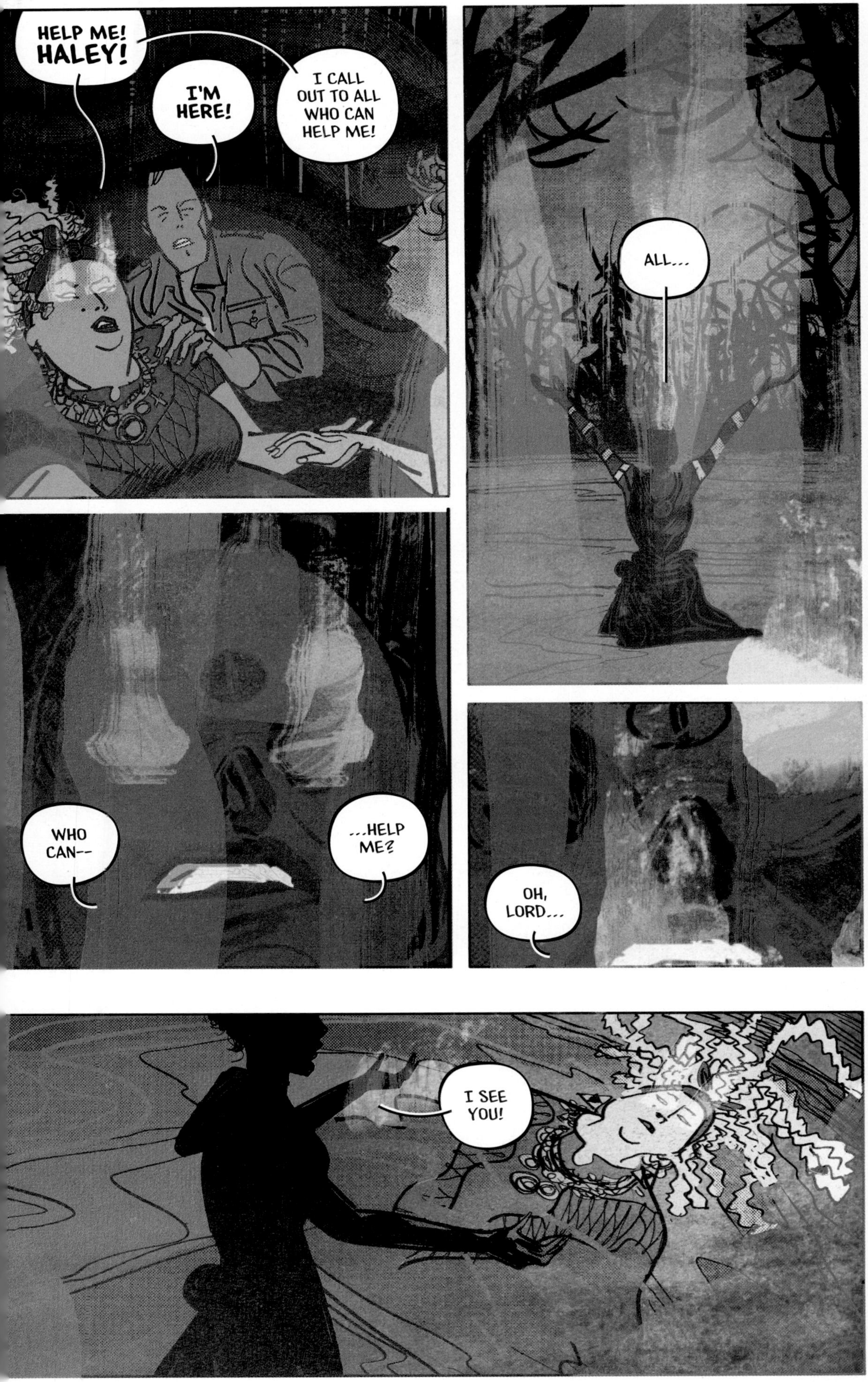
HELP ME! HALEY!
I'M HERE!
I CALL OUT TO ALL WHO CAN HELP ME!
ALL...
WHO CAN--
...HELP ME?
OH, LORD...
I SEE YOU!

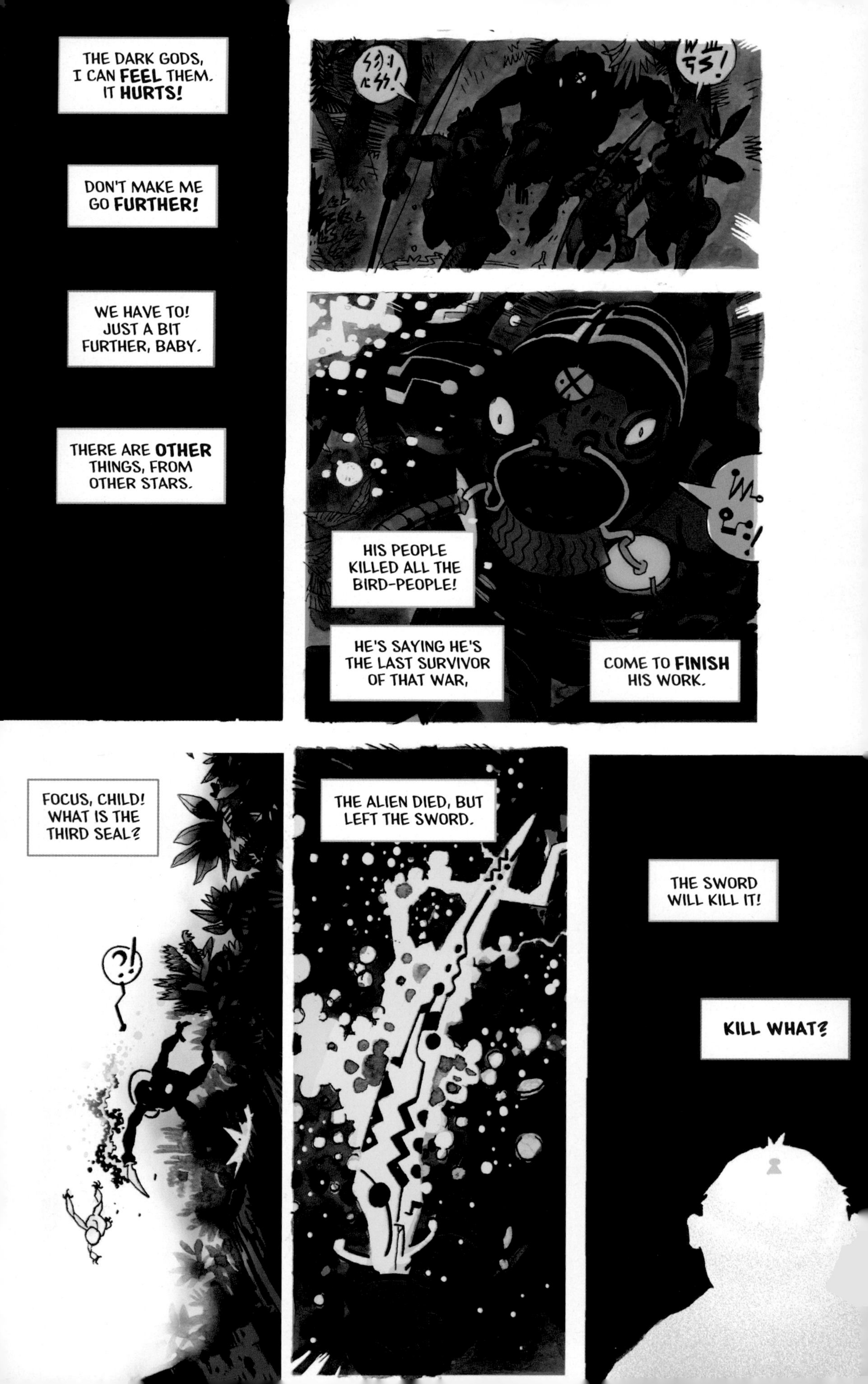
THE DARK GODS, I CAN FEEL THEM. IT HURTS!
DON'T MAKE ME GO FURTHER!
WE HAVE TO! JUST A BIT FURTHER, BABY.
THERE ARE OTHER THINGS, FROM OTHER STARS.
HIS PEOPLE KILLED ALL THE BIRD-PEOPLE!
HE'S SAYING HE'S THE LAST SURVIVOR OF THAT WAR,
COME TO FINISH HIS WORK.
FOCUS, CHILD! WHAT IS THE THIRD SEAL?
?!
THE ALIEN DIED, BUT LEFT THE SWORD.
THE SWORD WILL KILL IT!
KILL WHAT?

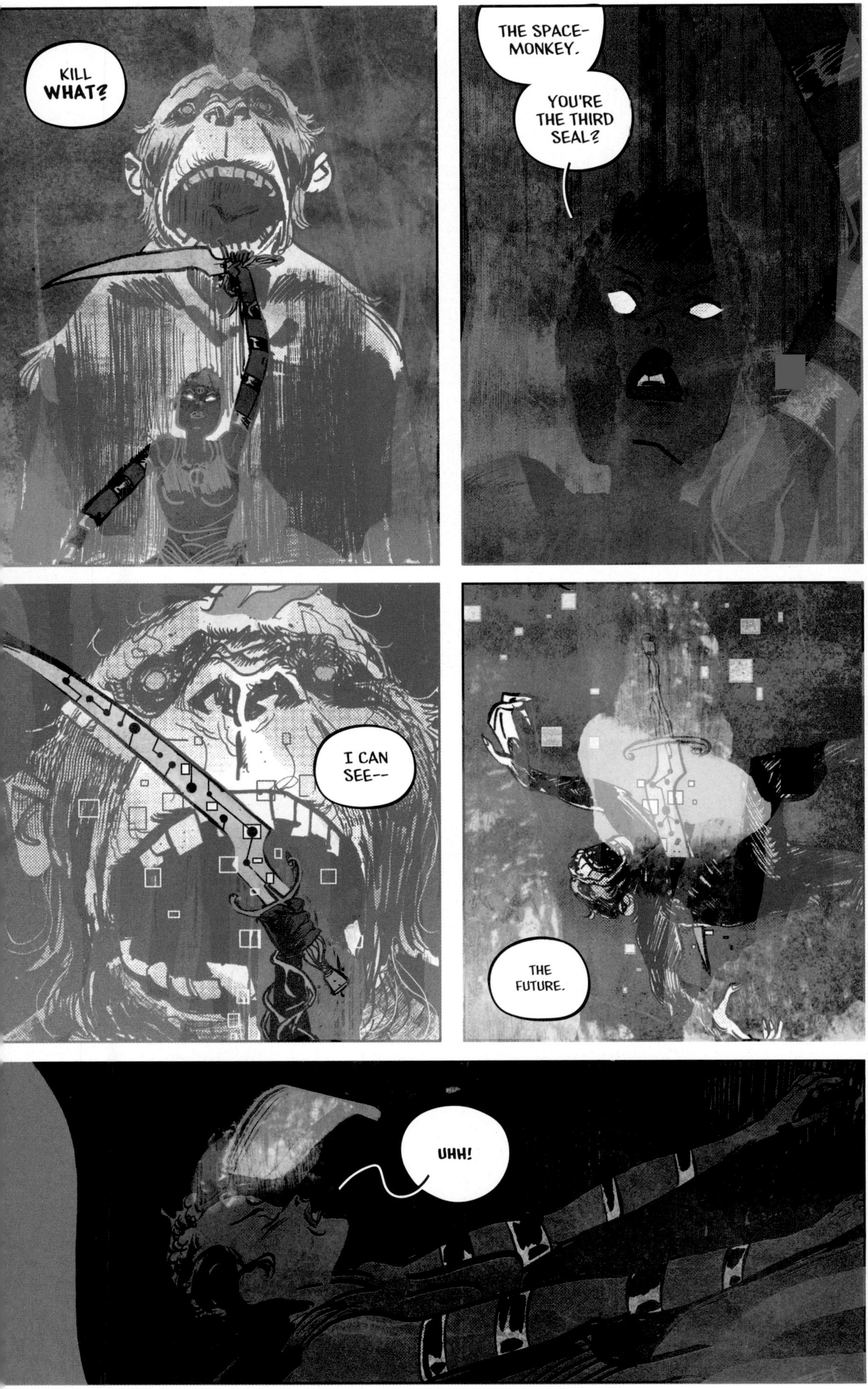
KILL WHAT?
THE SPACE-MONKEY.
YOU'RE THE THIRD SEAL?
I CAN SEE--
THE FUTURE.
UHH!

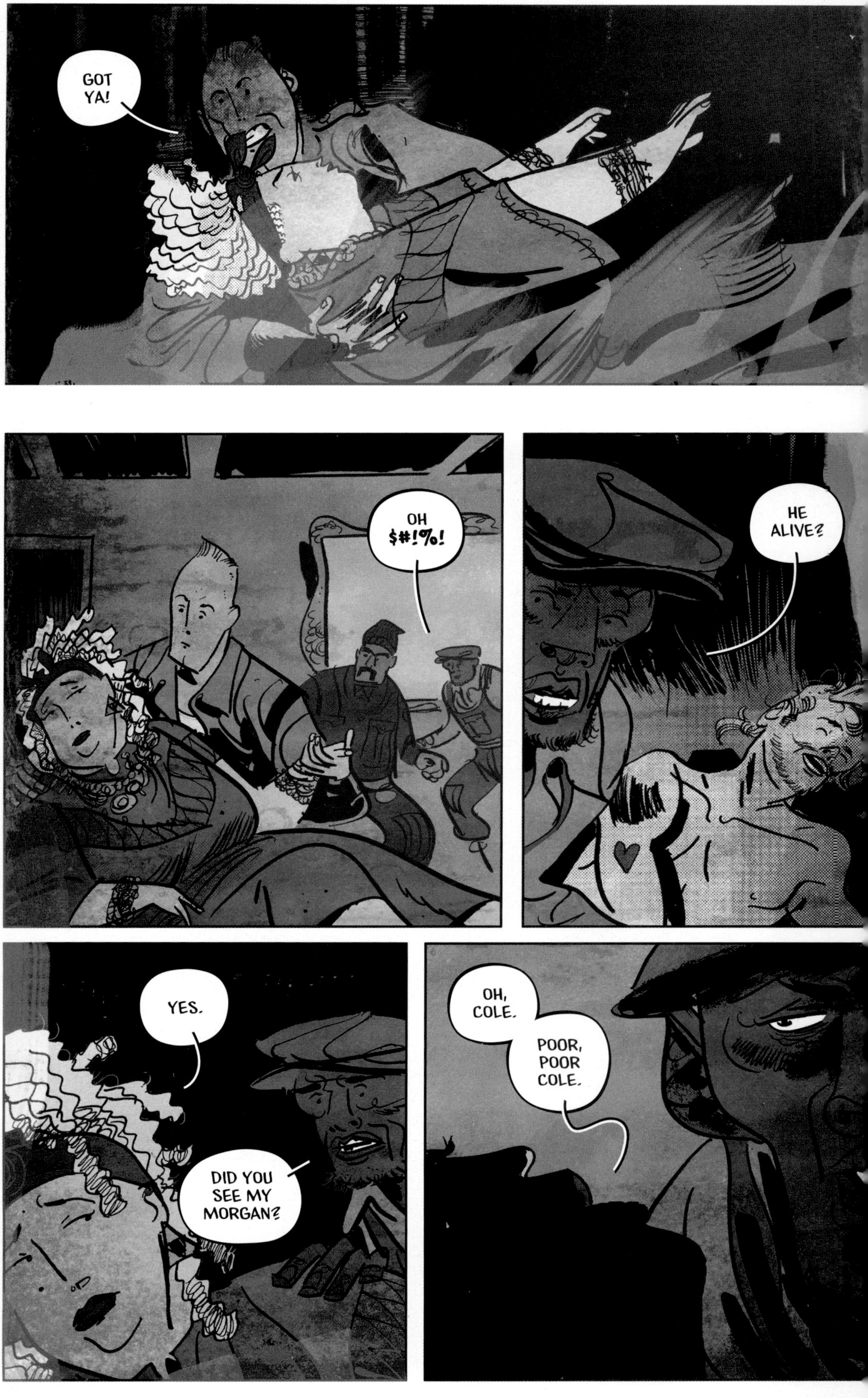
GOT YA!
OH $#!%!
HE ALIVE?
YES.
DID YOU SEE MY MORGAN?
OH, COLE.
POOR, POOR COLE.

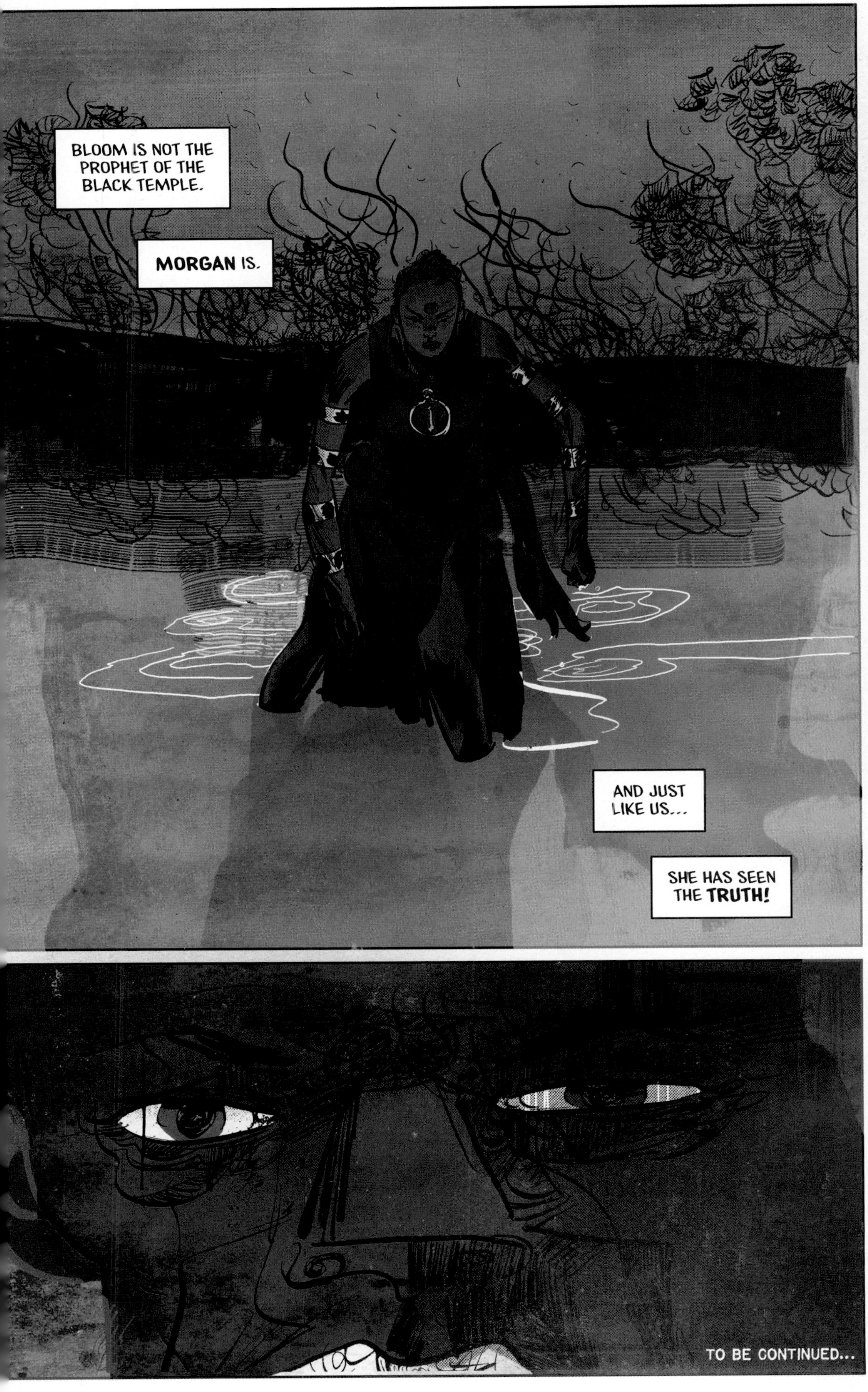
BLOOM IS NOT THE PROPHET OF THE BLACK TEMPLE.
MORGAN IS.
AND JUST LIKE US...
SHE HAS SEEN THE TRUTH!
TO BE CONTINUED...

THE GRAVE DIGGERS UNION

MONTHLY COVER ART GALLERY BY

Wes Craig

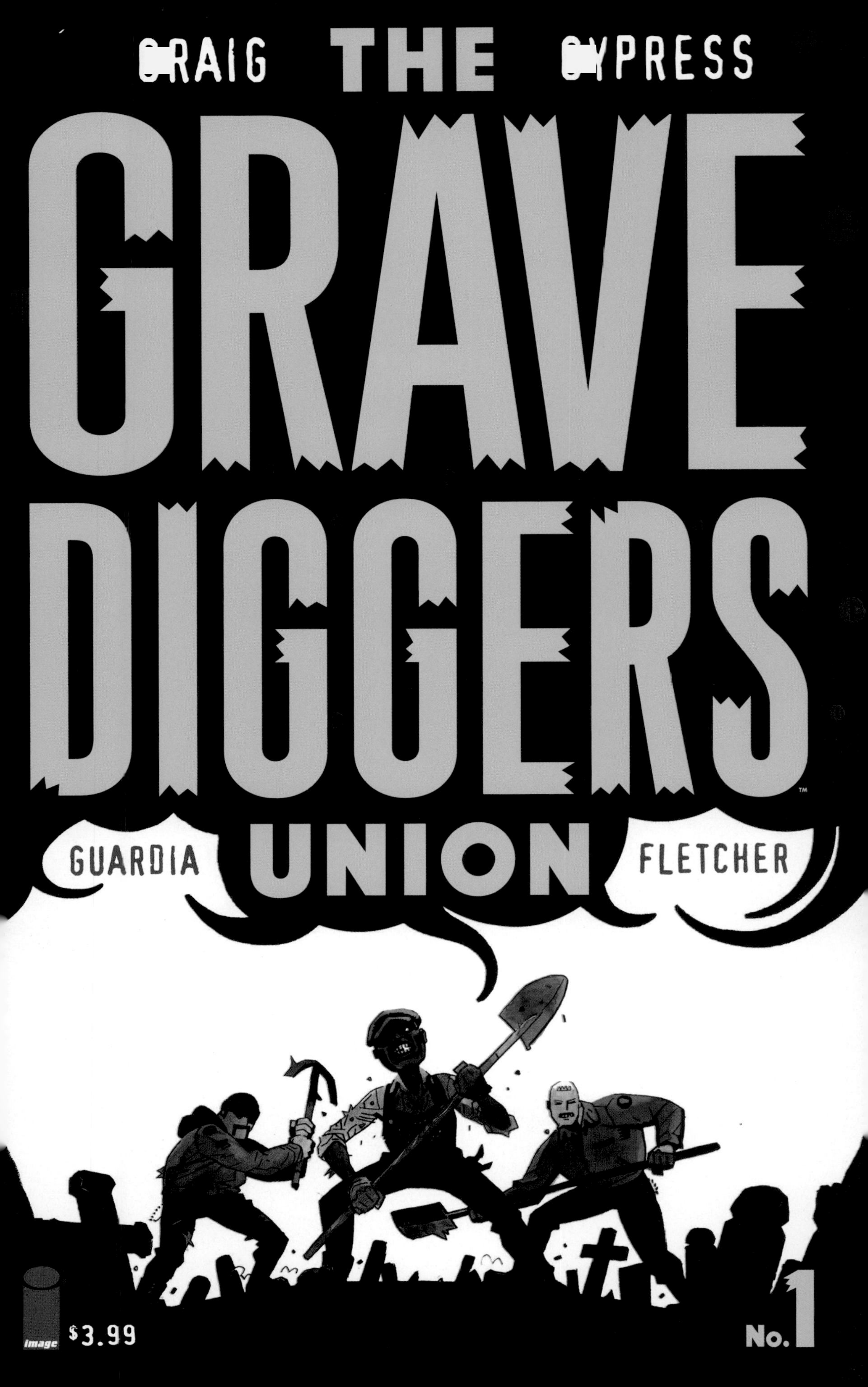

CRAIG THE CYPRESS

GRAVE DIGGERS

GUARDIA UNION FLETCHER

image $3.99 NO. 1

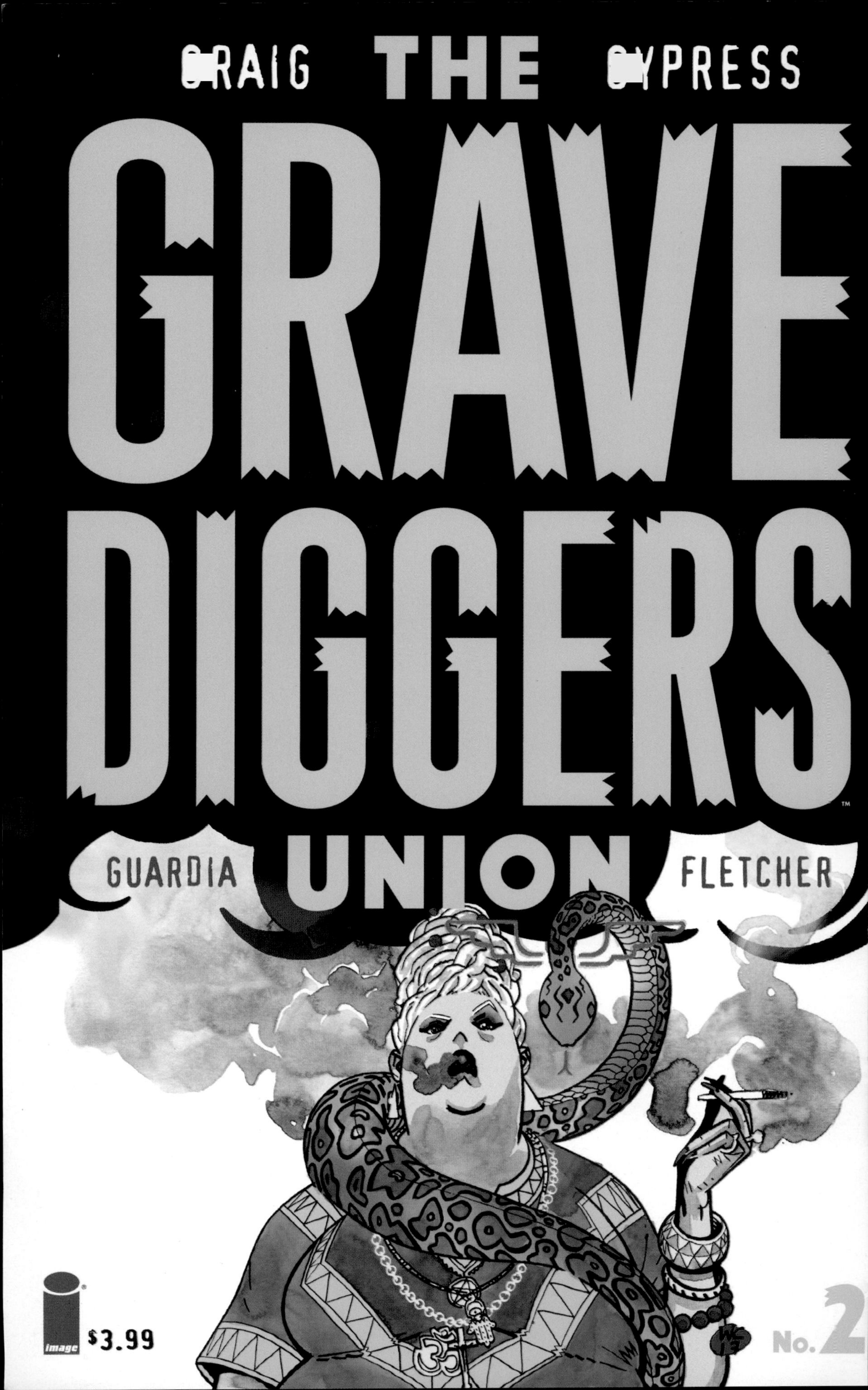

CRAIG THE CYPRESS

THE GRAVE DIGGERS UNION

GUARDIA UNION FLETCHER

$3.99

No. 2

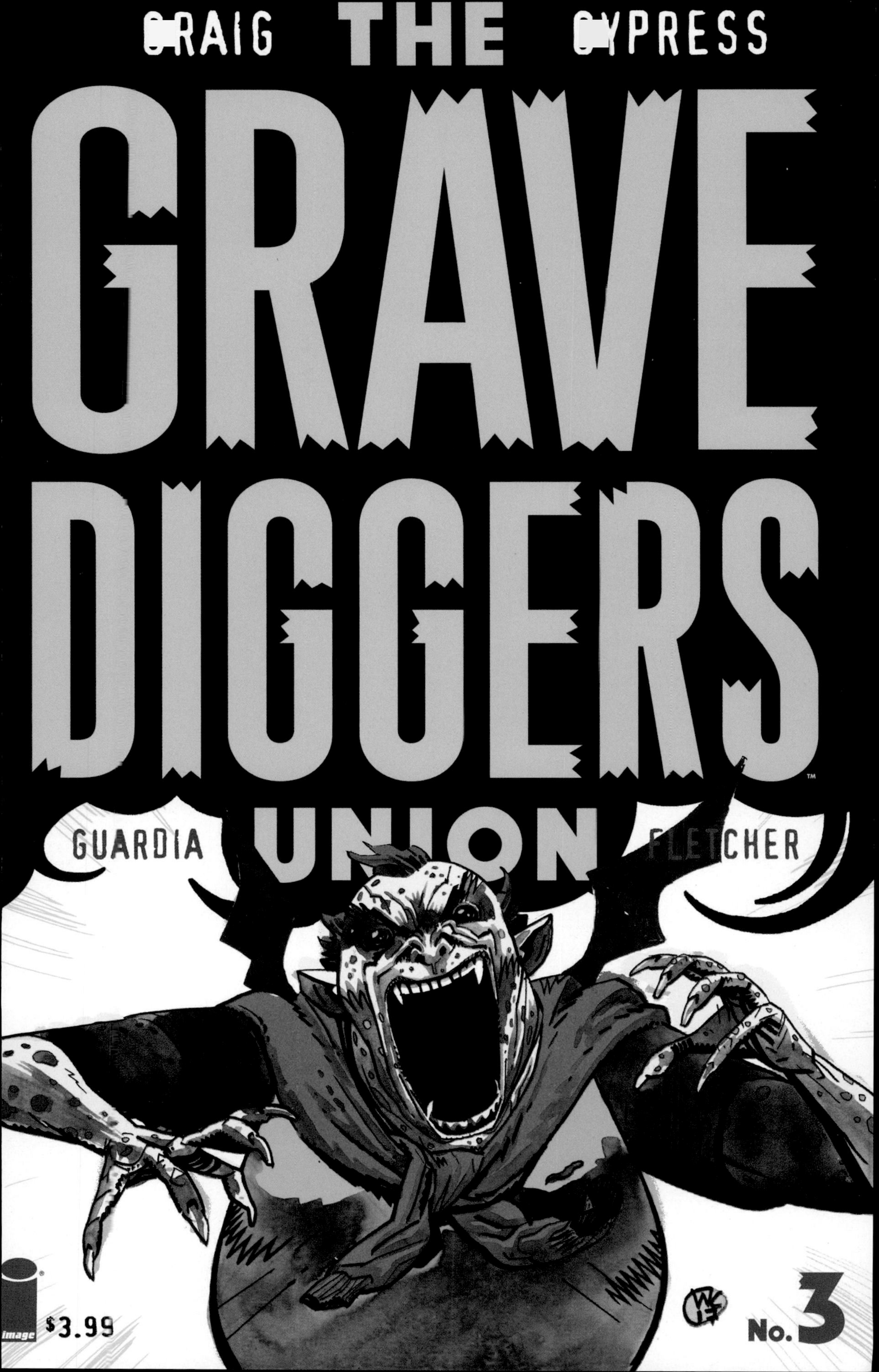
CRAIG THE CYPRESS
GRAVE DIGGERS
UNION
GUARDIA
FLETCHER
$3.99
No. 3

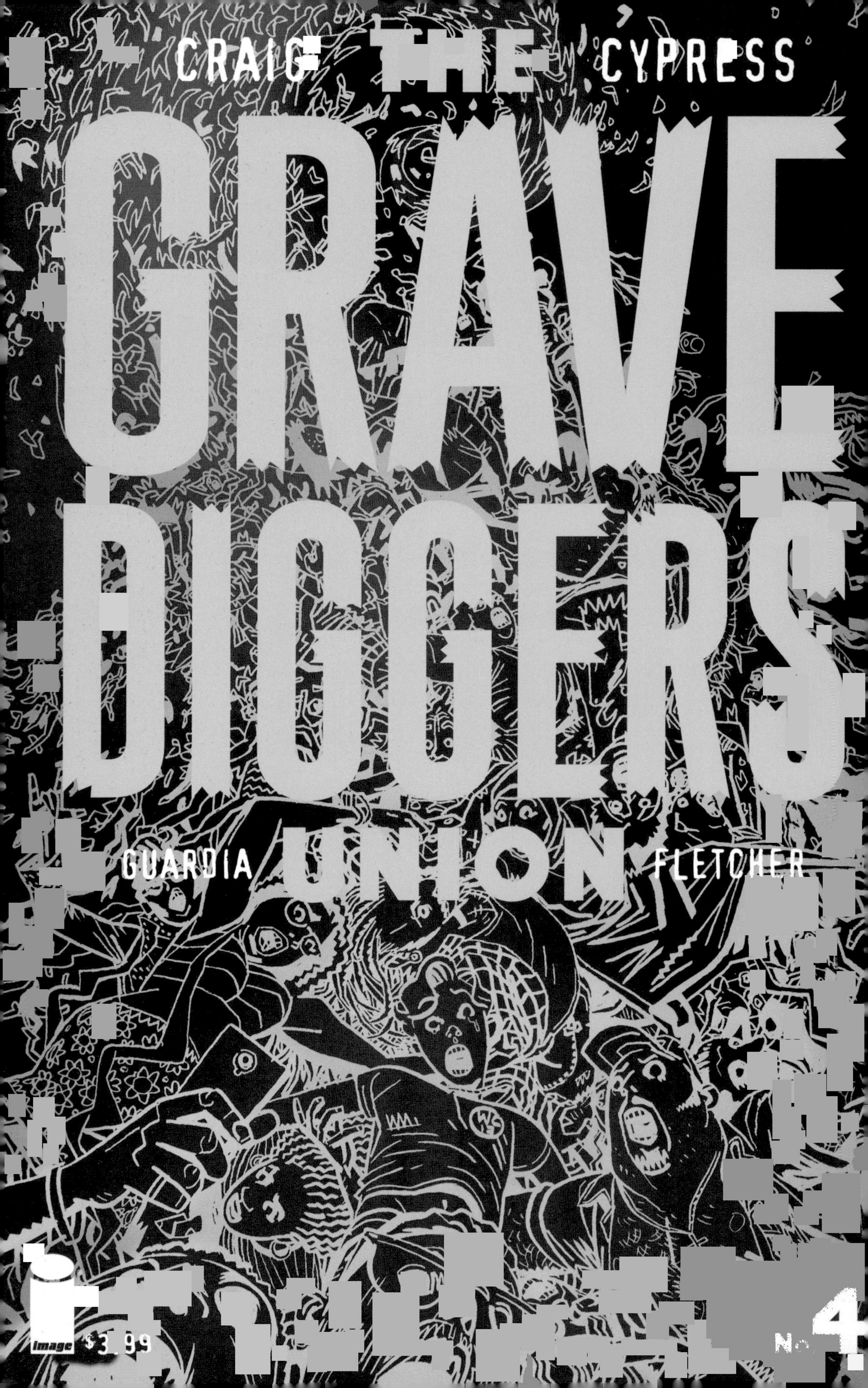
CRAIG
CYPRESS
GRAVE
DIGGERS
UNION
GUARDIA
FLETCHER
$3.99
No. 4

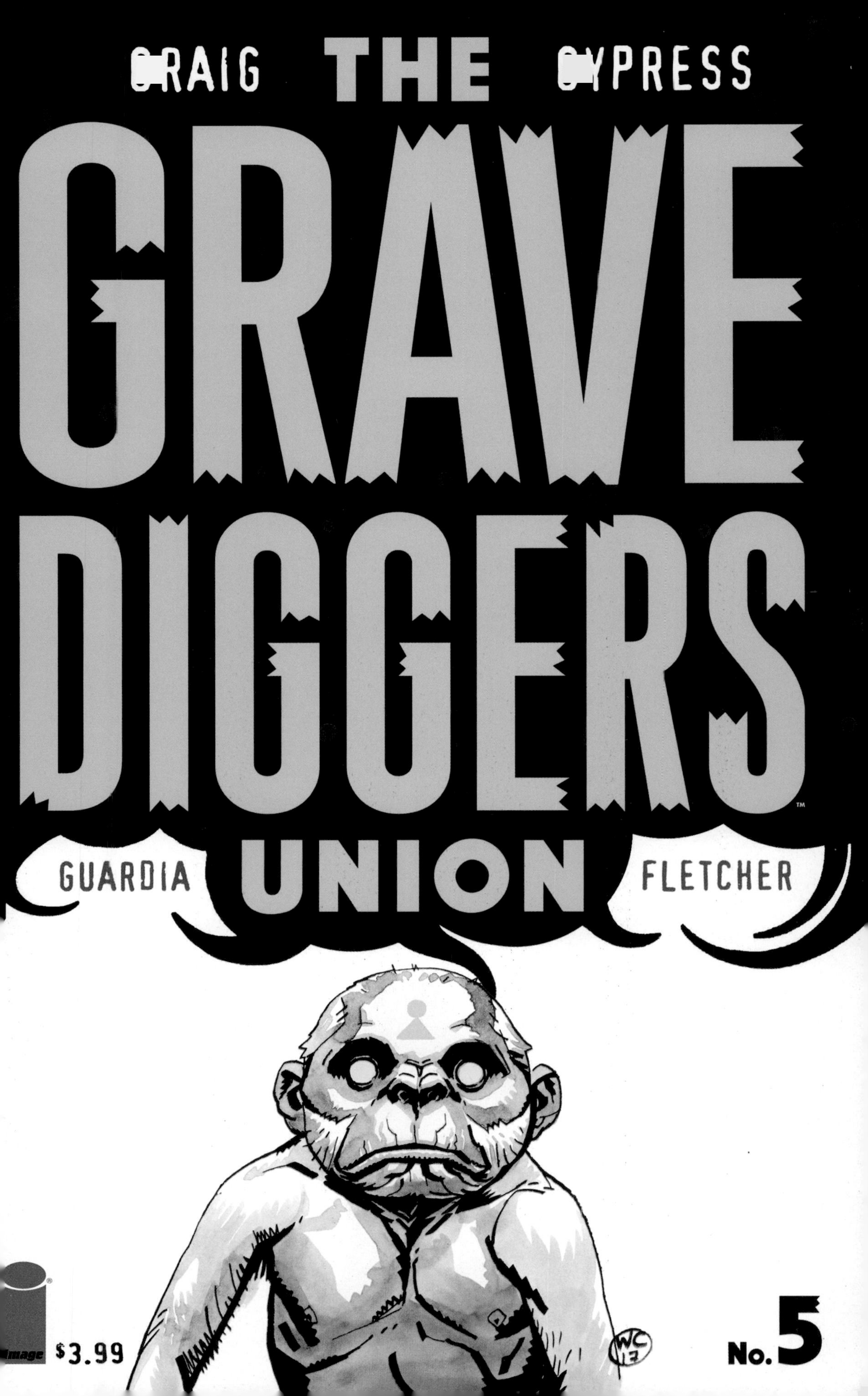

CRAIG THE CYPRESS

GRAVE
DIGGERS

GUARDIA UNION FLETCHER

$3.99

NO. 5

THE GRAVE DIGGERS UNION

ORIGINAL SHORT STORY
WRITTEN AND DRAWN BY

Wes Craig

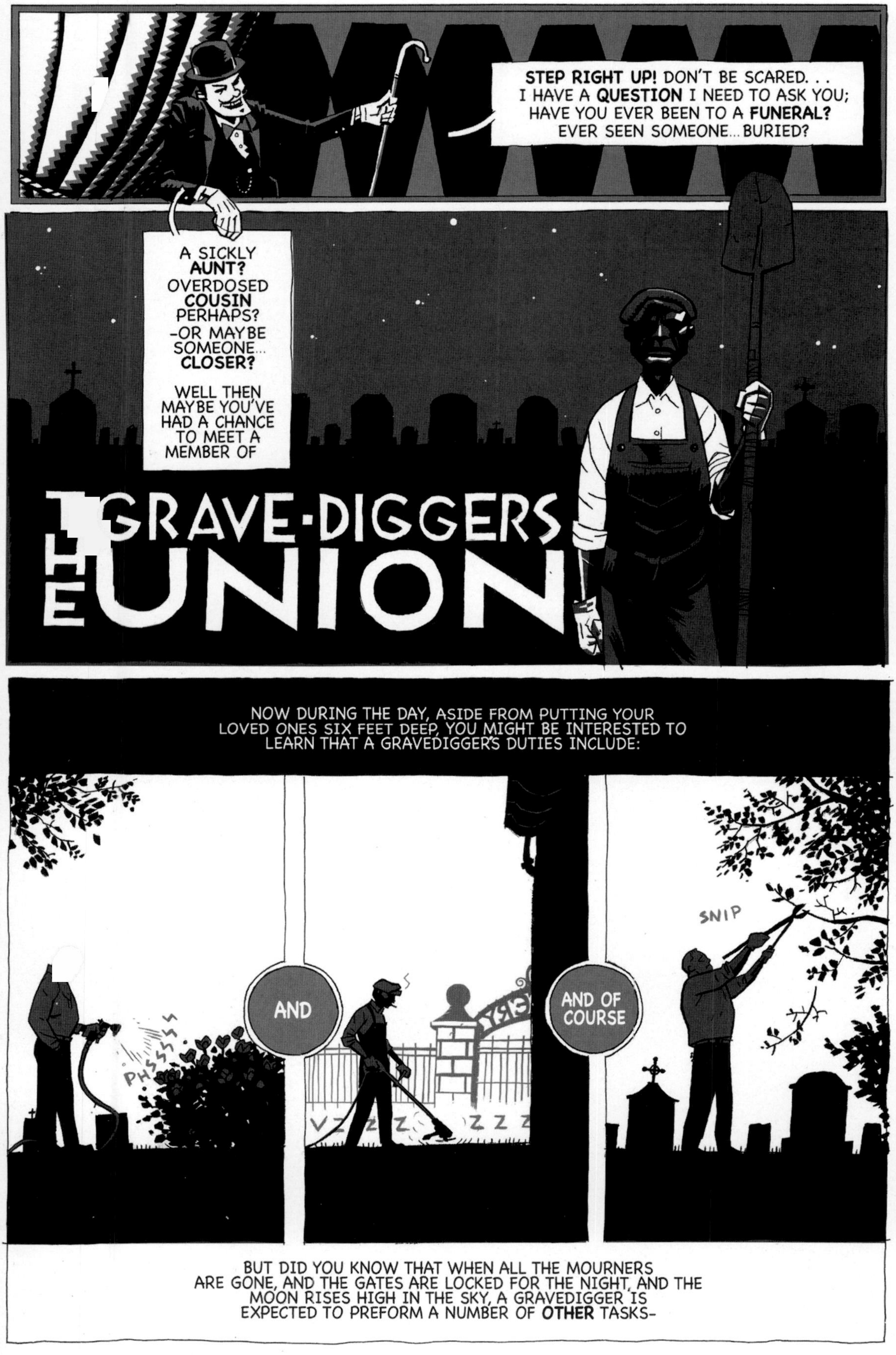
STEP RIGHT UP! DON'T BE SCARED. . . I HAVE A QUESTION I NEED TO ASK YOU; HAVE YOU EVER BEEN TO A FUNERAL? EVER SEEN SOMEONE... BURIED?
A SICKLY AUNT? OVERDOSED COUSIN PERHAPS? -OR MAYBE SOMEONE... CLOSER?
WELL THEN MAYBE YOU'VE HAD A CHANCE TO MEET A MEMBER OF
THE GRAVE-DIGGERS UNION
NOW DURING THE DAY, ASIDE FROM PUTTING YOUR LOVED ONES SIX FEET DEEP, YOU MIGHT BE INTERESTED TO LEARN THAT A GRAVEDIGGER'S DUTIES INCLUDE:
PHSSSSS
AND
VZZZ ZZZ
AND OF COURSE
SNIP
BUT DID YOU KNOW THAT WHEN ALL THE MOURNERS ARE GONE, AND THE GATES ARE LOCKED FOR THE NIGHT, AND THE MOON RISES HIGH IN THE SKY, A GRAVEDIGGER IS EXPECTED TO PREFORM A NUMBER OF OTHER TASKS-

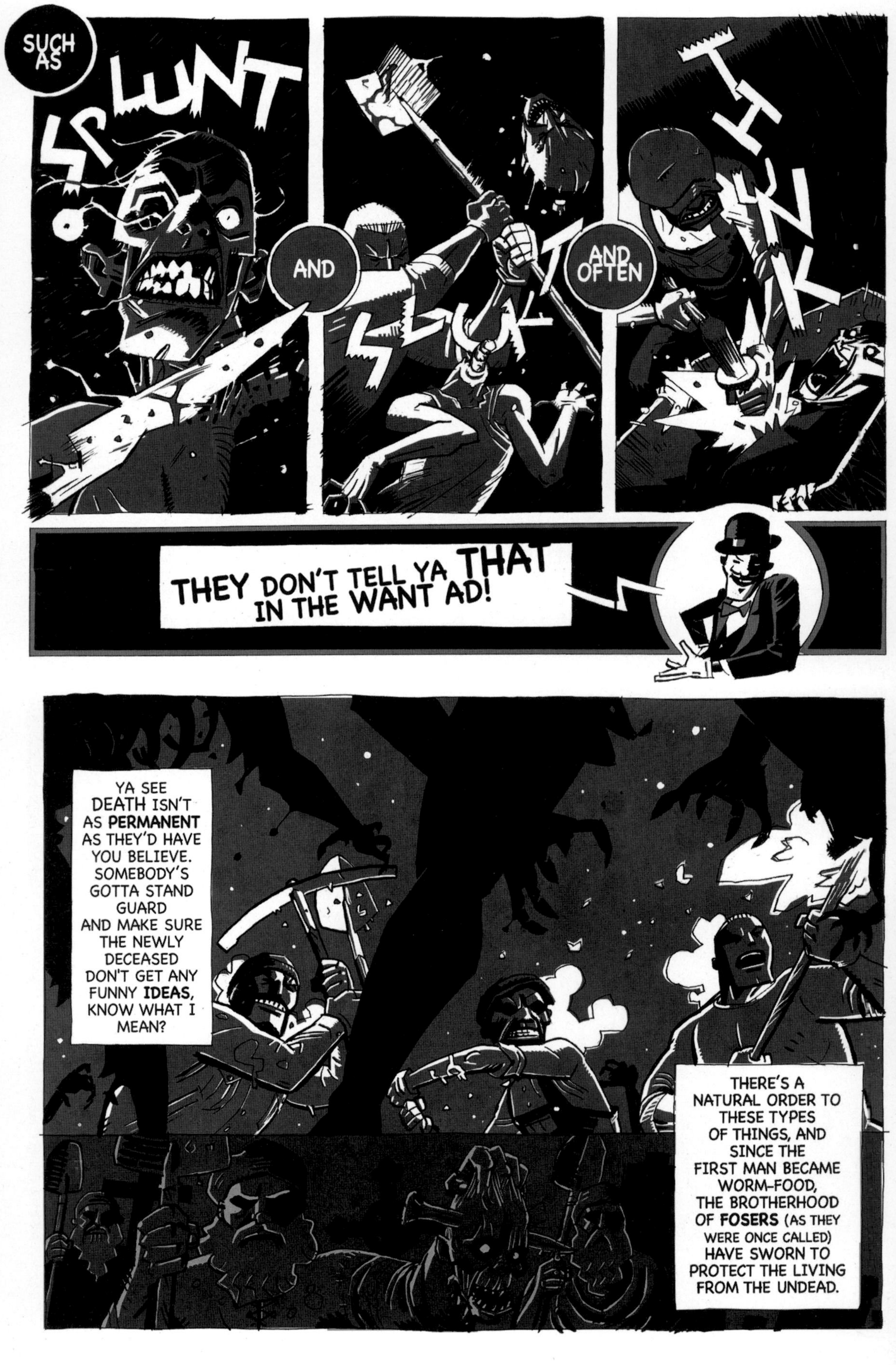
SUCH AS
SPLUNT
AND
SLUK
AND OFTEN
THUNK
THEY DON'T TELL YA THAT IN THE WANT AD!
YA SEE DEATH ISN'T AS PERMANENT AS THEY'D HAVE YOU BELIEVE. SOMEBODY'S GOTTA STAND GUARD AND MAKE SURE THE NEWLY DECEASED DON'T GET ANY FUNNY IDEAS, KNOW WHAT I MEAN?
THERE'S A NATURAL ORDER TO THESE TYPES OF THINGS, AND SINCE THE FIRST MAN BECAME WORM-FOOD, THE BROTHERHOOD OF FOSERS (AS THEY WERE ONCE CALLED) HAVE SWORN TO PROTECT THE LIVING FROM THE UNDEAD.

-OR ANY OTHER NECROMANTIC THREAT FOR THAT MATTER...

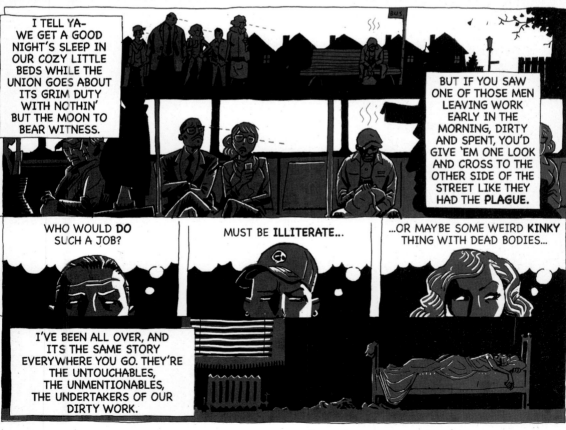

I TELL YA- WE GET A GOOD NIGHT'S SLEEP IN OUR COZY LITTLE BEDS WHILE THE UNION GOES ABOUT ITS GRIM DUTY WITH NOTHIN' BUT THE MOON TO BEAR WITNESS.

BUT IF YOU SAW ONE OF THOSE MEN LEAVING WORK EARLY IN THE MORNING, DIRTY AND SPENT, YOU'D GIVE 'EM ONE LOOK AND CROSS TO THE OTHER SIDE OF THE STREET LIKE THEY HAD THE **PLAGUE.**

WHO WOULD **DO** SUCH A JOB?

MUST BE **ILLITERATE...**

...OR MAYBE SOME WEIRD **KINKY** THING WITH DEAD BODIES...

I'VE BEEN ALL OVER, AND ITS THE SAME STORY EVERYWHERE YOU GO. THEY'RE THE UNTOUCHABLES, THE UNMENTIONABLES, THE UNDERTAKERS OF OUR DIRTY WORK.

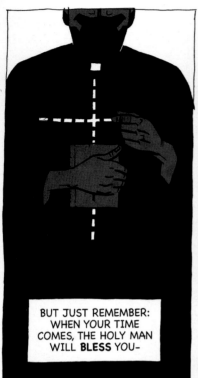

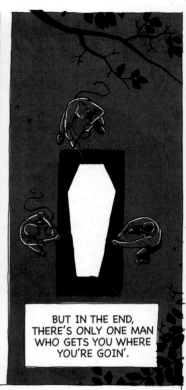

BUT JUST REMEMBER: WHEN YOUR TIME COMES, THE HOLY MAN WILL **BLESS** YOU-
AND YOUR FAMILY WILL **WEEP** FOR YOU-
BUT IN THE END, THERE'S ONLY ONE MAN WHO GETS YOU WHERE YOU'RE GOIN'.
WE LET THEM DO THE DIRTY WORK THEN WE TURN UP OUR NOSES AT THEM FOR **DOIN'** IT. PEOPLE HAVE ALWAYS BEEN THAT WAY, AND I DON'T SEE THEM CHANGIN' ANY TIME SOON.
BUT IF YOU ONLY KNEW WHAT THESE BRAVE MEN HAVE **STOOD** AGAINST- THE INJURIES THEY'VE **ENDURED**-
METAL PLATE
BUSTED NOSE
BUSTED NOSE
x4
BUSTED ORBITAL
BUSTED NOSE
x6
DIS-LOCATED SHOULDER
CON-CUSSION
x5

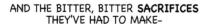

AND THE BITTER, BITTER **SACRIFICES**
THEY'VE HAD TO MAKE-

SHUNK

THEN MAYBE YOU WOULDN'T BE SO QUICK TO JUDGE.

SO NEXT TIME YOU SEE ONE HEADING HOME, HUNCHED
OVER FROM A LONG NIGHT'S WORK, DON'T TURN UP YOUR
NOSE, OR LOOK AWAY. INSTEAD BOW YOUR HEAD IN RESPECT, OR
SHAKE HIS HAND AND THANK HIM FOR ALL HE'S DONE.

BUT APPRECIATED OR NOT, IT DOESN'T
REALLY MATTER TO THEM. PUTTING A SHOVEL IN THE
SKULL OF ONE OF THE UNDEAD IS THANKS ENOUGH.

THE GRAVEDIGGERS UNION WILL BE THERE LIKE THEY ALWAYS
HAVE BEEN, TO PROTECT THE LIVING. THEY'LL BE THERE
FOR YOUR FRIENDS, THEY'LL BE THERE FOR YOUR LOVED ONES,

AND THEN- ONE DAY-

THEY'LL BE THERE FOR YOU.

THE END

THE
GRAVE
DIGGERS
UNION

WILL CONTINUE IN

VOLUME